Rebellious HEART

Books by Jody Hedlund

The Preacher's Bride
The Doctor's Lady
Unending Devotion
A Noble Groom
Rebellious Heart

Rebellious HEART

JODY HEDLUND

BETHANYHOUSE
a division of Baker Publishing Group
Minneapolis, Minnesota

© 2013 by Jody Hedlund

Published by Bethany House Publishers
11400 Hampshire Avenue South
Bloomington, Minnesota 55438
www.bethanyhouse.com

Bethany House Publishers is a division of
Baker Publishing Group, Grand Rapids, Michigan

Printed in the United States of America

Library of Congress Cataloging-in-Publication Data
Hedlund, Jody.
    Rebellious heart / Jody Hedlund
        pages   cm
    Summary: "When Susanna's heart for the poor and Ben's disillusionment with British rule cross paths in 1763 Massachusetts, the two find themselves bound in a dangerous fight for justice"—provided by the publisher.
    ISBN 978-0-7642-1048-8 (pbk.)
    1. Young women—Fiction. 2. Massachusetts—History—Colonial period, ca. 1600–1775—Fiction. I. Title.
PS3608.E333R43 2013
813'.6—dc23   2013016870

Scripture quotations are from the King James Version of the Bible.

This is a work of historical reconstruction; the appearances of certain historical figures are therefore inevitable. All other characters, however, are products of the author's imagination, and any resemblance to actual persons, living or dead, is coincidental.

Cover design by Jennifer Parker
Cover photography by Mike Habermann Photography, LLC

13 14 15 16 17 18 19   7 6 5 4 3 2 1

To my three beautiful daughters
Jenna, Jessica, and Joy

I pray that God will bless you with husbands who become
The Dearest of Friends

Chapter
1

BRAINTREE, MASSACHUSETTS
SEPTEMBER 1763

"He's guilty of murder." The judge's voice echoed through the meetinghouse. "I hereby sentence him to be hanged."

Murmurs of approval broke the tense silence.

But Susanna Smith's chest constricted with something close to pity. From her spot in the gallery, she had a clear view of Hermit Crab Joe, of the flicker of surprise that rounded his eyes and cracked the weathered skin of his forehead.

He might be a murderer, but that didn't stop her from feeling sorry for the lonely old recluse.

"Thank the Lord," Mary whispered. "Now we can finally sleep peacefully at night."

Her sister's words gave breath to her own thoughts, to the worries that had plagued her since several local farmers had discovered the battered, lifeless body of the young maiden along the rocky coast of the bay. The surrounding parishes had been able to speak of nothing but the murder for the past week.

Now perhaps they could resume normal life again.

Susanna folded her hands in her lap. "We need to pray for his poor lost soul." But even as the words left her mouth, her gaze strayed to the slumped shoulders of Mr. Benjamin Ross, sitting on the bench next to Hermit Crab Joe.

Mr. Ross had spoken eloquently and passionately on behalf of his client. His defense had been flawless, and he'd almost made her believe the aged seaman was innocent. Almost.

Yet no one else in their law-abiding community besides Hermit Crab Joe even came close to being a suspect. And it was too frightening to acknowledge the possibility that a murderer still roamed free, that perhaps one of the God-fearing men sitting in the box pews below was to blame instead.

"I hope we'll have the hanging today and be done with this awful affair." Mary tucked a loose golden curl back under the wide brim of her hat. Her usually pale cheeks were rosy from the stuffiness that had settled upon the square room. The clapboard building that also served as a place of worship was filled beyond capacity. Even with all three doors open, the crispness of the September afternoon had been unable to penetrate the interior of Braintree's Middle Parish Meetinghouse, including the gallery where the women sat.

"Poor, poor Joe," Grandmother Eve said, tears pooling in her usually merry eyes.

All along, Grandmother Eve had insisted Joe was innocent. If Susanna hadn't known better, she would have been tempted to draw the conclusion that Grandmother Eve was acquainted with the man. But that was impossible. Stooped at the shoulders, with his long hair tangled across the hump of his back, Hermit Crab Joe had always kept to himself in his dilapidated hovel near the shore.

"I'm sorry, Grandmother." Susanna reached for the woman's hand and squeezed her plump fingers. "We don't have to stay for the hanging. If you'd rather return home—"

"Honorable Justice Niles." The strong voice of Mr. Ross rose above the clamor that had swept through the meeting-house. "I plead for mercy on behalf of my client."

The young lawyer stood. His face was flushed, and beads of perspiration speckled his brow beneath the gray wig he wore tied into a queue like most of the other men.

The judge, who'd been talking with the beadle and consta-ble—likely making arrangements for the hanging—frowned at Mr. Ross and then raised his hand for silence. With the long ringlets of his white periwig, the bands at his throat, and his imposing black robe, Judge Niles was surely the picture of God himself.

The chattering among the crowd ceased, broken only by the distant call of a sea gull.

"Regardless of the sentiment toward my client," Mr. Ross said, his clear, clipped voice commanding Susanna's attention, as it did everyone's, "I plead *benefit of the clergy*. I would like to prove Joe Sewall can read the Bible and thus is a worthy candidate for reform."

The lawyer stepped forward. His back was stiff and unyield-ing, his expression earnest. But it was the penetrating keenness of his blue eyes that arrested Susanna more than anything else.

When she'd been a little girl visiting her grandparents at Mount Wollaston in Braintree, she'd seen Benjamin Ross on occasion. He'd delivered shoes to her grandparents' mansion for his cordwainer father, who like many of the other farm-ers plied a trade in order to provide for his family. And she'd always liked his blue eyes.

At the time, he had seemed so much older, and she'd been too young to pay him much notice. Except for one time . . ..

She pressed a hand against her embroidered stomacher as if she could push away the embarrassing memory.

She hadn't seen him since that long-ago day—when she'd been such a silly, childish girl and said such silly, childish things. Not long afterward, she'd heard his father had sold ten acres of farmland in order to send him to Harvard.

Over the ensuing years she'd forgotten all about Benjamin Ross and his keen blue eyes, until she'd learned he was defending Hermit Crab Joe. Only then had Grandmother Eve informed her Mr. Ross had finished his education at Harvard, along with his lawyer training, and had recently returned to Braintree.

Mr. Ross turned to address the gathered crowd. "As God-fearing Christians, do we not have the obligation to reform a wayward soul? Would you live the rest of your earthly days with this man's eternal death and condemnation overpowering your conscience? Would you not stay the execution and give this man a chance at reform first?"

He paused and looked over the wealthy gentlemen of the community—including her own grandfather Quincy—sitting in the front pews in their tailored suits and powdered coifs. Mr. Ross's impassioned plea reached out to the farmers and laborers sitting in the free pews, and even to the Redcoat officer who stood as straight as a sword at the back of the meetinghouse, likely there to keep the peace.

Susanna was surprised when Mr. Ross looked up at the balcony to the women, almost as if their opinion was important too.

When his gaze flickered over her, Susanna's breath caught in her throat. Did he recognize her? Did he remember the silly things she'd said to him those many years ago?

But his expression contained only his heartfelt passion for his client and his appeal for compassion.

Grandmother Eve clutched Susanna's fingers. "I think this might just work. I knew if any lawyer could help Joe, it would have to be Benjamin."

The dear woman scooted to the edge of the bench, inattentive to her fine satin petticoats imported all the way from London that had bunched together in an ungracious heap. Excitement flashed across her countenance and had obviously chased away her worry. And now she gripped the banister, ready to fly down and hug Mr. Ross if she could.

Susanna held Grandmother Eve's hand tighter, having no doubt her grandmother would find a way to fly if she could.

"Mr. Ross," Judge Niles finally said, "are you to have us believe this criminal can read?"

Mr. Ross nodded at Parson Wibird, who was sitting in the pew behind him.

The parson rose and tugged on the crisp tails of the white stock surrounding his neck before handing Mr. Ross a thick Bible.

"Honorable Justice, I would like my client to read the first lines of Psalm fifty-one." Mr. Ross opened the Bible and scraped through the pages. Then he slipped his hand under Hermit Crab Joe's elbow and assisted the man to his feet.

Everyone knew pleading benefit of the clergy was an acceptable and common method to avoid the gallows. If a criminal could prove his ability to read and thus his willingness to change, the judge might issue a lesser punishment.

Mr. Ross pointed a finger to the words on the page.

Susanna leaned forward, her stays pressing against her ribs and constricting her breath. Her thoughts jumbled together like tangled bobbins in a loom basket.

How was it possible that only moments ago, she'd been relieved Hermit Crab Joe was receiving the just dues of his crime? And now she was holding her breath, hoping the murderer really could read and that Mr. Ross would find a way to save the man's life?

"'Have mercy upon me, O God, according to thy lovingkindness.'" Hermit Crab Joe read smoothly and clearly like a learned man, not at all what she'd expected from a fisherman. "'According unto the multitude of thy tender mercies blot out my transgressions.'"

Susanna sat in stunned silence with the rest of the gathering, except Grandmother Eve, who beamed.

"As you can see," Mr. Ross said, closing the Bible with a thump, "my client can read quite well and is a natural candidate for reform."

Judge Niles studied Hermit Crab Joe, his expression clearly puzzled. Finally he spoke. "Mr. Ross, how can we be assured the criminal will reform his ways? We certainly don't want to set him free, only to have him kill another young woman."

The judge's words blew at Susanna like a chilly fall breeze, pushing her back, reminding her of the heinous nature of the murder.

Judge Niles was right. They had no jail in their community. What if Hermit Crab Joe decided to strike again?

Mr. Ross cocked his head at Parson Wibird. "Our own Parson Wibird has agreed to take Mr. Sewall under his mentorship."

The parson of Middle Parish squinted and smiled, revealing several blackened teeth.

"Not only will Parson Wibird study the Scriptures with Mr. Sewall, but he'll also provide accountability for Mr. Sewall's whereabouts."

"Are these your true intentions, Parson?" asked the judge.

"Most ardently," said the parson. "As the shepherd of this flock, I take my duty seriously. Since no one is beyond the concern of our loving heavenly Father, how can I do anything less than extend my own arms in an embrace of love toward a lost sinner?"

The judge pursed his lips together, staring first at the parson, then at Mr. Ross before bending to confer with the beadle and constable.

The beadle nodded and started down the aisle.

Susanna watched him weave through the crowd to the west door of the building, so much like the meetinghouse her father pastored in Weymouth. The interior was simple and free of artifacts and decorations. Their Puritan ancestors had sacrificed their lives to break away from the ornate and ritualistic Church of England in order to settle in America. And in the tradition of those early founders, they'd kept their churches pure. Not even a cross hung on the wall.

"Mr. Ross." Judge Niles stood, his long robe rippling about him. "Based on your plea for benefit of the clergy on behalf of your client, I have decided to lessen the punishment for Mr. Sewall."

Grandmother Eve released a pent-up breath at the same time Mary sucked in a sharp one.

"Instead of the gallows," the judge continued, "I hereby sentence Joseph Sewall to have both ears cropped and his right hand and cheek branded with M for manslaughter."

At the pronouncement of judgment, the meetinghouse broke into a commotion of protests as well as assent at the new verdict.

Susanna didn't speak. She wasn't sure if she should be upset a murderer was being set free or relieved that Mr. Ross had found a way to help his client.

Mr. Ross patted Hermit Crab Joe on the back and offered him a smile that said they had won.

Hermit Crab Joe's forehead wrinkled and his brows pinched together in a moment of unguarded sadness, obviously not sharing Mr. Ross's satisfaction with the new sentence.

She didn't blame the old man. The judge had spared his life. But now he'd spend the rest of his life maimed with a ghastly brand upon his face and hand. Perhaps death by the gallows would have been preferable to having the guilt of his crimes forever embedded upon his personage. No one would ever be able to forgive or forget what he'd done—least of all himself.

"This is delightful." Grandmother Eve broke into one of her cheerful smiles. "I think we shall have a party tonight to celebrate Mr. Ross's triumph."

Mary could only shake her head, her fair-skinned face paler than normal. "But Grandmother Eve, what about the young maidens? Won't we still be in danger as long as Hermit Crab Joe is alive?"

"You'll still be in danger all right, darling." Grandmother Eve was already standing and peering over the balcony. "But it won't be because of Joe. You were never in any danger from Joe." The spritely woman leaned over the railing and flagged her arms at Mr. Ross.

"Careful, Grandmother." Susanna grasped the folds of Grandmother Eve's sacque-back gown.

"Mr. Ross!" Grandmother Eve waved her arms wider.

The young lawyer was immersed in an animated conversation with a gentleman wearing a fashionable melon-colored coat that fell to the knees of matching breeches. Everything about the gentleman spoke of wealth, from his face, clean-shaven in the English style, and his spotless white cravat to his embroidered socks and polished silver buckles. In contrast, Mr. Ross in his plain, well-worn suit had a ruggedness that hinted at his ties to the land.

At Grandmother Eve's greeting, Mr. Ross glanced toward the gallery.

"Splendid defense, Mr. Ross," Grandmother called, bestowing a smile upon him.

"Thank you, Mrs. Quincy." He bowed his head.

"You'll come to Mount Wollaston tonight for a party, will you not?" Grandmother Eve dangled over the edge like a brightly lit chandelier. Susanna rose and took hold of her grandmother's arm to prevent her from plummeting to the first floor. Thankfully, Mary had the sense to do likewise.

"My two beautiful granddaughters will be there."

The well-dressed gentleman spun, and his eyes widened at the sight of her and Mary on either side of Grandmother Eve, holding on to the woman. His gaze swung from Mary to her, then back to Mary.

And of course that's where his attention stayed. On Mary. On pretty, fair-haired, fair-skinned Mary.

Not on dark-haired, olive-skinned Susanna.

Why would anyone give the moon a second glance when it was next to the sun? Who would want the seriousness of the ocean depths when they could have the freshness of a tinkling brook?

At least Susanna could derive some satisfaction from the fact that Mr. Ross hadn't given in to the temptation to stare at Mary. He had quite ignored both of them.

"And, please, bring your friends." Grandmother Eve nodded at the wealthy-looking gentleman. "I always say, the more the merrier."

"Thank you for the invitation, Mrs. Quincy," started Mr. Ross, "but I'll be helping my father drag in salt hay on the morrow. Regrettably I'll need to—"

"Attend the party for some of the evening," cut in the

friend, slapping Mr. Ross on the back without breaking his concentration on Mary. "My good friend, Benjamin Ross, needs to loosen his top button and enjoy life a little more."

Mary's cheeks had bloomed a fetching shade of pink. She smiled at her new admirer and lowered her lashes demurely.

Hadn't Mother recently lamented the lack of appropriate suitors? Mother had considered sending them both to Boston to live with wealthy Uncle Isaac for the sole purpose of finding husbands—men who had the degree of prestige and wealth suitable for Quincy blood.

And while Susanna never passed up an opportunity to travel the fourteen miles north to Boston to visit her aunt and uncle and all the friends she'd made there during her visits, she loathed having to go for the purpose of husband hunting.

The idea of flirting and flouncing and giggling in an attempt to attract a prestigious husband repulsed her. She detested when the local men pursued her with the hope of procuring a bride who could better their position. And she certainly didn't want to have to do the same.

But even as her heart rebelled against the status and wealth-seeking mentality, the rational part of her knew marrying up was inevitable. She really had no choice in the matter.

If only she could flirt as effortlessly as Mary . . .

Her sister lifted her lashes again and glanced at the young gentleman, who wore an enormous foolish grin and obviously couldn't tear his attention from her.

Susanna peeked at Mr. Ross. Had he noticed his friend's pathetic enamoring of Mary?

As if sensing her question, Mr. Ross finally looked at her. An intensity within his eyes pierced beneath her polite façade. Did he recognize her?

One of his brows cocked, and the corner of his lips arched

into the beginning of a knowing grin. But it was the kind of smile devoid of any warmth. Rather, the half grin only seemed to turn his eyes into ice.

So he *did* remember her and all the vain words she'd spoken.

Heat crept up her neck and into her cheeks. She wanted to lower her lashes as Mary had done. But instead she forced herself to stare back.

"Excellent." Grandmother Eve watched the two men and the interest they were paying her granddaughters, and her smile widened like that of a cat satisfied with its catch. "Then we shall see you both tonight."

Mr. Ross started to shake his head. "Thank you, Mrs. Quincy, but—"

"Of course we'll see you tonight," the gentleman friend said.

Before Mr. Ross could protest further, the beadle burst through the door with the blacksmith behind him. The smith's woolen cap was askew, and his leather apron hung low over his round belly. As the only tradesman busy enough to maintain a full-time shop, he'd likely already worked a long day. But he strode to the front of the meetinghouse, his boots clunking an ominous rhythm. In one soot-covered hand he carried a chisel and small anvil, and in the other a long brand that glowed red at the end.

Susanna took a quick step away from the rail. She'd never found any amusement in watching the punishment or suffering of another mortal. She understood the reasoning behind making criminals suffer publicly. Their agony was meant to deter others from sinning.

Nevertheless, she could not bear to watch or listen, just as she'd tried not to listen to the rumors about the young woman's death. But everyone had been talking about it for days. Of course no one had been able to identify the woman. She wasn't from Braintree or the surrounding countryside.

Some had said the young maiden looked like she'd been chased until she'd finally been unable to go any farther. Her bare feet had been mangled and bleeding and punctured with pieces of broken shell. But others said she'd been violated and choked to death.

Whichever way she'd died, it had obviously been painful. Once again silence descended over the meetinghouse.

Susanna sidled around the bench and flattened against the wall of the gallery. Her body tensed for the first tortured scream.

The ring of the anvil against chisel was followed by a deep-throated moan of agony.

She pinched her eyes shut, but her mind conjured up the image of the bloody stump of ear that remained.

When the smith finally laid the hot iron against Hermit Crab Joe's flesh with the *M* that forever branded him a murderer, she clamped her hands against her ears. But she couldn't block out his hoarse screams, no matter how hard she tried.

Her stomach swirled with revulsion.

She tried to remind herself he'd deserved much worse—that he didn't deserve any mercy. Surely the young maiden he'd killed had screamed for mercy and been shown none.

Even so, when she finally drew the courage to take her hands away from her ears, she found that her heart ached and her cheeks were wet with tears.

Chapter
2

Ben slipped through the half-open door of the sitting room and soundlessly closed it behind him.

He desperately needed a break from the guests.

Although he liked Mrs. Quincy, her circle of wealthy friends and family wearied him. They had their noses stuck to the ceiling just like they always had. After only an hour of them talking down to him like he was still nothing more than a cordwainer's son, he'd had enough.

He was ready to leave.

Only he couldn't go yet.

Cranch was too busy flirting with one of Mrs. Quincy's granddaughters. And he'd give Ben untold grief if he tried to make him depart so early in the evening.

Ben crossed the room, the thick carpet muting his footsteps. He passed behind two high-backed wing chairs positioned in front of a comfortable fire and made his way to one of the windows. He peered through the dozen panes over the large groomed grounds that graced the Quincy mansion.

The stately home still reigned over Braintree at the top of

gently sloping Mount Wollaston, just as it had when he'd been a boy roaming the hills. The late evening sky was streaked with remnants of the sunset and had ignited the changing leaves so that the reds, yellows, and oranges glowed.

He took a deep breath, tugged off his wig, and tossed it onto the half-moon table that flanked the window. The two candles in sleek silver holders had already been lit, and they glowed against the glass in the darkening shadows.

It had been a very long day. And it hadn't helped that the British officer quartered in Braintree had shown up halfway through the trial and had stood in the back of the meeting-house, listening to his defense.

Why had Lieutenant Wolfe come? Ben didn't want to think about the possibility that the officer knew of his involvement with the Caucus Club. How could he? Not when he and the other dissenters had worked hard to keep their meetings and activities clandestine.

Ben ran his fingers through his hair, combing it into the cord at the back of his neck.

Every time he remembered the agony and confusion in Joseph Sewall's eyes when the brand had touched his cheek, Ben's body tightened with fresh protest.

He'd wanted to scream with old Joe. He'd wanted to scream at all those gathered in the meetinghouse. They were too set in their ways, too prejudiced, too quick to judge. And even though old Joe hadn't committed the murder, Ben had known from the start—when Mrs. Quincy had approached him about defending old Joe—that he was taking on a losing case.

At the very least, he'd been determined to save the old man's life. And he'd accomplished that. He should be happy Joe was still alive and not swinging from the gallows.

"I should have done more," he whispered to his somber reflection. It didn't matter that his father had come up to him after the trial and given him the kind of look that said he was proud of him.

He still should have found a way to prove Joe's innocence.

He'd searched for alibis, anyone who had been with old Joe the night of the murder, someone who'd seen him elsewhere. But of course Joe had been home alone, like usual. Ben had also investigated clues that could lead him to the real murderer. But he'd come up empty-handed.

The problem was that everyone in Braintree was already afraid of old Joe. It was no surprise that when a strange young woman was murdered and dumped in front of Joe's sea-battered home, the community had blamed him for the death.

Ben could only shake his head at their foolishness. What murderer would leave a body outside his home in plain view of everyone? A real murderer would try to cover up the evidence or frame someone else.

But of course they hadn't listened to any of Ben's arguments. He'd known they wouldn't. Not poor Ben Ross, the son of a simple, uneducated farmer.

A movement in the reflection of the window cut short Ben's inner tirade, and his muscles tensed. Was someone else in the room?

He spun.

A young woman was in the process of rising from one of the chairs in front of the fire. Her eyes were wide and fixed on him, and she'd been moving in slow motion as if trying to escape from the room without being seen.

She froze halfway out of the chair. A volume of Milton lay facedown on the round pedestal table that stood beside the chair.

"I beg your pardon," she said. "I should have made my presence known the moment you stepped into the room."

He knew her immediately, just as he had at the trial. Susanna Smith. Mrs. Quincy's granddaughter. And she'd certainly grown into a striking young woman, hardly resembling the gangly, sick girl she'd once been.

In the growing dusk, the light from the fire cast a glow over her, illuminating her fine complexion and her eyes that were as dark as ink. Her raven hair fell in soft waves about her slender cheeks and was pulled loosely back by a ribbon.

She straightened to her full height, ironing the wrinkles from the silky layers of her skirt. The shimmering blue of the gown served to highlight the contrast with the darkness of her hair and eyes. And for a long moment he could only stare at her, completely speechless.

Her fingers fluttered to the triple strand of pearls at her neck.

The movement drew his attention to the pearls, to their perfection, to all they stood for. And that was all it took to break her spell over him. A chill slipped into his blood as it had earlier at the meetinghouse when he'd caught sight of her in the gallery.

"Susie Smith," he said, disregarding proper etiquette and using her childhood nickname. Susanna Smith may have turned into a ravishing beauty of a woman, but he'd never forget that she'd once been a spoiled, snobby girl.

"Mr. Ross." She tilted her head slightly, but it was enough to cause a tress of her hair to slide across her cheek. She brushed it back and tucked it behind her ear.

He couldn't keep from admiring the elegant curve that ran from her ear to her chin. And when she offered him a tentative smile, he almost found it charming the way her lips cocked higher on one side into the beginning of a dimple.

"So," he said, forcing himself to remember who she was, "I suppose you're happily engaged to the rich prince you told me you would marry someday."

Her half smile faded, taking the dimple with it, and a shadow of embarrassment flickered across her features.

For a moment, regret pricked him. After all this time, he didn't have to hold a grudge, did he?

She shifted her concentration to the blazing fire as if drawing energy from it. Then she met his gaze head-on again. This time her eyes sparked. "Of course I have a line of princes just begging to marry me. What else would you expect?"

Alas, her tongue was still quick. "I'm sure you've perfected putting into place all the poor farm boys you meet."

"I was already quite perfect at that, wasn't I?" Even though her response was tart, there was something in her dark expression that hinted at remorse.

He stared deeper, trying to probe into her heart. Was there a chance that over the years Susanna Smith had changed as much on the inside as the out?

"As you can see"—she waved her hand around the room and gave another half-cocked smile—"I'm the most popular young lady at the party tonight."

He didn't break his gaze from hers. He couldn't. He wanted to prove to her he wasn't a simple, uneducated farm boy anymore. He was a grown man, Harvard-educated, and determined to do whatever it took to earn a prestigious reputation.

Maybe he wasn't an important lawyer yet. Maybe he wasn't the perfect catch for a husband. But he was on his way. He was already beginning to make a name for himself. And if he worked hard enough, one day he'd be able to set up a practice in Boston.

He'd show her—he'd show everyone—that he wasn't a nobody.

Under his unrelenting examination, her cheeks seemed to darken their hue even though she didn't have the complexion of a blushing woman.

Good. She deserved to be uncomfortable—for just a moment.

Her long dark lashes fluttered, then swept down and hid her eyes. She shifted and ran her finger over the fraying spine of the book she'd been reading.

He was being a bit hard on her, but he couldn't seem to stop himself. "I don't remember that particular volume of Milton having any illustrations."

"Then you've remembered correctly."

"If it has no pictures to entertain you, then what are you doing with it? Practicing your posture?"

"Is it so impossible to believe that a young lady could read Milton for enjoyment?"

"You? Read Milton?" His tone was more cynical than he intended. "What need does a woman have for *Paradise Lost*?"

"And just what need would a *man* have for such a book?"

"Plenty." He stepped away from the window and crossed toward her. "The great classics challenge our minds, help us think, and force us to evaluate life so that we can better ourselves."

"Then you have spelled out chiefly why I'm reading the book." Although she calmly traced the gold-embossed lettering on the cover, her eyes were a tempest. "I'm challenging my mind to better myself."

He stopped in front of the pedestal table. She was less than an arm's length away, close enough to catch the tang of apple cider lingering on her breath. He could almost picture her when she'd been caught in the apple tree that last August before he'd left for Harvard.

She'd wedged the heel of her silk brocade shoe in the V of a branch and had twisted her ankle in trying to dislodge it. Of course she'd been too far from the mansion for anyone to hear her cries for help . . . until he'd come strolling through the orchard after making a delivery for his father.

Tears had streaked her thin face, her pinner cap had fallen away, and her hair had blown about her head in a tousled disarray. Her pink calico frock was dirty and torn in her unsuccessful efforts to free herself.

At first he'd taken pity on her. She'd appeared helpless and forlorn like a dainty injured dove.

He'd climbed the tree and quickly concluded the best way to pry her free of her prison was to first have her slip her foot out of her shoe.

She'd inhaled a sharp breath at his request as though he'd asked her to take off her gown instead of mere footwear. "I wouldn't dare bare my foot in front of you." Her voice contained all the haughtiness of a woman—not a frightened little girl.

"But it will allow me to twist the shoe without hurting your ankle." He wobbled on the branch next to her. Twigs poked his hat, knocking it askew, and bunches of ripening apples bumped his back.

"I won't give you leave to see my bare foot."

"But it won't be bare, will it?" He grinned, hoping to cheer her. "You're wearing stockings, aren't you?"

"Of course I am." Her dark eyes filled with the kind of look that said she thought he was ignorant for asking such a question. "But I'd much rather stay stuck up in this tree than give you a glimpse of my ankle."

He examined her finely crafted silk shoe, which was smaller than the length of his hand. She was only a girl of five, maybe six years, much younger than his fifteen. Did she really think he'd ogle over her ankle?

"Besides," she said, "I'm hiding here and I don't want to be found. Hence I'm never coming down."

He wiggled the stubborn heel of the shoe. "So you're planning to live in this tree?"

She nodded.

He prodded his clasp knife out of his pocket and bent closer to examine the branch. "And what has brought you to such despair that you'd resort to living in a tree like a bird?"

"My awful cousin said that no one would ever want to marry a skinny dark-haired girl like me." Her voice wobbled, and Ben glanced up just in time to see several glistening tears trickle down her cheeks.

He knew which *awful* cousin she was referring to. None other than the insufferable Elbridge Quincy. Every time the boy came visiting from Boston in his fancy ruby coach with the fine black horses, he stirred up trouble.

"Don't believe your awful cousin. He's the worst sort of liar I've ever met." Ben wedged the knife into the branch that held the heel captive. "If you were older, I'd marry you."

He didn't really mean it. He was just trying to say something that might make her big tears stop flowing. Having grown up in a family of all boys, what did he know about making little girls feel better?

She paused mid-sniffle. "Oh, I could never marry you." Her voice was low and serious and her eyes round with horror.

A chill breeze rippled through the leaves around him and then across his skin.

"You're a nobody." Her childish voice was once again

26

haughty. "You're nothing but a farmer and a shoemaker's son. I could never marry someone from the middling class. My mother would never allow it."

"Of course not," he said quickly, his muscles turning frigid. "I know *you* wouldn't marry *me*. I was simply trying to make a point that *someone* will want to marry you someday."

Suddenly anxious to be on his way, he dug the knife into the branch and worked faster at chipping away the bark. In fact, why should he help a little sour-milk pudding like her anyway? From what he could tell, she deserved to be stuck in the tree and rot away there.

"No matter what my cousin says," she said, wiping her cheeks dry, "I'm going to marry a rich prince someday. Or a nobleman. Or at the very least, a wealthy merchant like my uncle in Boston."

If he'd ever held any admiration for Mrs. Quincy's granddaughter even just briefly from a distance, every ounce of goodwill had drained out of him completely at that moment.

And it had never returned.

He'd been gone for many years—first to Harvard, then teaching school in Worcester before finally studying law under Putnam for two years. And since his return to Braintree, he'd been too busy setting up his practice. He'd all but forgotten about Susie Smith . . . until today when she'd made her appearance next to Mrs. Quincy after the trial.

And now at his presumption to stand so close to her, the rapid beat of her pulse echoed between them.

Did she still think she was too good for a man like him?

He moved his hand onto her book, letting his fingers slide down the worn spine until they brushed against hers.

At the barest contact, she drew in a breath, and her inky eyes darkened.

He dared her—no, taunted her—to pull away.

"Why do you need to better yourself, Susie?" he asked in a half whisper.

She held herself motionless.

He took another step closer, testing her, helplessly driven by the hurts of the past to challenge her. Mere inches apart, he was taking liberties, but he couldn't deny himself the chance to see if his lack of fortune and prestige still repulsed her.

With one hand against hers on the book, he lifted the other to the long slender line of her jaw. He skimmed his fingers along the curve, relishing the smoothness of her skin.

Her breathing turned softly ragged, the warmth of it spreading over his wrist, to his pulse. The darkness in her eyes was murky and unreadable, but there was the slightest flicker of something.

His own breath hitched in his chest. What passion simmered beneath the surface of a saucy woman like Susanna?

As if sensing the direction of his thoughts, she took a small step backward, breaking their connection.

"Last I remember," he said, "you already thought you were better than everyone."

She stared at the elegant geometrical pattern of the carpet. "Time has a way of showing us our true condition, Mr. Ross."

"Ben?" The door of the sitting room swung open, and Cranch peeked inside.

Susanna rapidly put several more feet between them. Her hand fluttered to her bodice and the lace that bordered her graceful curves.

A wicked grin spread over Cranch's face. "Ah, just as I told everyone." He sauntered into the room. "I figured you must have hidden yourself away with a pretty lady."

"You're quite mistaken, Mr. Cranch." Susanna tossed the

man a cutting glare. "Mr. Ross and I are only together by accident."

Was she embarrassed to be caught with him?

"Come now, Miss Smith," Ben said. "Admit it. You were waiting for the chance to be alone with me so that you could whisper sweet verses of poetry into my ear."

A retort formed on her lips, but before she could utter the witty response he'd hoped for, her sister glided into the room, followed by Elbridge Quincy—as insufferable as always.

Susanna's rich cousin had sat through the proceedings that afternoon, and his mocking gaze had followed Ben's every move.

Of course, Ben knew Elbridge was simply jealous. Even though the scoundrel had ranked higher in their graduating class at Harvard because of his family's social standing, Ben had outscored him on all the tests. Academically, Ben had come out third in his class, and Elbridge had ranked far below him.

But Harvard refused to let go of its antiquated and preju-dicial methods of arranging students—preferring to rank students according to family status rather than alphabetically or by academic achievements.

At the sight of him alone with Susanna, Elbridge's eye-brows shot up, nearly disappearing under his wig. "Just what do you think you're doing in the same room alone with my dear cousin?" Tall and athletic, Elbridge peered down at Ben over the tip of his long Roman nose.

During their time at Harvard together, Ben had always wanted to put a dent into Elbridge's proud, straight nose. But he'd learned he was a better fighter with his words than with his fists. "Miss Smith and I were discussing the merits of Milton. It was quite the intimate conversation, if I might be so bold as to say so."

Susanna grasped Mary's hand and whispered in her ear.

"I hardly think Susanna would want to share anything with you, Ross," Elbridge said, crossing toward Susanna, his sights focused solely upon her with a possessive glint that hinted at something more than familial affection.

Did Elbridge harbor aspirations toward the cousin he'd once tormented so religiously?

Cranch raised his tankard toward Ben. "I thought for sure you'd be trying to convince us again that Hermit Crab Joe is innocent."

Ben knew his friend well enough to guess his mug wasn't entirely filled with Mrs. Quincy's freshly pressed cider. Cranch had likely spiced his drink with rum as well.

Elbridge took his place next to Susanna and puffed out the silver-trimmed waistcoat that overlaid his fine linen ruffled shirt and pristine cravat. "I thought Ross would be trying to persuade us once again of the abomination of His Majesty's decision to prevent settlers west of the Appalachians."

"I don't need to do any more convincing." Ben forced arrogance to his words. During his years at Harvard, he'd had to learn to hold himself with more confidence than he felt inside. "Why would I need to entreat anyone when I've already done a substantial job?"

Susanna's bright eyes narrowed on him. "Then you disagree with King George's proclamation prohibiting colonists from moving farther west?"

"Of course I disagree. What freethinking intelligent man would agree with the king's decision?" He needed to choose his words carefully about King George and the new proclamation, especially around Elbridge, who was as loyal to the Crown as a native-born Englishman.

Nevertheless, over the past year since the end of the war

with France, Ben had been growing more disenchanted with the king and the policies directed toward the colonists. And he was having an increasingly difficult time keeping his seditious thoughts from having a voice.

"And just what about the king's proclamation do you find offensive?" Susanna asked. She stood in front of the large fireplace, and the dancing light from the flames cast a sheen upon her ebony hair.

Was she like Elbridge, only trying to entrap him into saying something treasonous? Or did she truly care to hear his thoughts about the proclamation?

Her eyebrows arched, and her level gaze didn't waver from his face. "The land west of the Appalachians is dangerous and the threat of Indian attacks constant. Do you not think the king is merely trying to protect men and their families?"

"I don't think King George cares one whit for our protection," he replied. "He's trying to protect his holdings in America from the French. He knows if he spreads himself overly thin, he risks losing all he's recently gained in the war."

"Even so," she said, "if the threat from France were to disappear altogether, the king would still prohibit expansion. The Indians are bloodthirsty. We've all heard stories of scalping and inhumane torturing of men, women, and children alike."

His body had sagged with fatigue since the branding at the trial, but now at Susanna's challenging comments, his pulse spurted forward with fresh energy. "Did the threat of danger from Indians and elements stop our Puritan forefathers from settling this very land we now call home, this land we hold so dear? Imagine if our ancestors had let the fear of the unknown dictate their decisions."

Her lips stalled around her response.

Cranch took a swig from his tankard and started toward Ben. "See. This is exactly why I count you among my favorite friends."

A glimmer in Cranch's eyes warned Ben to stop, but the words inside him seemed to have a life of their own. "We're here today in the colony of Massachusetts because of the courage of our relatives. I firmly conclude we can't let fear deter us from pursuing what we believe is the right course of action."

Cranch draped his arm across Ben's shoulders. "This is why I am loath to be apart from you for even the briefest moment. You're so talented at livening up a party." He squeezed, and the pressure of his fingers was enough to remind Ben of where he was and to whom he was speaking.

And that Elbridge was in the room watching him with calculating eyes.

Mary giggled and leaned her blond head against Susanna's dark one, whispering something into her sister's ear.

The girl was much shyer than Susanna, but she'd had no problem flirting with Cranch. The young ladies never had any difficulty talking with the smooth-tongued Richard Cranch.

He was English-born, handsome, and good-natured. He'd moved to Boston with his prosperous father, who'd come like so many others to invest in land, along with the shipping of the rum produced in the colonies. What girl wouldn't be impressed with him?

Certainly Mary's family would have no reason to object if Cranch came calling.

Elbridge gave Susanna one of his winsome smiles and held out his arm to her. "We'd better make our escape now before Ross begins to regale us with tales of his recent treasonous trial in Boston."

"There's nothing treasonous about defending the inno-cent," Ben said.

"And there's nothing innocent about stealing a horse from a British regular." Elbridge spoke as though he were an errant child.

Ben's body tightened with old insecurities. He fought the pressure to slouch and fade into the background. Instead he pushed himself to his full height and reminded himself why he was fighting against injustice—to give the downtrodden, like himself, a fair chance in a world in which those with the most power and wealth made the rules.

Susanna slipped her hand into the crook of Elbridge's arm, but she didn't move forward with him. Instead she threw one more question at Ben. "Are you joining the ranks of the treasonous, Mr. Ross?"

He could see disappointment in the slant of her eyes, and he wished he could ignore it. "Treason can be a subjective issue, Miss Smith."

"Obeying our ruling powers is hardly subjective," she countered. "Scripture commands us to obey our leaders and submit to those in authority. God's Word isn't open to subjective interpretation."

The intelligence and decisiveness of her responses were like a shot of energy in his veins. There was something entirely refreshing about a young woman who wasn't afraid to voice her thoughts and spar intelligent words with a man. Most women he'd met didn't have the slightest interest in the latest political situation involving the king, nor did they have any thoughts about treason or anything else important.

Elbridge tugged gently on her arm. "My dear cousin, I must advise against any more discourse with Ross. His impassioned speeches will only lead him to serious trouble one of these days."

"The greater the tyranny, the greater the treason." Ben couldn't prevent a parting retort.

"There you are, Mr. Ross" came a cheerful voice from the doorway.

In a glorious red gown, Hannah Quincy flounced into the room like a plump ripe apple ready for picking. She gave him the kind of smile that was meant to beckon him to her side.

He was all too willing to accommodate her.

"I came to congratulate you on your fine performance today at the trial."

"Why, thank you, Miss Quincy." *Performance?* He had in no way *performed* at the trial. Everything he'd done had been genuine and straight from all the passion in his heart. Nevertheless, he closeted his response into the recesses of his mind. He gave a slight bow and returned what he hoped was an adoring smile of his own.

Hannah Quincy was one of the most eligible young ladies inside and out of Boston. Not only was the Quincy family affluent, but they could trace their ancestry back to the founders of New England, to the landed gentry of England, and even to one of the signers of the Magna Carta.

That Hannah had taken an interest in him on the couple of occasions they'd been together recently was more than a little flattering.

It didn't matter that she was Elbridge's sister. She was as sweet as she was well-rounded. With her solid family connections and status, she was the kind of young woman he needed to marry if he wanted to increase his prestige.

As he approached her, she held out her hand to him. "I

don't care what Elbridge says, I think you have a very convincing way with words."

"Compared to your brother's oratory skills, mine do seem rather convincing."

Cranch guffawed and sputtered out a mouthful of cider.

Hannah only bobbed her pretty head while the hair coiffed high upon her brow remained perfectly still. Ben guessed she hadn't understood the jibe he'd leveled at her brother.

Surprisingly, Susanna's lips had twitched into a smile, which she promptly hid behind her hand.

Cranch wiped his mouth on his sleeve. "My stuffy old friend, I may hold out hope for you after all."

"Don't bother." Elbridge's nostrils flared. "Ross is such a bore that I'm afraid no matter how refined he tries to be, he'll always be nothing more than the son of a struggling farmer."

The words pummeled Ben in his gut just as Elbridge had likely intended.

"Oh, do stop being so cranky, you two," Hannah said, tugging Ben toward the door. "Let's go play. Aunt Eve always has such fun games at her parties."

Even though Ben wanted to toss another insult at Elbridge, he reined in his rebuttal. The firm pressure of Hannah's fleshy hand against his reminded him that he had too much at stake to alienate such a fine woman.

Sure, he'd had plenty of women show interest in him over the years. Yet he'd followed the advice of his friends and mentors who'd encouraged him to pursue his study of law with unequivocal devotion and without the encumbrance of an early marriage.

Now at twenty-eight years, with a growing practice, he'd decided it was time to find a wife. But not just any wife. He needed one with the right connections and social standing. So far he hadn't found anyone quite as fitting as Hannah Quincy.

He didn't really care that she'd started showing interest in him only after he'd won the case in Boston regarding the young man accused of stealing a horse from a British regular. All that mattered was that she favored him and wanted to be with him.

He pressed her hand and smiled down at her.

She lifted her pert nose and gave him a promising smile in return. She hadn't disdained him the way Susanna had.

Out of the corner of his eye, he saw Susanna watching him.

He patted Hannah's hand and bestowed a look of endearment upon her.

At the very least, he could make Susanna realize that just because she hadn't thought him worthy didn't mean every wealthy young lady would feel the same.

Chapter
3

Susanna peeked through the window at her younger brother, William, sitting under the tutelage of his teacher. Jealousy twined around her heart and pulled taut. What she wouldn't give to be inside the parsonage at the table, studying with him.

She tugged at the ribbon of her cape and loosened it, letting it droop from her shoulders. Due to the chill of the September afternoon, her mother had insisted she don the outer garment over her riding suit during their visits to the poor widows. But the heavy cape had only overheated her and now added to her irritation.

William twisted his pencil above his slate and stared at a faraway spot on the wall while his tutor read to him from the thick volume of *Rollin's Ancient History*.

Susanna had to swallow the bitter words she wanted to shout at her brother through the window. There he was, surrounded by their father's massive library with a knowledgeable teacher at his leisure, and yet he failed to apply himself or appreciate the privilege of his education.

He was an ungrateful boy.

She spun away from the parsonage before she gave liberty to her unkind words. Her father had always admonished them to say all the handsome things they could of people and never to speak ill of anybody.

But sometimes Father's instructions were too difficult to follow, like now when she wished she could trade places with William.

She'd begged her parents to send her to one of the rare academies in Massachusetts that admitted girls. When they'd refused, she pleaded for the chance to at least sit with William during his lessons. And while her father had been open to considering the arrangement, her mother had insisted on training her daughters properly. Mother had instructed her and Mary in simple writing and arithmetic, as was appropriate for preparing young girls to manage their own homes someday. Anything beyond the basics was deemed unnecessary and even ostentatious.

"Reading books is a waste of time for girls," Mother said too often. "As long as you know how to read the Bible, then what more do you need?"

If it hadn't been for Grandmother Eve's encouragement and additional instruction, Susanna was sure she would have withered up and died by now. As it was, every time she'd visited Grandmother Eve at Mount Wollaston, the dear woman had provided excellent lessons in her unique way of blending learning and amusement. She'd not only instilled in her a love of reading, but of writing and thinking deeply.

"Susanna Smith," her mother called from the garden where she'd stopped to give instructions to Phoebe, who was finishing picking the root vegetables. "If you're going to stay outside, you must wear your cloak."

"Yes, Mother." Even as she pulled the cloak back over her

shoulders, her heart rebelled against the action. She was nineteen years old, and Mother still treated her like she was nine.

"In fact," Mother continued, "I suggest you go straightaway into the house. You've been out long enough, and we don't want to chance you getting ill."

"I beg you not to worry." Susanna moved away from the window, away from the parsonage and toward the gate. "The ride and the fresh air have invigorated me. Besides, I've promised Phoebe I'd gather a basket of fresh apples so she can make apple tansey tonight."

Susanna unlatched the gate and slipped through before her mother could intercept her.

"Don't be gone overlong," Mother called after her. "It isn't safe."

As Susanna had predicted, after yesterday's trial and Hermit Crab Joe's freedom, Mother had worried about traveling without a male chaperone. She'd insisted Tom accompany them, even though he was already busy enough with all his harvesting duties.

Susanna started toward their old slave whose slumped shoulders were outlined in the shadows of the barn as he tended the needs of the horses they'd ridden that afternoon during their visiting around Weymouth's North Parish.

Even if Susanna balked at Mother's overprotectiveness, she more than willingly joined her mother's charitable efforts to provide relief to the poor women who had no trade or means to earn a living for their families. As the minister's wife, Mother took her duties to look after the widows and orphans quite seriously.

She admired Mother's determination to care for the needs of the women who'd lost their husbands during the years of fighting with the French and the Indians. Although the

Treaty of Paris had brought an end to the hostilities earlier in the year, it hadn't brought any solutions to the suffering of the widows.

More important than the food and cords of wood they distributed were the supplies for spinning yarn and weaving cloth they gave the women. When the widows finished spinning and weaving, Mother sold the cloth and was in turn able to pay the women.

"Miss Susie," Tom said with a gentle smile as she stepped into the barn. "Let me go get the apples. I don't like seeing you go against your mama's wishes."

"She's still anxious about the murder." Susanna stretched for one of the woven baskets hanging from a hook in an overhead beam. The dust of the recently cut hay sprinkled down and tickled her nose.

Tom paused in unhitching a bridle. His warm brown eyes probed her.

"She has to realize sooner or later I'm not a child anymore." Susanna dangled the empty basket from her arm. "I can make some of my own decisions, can I not?"

"She just loves you. That's all."

"And she shows you an abominable lack of consideration." Susanna had long ago asked her parents to give Tom and Phoebe their freedom. She couldn't understand why any human being needed to be owned by another. But as a Quincy, her mother had grown up with slaves and didn't see any reason why they needed to make changes to their circumstances—not when they treated their slaves as well as any servant, if not better.

"It's all right, child." Tom resumed his care of the fine mare she'd ridden earlier. "Your mama's a good woman. 'Sides, you know she's not my real Master."

Susanna nodded and patted the mare's flank. She'd heard Tom's explanation her whole life, and she loved him for it.

"My real Master, He rules from heaven, and I take my orders from Him. And as long as He says to serve and obey my earthly master, that's what I'm gonna do."

Susanna knew she would ultimately do the same too. She would never willfully disobey God or her parents. Mother was only doing what she thought was best for her—even if she became slightly smothering at times.

After all, Mother had allowed her to conduct her dame school in the kitchen for the local girls. She'd helped provide the supplies and was supportive of her efforts to teach the young girls, although the schooling only consisted of basic writing, reading, and sampler work.

"Susanna!" Mary's call came from near the parsonage.

Susanna gave the mare a parting slap and retreated from the comfortable shadows of the barn into the fall sunshine. The clouds half covered the sky, rendering it the same misty gray as the distant waters of the Massachusetts Bay. The breeze blowing off the sea and the long estuary brought a damp chill.

Mary stood by the garden fence, tendrils of her fair hair dancing with the wind around her face and highlighting the excitement in her features. "You'll never guess who has sent me a letter."

Susanna's thoughts returned to the party at Grandmother Eve's and the attention Richard Cranch had lavished upon her sister all evening. "You're right. I'll never guess. I can't even begin to imagine who would send you a letter."

With a dreamy sigh, Mary pressed a sheet of paper to her breast.

Long into the night, when they'd finally snuggled under the coverlet in their bedchamber at Grandmother Eve's, Susanna had listened to Mary whisper about Mr. Cranch and how kind and thoughtful and funny he was.

Unfortunately all the talk of Mr. Cranch had only made Susanna think about Mr. Ross. She'd given herself a lecture numerous times, telling herself to put all thoughts of him aside. He was after all, by his own admission, in disagreement with the policies of the king. What if he decided to join the ranks of those who were growing discontent with British rule? Everyone knew the men who spoke of rebellion were either fools or hotheads.

Besides, Mr. Ross had paid altogether too much attention to Hannah. And most suitors who were enamored by her witless cousin were usually seeking her dowry.

"Wealth, wealth, wealth—it is the only thing that is looked after now," she'd whispered as she watched him at the party hovering over Hannah, jumping at her every insignificant whim, and smiling at her every boring word.

Susanna knew she couldn't be too harsh on Mr. Ross for his conjugal aspirations. After spending the afternoon delivering goods to the poor with Mother, she was reminded again that they could only offer such assistance because of their affluence. If she hoped to carry on the work of helping young women, then she herself would need to have substantial means. That meant only one thing. She must do her best to find a suitable husband.

As much as she'd liked to think she was no longer the same silly girl who had once dreamed of marrying princes and rich merchants, what other choice did she have besides making a good match?

"Mr. Cranch has asked to come calling this evening," Mary called breathlessly. Of course, Mary had never been at a loss for suitors, but so far none had captured her attention quite the way Mr. Cranch had. "Father has agreed to let me invite him to dinner this evening."

"Then I really must make haste to pick apples for Phoebe so your Mr. Cranch can enjoy her apple tansey."

"*My* Mr. Cranch?"

"Yes. *Your* Mr. Cranch. You know you've already won his heart."

At least Mr. Cranch wasn't self-seeking like so many of the men who came calling. He had enough prestige and prosperity of his own that he didn't need Mary's. Instead he seemed genuinely enamored with her.

Was it too much to expect the same, to find a man who would love her for her inner qualities rather than her outward assets?

Susanna wound her way up the gently rolling hill behind their large home to the orchards. She strolled among the trees laden with apples and pears, but didn't stop until she'd crested the hill.

She took a breath of the crisp air, inhaling the sweet tang of the apples that had fallen and were already fermenting beneath the trees. She feasted upon the surrounding farmlands, on the old clapboard houses weathered by the sea sitting upon their one- or two-acre plots. In the distance, wetland swamps and beaches were coated with seaweed the farmers would cart away to restore vitality to the soil.

Everything entreated her to stay and relax. Even the nearby wooded heights among the granite outcroppings gleamed with the vibrancy of the changing leaves.

She dropped her basket into the yellowing grass and wished she'd thought to bring her newest book from Grandmother Eve. As it was, she dug into her pocket and retrieved the small volume of poetry she'd managed to hide. In spite of the slight chill, she needed the peace to read without Mother hovering over her.

Susanna shrugged out of her cloak and spread it on the grass. Surely she had nothing to fear. Even as she glanced around and attempted to reassure herself she was completely safe, a twig snapped nearby.

She jumped and searched the sloping orchard for signs of danger. She tried to silence the hard thump of her pulse and listen for any other sounds.

Except for the *dee-dee-dee* of a chickadee, the orchard was silent.

A chill breeze rippled the ruffles of her sleeves and sent shivers up her arms.

Out of the corner of her eye she caught the slight movement of a dark shadow. But when she turned her head, she saw nothing but the peaceful orchard.

"Everything is just as it should be," she whispered. She was only nervous because of yesterday's trial. She had no reason to worry. Mr. Ross and Parson Wibird had insisted Hermit Crab Joe was no longer a threat.

Nevertheless, she picked up her basket and gathered her cloak and decided not to linger.

As she plucked the ripe apples, every flitting silhouette seemed to jump out at her until she found herself picking faster and glancing around more often, gleaning little enjoyment in the task she usually found so pleasant.

She'd only filled her basket half full when another twig snapped, this one louder and more distinct.

She stopped, her hand midair. She spun and saw what appeared to be a young woman before the form slid behind a trunk, obviously trying to escape from the orchard undetected.

"May I help you?" Susanna called.

The woman darted forward, her apron bulging with apples.

"Please, don't go." Susanna started after her. "I mean you no ill will."

The woman tripped, stumbled to her knees, and gave a cry of pain. The apples in her apron tumbled around her.

Susanna dropped the basket, picked up her skirts, and bolted toward the stranger.

The woman looked over her shoulder, giving Susanna a glimpse of beautiful but delicate features etched with fear.

"Please don't be afraid." Susanna held out a hand, hoping the stranger would see it as a gesture of peace.

"I'm so sorry." The woman crawled forward, scrambling to rise and get away at the same time. Her feet were bare, which wasn't unusual for a poor maiden, not on fair-weather days when one might attempt to conserve a pair of shoes.

What was unusual was the condition of the young woman's feet. The heels, arches, and toes were slick with blood and dirt. In places, the flesh was sliced open.

Susanna pushed her hand against her mouth to stifle a gasp.

The stranger rose to her bloody feet, but not without another cry. She grabbed a low branch to hold herself upright, but it broke like dry kindling and she crumpled to the ground again.

Susanna hastened to the woman's side and knelt next to her. "My dear woman, you're in need of a doctor."

"No!" Her thin cheeks were streaked with dirt, her bodice ripped in several places, and her hair hung in a loose, snarled mess beneath her dingy muslin cap. "Please don't call anyone."

Susanna was familiar with all the poor women who lived around Weymouth, and she was certain she'd never seen her before.

"Please just let me be on my way," the timid soul begged Susanna. "I promise I won't steal any more apples."

"But you're hurt." Susanna studied the woman's face and guessed her to be less than her own nineteen years or at least close to it.

The stranger's gaze darted around the orchard as if she expected someone to jump out and grab her.

"We're alone." Susanna prayed they truly were alone, that whatever haunted the woman wasn't lurking nearby.

"I must go."

"I beg you to let me help you."

"You're very kind, miss. But I'm not wanting that anyone should know my whereabouts, you see."

Susanna nodded, but she didn't see. Was this woman wanted for a crime? Was she a thief? She had, after all, been stealing apples from their orchard.

But even as Susanna mulled over the thought, she cast it aside. There was something too soft and kind in the woman's face to label her a thief. She was likely taking the apples to satisfy her hunger.

"Please, please, don't tell anyone you saw me. Please promise you won't breathe a word about my being here."

Susanna hesitated. Was she running away from something or someone? "Won't you come down to the parsonage and let me help you?"

"Oh, I couldn't, miss."

When the woman started to rise again, Susanna touched her arm. "If you won't let me help you, then you can at least take these."

Susanna began to untie her leather buskins.

"Not your boots, miss. Oh, I couldn't. Just couldn't."

But Susanna had already slipped her foot out of one and

was unlacing the other. "I'm venturing we're about the same size."

A sob broke from the woman's lips, and tears began to slide down her cheeks, making trails through the grime.

Susanna unrolled her silk stockings and slipped them off. "You'll need these also."

Susanna refused to take the boots and stockings back even when the young woman pushed them at her. Instead she helped rip strips from her petticoat, bandaged her cuts as best she could, then assisted her into the buskins. She then refilled the stranger's apron with apples and watched her stumble away.

"If you need anything—anything at all—you must come find me at the parsonage," Susanna called.

Even with boots on, the poor woman could hardly walk, and Susanna had to fight the urge to run after her and aid her further—but aid her how?

Susanna started to follow, but the pricks in the tender skin of her feet stopped her. She couldn't remember the last time she'd walked outside in bare feet.

She had a vague recollection of having taken off her shoes once at Grandmother Eve's urging, likely because her grandmother had bared her own feet. Of course, Mother would never have allowed such scandalous behavior.

Susanna peered down at her toes poking out from the hem of her petticoats. The long grass tickled her skin, and the coldness of the damp earth pressed against her soles.

"Whatever will I tell Mother now?"

Chapter
4

Ben pressed his thumbs into his temples to ward off the ache that was creeping into the inner reaches of his head. He wished he could discard his waistcoat down to his shirtsleeves, toss off his wretched wig, and simply be himself.

Instead he was stuck in the parlor of the Smith home, attempting to make polite conversation about matters that held no interest to him.

He hadn't wanted to come, but as usual Cranch had convinced him to accompany him. He'd long ago decided Cranch should have been the lawyer. Somehow his friend could always talk his way into getting what he wanted.

Ben knew he shouldn't complain about the visit. Making the trip to Weymouth had given him the perfect excuse he'd needed to schedule a meeting with the Caucus Club at Arnold Tavern out on the coastal road. It had been several weeks since he'd last met with the men.

He sat back in the uncomfortable parlor chair, and to his dismay it creaked rather loudly, drawing Mrs. Smith's attention.

"So, Mr. Ross." Mrs. Smith sat in a chair next to the marble fireplace, near her husband, the Reverend Smith, who was pacing the length of the Oriental carpet centered on the wood floor. "We're not overly pleased with the results of the trial yesterday."

Ben had already received plenty of negativity for invoking the benefit of the clergy for old Joe, and he was tired of it. But he stuffed down a caustic remark and forced himself to answer politely. "You can rest assured, I'm not pleased with the results either."

Mrs. Smith's elegant eyebrows lifted. "Is that so?"

"Mother, please," Mary said, "may we please talk of something besides the trial?"

"No, dear," Mrs. Smith cut off the girl. "I'm sure we'd all like to hear Mr. Ross explain himself." Her tone was condescending, and it was obvious she didn't like him. He'd seen it in her face when Cranch had introduced him. She was probably wondering—like he was—why he was there.

He hesitated, but the pressure to defend himself was too great. "I'm not pleased with the results of our court system. We ought to all be ashamed when justice is usurped and decisions are based on the feelings and whims of the fickle populace instead of careful consideration of the facts."

Mrs. Smith's lips formed around a word, but she clearly couldn't find an appropriate response and instead turned to her husband. "What do you think, Reverend Smith?"

Just as she uttered the question, her attention snapped to the hallway outside the parlor and she gasped. "Susanna!"

There in the hallway, in the process of tiptoeing past the doorway over squeaking floorboards, was Susanna.

At her mother's sharp call, the young woman froze.

"Ah, there you are, my dear Susanna," called the reverend,

coming to a halt in his pacing. "I was telling the gentlemen you were likely hidden away somewhere reading. And it looks like I was correct."

"Yes, Father. You know me well." Quickly Susanna tucked a small book into the folds of her skirt. She kept her head down and turned away from her mother, who was rising from her chair. "If you'll excuse me while I change into dinner apparel, I'll join you shortly."

Without waiting for her parents' dismissal, she started to rush to the stairway.

"Susanna Smith!" Mrs. Smith's voice was laced with horror, and Susanna jerked to a halt again.

The carpet muted Mrs. Smith's firm footsteps. But tension radiated in each thump the woman took toward her daughter. She stopped in front of Susanna and peered down at the girl's shoes . . .

Or lack thereof.

Ben sat straighter and couldn't keep from staring at the dirty foot peeking out from beneath the hem of Susanna's gown.

"I can explain," Susanna said.

But Mrs. Smith was already pushing aside the layers of muslin, revealing Susanna's other bare foot. "My gracious, what has happened to you?"

"I'm perfectly fine, Mother. Nothing unseemly has happened."

The slender curve of her ankle and the pure creamy skin had likely never seen the light of day.

Or the sights of any man.

At Mary's soft intake of breath, Cranch chuckled.

Only then did Susanna glance into the parlor, first to Mary, then to Cranch sitting next to her sister on the settee. Beneath a tumble of wind-tossed waves of hair, Susanna glared at the man, rebuking him for his impropriety.

Cranch wiped away his grin, but his twinkling eyes laughed at her.

Ben gave a muted cough, unable to resist the temptation to goad her.

Her gaze shifted to him, and her eyes widened with surprise that was rapidly chased away by embarrassment when he made a point of looking directly upon her bare feet and her slim ankles that her mother's fussing had revealed.

She jerked away from her mother and yanked her petticoats down, tucking her feet and ankles out of sight.

Had she remembered her childhood declaration, that she'd much rather stay stuck in a tree than show him her ankles?

He couldn't contain his grin.

She glanced away, but not before he caught sight of the mortification rounding her features.

"Susanna, I'm speechless," Mrs. Smith said. "Absolutely speechless."

"I can explain—"

"There is no excuse for appearing in this condition."

Susanna swept aside the waves of hair that fell about her head in abandon, revealing her flushed cheeks and windswept beauty.

Ben's heart gave an unexpected thump. There was no denying Susanna Smith was indeed an attractive woman, from her wildly flowing hair all the way to her lovely, dainty toes.

"However, to show up in this . . . this deplorable condition? When we have company?" Mrs. Smith continued, her tone rising a notch. "This is completely unacceptable behavior."

"I agree." Susanna straightened her shoulders. "If I had known Mr. Cranch was arriving so early—and bringing a guest with him—I would have made a point of returning much sooner."

"You knew I didn't want you lingering out of doors."

Susanna pressed her lips together, having the grace not to disagree further with her mother in front of everyone, even though her eyes flashed with a rebuttal Ben would have enjoyed hearing.

"And exactly where are your boots?" Mrs. Smith asked.

For a long moment, Susanna didn't say anything. The clink of dishes in the dining room where the slave was preparing their table seemed to grow louder. The thick aroma of roasted veal and cabbage had already penetrated the parlor, stirring Ben's stomach with hunger.

Finally Susanna lifted her chin. "I've given my boots to a poor beggar woman who had much more need of them than I did."

"You did what?" Mrs. Smith sputtered the words.

"I gave them away."

"That was very generous of you, Susanna," Reverend Smith said. "I'm sure your dear mother would have done the same thing had she been in your situation."

Ben couldn't imagine Mrs. Smith ever doing something such as that. She seemed too proper and sophisticated to bare her feet. But then again, he never would have expected spoiled Susie to take off her boots either.

Maybe she had changed more than he'd believed possible.

"We shall have a new pair of boots cobbled for Susanna to reward her benevolence." Reverend Smith smiled at his daughter. "I'm sure she's due for a new pair anyway."

Susanna returned her father's smile. "Thank you, Father. But I have plenty of shoes—"

"No, Susanna. That was your only pair of buskins." Mrs. Smith stood with the regality of a dowager queen. "We shall have to have new ones made. Perhaps Mr. Ross can take Susanna's measurements tonight."

Her words slapped him in the face.

"You're still living with your parents, aren't you, Mr. Ross?"

"That's correct." At twenty-eight he wasn't exactly proud he'd taken up residence with his father and mother. But he wasn't a freeholder and didn't have the means to buy any property of his own. Ben had been grateful his father had offered him the back room of the house for his law office.

"Your father still is a cordwainer, is he not?"

From the gleam in her eyes, he could tell they both knew what she was doing. She was attempting to put him in his place. He forced a cold calmness to his tone. "If you'd like to send your daughter's foot measurements with me, I'll be sure to pass them along to my father."

"Very well. I give you permission to take Susanna's measurements before you leave," Mrs. Smith said. "And I do hope your father will appreciate our solicitation as we will be neglecting the cordwainer here in Weymouth."

Ben wanted to tell her his father wouldn't want to make Susanna's buskins, that they could take their business to the Weymouth shoemaker. But even as the words pushed for release, he held them back. The truth was, he could use another excuse to return to Weymouth for a future Caucus meeting. Delivering the buskins for his father would give him the cover he needed without arousing suspicion.

"Thank you, Mrs. Smith," he said stiffly. "As long as your daughter is willing to allow me access to her foot . . ."

Susanna's gaze snagged his. "Since you've already taken the liberty of viewing my feet, I don't see any reason to guard my modesty further."

Framed in the doorway, with her long hair swirling about

her elegant face in wild waves and her eyes flashing, she was a sight to behold. He had an urge to stand, stride across the room, yank her body against his, and show her . . .

Show her what?

He swallowed the swift desire that rose at the thought of holding her.

She lifted her nose just slightly with a pride that challenged him and stirred his blood.

Yes, he'd show her . . .

Show her that she wasn't better than him anymore.

If only the evening would come to an end.

Susanna twisted her spoon next to the uneaten plum pudding left at her spot from the first course. The molasses and butter had melted and formed a river around the mound.

But neither of the two courses at dinner had tempted her, not when she couldn't stop thinking about the young woman she'd met in the orchard.

Of course, her lack of appetite had nothing to do with Mr. Ross and his presence across the wide dining room table.

She'd avoided looking at him during the meal. And she'd had the distinct impression he'd done the same. Except for glancing at her as she'd made a grand entrance into the dining room earlier, after she'd returned properly attired, he avoided her as if she'd contracted smallpox.

Susanna had prayed that in her elegant silver evening gown the guests would forget how uncivilized she appeared when she'd arrived home without boots. From the gentle easing of the strained lines on Mother's face, Susanna could only hope the diversion had worked.

She twisted her spoon again, this time clinking it against

the fine porcelain plate. With her father on one side and her brother William on the other, she'd had altogether too little conversation and too much time to brood.

Mr. Cranch's lively voice rose, followed by Mary's delighted laughter.

He'd arrived much too early. And why had he brought the impossible Mr. Ross with him?

She tried to conjure grievousness toward Mr. Ross for his earlier impudence toward her. She wanted to be offended at him for the impropriety of brazenly staring at her bare feet. After all, any gentleman would have averted his attention or at the very least pretended not to notice.

But inexplicably she couldn't maintain her feelings of insult, not with the memory of the past evening and the way his blue eyes hadn't been able to let go of hers, or the way his fingers had skimmed her cheek.

She peeked at him from beneath her lashes, at the strong square line of his jaw and the seriousness with which he held himself. She couldn't deny that he'd turned into a fine-looking man.

Mr. Cranch swung his new watch by a silver chain, having amused them with the story of how a street urchin had stolen his previous watch right out of his pocket and how he'd been forced to buy this new one. "And to think I could have purchased this beauty for half the price in London."

"I'm sure you could have purchased it for half here too," Mr. Ross said, tossing out another of his cantankerous comments. "If only you were less gullible and had more business sense about you."

"Indeed." Mr. Cranch flashed a winsome smile. "Mr. Ross is correct. The shopkeepers love to see me because they know they'll make a hefty profit whenever I visit."

Mary laughed and she leaned closer to Mr. Cranch. Her pale face was flushed, and her eyes had a lovesick droop to them. From the smile that graced Mother's lips, Susanna decided Mary need not worry about Mother disapproving of the match.

Susanna stifled a smile of her own, knowing later in bed Mary would keep her up again whispering about the wonderful Mr. Cranch.

"The British have continued to raise the prices of their imported goods," Mr. Ross said, "and there's no use pretending otherwise."

"'Twould seem only natural to me that they do so." Father sat back in his chair and took a sip of his Madeira. "Considering the enormous cost of the war with France."

"But raising prices and subsequently demanding the colonists purchase all their goods only from England will create trouble." Mr. Ross's retort was decisive. "The king is a fool to make more demands without first consulting us for input and cooperation."

The conversation grew suddenly silent. The crackling of the logs burning in the wide fireplace and the distant clank of pans in the kitchen sifted through the awkward silence.

Mr. Ross's words bordered on seditious, and they all knew it.

"Erelong," he continued, apparently undaunted by the controversial topic, "the British will be adding taxes to everything."

She squirmed, waiting for one of the other men to speak.

But Father only sipped his wine, and Mr. Cranch was whispering something to Mary.

If no one else would challenge Mr. Ross's rebellious thoughts, then they left her little choice but to speak up.

"Why shouldn't the British add taxes? Our mother country has incurred a staggering debt as a result of the war—a war they fought on *our* behalf."

"Oh, you can be sure the war was not entirely for our benefit," he countered.

She toyed with the edge of her napkin. "Why should the people of England be held responsible and suffer for the cost of *our* war? Surely we can abide a few extra taxes to alleviate the burden that should rightly be ours?"

In the glow of the candelabras on either side of the long table, Mr. Ross's eyes turned into smoldering embers.

"That's easy for you to say, Miss Smith." His voice was taut. "You and your family can easily bear the burden of higher prices and taxes. But what of those who cannot?"

"The British army in the colonies benefits us all, poor and wealthy alike."

"I'm not entirely sure having ten thousand Redcoats upon our shores is beneficial to *anybody*."

Mother peered at her over the edge of her glass. She leveled a frown at Susanna, one that said she'd overstepped the bounds of propriety again.

But Susanna couldn't seem to stop herself from expressing her thoughts as Mr. Ross sat back in his chair, steepled his fingers under his chin, and watched her, inviting—even anticipating—her rebuttal.

"Should we not be grateful for the protection of so fine an army?" she asked.

"The requirement to quarter them only adds to the burden of the colonists, especially during a time of peace. I'm beginning to think the soldiers are here not so much for keeping peace as they are for enforcing the king's unpopular policies."

His responses were as quick and intelligent as they'd been

at the trial—and entirely stimulating. She pretended not to see Mother's deepening frown. "God has meant for men to obey their kings. Do you really think you know better than the king and the learned men of parliament?"

"How can men three thousand miles away know our needs better than we do?"

"And just how can God up in heaven know what's best for us? Surely we must trust He has our best interests in mind even when we don't understand His ways."

Mr. Cranch gave a soft whistle. "Ben, my stuffy old friend, I do believe you've finally met your equal in Miss Smith's convincing tongue."

"I've always thought Susanna overly forthright," Mother said, rising from the table, signaling the end of their meal and conversation.

But Mr. Ross didn't move. Instead he held Susanna's gaze, and a slow, satisfied smile crept across his lips, one that spread into his eyes, one that seemed meant for her alone.

For the first time since their encounter yesterday, a small blossom of hope unfurled inside her. Was it possible they didn't have to be enemies anymore? Could he find the charity within himself to forgive her for her past mistakes?

Tentatively she offered him a smile in return. She might not agree with his seditious leanings, but she could appreciate a fine mind when she encountered one.

As they exited the dining room and congregated in the front parlor, she caught herself watching him on more than one occasion. Mary played the spinet and sang. Then Father concluded their evening by reading a passage of Scripture. When he was done, he managed to convince Mother and William to accompany him to his study.

Susanna concealed a smile behind her hand at Father's

clever maneuvering to allow Mary some time alone with Mr. Cranch. Of course, Mother hadn't protested too loudly, another sign that perhaps Mary had finally captured the attention of a man that lived up to Mother's high standards.

After they were gone, Mr. Cranch wasted no time in pulling his chair next to Mary's.

Mr. Ross rose from his seat by the fireplace and glanced first to the window, then to the door. From his caged expression, she guessed he'd rather be anywhere but there.

Susanna shifted against the hard seat of her chair, wishing she could sneak off to the warm kitchen hearth and read. But she was a prisoner in the room too. Although her parents hadn't said the words, she knew they expected her to remain with Mary and act as her chaperone.

Mr. Ross glanced in her direction.

Quickly she pretended to be busy tucking a stray hair back into the smooth coiffure Phoebe had managed to help her arrange in spite of the earlier tangles. The slave had even added a white rosette to the coif, a larger version of the striped ribbon rosettes sewn among the pleated robings of her sleeve.

When he stared at her again, this time longer, her heart sputtered. She ought to stare right back at him to show him he wasn't having any effect on her. But she had the impression he'd see through her façade.

Instead she focused on the embroidered edge of her gown, which opened in the front to reveal her silky petticoat beneath.

Out of the corner of her eye she could see him crossing the room. When he stopped in front of her, she couldn't resist lifting her gaze to meet his keen one.

"Alas, Miss Smith," he said, "it appears we've been relegated to act as chaperones to our enamored companions. Hence we may as well make the most of it."

"They are enamored, aren't they?" Although she was happy for her sister, a twinge of jealousy tugged at her nonetheless. Young men paying court to Mary had always been as plentiful as herrings. And since Mary must wed first, Susanna had conceded her beautiful fair-haired sister to the suitors. None had appealed to her anyway. None had what really mattered—justice, honesty, prudence—among other virtues. Instead they were governed by self-interest.

"Have you read any Milton today?" He lowered himself into the chair next to her.

She shook her head, testing the sincerity of his words. Was he planning to belittle her again for reading? Or perhaps he would snub her as so many men did when they learned of her love of books. Most men didn't want a wife who was an independent thinker or more knowledgeable than them.

"Are you planning to condemn me, Mr. Ross, like so many of your sex?"

"That depends."

"And what exactly is so wrong about a woman learning to read something other than the Bible? Isn't a woman's mind equal to that of a man?"

"I can see that yours is."

"The intellectual capabilities of *all* women are no less than those of men," she insisted. "If we weren't denied the same opportunities of education, then we would at last have the chance to prove it."

"So what are you saying, Miss Smith? That girls should be able to attend school alongside the boys? Perhaps even Harvard?" His voice held the hint of laughter. "What next? Women opening law practices or becoming ministers?"

"You're mocking me."

"Then what reason could women possibly have for higher learning?"

"Education has the capability of making women better wives and mothers. Since families are the cornerstone of our society, we should strengthen women's abilities to teach their children because then we strengthen our society as a whole."

He sat forward and studied her, the humor fading from his countenance.

She held her breath, waiting for his response, wondering how he could possibly argue with her further.

"Go on. Perhaps you'll convince me yet."

"Very well." Her heart quavered. Never had a man cared what she had to say on anything, let alone when it came to providing girls with educational opportunities. "In youth the mind is like a tender twig, which you may bend as you please, but in age it's like a sturdy oak and hard to move."

He nodded, the earnestness of his expression spurring her on.

"Therewith young girls ought to sit alongside their brothers and gain the same knowledge while they are in their youth. Why are they any less deserving?"

"Am I to surmise you've been denied this very thing?"

She pushed down the bitter disappointment that surfaced whenever she thought about the education her parents had given to William but refused her. "My father has always been lenient about my use of his library. And Grandmother Eve has done her best to take me under her limited tutelage."

"But that hasn't been enough, has it?" he finished for her softly, his expression almost tender.

The question echoed the pain in her heart and sent a lump into her throat.

Amidst the glow of the fireplace and dim light of several candles, the intense lines of Mr. Ross's face had disappeared. And when he leaned forward and rested his elbows on his knees, she had the urge to scoot her chair closer to him.

Mary's happy laughter drifted toward them, followed by Mr. Cranch's.

His eyes went to the couple, and Susanna's followed. "I certainly hope Mother will approve of Mr. Cranch," she whispered. "Otherwise I'm afraid Mary shall have a broken heart."

Mr. Ross's eyebrow quirked. "Ah, yes. Your mother has great aspirations for whom you marry, doesn't she?"

The sudden tense undercurrent in his tone brought Susanna back to reality and to the fact that she was conversing with Benjamin Ross, whom she'd so foolishly degraded those many years ago.

"I wish I could say Mother doesn't have such high standards," Susanna said, "but I'm afraid that wouldn't be truthful."

A chill from the September evening slithered across the floor and wound its way between them, chasing away the warmth.

"Surely your standards aren't much different than hers."

She hugged her arms to her chest. "I admit, I'm caught in the trap of having to make a beneficial match." As much as she longed to be free from the constraints of the way things had always been done, some chains were not meant to be broken.

"So you're still waiting for your rich prince after all."

The truth of his words pierced her and pushed her to her feet. "And just how are you different from me, Mr. Ross? I saw you with my cousin Hannah Quincy last evening. You weren't hanging over every word she spoke because of their brilliance."

He sat back as if surprise over her words had pushed him there.

"Don't pretend you aren't interested in status. An important Quincy like Hannah would be a fine catch for an aspiring lawyer like you."

He didn't say anything for a long moment. "I call for a truce, Susanna."

At the sound of her given name, all traces of her indignation blew away.

"In fact, I concede to your superior skill at arguing a case."

Somehow in an instant all the earlier warmth returned with the heat of a late summer day.

"Please." He motioned at her chair. "Sit back down."

"Very well, I accept the truce." He was infuriating and intriguing and altogether likable at the same time. And she felt helpless to do anything but lower herself.

He slid off his chair and onto one knee before her. With a devilish grin, his eyes glimmered with unspoken challenge. "Since we've called a truce, then I guess you won't object if I view your foot."

Her breath caught in her throat.

"If we want to keep the peace"—he dangled the measuring tape Mother had given him after dinner—"then we dare not disobey your mother's wishes that I take your measurements."

"If you think I'm still overly prude to bare my foot, then you're sorely mistaken."

"Then let's see you do it." His voice was low, and the blue of his eyes darkened to the shade of the sky at eventide.

She knew she couldn't refuse his challenge, that she needed to prove she was no longer the same silly girl who'd denied him a look at her foot. Nevertheless, her legs trembled, and she was grateful for the layers of her petticoats that hid her embarrassment.

"I don't think you can do it," he whispered.

"Of course I can." Before her rational side could convince her otherwise, she crossed her legs at the knees, plucked off her worsted damask shoe, and lifted her skirt and the layer of petticoats underneath. She bunched the satin to her knee—much higher than necessary, a spurt of defiance giving her fresh boldness. When she reached the top of her fine silk stocking, she plucked the ribbon of the garter and loosened it. Then she began to roll down the delicate material, deliberately slow, inch by inch revealing her smooth untouched skin.

He followed the path her stocking made, his expression remaining calm as though he made an everyday occurrence viewing the bare legs of women.

As she passed her ankle, her heart quivered. She was relieved when he stopped her with a touch of his hand.

"I need to take your measurement with your stocking on, Susanna."

"Of course." She lowered her lashes to hide the mortification that was sure to be in her eyes. Had she really almost willingly bared her foot to Benjamin Ross?

She suspended her foot before him, resisting the overwhelming urge to pull her stockings back up to her knees and tuck her feet back into the safety of her petticoats.

If he could view her leg and foot with unabashed boldness, then surely she could sit for a moment without squirming.

He lifted his hand toward her foot, but hesitated. Only then did she notice him swallow hard. The tips of his fingers made contact with the sensitive skin of her sole before moving to trace the edge of her arch. Through the thin layer of silk his touch still sent ripples of warmth up her leg into her stomach.

Jody Hedlund

"I guess I finally must admit you're quite grown up." Only then did he look up.

His gaze caressed her just as surely as his hand on her foot.

She shivered at the intensity of the intimacy, the heat in her stomach tightening. She knew she ought to pull away, that she ought not to encourage him, that she needed to keep their interaction businesslike.

But even if his hold on her foot was feather soft, his grip on her heart was like a balled fist. She couldn't breathe, couldn't move, couldn't think.

"You've turned into a beautiful woman, Susanna" came his whispered confession, almost as if he were helpless to say anything else.

The words stirred something inside her, something she couldn't explain, which made her want to lean closer to him. She was sure he could hear the rapid tapping of her heartbeat against her ribs and see the longing in her eyes.

She tried to form her lips into a smile. "Does this mean you've forgiven me for my past mistakes?"

His gaze dropped. He fumbled for the measuring tape and lifted it to her foot. All the warmth of his touch evaporated and in its place was the brusqueness of a cordwainer.

Had she read more into his words than he'd intended?

"I truly am sorry for the intolerably rude things I said to you when we were younger."

"Let bygones be bygones." He stretched the string across the length of her foot from her heel to her big toe.

"Then you shall forgive me?" She wasn't sure why she coveted his forgiveness, but suddenly she longed for it with a sharpness that set her on the edge of her chair.

He flipped the measuring tape to the width of her foot but didn't respond.

An ache crimped a corner of her heart.

Finally he sighed. "I forgive you, Susanna. But that doesn't change who we are, does it?"

Why did they have to consider who they were or what families they were from? But even as she asked herself the question, she knew it did matter—to both of them.

"Perhaps we'll be able to be friends?" she offered.

"Perhaps." His answer had a hollow ring to it.

And much to her surprise, the uncertainty of his response left an emptiness in the middle of her chest.

Chapter
5

Ben pitched another forkful of salt hay onto the heaping mound in the wagon. His hands were blistered and his muscles throbbed, but he felt invigorated in a way that he hadn't since his return to Braintree earlier in the fall.

"You're keeping up with your brothers better than I thought you would," his father called down from the top where he straddled the tall stack, his feet sinking deep in the hay. The tidal waters infused the sea grasses with salt and nutrients that would keep the cows and sheep healthy and well fed during the coming winter.

"I'm surprised too." Ben stopped and wiped his brow, letting the cool breeze off the bay bathe his face. They'd been working in the marshes for several days. He had to admit that as much as he loved his books and practicing law, he'd also missed the satisfaction that came from spending a day under the wide-open sky. The wet scent of the wind and the sand surrounded him at every turn, filling his senses, reminding him of the many autumns he'd spent along the shore doing the same thing.

"I appreciate your help," his father said, looking out at the whitecaps rolling in over the distant beach. In an unguarded moment, Ben caught a glimpse of the all too familiar anxiety in his father's eyes.

"I'm more than pleased to assist," Ben replied. Since his return he'd noticed the grooves in his father's forehead and the slump of his shoulders. Even though his father never complained, Ben had overheard plenty of locals talk about how difficult the past year had been. With the continually rising price of British goods, his father—like many farmers—hadn't been able to afford to hire help for the haying or the other work.

With a frustrated shake of his head, Ben sank his fork into the cut grass his younger brothers had left behind for him to pitch into the wagon. They were already well ahead of the horse and wagon, doing the hard work of mowing the hay with the blades of their scythes.

"Heard a rumor that the British officer was moving out of Braintree," his father said. "Guess the rumor was right."

Ben followed his father's gaze to the coastal road. At the sight of Lieutenant Wolfe and his assistant, along with several other soldiers, Ben straightened. Their horses were loaded with their haversacks and supplies. They were clearly moving out of Braintree.

He hadn't rested easy since the officer had taken up residence in their community during the past month. The lieutenant had demanded accommodations under the antiquated Quartering Act, which hadn't pleased any of the farmers who were already struggling. Having to give free lodging and meals to the lieutenant and his men had only strained their empty purses all the more.

No one had been able to understand why the British had

sent the lieutenant to their community. But Ben suspected the king was attempting to determine exactly how much smuggling was going on up and down the coastline outside of Boston, especially if parliament was getting ready to enforce the Molasses Act and put an end to the illegal activities the colonists relied upon.

Ben didn't want to think about what would happen to tradesmen and farmers like his father if they had to depend solely upon British imports. The king already picked the colonists' pockets every day. Without the option of smuggled goods, the king's stealing would grow even worse.

"Have you heard where the lieutenant is going next?" Ben asked, tossing hay up to his father.

His father shook his head. "No one knows."

"Hopefully he's taking his red monkey suit and his puppets back to Boston."

The lieutenant swerved his horse off the road and began galloping toward them, almost as if Ben's quiet muttering had traveled across the field and reached his ears.

Ben plunged the tip of his pitchfork into the muddy marsh and stared at the approaching officer, unwilling to let a king's soldier scare him.

"Be careful, son. There's a time for war and a time for peace. And we need to know which is when."

Ben hadn't discussed his involvement with the Caucus Club with his father, but he didn't doubt his father had guessed his leanings. Ben had always harbored dissatisfaction with the methods the British used in governing the colonies. But since his days in law school, as well as his growing friendships with Boston merchants like Cranch, his frustrations had only increased.

"Esquire Ross," the lieutenant called as he drew near.

Ben's muscles tensed. Even though he wasn't technically involved in any of the smuggling, he'd agreed to act as the liaison between the Boston merchants and the smugglers. Had the lieutenant learned of his role?

The officer reined his horse and nodded at Ben. "Congratulations are in order for your defense of Mr. Sewall earlier in the week."

"Thank you, Lieutenant. It's easy to defend someone who's innocent."

The officer sat straight. His tall, cocked officer's hat lent him another foot of height, making him even more imposing. But it was his sharp piercing eyes that sent a shiver of unease up Ben's back. The hard glint was anything but congratulatory or friendly.

"Seems you are gaining quite the reputation for defending rascals both in and out of Boston."

"Everyone deserves a fair trial, rascal or not."

The lieutenant studied him a moment, taking in his sweat-stained hat down to his mud-caked boots. A derisive grin formed at the corners of the officer's pinched lips. "You have a way with words, Esquire Ross. It's lamentable that you have to waste your eloquence on the guilty."

"And I suppose you're qualified to act as judge?"

"Much more qualified than you. Then again, even the swine need someone from among their own to defend them."

A sharp rebuttal rose swiftly.

"Is there something we can do for you, Lieutenant?" his father interjected before Ben could utter his response and shot him a glance that issued caution.

The lieutenant didn't bother to acknowledge his father's question, but instead pinned Ben with a final glare before spinning his horse and trotting away.

"What was that all about?" his father asked when the lieutenant was back on the road with his regiment.

Ben lifted his pitchfork and wished he could send it flying into the air after the lieutenant. "Just one more example of someone with power thinking he can intimidate those without it."

His father slid down the hay mound, sending a spray of dust and grass into the air. "Let him go, son. He's not worth the frustration."

"He was intolerably rude to both of us. Doesn't that bother you?"

"It isn't worth my time." His father raised one of the horse's hand-hewn mud boots intended to keep the mud from weighing the beast down. He combed his fingers over the boot and dislodged a clump of thick sludge.

Ben shook his head. All too familiar anger and helplessness twined through his gut like leather stitching. He was weary of the mockery from those born to a higher class. More than that, he was weary of watching his family struggle to survive year in and year out.

His father had made incredible sacrifices for him to go to Harvard, to make sure he was never in want of books or anything he'd needed in his pursuit of education.

Surely now he could make his father proud of him by rising higher, gaining more, and becoming someone great. If he bettered himself, then he'd be able to help his family. He could repay his father for all his sacrifices. He could keep men like Lieutenant Wolfe from making a mockery of them.

Ben swiped off his hat and knocked the dust from it. "We're all created equal, Father. And I can't sit idly back and let men or kings deny us our fundamental and unalienable rights."

"I know you can't sit back, son." His father's eyes lit with pride. "You're different than me, and you're destined to do more than I ever could."

Fresh determination surged into Ben's blood. He knew he couldn't rest. He had to continue to work with all the industry and ambition he'd always employed.

And of course the right match with the right woman wouldn't hurt either.

"I'm very pleased with your progress learning your letters, Anna," Susanna said to the last of the young girls who remained in the big kitchen. In the dismal gray afternoon, the light from the hearth and several large candles added a homey glow to the back room of the parsonage.

"Thank you, Miss Smith." Anna wrapped her worn cloak about her shoulders, but her eyes were riveted to the oak hornbook with the faded sheet of yellowish horn covering a printed page of letters, syllables, and the Lord's Prayer.

"Would you like to take the hornbook home with you?" Susanna closed her copy of the *New England Primer*, which she preferred versus the old hornbook that had once belonged to Grandmother Eve.

Anna nodded eagerly. "Oh, would you let me?"

"Of course." Susanna fanned her overheated face with her apron. The warmth from the enormous stone fireplace permeated the kitchen, along with all the tantalizing scents of Phoebe's preparations for the evening repast—corn chowder and roasted duck.

"I promise I'll be careful. And I'll keep it dry." Anna tucked the hornbook into her cloak to protect it from the cold drizzle that had started falling during school time.

"I have every confidence in you," Susanna said, wishing each of her girls was as eager to learn as Anna Morris.

She glanced at the open door to the other girls already well on their way down the winding road. At least they came to her lessons when they could. "Hurry now and catch up with the rest." Susanna ushered the girl toward the door.

"I want you girls to make sure you stay together." Even though nothing had happened over the past week since Hermit Crab Joe's trial, she couldn't shake her fear that it was only a matter of time before someone else was hurt. "Please be careful."

"Yes, Miss Smith." Anna pulled up the hood of her cloak and started outside.

Susanna put a hand on her arm. "Wait." She grabbed an apple tart from the long plank worktable and held out the delicacy to Anna. "Take this too."

"Thank you." Anna's face was etched with a hunger that was all too common among the children of the poor widows of the parish.

Even though Susanna made certain the girls had something to eat—usually bread, cheese, and apples—when they came to her dame school, she knew they were always battling hunger. Their mothers couldn't earn enough to provide for all their needs, even with the spinning and weaving work Mother provided.

"Go on now." Susanna nodded toward the other girls.

Anna tucked her hands into the folds of her cloak, hiding the tart, and then she skipped off into the cold autumn afternoon.

Susanna leaned against the open doorframe, letting the cool mist brush her hot cheeks. She derived great pleasure from imparting knowledge to the impressionable young minds and only wished she didn't feel so inadequate as their teacher. After all the time she poured into helping the girls, she'd hoped to see more progress by now.

Yet regrettably she expected most of them came because she fed them and because they could socialize away from the unending work they faced at home.

Deep inside she'd wanted to prove that the poor young girls of the community could learn just as well as the boys, that girls were worthy of an education too, that the naysayers were wrong.

But what if they were correct after all? What if men's minds really were stronger? It was altogether too grievous to embrace the possibility that women weren't meant to give themselves over to reading and writing, that they truly were more useful focusing their attention on household affairs.

With a sigh Susanna closed the door and then leaned against it. "I don't know, Phoebe. What if all my work with these young girls is merely a waste of time?"

"Don't say things like that, Miss Susie," Phoebe said sharply as she slipped one apple slice after another onto the twine above the fireplace where she would dry them in readiness for their winter stores. "You're doing a good thing for them, and that's all there is to it."

"But they don't seem to be excited about learning."

"Don't you go thinking that anyone's gonna be as excited about learning as you." Phoebe's dark skin glistened with the heat from the hearth. "'Sides, you're helping them better themselves. And that's all that matters."

"Maybe they don't want to better themselves. Maybe they're content without an education."

"Sometimes people don't know what they need till they have it." Phoebe didn't break her steady rhythm in stringing the apples. Since she was tall and thin, she could easily reach the twine, except that her turban continually bumped against the bundles of herbs dangling from the beams in the ceiling.

Susanna smiled at the slave who was as dear to her as Tom. "How'd you become so wise, Phoebe?"

Phoebe wove the last piece of apple and then flashed her a sly smile. "Those girls aren't the only ones getting a learning from you. I might be busy in here with all my work, but I got my eyes and ears wide open."

"Good." Susanna pushed away from the door and crossed the room to the table where she'd left her supply of books and teaching materials. "I only wish you'd let me teach you properly."

"Maybe someday." Phoebe sprang toward the bubbling pot on the hearth, stirring it before bounding over to the last bushel of apples and dumping them onto the chopping block. Susanna had never seen Phoebe walk. She always moved at top speed, never rested, never stopped working.

"You work more than anyone should have to."

"I like my work. It's good to work hard." Phoebe sorted through the apples, rapidly setting aside the ones too bruised or wormy that she would later make into vinegar. "Besides, we've got to know which things we can change, and accept the things we can't."

Phoebe had been Mother's slave forever, had grown up with Mother over at Mount Wollaston. And when Mother had married and moved to the Weymouth parsonage, Phoebe had come with.

After so many years, Susanna wished Mother would free Phoebe and pay her a fair wage like so many of their peers were beginning to do. At the very least, she'd asked Mother to hire more help so that Phoebe didn't need to shoulder so much of the work all the time.

But Mother had insisted she and Mary learn the chores and assist Phoebe so they would be well equipped to manage their own homes someday. Sometimes Susanna wondered if Mother used the work as one more excuse to keep her out of Father's study and away from the books. After all, William didn't have to do manual labor. Everyone assumed he'd have slaves and servants to do his work for him.

A light tap on the back door startled Susanna, and one of the books slipped from her pile and fell to the floor with a smack.

Her first thought was one of dread, that something had happened to the girls on the walk home.

She rushed back to the door and swung it open, letting the cold misty air hit her again.

A cloaked figure of a young woman hunched against the siding. Peering out from the shadows of the hood was the same lovely face of the young woman Susanna had met in the apple orchard the previous week, only this time she was thinner and more haggard, and her lips were blue from the cold.

"Miss," the woman greeted her hesitantly. Her cloak was damp, and strands of her wet hair stuck to her neck. "I don't know if you remember me. . . ."

"Of course I do." Susanna opened the door wider. "Please, come in."

"Oh, I can't, miss. I can't—"

"Please." Susanna had no doubt the woman was starving. "I insist."

The young woman stared into the warm kitchen, the longing to come inside palpable.

"Only for a few minutes," Susanna offered. "You don't have to stay long if you don't want to."

The woman started to shake her head and shrink back, until she spotted the tarts on the worktable.

"I'm sure Phoebe will be able to find something for you to eat."

Phoebe was already slicing more apples. The steady chopping of the knife against the cutting board didn't slacken, even as the slave's gaze flicked over the stranger. At the sight of the fine leather boots poking from beneath a mud-splattered hem, Phoebe's eyes sparkled. "Miss Susie, I see I have a reason to be proud of you."

Susanna nodded. "Yes, you do."

"She needs a bowl of my corn chowder." Phoebe set aside her apple slicing and wiped her hands on her apron.

Susanna grasped the young woman's arm and tugged her inside. She was too tired and hungry to resist as Susanna settled her on a bench near the hearth. Phoebe put a tankard of hot cider into the woman's hands, along with a bowl of chowder and a thick slice of bread slathered in the butter Susanna had helped churn only that morning.

"May I inquire after your name?" Susanna draped the woman's wet cloak over another bench in front of the fire to help it dry, doing her best to pretend the young woman wasn't devouring her food in large gulping bites.

"Everyone calls me Dotty." The young woman swallowed her mouthful.

"And I'm Susanna."

Dotty was slurping the chowder as though it would disappear if she didn't eat it quickly enough.

Susanna fidgeted with the cloak, all the while peeking at Dotty. Her bodice was still ripped and in need of a washing.

Her muslin cap was askew and streaked with several days' worth of grime. And the boots that had once been clean and tidy were now scratched and caked with mud.

"How are your feet?" Susanna asked gently, not wanting to frighten the woman with too much prying.

"Very well, miss. Very well. Thanks to you."

"I'm glad to hear it." Susanna moved to the table and began to cut another piece of bread. "I do hope you have a warm place to stay."

"It's not so bad, miss. Except that it's turning a mite cold at night now."

Susanna attempted to make a mental list of the places the young woman might be staying but could think of nowhere suitable. Was it possible Dotty was a vagrant and that she was living wherever she could find refuge?

"It most certainly *is* turning colder." Susanna spread a thick layer of butter across the bread and handed the extra piece to Dotty. "It won't be long now until a person could freeze to death if out in the cold all night."

Dotty took the bread but only looked at it. A shadow fell across her delicate features. "Aye, freeze to death. That they could, miss. That they could."

From the front of the house, the tinkling music of the spinet echoed a dismal tune, indicating that Mary had begun her daily practicing and was apparently choosing the music to reflect her mood. She'd been moping over Mr. Cranch's absence all week long.

Dotty glanced at the interior kitchen door and fear flashed across her face—the same fear Susanna had seen on her face the day in the apple orchard. She stood and folded the extra piece of bread.

"You don't have to leave yet," Susanna said.

But Dotty was already gathering her cloak. "I can't stay. I really can't."

"But you're welcome to have more to eat. Surely you haven't had enough. And your cloak is still damp. Can you stay until it's dry?"

"Thank you, miss. You're very kind. Very kind." The young woman tossed her cape around her shoulders and strode to the door. "But I've already been here overlong, and I can't chance anyone finding me."

Susanna was tempted to run to the door and throw her body across it to force Dotty to stay, at least until she was warm and well fed. But the young woman was already skittish and didn't need Susanna trapping her and adding to her fear. Dotty was obviously hiding from someone.

Was she a runaway?

Susanna wanted to ask, but if Dotty was indeed running away, Susanna's prying would make her bolt from her for good.

Even if plenty of indentured servants and slaves attempted to leave their masters every year, running away wasn't easy and was rarely successful.

"If you must leave so soon, then won't you at the very least take the rest of this loaf with you?" Susanna glanced at Phoebe, silently pleading her forgiveness for giving away the entire loaf.

Still chopping apples, Phoebe nodded. "Give her several of the tarts too."

Susanna wrapped as much as she could fit into a linen towel, tied it in a knot, and gave it to Dotty at the door.

"Please take it." Susanna pushed it into Dotty's arms. "And if you need anything else, I don't want you to be afraid to come here and ask for me."

"I don't know how to thank you, miss."

"You can thank me by promising to take care of yourself."

"I'll do my best, miss. Aye, that I will." Dotty pulled up her hood, opened the door, and slipped through. After a darting glance around the fenced yard of the parsonage, she ducked her head and dashed toward the gate, limping only slightly on her injured feet.

"By the way," Susanna called after her, "the barn door is never locked at night."

Dotty didn't stop to acknowledge that she'd heard. Instead she scrutinized the deserted yard, then let herself out the gate and sped toward the apple orchard.

Susanna watched her until she disappeared before finally turning back to the kitchen and closing the door.

"That girl's in a heap of trouble." Phoebe had laid aside her knife and apples and stood in front of the hearth. She swung the crane away from the fire and dipped a long wooden spoon into the kettle that hung from the trammel.

"Regrettably I must concur." Susanna pressed the back of her hand to her forehead. "I wish I knew more about her troubles so that I could be of better assistance."

"She's a runaway."

"Do you think so?"

"No doubt about it."

"I had almost come to the same conclusion myself. But how can we be sure?"

"She's got the look—the haunted look." Phoebe took several quick slurps from the spoon. "'Sides, she's hiding out and doesn't want anyone to find her. If that ain't a runaway, I don't know what is."

"You should have seen her feet when I met her the first time." Susanna pushed away from the door and started toward her discarded stack of books. "Her soles were cut and battered so badly she could hardly walk."

Phoebe pursed her thin lips together and gave a curt shake of her head. "Then it's a good thing she ran away from her master."

Susanna wanted to agree with Phoebe, but something held her back.

If Dotty were indeed an indentured servant who was running away from her master, then she was most definitely in a *heap* of trouble. And Susanna would be too if anyone discovered she was helping the young woman.

The contract of the indentured servant was binding by law. The servant agreed to work for a specified number of years for someone in exchange for the cost of the ship passage to America. If the servant broke the agreement by running away, then she was disobeying the law and subject to stiff penalties, including additional years of indenture, whippings, brandings, and in some cases execution.

And the penalty for assisting or harboring runaways was often severe too.

"No doubt that girl's got a reward out for her." Phoebe started stirring the chowder again in swift, jerking motions. "That's why she's hiding. She knows if someone spots her, they'll turn her in and get some money for it."

Susanna had seen the advertisements in the *Spectator*, the notices of rewards for runaways.

If Dotty had run away, then she was also now a criminal. And Susanna had no business assisting her. Hadn't she always believed God commanded them to obey the laws and leaders appointed to guide them?

She'd recently rebuked Mr. Ross for his subjective view of Scripture. And if she'd meant what she said, then surely she oughtn't to twist God's Word to fit her situation.

"What should we do, Phoebe? If she comes again, should I tell her to return to her master? Even if he's deplorable, at least she'll have a better chance of survival in a warm home than she will out here roaming the countryside." Susanna stared at the blue flames of the burning hickory and pictured Dotty's blue-cold lips.

"Don't you think she's already thought of returning?" Phoebe adjusted the crane, and the iron hook squeaked as she swung the kettle back over the low flames. "Seems like she's chosen to die out here instead of having to go back and face whatever made her run in the first place."

"Surely there are other recourses besides running away—"

Phoebe's constant motion came to an abrupt halt. Her face grew rigid and her eyes stony. "We both know what happened to my sister."

Susanna nodded solemnly. Even Mother had been grieved when she'd heard the news of Phoebe's sister's death at the hands of her master.

The fact was, Phoebe's sister would have done better to run away. But she'd stayed, even when the conditions had become deplorable.

And in the end, she'd been brutally tortured and murdered.

"If she'd run, she might still be alive." Anguish tightened the muscles in Phoebe's face as she stared out the window to a different time and a different place.

Susanna didn't know what to say. She never did when Phoebe talked of her sister. Susanna couldn't imagine such cruelty, but she supposed Phoebe had witnessed it and had decided that compared to what her sister had lived through, she'd been blessed. Mother might be a demanding mistress, but she was still kind to Phoebe and Tom. Susanna guessed that was one of the reasons Phoebe never talked about running away herself—even though if anyone could escape and survive, Phoebe was a likely candidate.

Phoebe spun back to the worktable, to the apples that still needed slicing, and resumed her chopping with sharp, even taps of the knife against the cutting board.

Susanna lifted the stack of books she'd used in her dame school and started to leave.

"Only one thing to be done for that runaway." Phoebe didn't miss a beat in the steady chops.

Susanna stopped.

"Help her."

As frightening as that prospect was, Susanna didn't know how she could possibly do anything less. "What shall I do?"

"Whatever you can."

"But what if I get in trouble?"

"If we're careful, no one will find out. And I'm sure Dotty won't stay long before she decides to move on."

Susanna tried to still her rapid pulse by telling herself there was nothing wrong with providing mercy and kindness to one so clearly in need, even if she was a criminal.

And if Dotty had been mistreated, perhaps there were legal recourses they could take to help her. Maybe they could press charges against her master and perhaps even win her freedom.

Susanna's mind spun with the sudden possibilities. She knew she couldn't tackle the problems herself. She'd need a good lawyer—one who was willing to help the less fortunate, one filled with compassion and mercy.

That ruled out Elbridge. Her cousin may have matured over the years. As a distant cousin and a Quincy, he was the kind of man who would meet Mother's approval for a suitor. But she doubted he'd be willing to defend a poor woman like Dotty.

Susanna stood up straighter. What about Ben Ross?

He'd treated Hermit Crab Joe with such civility, even though the man was an outcast. If anyone could help Dotty, surely Ben would. If she sent him a secret letter and explained the situation without giving him all the details, he would be able to advise her.

"I know what I'll do," Susanna said. "I shall write a confidential letter to Mr. Ross."

But even as her mind began to compose the letter to him, her heart quavered with uncertainty.

Did she really dare help Dotty? She'd not only risk endangering herself, but she might bring trouble upon Phoebe too, perhaps even her whole family.

Or was it better to stay safe and abide by the law as she'd always done?

Chapter
6

Ben leaned back on his elbows on the blanket spread over the warm sand and peered into the endless blue of the Massachusetts Bay.

He was doing his best not to stare at the beautiful woman sitting beside him on the blanket. But with each passing moment, he was finding it harder to keep his attention from straying to Susanna Smith. In a light yellow gown, her dark eyes and hair seemed only darker and more ravishing.

Cranch hadn't made the situation any easier when he'd pulled Mary up, claiming he was taking her for a walk down the beach. At least when they'd all been together, Ben had other distractions.

But now that he was alone with Susanna . . .

He nodded at the couple ambling away from them, Cranch having kept his hold on Mary's hand. "I think those two dragged us out here this afternoon so they could have time alone."

Susanna tipped up the wide brim of her straw hat decorated with ribbon and silk flowers that matched her dress. Her gaze followed the couple and strayed to their linked fingers before it dropped to her gloved hands folded in her lap. A smile hovered over her lips. "I don't blame them for wanting a moment of privacy, not when my mother won't let them be alone together for a single moment."

"So you don't mind getting coerced into playing chaperone again this afternoon?"

"I don't mind." She peeked again at the couple. "After having to watch Mary mope for the past week, wondering when she would get to see Mr. Cranch, I'm relieved to see her smiling again."

"She likes him, then?"

"Very much."

The squawk of a sea gull drew his attention back to the ocean and to the bird swooping above the gently lapping waves.

"At least they've picked a favorable day for their excursion," he said, having already discarded his cocked hat to let the sun's rays warm his face. And thankfully this stretch of Weymouth beach was fairly clean of the usual seaweed that lined the shore.

Some of the local farmers had likely hauled the slimy grass back to their fields to use as fertilizer. After gathering the salt hay, he had in fact helped his own father pick up seaweed along the coast near their farm in Braintree.

"Am I to presume, then," Susanna said, brushing at the sand that had made its way onto their blanket, "that you're not irritated with Mr. Cranch for dragging you along today?"

He shrugged. "I could think of worse things I could be doing." The truth was, since his father wasn't finished making Susanna's buskins, he'd needed an excuse to ride over to Weymouth. Cranch's invitation to accompany him on an outing with Mary had provided the cover he needed to attend a meeting with the Caucus Club.

"Are we that detestable to you, Mr. Ross?" Beneath the brim of her hat, her inky eyes met his and did strange things to his stomach as they had the last time he'd been with her in the parlor when he'd touched her foot.

"I'd be a liar if I said you were detestable, Miss Smith." Heat made a fist around his gut at the memory of the slender leg and delicate ankle she'd bared to him.

"If I'm not detestable, what am I?" Her lips curved up on one side and led to a dimple.

"Well, I wouldn't call you despicable either. Nor disparaging."

"I'm relieved to hear it. You sure know how to put a girl's heart at ease."

He grinned. He'd never prided himself at flirting—he'd always been so much better at arguing. But he had to give himself credit. He was doing a fine job flirting with Susanna Smith.

"I am rather advanced at paying compliments," he teased. "If you ever need one, don't hesitate to ask."

At his words, her smile dimmed and she refolded her hands in her lap, neatly, just like a well-trained lady. "I don't need a compliment today," she said quietly, with an urgency that hadn't been there before. "But I do need your advice."

"Then you're in luck, because I'm quite advanced at giving advice too—particularly when it's unwanted."

His words didn't elicit the dimple he wanted to see again. Instead she lowered her voice even more. "Did you receive the letter I sent with Tom yesterday?"

"Yes, I received it."

Alas, he'd done more than receive it. He'd kept it in his waistcoat, reading it more times than he cared to admit.

"I hope I wasn't presumptuous to send it to you."

"Of course not." He'd been more than a little surprised—and slightly flattered—when the Smith slave had stopped by the farm to deliver the letter while on his way to Boston for supplies.

"And . . . what do you think?"

"First, I think that in any future correspondence, you should refrain from using our given names. If such letters should happen to fall into the wrong hands or be read by prying eyes, you would put yourself in great danger."

If the girl in reference was a runaway indentured servant as Susanna presumed, then aiding the young woman would indeed be a risky venture.

Interestingly, his first reaction to Susanna's letter was to tell her to have nothing to do with the runaway. For a reason he couldn't explain, he didn't like the thought that Susanna might put herself at risk.

On the other hand, his esteem of her had risen. He hadn't thought her capable of doing something quite so noble as to sacrifice her own safety for someone less fortunate than herself.

"Then I shall assume a pen name." Her brow wrinkled in thought. "I shall be Diana, after the Roman goddess of the moon."

"So you think you are a goddess, my lady?" The sarcastic comment escaped before he could stop it.

Her long lashes fell to her cheeks and she tipped her head away from him, revealing her slender neck. He wasn't sure if her hat cast a becoming shadow over her cheeks or whether she was blushing. Either way, the picture she made, sitting on the beach under a bright blue sky in her fashionable hat and dress, was enough to make him forget about anything and anyone else.

"Forgive me, Susanna. I shouldn't have spoken so crossly." Hadn't she declared that she'd changed from the spoiled little girl she used to be? And hadn't he told her he'd forgive her past mistakes?

A ringlet of her dark hair dangled against her ear. The gentle sea breeze teased the loose curl, tantalizing him to sweep it away and let his fingers caress her skin instead.

"I suppose you've been reading Cicero this week," he said, wanting to make amends for his comment. "If I do say so, Cicero was rather fond of the goddess Diana."

Her mouth cocked into a half smile. "You've uncovered my secret sin. I beg you not to tell my mother I've been reading again."

"Our dear Cicero, the great Roman philosopher, says: 'Read at every wait; read at all hours; read within leisure; read in times of labor; read as one goes in; read as one goes out—'"

"'The task of the educated mind is simply put: read to lead.'" She finished the quote for him.

Satisfaction flooded his soul. How utterly fascinating to find a young woman who could quote Cicero as easily as himself. "Perhaps you truly are the goddess Diana."

"I consider myself a moon compared to my sister Mary's radiant sunshine." Her tone held the barest hint of envy.

"There's nothing wrong with being a moon. I've always considered the moon a steady light, ready to guide us through the darkest of nights."

"I like your analogy, Mr. Ross. Perhaps I need to have more faith that God will use me someday to be a steady light for someone going through a dark travail." She glanced down the shore again at Mary and Cranch, whose shoulders brushed together in their ever-slowing walk. Then as if shaking herself from her melancholy thoughts, she smiled at him, almost too brightly. "And if you need to correspond with me in return, what pen name shall you choose?"

Under the beam of her smile, his heart did another silly flip. "I shall take the name Lysander." He fumbled to find his smooth tongue. "Yes. Lysander, after the poor plain Spartan statesman."

"So you're willing to secretly advise me?"

"I'll do my best." He wasn't sure there was much he could do. Even though indentured servants had a few rights, the law essentially treated them like slaves, giving the masters jurisdiction to treat—or mistreat—them as they wished. One poor woman wouldn't have a significant case against her master, not enough to justify her running away.

But at least if he involved himself with the case, he could oversee Susanna's actions and hopefully keep her safe.

Susanna leaned toward him. "If I see her again, what should I tell her?"

"Try to get a clearer picture of her situation." A movement down the beach the opposite direction of Cranch and Mary caught Ben's attention. He pushed himself up. "There is no sense in plotting overly far ahead until we know more about her."

"Yes," she replied. "I suppose you're right."

He could make out the forms of two men on horseback riding their way. He sat up straighter. They were dressed in red—the unmistakable red that belonged only to the soldiers of King George.

"Do you think I should offer to help her," Susanna asked, "even if she's a runaway? After all, I don't want to break the law."

Had Lieutenant Wolfe relocated to Weymouth? Ben's muscles tightened in protest.

"If the law is unjust and oppressive, then perhaps it deserves to be broken." His tone was clipped. But there were much bigger issues at stake and much bigger laws that were unjust and oppressive than those having to do with runaway servants.

Susanna turned and saw the approaching soldiers astride their horses. She sat up, shifting her gown and smoothing it over her ankles.

Their modern muskets with bayonets served to remind Ben of how ancient the colonists' weapons were. His own flint-lock, an old squirrel gun, had been handed down to him from his grandfather, and likely from his grandfather before him. The old gun was typical of what many of the farmers had.

The stiff shoulders and pinched face of the man riding the center horse belonged to only one man—Lieutenant Wolfe. If the lieutenant had relocated to Weymouth, then that meant only one thing. The king was indeed growing more serious in his attempts to stop the colonists' smuggling.

"Just what we needed," Ben said. "A visit from the dressed-up red monkey himself, Lieutenant Wolfe."

"Why, Mr. Ross, I don't understand the disrespect. These are the king's soldiers."

"Exactly." Had Lieutenant Wolfe discovered the secret meeting they'd held earlier in the day? Had he come to interrogate him about it?

Lieutenant Wolfe trotted his horse in their direction, reining it just short of their blanket, close enough for the hooves to spray sand at them. The sergeant riding with him stopped a respectable distance away.

"If it isn't the esteemed Esquire Ross, the lover of horse thieves and hermit crabs." The lieutenant peered down at him with sharp eyes. "Fancy seeing you here today in Weymouth."

"Yes, fancy that."

"You seem to have a penchant for beaches."

"Who can resist the sand and waves one last time on a warm fall day?"

"Perhaps your love of beaches isn't for the sand and water as much as for what the tide brings under cover of darkness?"

The glint in the lieutenant's eyes spoke more than his words and speared Ben with an urgency to warn the Caucus Club of the danger the lieutenant was bringing to Weymouth.

Lieutenant Wolfe looked at Susanna, and even though he was old enough to be her father, sudden lust flickered across his features. "Or am I to presume you're here for pleasure, and pleasure alone?"

"What do you think, Lieutenant Wolfe? Why else do you think I'm on the beach with a lovely young lady?" How dare the lieutenant leer at Susanna that way. Who did he think he was?

The lieutenant's eyes narrowed. "Perhaps you got word of my presence in Weymouth and decided to warn the smugglers to be on the lookout?"

Susanna drew in a breath. "Smugglers?"

Ben gave her a sideways glare that he hoped conveyed his desire for her to stay silent.

"I beg your pardon, Lieutenant," she said with the tone of one who had been offended. "If you think any of the dear people of my father's parish are involved in smuggling or any other illicit activities, you're sorely mistaken."

Once again Lieutenant Wolfe stared too freely at Susanna, and Ben had to restrain himself from standing up and shouting at the red monkey.

"Who is your father?" the lieutenant asked coldly.

"The Reverend Smith of the North Parish. And I assure

you, if any smuggling was occurring along Weymouth's shores, my father would have called on his parishioners to stop."

Ben bit back the terse words he'd had ready for Susanna. If he stayed silent, perhaps her innocence and ignorance, along with her fervor for the king, would be just the convincing Wolfe needed to leave them alone.

"We're a law-abiding community," she insisted.

Of course, the smuggling of molasses, sugar, and rum had been ongoing for years and years, ever since the Molasses Trade Act was passed thirty years ago. The trade laws had the intent of forcing the colonists to buy and sell only with Britain. But always in the past, the king's customs officials had turned a blind eye after the smugglers had paid them handsomely to ignore the illegal cargo coming in from the West Indies where the merchants could trade fairly.

But now that the king had grown more desperate for revenue, he was apparently intent upon enforcing the old Trade Act. Ben had heard rumors the prime minister had begun to pay the customs officials higher wages, which would only make them less likely to succumb to bribes from the New England merchants.

Had the prime minister also given officers like Lieutenant Wolfe more power to enforce the outdated Molasses Trade Act? It made sense, but only irritated Ben all the more that the king would stoop to such subversive tactics rather than openly discussing the problem with the colonists.

"Our community prides itself on loyalty to England and to the king," Susanna continued, impassioned with what she obviously believed to be true.

Ben focused on a crab scurrying near the water's edge, where the incoming tide threatened to draw it under. He didn't dare let Susanna look into his eyes for fear she would see the truth there.

What she didn't know wouldn't hurt her. Her patriotic declarations were just what he needed at that moment to distract Lieutenant Wolfe from the trail he was pursuing, for the man was indeed getting much too close to the heart of the illegal activities.

The distilleries in Boston depended on the cheap tax-free molasses that was smuggled in. They needed it for making rum.

And it wasn't that Ben approved of the rum. Even though the strong drink was used in preserving food and treating ailments, he'd also seen the effects of its overuse—many lives wasted as a result of imbibing too freely.

He'd wanted to speak out against the ill effects of strong drink, but the life of the colonies depended upon the income the rum brought. If the British cut off the smuggling, they would impoverish the colonies and make them even more dependent on their mother country.

And that was exactly what Ben and the other members in the Caucus Club were determined not to let happen.

"Miss Smith." Lieutenant Wolfe gave a strained smile, one that was more of a grimace. "I would expect nothing less of this community than its utmost allegiance to His Majesty, King George the third. This is to be expected."

"As it should be," she said, tipping up the brim of her lovely hat.

"Parliament has commanded that General Gage search out and destroy any sedition. He's been given the power to send any man involved in plotting revolt back to England to stand trial."

Susanna's response stalled as she glanced at Ben.

He wanted to frown at her, to tell her to continue with her passionate soliloquy of loyalty rather than giving the lieutenant more reason to suspect Ben's seditious leanings. An arrest by the lieutenant would put a certain end to all his aspirations and hopes, for a trial in England would be nothing but a parody followed by certain death on the gallows.

Lt. Wolfe's lips curled into a disdainful smirk. "Miss Smith, since you are such a loyal subject of the Crown, I expect you will be the first to report any signs of treachery."

Ben's pulse quickened. Susanna wouldn't share her suspicions about him with this officer, would she? Surely she had more class and kindness than to betray him.

Susanna looked beyond the lieutenant to the young sergeant. He had the youthful features of a boy with freckles sprinkled across his pale face. Sprigs of wiry red hair had come loose from the tight braid at the back of his neck. His eyes held an apology, as if he was embarrassed by the lieutenant's interruption of what probably appeared to be an intimate moment.

"How long will you and your soldiers be in Weymouth?" Susanna asked.

"As long as it takes," Lieutenant Wolfe replied, his eyes fixed on Ben.

Ben smiled back at the lieutenant, hoping to prove to the proud man that he wasn't so easily intimidated.

"Rest assured, Lieutenant," Susanna said, "I will be the first to alert you should I have any knowledge of illegal activities."

Irritation slithered through Ben. From everything he'd learned so far about Susanna, he had a feeling she truly would be the first to notify Lieutenant Wolfe of any smuggling, which meant he would have to guard what he said around her much better than he had so far.

The lieutenant only nodded at her briefly before spurring his horse and kicking more sand at them.

Once Lt. Wolfe had ridden away, Ben leaned back, rested his head against the blanket, and closed his eyes.

For a long moment, Susanna didn't speak.

The gentle rush of ocean waves filled the silence between them, along with the occasional cry of a sea gull.

"Mr. Ross," she started softly.

"Don't ask me any questions. It's quite clear the less I say around you, the better."

"But you heard the lieutenant. Those harboring thoughts of rebellion against the king will only put themselves in grave trouble."

"Then you have nothing to worry about, do you?"

"But *you* do."

"I can take care of myself."

"Hence I prefer not to know your involvements. If I remain unaware, then I won't have to report anything, will I?"

He snorted. "How very noble of you."

"As opposed as I am to any kind of sedition, I certainly don't want to see trouble befall you."

"Liberty must be supported at all hazards," he said, "even to life and limb."

"But we already have liberty." Her fervent voice hung above him.

He opened his eyes and found her leaning over him. In spite of his irritation, he couldn't keep from admiring her pretty face above his, her flashing eyes and the sincerity of her expression. Did the narrow crease between her brows mean she was worried about him?

"We have only as much liberty as the king is willing to give," Ben said, unable to restrain his tongue even though he knew he should. "And true liberty shouldn't be handed out by a king at his whim. Freedom is an inherent right we all have derived from our Maker. Our fathers have earned and bought it for us at the expense of their ease, their estates, their pleasure, and their blood."

He expected one of her quick rebuttals. But her eyes were deep, murky pools, as if she were swimming in his words and trying to make sense of them.

Was there hope for her after all? Was she wise enough to listen and learn?

Perhaps more colonists would be willing to take a stand against British oppression if they learned to think for themselves. Perhaps he and Gridley and Otis and others like them needed to make more of an effort to educate the people. Was the true source of their suffering because they were timid— too afraid to read, think, speak, and write?

"Freedom as an inherent right," she repeated, her lips seeming to taste the words.

He couldn't keep from staring at her lips and the delicate way they formed around each of the words. What would it be like to kiss Susanna Smith? Would she hold herself stiff and offer him a peck like Hannah Quincy had done the last time he'd visited her?

Susanna hovered close enough that he could reach his arms up and easily bring her down on top of him for a kiss before she had time to realize what he was doing.

Would she pull away or would she melt into him with all the passion that simmered beneath the thin disguise of her gentility?

As if hearing his thoughts, her lips parted, just enough for her to release a soft, quick breath.

His gut twisted with the sudden overwhelming need to

test her passion, to find out for himself how she would react to him.

He lifted his fingers to the errant strand of her hair that had tantalized him earlier. He touched it, letting his fingers graze her neck in the process.

Her eyes widened.

He held her gaze, refusing to break the connection. He couldn't think. All he knew was that he was reacting to this woman in a way he'd never responded to anyone else. His need to kiss her and mingle his breath with hers was so keen it almost made him tremble.

"You old dog!" Cranch's boisterous voice sliced the thickness of the passion between them.

With a sharp intake of breath, Susanna pushed away from Ben, breaking his contact. She dipped the brim of her hat and hid her face.

The move was enough to awaken him from the spell she seemed capable of casting over him whenever they were alone together.

"Good thing Mary and I came back when we did," Cranch called, walking swiftly toward them with Mary at his side. Cranch grinned at him wickedly.

A rush of embarrassment pushed Ben off his back. He sat up and tried to return what he hoped was a nonchalant grin.

"Maybe you two are in need of a chaperone more than we are." Cranch's teasing was merciless.

"I don't know," Ben called. "From all appearances, you were getting mighty cozy with Miss Smith."

Mary blushed prettily.

Susanna was already making a move to rise.

Ben jumped to his feet and held out a hand to assist her to her feet.

Hesitantly she placed her fingers against his. Her touch was enough to make him forget reason again. And as he helped her stand, he couldn't keep himself from leaning just a little closer and inhaling the sweetness of rose balm in her hair.

When she was solidly on her feet, he didn't relinquish her fingers.

She gave him a shy smile. "I do hope you and Mr. Cranch will be joining us for dinner this evening."

Cranch groaned. "I'm sorry to say, we won't be able to stay. I'm very sorry, but Ben has promised Hannah Quincy we would join her at your grandmother's house this evening."

"Oh." Susanna's smile faltered. "Dear cousin Hannah."

Ben shook his head at Cranch, warning him against saying anything else. But Cranch was looking only at Mary. "I promised Ben I'd go with him to visit his girl, so long as he agreed to come here with me so that I could see mine."

Susanna slipped her fingers out of Ben's, and her smile disappeared completely. "Your girl?"

Ben shrugged and tried to cast aside the guilt that suddenly plagued him. What could he say? He certainly couldn't deny Cranch's declaration, could he? He was pursuing Hannah at every possible opportunity. He'd set his attentions upon having her as his wife, and she'd been cooperating very nicely.

"Oh, that's right," Susanna said. "You're bowing and scraping at Hannah's feet."

"I've never made any pretense about my interest in her." But as his explanation left his mouth, it sounded weak, even to his own ears. If he wanted to pursue Hannah Quincy, why was he lying on the beach next to Susanna, longing to pull her in his arms and kiss her senseless?

"Of course you've not made any pretense." Susanna stepped away from him. "You've made it quite clear you're just like all the other gentlemen seeking to better themselves by marrying after status and wealth."

Susanna's disapproval shoved against his chest. Perhaps he *was* seeking to better himself, but not for the reasons she believed. Not for himself alone.

Nevertheless, he shouldn't have been so forward with Susanna. It wasn't fair to her, and he certainly wasn't exhibiting faithfulness in his ardor toward Hannah Quincy. If he hoped to win Hannah's hand in marriage—which he surely did—then he couldn't allow himself to get distracted.

He couldn't lose sight of the bigger goal, the larger purpose he had planned for his life.

"I'm sorry, Susanna."

But she'd already turned her back upon him.

He wanted to grab her, spin her around, and . . . and what?

Instead he folded his arms across his waistcoat, feeling the crinkle of her letter in the pocket, and forced himself to do the right thing.

He let her walk away.

Chapter 7

The early morning mist snaked around Susanna. The chill of it soaked through the cloak she'd thrown over her nightdress.

She hadn't dared to light a candle. Without the moon and stars to guide her, she stumbled over a twig buried among the damp leaves that carpeted her path.

The sharp poke against the soft satin of her slippers reminded her that Ben still hadn't brought her new boots. Nor had he sent her a letter yet, even though several days had passed since their exchange on the beach.

She breathed out an exasperated sigh and stumbled again, this time bumping her outstretched hand against the barn. Her fingers made contact with the grainy weatherworn boards, and she shuffled along the wall until she found the side door.

Her insomnia had finally pushed her from bed. Unfortunately sleeplessness was a malady she suffered from all too often, but of late it had troubled her more frequently.

As she'd lain in bed wide awake, she decided it was past time to meet with Dotty again and find out more about the young woman. Perhaps Ben was waiting to write to her until she provided him with the additional information he'd requested. He couldn't very well advise her unless he knew more about the situation.

She paused at the door. From the mussed hay in the loft, she suspected Dotty had taken her offer to stay in the barn, but she hadn't seen her there. Tom hadn't seen the young woman either.

If Dotty had been staying in the barn, she'd certainly kept her presence clandestine—which was for the best, at least until Ben could advise them.

Susanna pushed open the door as stealthily as possible. Even so, the rusty hinges squeaked. With a cringe she glanced over her shoulder to the dark outline of the sprawling parsonage. If she didn't make any noise and she didn't stay overlong, she could return to the bed she shared with Mary before anyone awoke.

Leaving behind the chill of the autumn night, Susanna slipped through the door and let the damp warmth of the barn envelop her. The cows, horses, and sheep were quiet in their stalls. Though she couldn't see them in the blackness of the interior, their soft snorts greeted her along with the familiar scents of animal flesh and freshly cut hay.

A soft thump in the loft overhead drew Susanna's gaze upward. "Dotty?" she whispered, praying the noise came from Dotty and not merely the barn cat prowling on his nightly mousing.

Susanna stood still for a while, letting the faintness of dawn penetrate the inside of the barn through the crack in the open door. After several moments, her eyes began to adjust to the darkness. And as she glanced around the barn, to the ladder that led to the loft, she could find no sign of Dotty.

"Dotty?" she whispered louder. "It is I, Susanna Smith. I have provisions for you."

At her declaration, the scuffling overhead resumed, and after a moment a face peeked out from the loft, followed by the creaking of the ladder rungs as Dotty made her way down.

Susanna drew near the young woman. "How do you fare?"

"I'm getting by." Her tone was weary. "I'm grateful to have a warm place to hide . . . I mean, sleep at night."

Susanna untied the towel and retrieved one of the hard buns Phoebe had given her. "Here. Eat this." She pushed it into Dotty's hands.

Dotty tore off a hunk and stuffed it into her mouth. Susanna suspected it was the only food she'd had since the last visit.

"I'd hoped you were sleeping in the barn, but I wasn't certain," Susanna said. "But now that I know, I'll leave something for you to eat in the loft." It wouldn't be illegal to place a few food items in the barn every day. Surely not.

"Thank you kindly, miss," Dotty replied between bites. "You're very kind."

"It's the least I can do." Susanna hesitated. "Actually, if you'll let me, I'd like to do more for you."

"You've done enough already, miss. More than enough."

Through the darkness, Susanna reached out and touched Dotty's arm. "You're in trouble, aren't you, Dotty?"

The young woman stopped chewing and grew silent so that the whooshing breath of the nearby mare in her stall sifted around them.

"I want to help you," Susanna continued before Dotty could pull away. "I have a friend who's a lawyer. He's compassionate and kind, and he's indicated he may be willing to defend you—"

"I can't pay a lawyer, miss. I've got nothing. Nothing at all."

"Don't concern yourself with the fees. We'll take care of

everything." Susanna wasn't sure how, but that was the least of their worries at present.

Dotty let her hand fall to her side as if having lost her appetite for the half-eaten bun. "Why would you help me, miss? I'm just a poor woman on the run."

"On the run from your master?"

Dotty took a step back. "It isn't what you think."

"I promise you're safe with me," Susanna said quickly. "It's just that if I'm to help you, I must know more about your circumstances."

The young woman didn't say anything, and Susanna feared she might bolt past her and out into the early morning never to be seen again.

"If you've run away from your master, then you must have a reasonable explanation for why you did so. And if you would share your story with me, I'll be able to relay the information to Mr. Ross."

Dotty took another trembling step back.

"Please. I promise to keep your confidence. I won't tell anyone except Mr. Ross, and only so that he might bring justice to your cause."

"I don't know . . ."

"You can't live like this—running and hiding—forever. Don't you want to have a normal life again? A home to live in? Certain work?"

"I can't remember what normal is." Dotty's voice was hoarse. "I never had a real home, at least not that I remember. My brother and I lived wherever we could on the streets of London, until we were rounded up with some of the other children and put on a ship."

"You poor dear," Susanna murmured. She'd heard tales of young vagabonds being captured off the streets of London and brought over to the colonies for use as indentured servants, but she'd never quite believed the stories.

"We didn't know where we were going or what was happening to us till we arrived in Boston. And then I was sold for an indenture of seven years to Merchant Lovelace."

Susanna searched her mind for the name, trying to find familiarity with it from the times she'd visited her aunt and uncle in Boston, but he was apparently not among the circles of her family's association.

"I think my brother was sold to a farmer who lives on the distant borders of the colony. I haven't heard from him in five years, and I can't help thinking he's dead."

"Perhaps we can send out notices—"

"No," Dotty said too loudly before catching herself. She hunched her shoulders and glanced around as if expecting someone to spring out of one of the stalls. "If he's still alive after all this time, then he's made a new life for himself, and I can't bring my troubles upon him."

Susanna knew she was prying, but she had to learn more. "Can you return to Mr. Lovelace?"

The girl shuddered. "I'd rather die first."

"Then he harmed you?"

For a long moment, Dotty was mute, as though she couldn't speak of the horrors she'd lived through. Finally she whispered so softly Susanna had to still her breath to hear her. "I suppose I was yet a child when he first purchased me. But now . . ."

Susanna rapidly calculated the passing of time. If Dotty had been a young girl of twelve or thirteen years when she'd been indentured, then over the past five years she had matured into a becoming young woman. No doubt her loveliness had attracted the attention of plenty of men, including her master.

"I heard rumors of the things he did with the other female servants," Dotty said, "but I never expected him to . . ."

A sick ache formed in the pit of Susanna's stomach.

"I ran away once before," she continued. "But he found me, whipped me, and locked me up for a while . . . and as punishment he let his friends have their way with me."

Susanna gulped down the revulsion Dotty's words elicited. "So you ran away again the first chance you had?"

"Aye." The word was laced with all the pain and sorrow her young life had seen. "This time I knew I had to get out of Boston, as far away as I could."

"Do you think Mr. Lovelace is still searching for you?"

"He hired a man to hunt for me. I made it as far as Braintree when the man captured me." Dotty's voice shook. "Then he took my shoes and set me free."

"Whatever for?"

"For the sport of it. Apparently he likes the hunt."

"That's why you were without your shoes?"

"Aye."

"And is this man still searching for you?"

"I don't know."

Susanna couldn't imagine anything more perverted. Surely with the information Dotty had shared, Ben would have enough to make a case against Mr. Lovelace, enough to set Dotty free from her contract of indenture. She'd compose another letter to Ben this very day and find a way to have it delivered to him promptly.

Surely God would expect her to make this small effort for Dotty. Yes, God commanded His people to obey their rulers, but He also commanded them to show compassion to those in need.

The barn door squeaked, and the flickering light of a candle fell upon them.

Dotty scrambled back into the shadows of the haymow.

Susanna's breath caught in her throat. Had someone discovered them?

Tom's face appeared in the doorway, illuminated by the candlelight. "Miss Susie?"

Susanna released her breath and gave the slave a wobbly smile. She motioned him in and put a finger to her lips, signaling his silence.

But even as she turned to introduce him to Dotty, she knew the young woman was already gone, that she'd disappeared into the early morning through the side barn door that was unlocked.

"Your mama's not gonna like this at all," Tom said after Susanna had quickly explained the situation to him.

"I don't want Mother to know. I don't want anyone else to suspect anything," Susanna whispered. The fewer people who knew, the safer Dotty would be—at least until Ben could find a way to help her.

Tom only shook his head. The uncertainty in his brown eyes brought Susanna's racing thoughts to a halt.

"I don't like sneaking around," Tom said. "I figure if we have to sneak around, then something's not right about it."

"Then let me do the sneaking."

"Oh, Miss Susie. This is no good. You're only gonna get yourself in trouble."

"Not if we're quiet about it." But she knew there were no guarantees, that harboring a runaway was dangerous business for all those she involved. "I beg you not to tell Mother. And I beg you to keep this our secret."

In the flicker of the candlelight, the doubt etched upon his face cast a shadow over her plans. Slowly he nodded his head. "I don't like this, but I won't breathe a word, Miss Susie. So long as you promise me you'll be praying hard about this and doing what the good Lord wants."

"I'll pray." She would pray that somehow, someway, Providence would make clear to her what she should do before she brought peril upon herself and everyone she loved.

"I think I'm going to ask Mary Smith to marry me." Cranch closed the door of his father's Boston counting house on King Street.

Ben stopped short on the cobbled street. The heavy clatter of a passing coach drowned out Cranch's next sentence, which Ben guessed was something about riding out to Weymouth again at the week's end to propose.

"What do you think, old friend?" Cranch stepped next to him, straightening his cherry-red coat and then his lacy collar. "Do you think she'll be able to resist me?"

"She won't be able to resist you—not if you ride out there looking like a big shiny cherry with cream on the top."

Cranch grinned. "You're just jealous."

The length of King Street bustled with merchants as well as the sailors, porters, and riggers who worked on Long Wharf. The wharf ran for half a mile from King Street to the sea. The whistle of a distant boatswain and the tap of a shipwright's hammer fueled Ben's blood, reminding him of his mission.

Yes, he was in Boston to take on another case, this time from one of the wealthy merchants who'd heard of his oratory skill. But he was also there to pass along messages from the Caucus Club to the secret group that met in Boston.

"Admit it." Cranch socked Ben in the arm. "You're jealous."

"Why would I be jealous of you, you big cherry?" Ben

started up the street in the direction of Town Hall, an imposing brick building that stood at the head of King Street.

Surprisingly, in spite of Cranch's wealth and prestige, Ben had never experienced even a twinge of envy toward his friend. He supposed Cranch's carefree spirit and kindness made him the type of man anyone could like. There wasn't a hint of the petty superiority so many of Ben's companions exhibited.

"You're jealous because I'm going to taste sweet wedded bliss before you." Cranch strode alongside him, his shoes clapping against the cobbles as loudly as the horses passing by.

They passed Cranch's father's warehouse and then a coffee shop, the strong scent of the coffee overpowering the usual seaside odor of pickled herring.

"I won't be far behind you in tasting sweet wedded bliss." Ben thought back to his recent visit with Hannah Quincy. She'd been more than encouraging; she'd even let him sneak another kiss when he'd said good-night. He'd told himself it didn't matter that kissing an apple would have been more pleasant. He decided he only wished Hannah had been Susanna because he'd just spent the afternoon with Susanna on the beach.

Surely Hannah's cold, stiff lips would warm and soften to him eventually.

Cranch's grin widened. "Why, you old dog. Don't tell me you're thinking of proposing too."

"I am." Ben had to before someone more qualified beat him to the proposal.

"Maybe we can have a double wedding."

"Maybe." Although he doubted Mrs. Smith would want him to overshadow Mary's wedding in any way.

"I'm sure Mary would be delighted at the prospect of having a wedding with her sister."

"Her sister?"

"Don't deny it. You've had your eyes on Susanna. In fact, you can't take your eyes off her."

Ben couldn't deny it. But Cranch didn't need to know that. "You know very well I'm not planning to propose to Susanna. I'm asking Hannah Quincy to marry me as soon as I see her again."

Cranch groaned. "That's what I was afraid of."

"She'll make a fine wife."

"For a blockhead."

Ben stifled a smile.

"You know she'll bore you to your death."

Cranch was right. Hannah Quincy was interested in the number of rosettes a dress should have and how much powder a wig needed—the sorts of topics that put Ben to sleep.

"She's exactly the kind of woman a man like me needs." At least that's what he told himself every time he was tempted to yawn at her dull prattle. He reminded himself she was kind and sweet and endearing, and that surely his affection for her would grow over time.

The important thing was that she would bring him the status necessary to move up in Boston circles. If he married her, he wouldn't have any more trouble getting the kinds of cases that could help him make a name for himself. With the prestige he would finally be able to hold his head high, have the means to help his family, and repay his father for all his sacrifices.

"She might be the kind of woman you need if you want to turn into an old prune." Cranch doffed his hat to several young ladies passing in an elegant chaise, the feathers and flowers on their fancy hats blowing in the breeze.

They giggled at Cranch.

Ben couldn't begrudge his friend his charm. It oozed from him. But Ben had none. All he had was his intelligence and ambition and determination.

Hannah obviously saw the potential in him. And she had a large enough dowry that she didn't need to worry about his lack of means. She was spoiled and pampered by her parents, and everyone knew they'd let her marry whomever she chose, even a poor man like himself—at least that's what he was counting on.

And at present he'd somehow gained her favor. He needed to act quickly to secure a promise of marriage from her before some other man caught her attention.

"Susanna Smith, on the other hand," Cranch said, "now, she's the kind of woman who will sharpen you into a sword that's capable of challenging the most daunting of foes."

Ben couldn't disagree with his friend. Susanna was the most stimulating woman he'd ever met. Even thinking about the conversations he'd had with her stirred him. But . . .

"Mrs. Smith might adore *you*," Ben said, "and embrace the prospect of *you* becoming her son-in-law. But she'd never accept *me*."

"Give her time." Again Cranch doffed his hat, this time to a group of merchants striding past them. Even the autumn sunshine glinted off his fair head, setting him apart and favoring him.

"I could give her a hundred years and she'd still never approve." Ben was smart enough to know how the system of *marrying up* worked. While the Smith girls would have sizable dowries, theirs couldn't compare to Hannah Quincy's. They didn't have the liberty to marry anyone they fancied the way Hannah did. In order to ensure a comfortable lifestyle, the Smith sisters would have to marry men who could also bring their fortunes to the marriage, and a fortune was something he didn't have.

In fact, he didn't own anything.

It would never matter how stimulating Susanna was. It would never matter that she was one of the most stunning women he'd ever seen. And it would never matter if he did grow to care about her.

Her mother wouldn't approve of a man like him. Hadn't Susanna said it herself those many years ago when she'd been stuck in the tree? *"I could never marry beneath my class. My mother would never allow it."*

Perhaps Susanna Smith had changed over the years. But the fact that they were worlds apart had not changed. She would still never be able to marry a man like him.

"Speaking of Hannah Quincy," he muttered. Striding toward them from the direction of Town Hall was Elbridge Quincy, Hannah's brother, his tall, broad shoulders and proud carriage setting him apart from the others.

"Ah yes," Cranch said, "marrying Hannah would make you a relation to the most brilliant lawyer in Boston. That's a charming prospect, isn't it?"

Ben guffawed. He wanted to avoid an encounter with Elbridge altogether, but from the man's increased pace, he'd obviously seen them and was determined not to miss speaking with them.

Ben eyed the tavern they were passing, tempted to duck inside.

"You can't let him intimidate you forever," Cranch mumbled, steering him forward.

Elbridge stopped in front of them and peered down his Roman nose at Ben just as he always had. "I see you're back in Boston searching among the dregs of society for another case to represent."

"Good day to you too, Elbridge." Cranch tipped his hat at the man.

"Someone's got to represent those truly needing justice and mercy," Ben said, thinking again about Susanna and the young woman she was helping. He'd been expecting another letter with more information and could only pray Susanna wouldn't do anything rash until he'd had time to advise her.

A mocking smile turned up the corners of Elbridge's lips. "Yes, I suppose someone must do the dirty work. I'll send all the drunks, thieves, and murderers your way, Ross. I'm sure you'll find something good and noble within them."

"It's a good thing one of us can see the worth in people." Ben attempted to toss off Elbridge's barbs. Once he married Hannah, Elbridge would have to finally accept him.

Elbridge sniffed and his nose lifted higher. "And now that Lieutenant Wolfe has been sent to investigate subversive activities south of Boston, you may find yourself with more treasonous reputations to defend."

"Lieutenant Wolfe is only going to find himself watching the coming and going of the tide." At least Ben hoped that was all he'd find. For the time being, they'd sent word to the smugglers that goods would have to be unloaded and stored in warehouses near Plymouth, which would make the process of getting the molasses into Boston more difficult. But he and Cranch and the others had already met to discuss the options.

"If I were you, I wouldn't underestimate Lieutenant Wolfe," Elbridge said. "From what I've heard, he's a clever man."

"From what I've seen," Ben countered, "he's just wasting his time patrolling the coast. But I guess that's not surprising since the rest of the British army is wasting their time here as well."

Cranch elbowed him and cocked an eyebrow in warning.

Cranch's father was one of the biggest purchasers of smuggled molasses in Boston. Cranch had a great deal at stake with Lieutenant Wolfe's prying.

Ben knew he needed to watch what he said around Elbridge. The man would plunge a dagger into his back if he could. Even so, Ben couldn't stop himself from tossing a parting shot. "From what I can tell of Lieutenant Wolfe—from his time in Braintree and now in Weymouth—he's more concerned about leeching off the poor tavern owners all he can with naught a concern for how their quartering him and his men affects business."

Ben couldn't deny that Lt. Wolfe was indeed a great threat to their operations. After the past several days in Boston, Ben had heard rumors that Lt. Wolfe's superiors were dissatisfied with his conduct regarding the smuggling, that they were giving him one last chance to prove himself, and that if he failed to bring them vital information, they would likely send him back to London in disgrace.

If Lieutenant Wolfe was on a mission to save himself, then that would make him all the more dangerous.

Elbridge tipped his hat at another gentleman passing by, then turned to face Ben. "There are many who believe that after all the British army has done for us, the very least we can do is make them feel at home on our soil for the duration of the time they're away from their families."

"All they've done for us?" Ben started, but Cranch's sharp tug on his arm pulled him forward, away from Elbridge.

"Friends," Cranch said, "as much as I'd love to stay and discuss the merits of the British army with the two of you, I'd find it pleasanter to go home and prick my eyes out with roasting skewers."

Without waiting for another word from Elbridge, Cranch propelled Ben down the street toward Town Hall.

"Really? Prick your eyes out with roasting skewers?" Ben asked, allowing Cranch to drag him along. "If you're going to speak of self-mutilation, I'd expect you of all people to be a bit more romantic about it."

"True." Cranch gave a short laugh. "If I planned to harm myself, I'd likely choose an overindulgence in chocolate instead of skewers. I don't know what I was thinking."

Ben smiled.

But when Cranch's gaze met his, there was a hint of seriousness in them that reminded Ben they were no longer just school friends playing a simple game of cards. They were grown men. The game they were playing now was far more dangerous and the stakes much higher.

And the danger would likely get considerably worse before it got better.

Chapter
8

Susanna pressed her ear against the door of the study. "*S'il vous plaît*," she whispered, repeating the master as he gave William his French lesson. Even though she'd been trying to teach herself the language, she was having trouble with pronunciations.

Her brother's tutor spoke again, his voice muted through the thick walnut door.

"*Auriez-vous l'obligeance*," she mimicked.

With the bits of the language she heard during those occasional times when she was able to listen to William's lessons, she was making some progress.

But it wasn't enough. Her fingers strayed to the door handle.

If only she could sit with William instead of having to consign her learning to the rare times Mother was absent.

Mother hadn't denied her permission to eavesdrop on William's lessons . . . yet. So she technically wasn't doing anything wrong by listening. Nevertheless, she'd kept her activities to herself, unwilling to give Mother the chance to ban her from the small pleasure of learning more.

Down the hallway, the front door rattled and swung open. A brisk gust of wind swept it wide and banged it against the wall.

Susanna jumped and then strode away from the study, trying to put as much distance as possible between herself and any evidence of her indulgence.

When her father stepped through the front door, the tension eased from her body. If Father suspected she'd been listening to William's lessons, he would pretend not to notice as he usually did.

"Good afternoon, Father."

He blinked into the dim interior and, upon seeing her, smiled. "Susanna. How's my sunshine today?"

"I've finished dame school and sent the girls home already." She took his hat and assisted him out of his overcoat.

"I admire your determination to teach those poor young girls. You're a remarkable woman." He planted a kiss against her forehead. The spiciness of tobacco lingered on his breath.

"And how is Mr. Arnold today?" she asked, patting his cheek.

He glanced around the deserted hallway to the open doorway of the parlor.

"Don't worry. Mother is still gone calling with Mary." They both knew Mother didn't approve of him smoking his pipe at home, and that in order to keep the peace, he often went to Arnold Tavern to smoke.

Father patted her cheek in return. "I saw your friend there today."

"My friend?"

"The lawyer. Mr. Ross."

Her heartbeat lurched forward. "Mr. Ross is in Weymouth today?"

"He had a message for Mary from Mr. Cranch."

Did Ben have a message for *her* also? But even as the words formed on her tongue, she held them back. She couldn't appear overly eager and risk exposing her involvement with Dotty.

"It appears Mr. Cranch would like to visit on Saturday afternoon."

"I'm sure Mary would love seeing him again." That was an understatement. Since the time on the beach last week, Mary had been unable to think of anything or anyone but Mr. Cranch. Susanna refused to admit she'd done likewise with Mr. Ross. If she'd thought about him at all, it was only in regard to the situation with Dotty.

Maybe she could find an excuse to take the letter to him at Arnold Tavern. She had been growing increasingly desperate to apprise him of the information she'd learned about Dotty's master.

Father strode down the hallway.

"After lessons today, one of my girls said her mother is out of wool," she called after him, her mind scurrying to find any reason at all to visit Ben. "When Mother gets home, would you tell her I've gone to deliver more supplies to Anna Morris?"

"Of course." Her father waved at her. "You're just like your mother, always thinking of those poor women and caring for them. They're blessed to have your assistance."

Susanna quickly shoved aside her guilt at the small deception. She would take Mistress Morris more wool, and if she just happened to ride past the tavern, there would be no harm in stopping for a few seconds to deliver the letter to Ben.

She packed a bag of supplies and tucked her letter inside. She was thankful Tom was accompanying Mother. She didn't want to face his probing eyes, reminding her of the danger and deception of what she was doing. He'd surely insist on riding along, even though no one had suffered any further problems since Hermit Crab Joe's trial three weeks ago. Apparently Braintree's Parson Wibird was having great success in reforming the man—much more than she'd anticipated.

Even so, as she sat in her sidesaddle and straightened her petticoats, a whisper of warning shimmied up her backbone. She forced herself to ignore the unease and kicked her mare into a canter down the road that would take her to the coast and Arnold Tavern.

The wind rattled the leaves, blowing them from the trees, sending a whirl of scarlet, burnt orange, and fiery yellow onto the road, covering it like a carpet. The cool breeze lashed her cheeks and hair, determined to wrest every stitch of civilization from her and turn her into a wild woman.

After several miles, she turned her horse onto the coastal road. At the sight of two of the king's soldiers coming from the opposite direction, she slowed the mare and maneuvered to the side of the road.

She recognized the stiff shoulders and proud carriage of the soldier in the lead—Lieutenant Wolfe.

He brought his horse to a sharp halt next to her and peered down at her with a condescension unfamiliar to one of her class.

"If it isn't Miss Smith." His voice was every bit as brusque as it had been with Ben that day on the beach.

"Good afternoon, Lieutenant Wolfe." She pulled herself up, wishing she'd had time to reassemble her hair, which had tumbled from the neat knot Phoebe had arranged earlier and now whisked about her face in disgraceful abandon.

"Oh yes. Let's not forget to mention," Lieutenant Wolfe added, his eyes narrowed upon her, "you are the *loyal* Miss Smith."

"That is right. I am." Certainly he wasn't questioning her loyalty.

"And just why are you frequenting the coastal road on this autumn afternoon?" He eyed the bag of supplies she'd looped over her shoulder.

Since when did the colonists have to give an account of their comings and goings to British soldiers? Were they not free to travel about as circumstances dictated?

She bit back the sharp words she wanted to give him. Instead she forced calmness to her tone. "If you must know, I'm taking more wool to one of the women who spins for my mother."

His attention remained fixed on her bag, and for a long moment Susanna feared he would ask her to open the sack and empty its contents. And she would have readily done so. She wasn't smuggling anything and had nothing to hide from him.

Except the letter to Ben . . .

Of course she'd used the pseudo-names they'd previously decided upon, and she'd tried to remain as vague as possible about Dotty's situation and hadn't mentioned the girl's name. But that wouldn't explain why she had such an incriminating letter on her personage.

"I really must be going, Lieutenant." She shifted into a proper riding pose in the sidesaddle, hoping she appeared more collected than she felt. She mustn't allow the lieutenant to discover her letter to Ben. He might be on a mission to catch smugglers, but she doubted he would turn a blind eye if he found out she was harboring a runaway indentured servant.

Lieutenant Wolfe didn't move but focused now on her face as if reading the guilt written clearly there.

The young soldier who had reined his steed next to the lieutenant nodded at her. His face was pale in contrast to his red hair, yet his eyes were bright and kind. "Take care that you don't stay out overly long this afternoon, Miss Smith. From the way the wind is blowing, I sense a storm brewing."

The distant horizon of the ocean was the calm blue of the now-fading hydrangeas that grew along the parsonage.

But just because there wasn't a sign of a storm didn't mean one wasn't coming. The storms could arise seemingly out of nowhere and unleash dangerous fury.

"Thank you." She gave her mare a nudge with her heel. "Now, if you'll excuse me, I'll be on my way."

She urged her horse past the soldiers, even though Lieutenant Wolfe didn't offer her the courtesy of moving aside. As she trotted away, she didn't have to look to know the lieutenant was watching her, searing her back with a hundred questions.

By the time she'd ridden north along the coastal road and dismounted at Arnold Tavern, she'd put plenty of distance between herself and the soldiers. Yet her heart still pounded loudly, and she berated herself for not finding a better spot to secure the letter.

The plain weathered tavern stood along a rocky section of King's Cove where steep cliffs and jagged shoals made navigation by water difficult and treacherous.

She breathed in the sea air laden with moisture and peered at the crashing waves on the rocks far below. How could Lieutenant Wolfe have reason to believe anyone was engaging in smuggling here? There were stretches of beach that were smooth and sandy elsewhere along the coast. But the Weymouth shores were less than ideal for unloading goods.

Hopefully the lieutenant would realize his mistake and return to Boston soon.

With a shudder, Susanna pushed open the tavern door and was greeted by the musty odor of tobacco smoke.

She stopped short at the sight of the empty taproom, the wooden tables cleared and the benches deserted. Along one wall an iron pot hung in a huge stone hearth, and the waft of bubbling stew permeated the room. On the opposite wall sat barrels of beer, rum, and cider with a shelf above them lined with tankards.

Perhaps the usual crowd of men had been scared away by the lieutenant and his men. Or perhaps they'd sensed the coming storm and had gone home to take refuge.

If no one else found the afternoon conditions fit for riding, what was she doing out? She oughtn't to have left home. She should have waited to give Ben the letter on Saturday, that is, if he came calling with Mr. Cranch.

She took a step backward to exit, but hurried footsteps in the kitchen behind the taproom halted her.

Mr. Arnold's head peeked around the doorframe, his expression wary. "Miss Smith?" He straightened and made a pretense of wiping his hands on his apron, although they were neither wet nor soiled. "Mighty surprised to see ye out today, that I am."

"I was . . ." What could she say? She couldn't very well tell him she needed to deliver a letter to Ben Ross.

"The good reverend, yer father, has already left some time ago," he continued. "And as ye can see, the rest of me customers have already gone home for the day, what with the squall brewing and all."

Behind him, slabs of ham and beef dangled from the ceiling. The kitchen was crowded with barrels of salted fish, jars of honey, and wheat in sacks—all of the many provisions he needed to run his tavern.

"I shouldn't have come." She put her hand against the door. "It's just that my father mentioned he'd talked with Mr. Ross, and I'd hoped to find him here."

Mr. Arnold cast a glance over his shoulder.

Of course, she hadn't seen Ben's horse tied out front. He'd likely already gone on his way.

She started to open the door. She'd been a fool to attempt to track him down. "I beg your pardon, Mr. Arnold. I'll be on my way—"

"Susanna." Ben stepped around Mr. Arnold. He glanced to the dusty window and to the coastal road that ran in front of the tavern.

"Ben," she breathed with relief. She let the door close with a thump and crossed toward him.

The anger radiating from his eyes brought her to an abrupt halt. "What are you doing here, Susanna?"

"I heard you were in town and—"

"You shouldn't have come here." He looked out the window again.

"But I needed to see you." For a reason she couldn't explain, his tone and his attitude left an embarrassed sting upon her cheeks. Maybe she hadn't expected him to jump for joy at the sight of her, but she hadn't anticipated his anger.

Hadn't they moved beyond the past hurts?

"Don't seek me out here again," he said curtly.

Her shoulders stiffened. "Very well." If that's the way he wanted to be . . .

Mr. Arnold moved across the room to one of the big multi-paned windows and peered down the road. "They're coming."

With that, the tavern owner rushed to the barrel of cider, grabbed a tankard from the shelf, and began filling it. His hand shook, and splashes of cider spilled onto the already sticky floor.

Ben gave an exasperated sigh. Then he strode toward her, seized her arm, and dragged her to the nearest table.

"Who's coming?" she asked, too surprised by his actions to resist.

"Lieutenant Wolfe and his assistant." Ben plopped onto the bench.

Before she knew what was happening, he'd tugged her down, leaving her little choice but to land upon his lap.

"Mr. Ross!" She gasped. "Whatever is the meaning of such familiarity?"

He slid one arm around her and at the same time began unbuttoning his waistcoat.

Heat crept up her neck into her cheeks. She pushed against his shoulders and attempted to rise.

"Stay put." His arm around her waist pinned her, holding her prisoner.

Mr. Arnold plunked two tankards down on the table before them, sloshing the frothy liquid onto the table in his haste. "They're tying their horses."

"Who's tying horses?" She squirmed to dislodge herself from Ben's lap, her mortification increasing with each passing second.

Mr. Arnold skittered out of the room to the kitchen where he proceeded to bang pots together, clearly wanting to give the impression that he was in the midst of fixing the evening repast.

Ben glanced at the window and then grabbed both her arms. "Stop fighting me," he whispered harshly. "Put your arms around me. I need you to pretend we're lovers."

"Lovers? I absolutely will not—"

"We have no other choice." He reached up to her chin

and yanked at the ribbon of her wide straw hat. "Lieutenant Wolfe has followed you. What other reason can you give him for seeking me out here?"

Her mind spun but came up with nothing. She certainly couldn't tell the lieutenant she was delivering a letter about a runaway indentured servant.

At the heavy slap of boots on the front step of the tavern, Ben lifted her hat, flung it on the table, and dug his fingers into her loose hair. "I hope you're a good actress, Miss Smith." His warm breath fanned her cheek, and his eyes turned stormy.

The seriousness in each of his clipped words sent a tremor through her. "Of course I am." Had she brought them both to danger with her foolish trip?

"Then put your arms around me and act like you're enjoying my attention."

Hesitantly she lifted her hands to his shoulders.

The door scraped open.

And even though Ben had warned her, she was unprepared for the swiftness with which he brought his mouth against hers and the force of his lips as they crushed hers.

One of his hands pressed against the small of her back, giving her little choice but to arch against him. The other hand was intertwined in her hair, capturing her head and maneuvering her against the pressure of his lips.

The force of the kiss sent a torrent of flutters to her belly. Even though they were only acting, there was something about his fervor and the intensity of his hold that made her want to respond and almost made her forget she was only pretending.

She leaned against him, wrapped her arms around him, and let his lips guide hers with a passion that seemed almost more dangerous than facing Lieutenant Wolfe.

He broke away from her only to make a trail of kisses across her chin to the hollow of her neck. She closed her eyes and wanted to gasp.

The door slammed.

His mouth hovered in her ear, and his voice was strained and hoarse. "You have to hop up and act embarrassed." He nudged her.

She broke away from him and jumped to her feet. With true mortification cascading over her, she took a rapid step away from Ben.

In their crimson coats, Lieutenant Wolfe and his assistant stood at the entrance of the tavern. The young redheaded soldier had the grace to divert his attention to his shiny black boots. But Wolfe stared with frightening boldness.

"Lieutenant Wolfe," she said breathlessly, trying to infuse her words with surprise. "I didn't expect to see you again so soon."

"We decided we should make sure you delivered your *supplies* safely." His gaze loitered overlong upon her lips, which tasted of Ben and were swollen from his kiss. "But you weren't really delivering supplies, were you, Miss Smith?"

How could she answer the lieutenant without giving away the truth of the situation?

"What do you expect, Lieutenant?" Ben grabbed the tankard of cider and took a slurp. "She wanted to see me. You don't blame her, do you?"

"And she must sneak around to do this?"

"What would you have us do when her parents oppose a poor country lawyer like myself?"

"You told me you were leaving town."

"If I came here to see her, why would I leave before I've had the chance to do so?"

"You would have me believe the sole reason you came to Weymouth today was to meet with this woman?"

"I told you earlier when you rudely dispersed Mr. Arnold's customers that I came to deliver the riding boots my father fashioned. For Miss Smith."

Susanna trembled, whether from her contact with Ben or her fear of the lieutenant, she couldn't tell.

The look in Ben's eyes beseeched her to help him in the charade they were playing.

Her normally quick tongue felt stuck, and she fought to loosen it. "Lieutenant Wolfe, I don't understand this line of questioning. We've done nothing to provoke you, and yet you've treated us without any respect."

The lieutenant fingered the hilt of his saber sheathed at his side.

She lifted her chin and hoped he couldn't see the alarm running through her limbs.

His lips twitched with a semblance of a stiff smile. "The king has given me the mission of eradicating illegal activity and weeding out dissidents. I'm sure one as loyal as yourself can understand just how difficult and unpleasant that task can be at times."

"I'm sure it can be very difficult—"

"And it will go much easier for you, Miss Smith, if you have nothing to do with those who are involved in treason."

"If I learn that anyone is involved in treason"—her gaze slid to Ben before she could stop it—"then I shall indeed heed your warning."

Ben took another gulp of his cider.

The clatter of a kettle in the kitchen echoed in the emptiness of the taproom.

Mr. Arnold was obviously listening to them. She tried not

to think about how much fodder she was giving him to share with his guests, including her father, next time he came to smoke his pipe. She would be utterly mortified if he learned she'd been sitting on Ben's lap, kissing him.

Ben lifted his tankard toward the lieutenant, toasting him and giving him what was nothing less than a smirk. "And of course I shall heed your warning as well."

Wolfe's saber inched out of its sheath.

The young soldier cleared his throat. "Lieutenant, might I suggest that we be on our way before the storm hits?" He nodded his head to the window. "From the way the wind is blowing, I'm afraid we're in for a dangerous squall."

Through the hazy glass, Susanna could see that dark, billowing clouds had begun to amass over the bay. She knew she ought to return home at once, but since she'd already put herself at risk to deliver the letter about Dotty, she may as well see it safely into Ben's hands before she left.

With a last threatening glare at Ben, the lieutenant spun on his heels and stomped out of the tavern. The redheaded soldier tipped his hat at them and then followed.

For several moments after they were gone, Susanna couldn't move. She watched them mount their horses and start down the coastal road, the wind whipping at the tails of their coats as the beginning fat drops of rain splattered the road.

Ben didn't budge from his spot either.

In their quiet, peaceful community of Weymouth, she'd never had much interaction with the king's soldiers. And now after her encounters, she had to admit, being around them was much more intimidating than she'd imagined.

She supposed she wouldn't have anything to fear if she hadn't been breaking the law. After all, the lieutenant was only trying to ensure obedience to the king as he rightly should.

With trembling fingers she combed back her wild tangled hair.

Was God trying to tell her she'd gone too far in her efforts? Perhaps she needed to issue more caution as Tom had suggested. On the other hand, Phoebe had admonished her that the only thing to be done was to help the young runaway.

Mr. Arnold stepped out of the kitchen and once again wiped his dry hands on his apron. "That was a close one, I'd say."

Ben's shoulders slumped. "Very close."

"Do ye think he believed ye was here to visit Miss Smith?"

Only then did Ben turn to look at her, staring directly at her mouth.

She focused on the floor to prevent him from seeing her embarrassment over their moment of shared passion and the strange reaction it had produced within her.

"Lieutenant Wolfe is a very smart man," Ben finally said. "We won't be able to fool him. At least not for long."

"Should I tell the others to go?" Mr. Arnold asked while peering out the front window.

The rain was falling harder now, and a flash of lightning lit up the darkening sky.

Ben nodded. "We'll cancel our meeting for today. The storm will give them the coverage they need to disperse without drawing the lieutenant's attention."

Mr. Arnold returned to the kitchen.

"What *others*?" Susanna asked.

"I told you not to ask me any questions," Ben said. "The less you know, the better. Remember, you've made it your duty to cooperate as fully as possible with Lieutenant Wolfe." He shoved away from the table and stood.

"You don't need to be so rude." She didn't know what she'd

done to anger him, but his attitude bordered on hurtful. "I only want to do my best to obey the king."

He snorted.

She shouldn't have come. Benjamin Ross was impossible.

"I'm sorry I thought you'd be willing to help me." She grabbed her hat off the table and started toward the door, trying to push down the lump of disappointment that lodged in her throat. "I'll be on my way."

"You can't go now. You won't be able to outride this storm."

"I'd thank you not to interfere." She slapped her hat on. Without bothering to tie the ribbon, she reached for the door handle.

In two long strides Ben crossed the room and stuck his foot against the door, wedging it shut with the tip of his boot. "You'll have to wait out the storm here."

She spun to face him. "Excuse me, Mr. Ross, but you have no right to advise me. Not after telling me I shouldn't have come and that I shouldn't seek you out again."

A booming crack of thunder shook the frame of the building. And a gust of wind beat against the windows, rattling the panes. She ought to stay, but she was too angry to admit it.

He examined her face, and the tight lines in his face softened a bit. "It's not that I don't want to see you, Susanna, because, God help me, I do."

At the gentle confession she leaned against the door, suddenly conscious of the fact that they were less than an arm's length apart.

"I like seeing you," he whispered. The blue of his eyes darkened with something she didn't understand but that set her heart tapping erratically. "I like being with you more than is good for either of us."

When his gaze dropped to her lips, she could feel the warm pressure of his kiss all over again.

"But this place, this time, and all that I'm involved in—it's dangerous for you." He took a step back. "*I* am dangerous for you."

She started to shake her head.

"I shouldn't have made Lieutenant Wolfe believe we were lovers. Now he's going to be even more suspicious of you."

"I can only imagine the damage to my reputation henceforth when word regarding our indecent behavior spreads throughout the countryside."

"We certainly wouldn't want *your* precious reputation being damaged on account of me."

"Not on account of *you*," she said quickly. "Rather because of our . . . well, when I sat on your lap, when you—"

"When we kissed?" He quirked a brow. "I suppose you don't want anyone to know you kissed a poor nobody of a lawyer like me?"

"Oh, stop feeling sorry for yourself." She squirmed at the boldness of his words but tried to hide her discomfort. "You're *not* a nobody. You know I don't think that anymore now that I've grown up. Maybe it's time you grow up as well."

His lips curved into the beginning of a smile. "You're a sauce bucket."

"And you're a wet handkerchief."

The wind blew with a fury, whining down the chimney into the fireplace. A flash of lightning lit up the room, which had grown increasingly dark with the approach of the storm.

"So you're not offended that I kissed you?" His voice was low and his smile widened.

"I hardly think that's an appropriate question to ask a lady." She fought against her own smile.

"I think you liked my kiss."

"It was fair enough—"

"Fair?" He leaned a hand against the door next to her head. "Admit it, Susanna. My kiss was swoon-worthy."

He was right, and he was altogether too close. She glanced at the unhooked buttons of his waistcoat, unwilling to let him see the truth in her eyes. "As hard as it will be to contain your kisses around me, I must ask that you do your best."

He chuckled.

The sudden crash of breaking glass split the air around them. She startled.

But Ben pushed his body against hers, shielding her from the shattering of the front window. Glass and debris flew into the room, followed by a roaring wind and driving rain.

"I think ye better take Miss Smith to the cellar," Mr. Arnold shouted from the door of the kitchen. "Sounds like this storm wants to take me tavern apart board by board."

The wailing wind thrashed at them as Ben led her around the shards of glass. He hustled her into the kitchen to a trap-door in the floor that led to the cellar. She climbed down a ladder, and when her feet were planted firmly on the dirt floor, he lowered a candle to her.

"Stay underground until I come for you."

"Aren't you coming down with me?"

"I must help Mr. Arnold salvage his supplies before the wind blows them out into the sea."

"But it's unsafe. You could get hurt."

"Why, Miss Smith, I think I detect concern. I'm touched."

She was glad for the darkness that concealed the flush spreading over her cheeks. "Of course I'm concerned. For both you *and* Mr. Arnold. The *two* of you shouldn't be taking any chances."

"My dear girl, you can confess you had aspirations to get me alone in the dark and claim more of my kisses."

"I will confess to no such thing." Although the thought of such an encounter sent strange flutters through her middle. "Since you're the one mentioning it, I have to believe those are your aspirations."

He grinned and said nothing to deny her accusation.

Her stomach flipped.

Another crash echoed through the kitchen above. His brow furrowed and he backed away from the door. "Don't come up, Susanna. Please."

With that, he disappeared.

Chapter
9

The cold dampness of the cellar wrapped around Susanna. Crude wooden shelves full of jars and casks lined the walls. Barrelsful of the rum and cider Mr. Arnold sold to his customers crowded the floor. Crates overflowed with apples, onions, and potatoes. The earthy scent of them mingled with the mustiness of the damp boards and stones that littered the floor.

She lifted the candle, sending its glow to the corners of the cramped space. To her surprise, one of the dusty shelves leaned away from the wall, exposing a large hole.

Winding her way through the maze of supplies, she investigated behind the shelf. Indeed there was a hole. In fact, it was more of a tunnel, certainly big enough for a grown man or woman to crawl into.

She held out the candle to peer into the chasm. As she leaned forward, she grabbed on to the shelf to keep her balance and was startled when the entire structure slid away from the wall farther, almost as if it were on wheels of some kind.

When Mr. Arnold and Ben had referred to the "others" earlier, was this where they'd been? Down in the cellar? Perhaps having a secret meeting?

She knelt and poked her head into the hole. She had the suspicion Ben wouldn't tell her anything more about what was going on than he already had. Hadn't he said the less she knew the better?

She glanced to the opening that led to the kitchen.

He was busy, likely closing shutters and attempting to protect any more of the costly windows from breaking.

He wouldn't need to know that she'd taken a peek.

Yes, that's all she would do. Just take a peek.

She discarded her hat, sank to her knees and, holding the candle with one hand, began crawling forward.

The tunnel sloped downward. The dirt was cold and damp, and the dim light of the candle revealed the misshapen but smooth path that didn't appear to run farther than the length of the tavern.

In only a moment she reached the end and found herself peering into what appeared to be another dug-out cellar.

As the flickering light illuminated the cavern, she gasped.

The room was much bigger than Mr. Arnold's other cellar, and it was packed with more barrels than she'd ever seen in one place.

Slowly she stood and smoothed her skirt. With trembling legs and a heavy, sick load pressing upon her, she held out the candle to the nearest barrel.

The print painted across the stave was in French. She tried to read the words, but her grasp of the French language was still frustratingly minimal.

Yet even as she stared at the barrels upon barrels, the sick ache inside deepened. If the containers had been purchased from the French islands in the West Indies, then that could only mean one thing.

They were likely filled with molasses that had been smuggled into the colonies. Prohibited, French-made molasses.

Susanna shook her head, hoping she was mistaken, that the barrels were empty, that they weren't full of the illegal goods Lieutenant Wolfe was trying to locate.

Of course she wasn't naïve. Everyone knew there were those unsavory traders who blatantly disregarded the law and had done so for many years along the coast. There were too many greedy merchants who thought only of wealth and were unwilling to pay the tax the king had levied upon the British molasses.

And yes, she understood that the colonies depended upon the molasses for many things.

But the men of Weymouth were God-fearing, law-abiding, and loyal subjects of the king. Were they not?

They wouldn't stoop to illegal smuggling.

But as she looked around the chamber, she located another steep tunnel sloping away from the chamber. She guessed it led to the rocky coastline somewhere below the tavern and that somehow under cover of darkness the barrels of molasses were brought ashore, unloaded, and stored in the bowels of the earth beneath Arnold Tavern.

The smuggling was going on right here in her peaceful seaside town. In her father's parish. Among men she'd known and respected her entire life.

"How could they?" she whispered.

"Susanna?" Ben's voice came faintly from the root cellar on the other side of the tunnel.

And apparently Ben was involved in the smuggling.

From all he'd said, as well as what he'd left unspoken, she'd known he held seditious thoughts. But he was obviously much more involved in the illegal activities than she'd imagined.

"Susanna?" he called again, this time louder, his voice echoing in the tunnel.

What would she say to him? She couldn't deny that she had wanted his advice—perhaps even his friendship.

But now?

He poked his head out of the tunnel. "What are you doing?" His voice was tight, and his eyes flashed with restrained frustration. "You shouldn't have come in here."

"Why? Because you didn't want me to see your criminal activities?"

He crawled out of the tunnel and rose to his feet. In the darkness of the cavern lit only by the flickers of her candle, his shadow was tall and broad like that of a Greek Minotaur come to devour a helpless maiden.

The dripping of groundwater somewhere in the damp hovel told her the storm was still raging above them. But the deeper, darker storm brewing down under the earth suddenly seemed far more dangerous.

"I'm astounded by all of this." She waved her hand at the barrels. "Here in Weymouth? It's unthinkable."

"Perhaps to someone like you who's always been sheltered and had everything you've ever needed or wanted handed to you at your whim."

"Perhaps to someone who thinks we should obey the law instead of bending it whenever we wish to fulfill selfish gain."

"This isn't about selfish gain."

"Why else would you avoid the British taxes if not to fill your pockets with more money?"

He gave an exasperated sigh. "You obviously don't know the first thing about the whole conflict."

"Why? Because I'm an ignorant woman? Because I'm not as educated as you?"

"Now who's feeling sorry for herself and in need of the handkerchief?"

"Well, if I'm not stupid, then I suppose you'll tell me the truth about what's going on here. Are you involved with the smuggling or not?"

He pursed his lips together and didn't say anything.

"Your silence implicates you."

He studied her for a long moment. "I'm not involved in the way you think."

"I don't know what to think." She'd wanted to like Ben—had started to like him. And she'd wanted to respect him.

But how could she respect a criminal?

A rat scurried between two barrels, and she drew in a startled breath.

He nodded toward the tunnel. "Come on. We need to get out of here."

She didn't budge. "Why? So that Lieutenant Wolfe doesn't discover what you're doing?"

"We're careful. He won't discover anything."

"He might now."

Ben stiffened.

"I told him that I would report illegal activities to him."

Ben started across the cavern toward her. In the flickering shadows, the hardness of his face and the blazing in his eyes had indeed turned him into a towering Minotaur.

She backed up a step and bumped into a barrel. "In fact, I distinctly remember telling Lieutenant Wolfe I would be the *first* to alert him should I become privy to criminal activity."

He didn't stop until he was mere inches from her. His presence threatened to overpower her.

She forced herself to stand her ground. "Would you have me lie to him?"

"I would have you stay silent, Susanna."

"What you're doing is wrong and I won't stay silent about it." She took a side step to maneuver around him, but he shifted and grabbed her arm, pinning her in place.

"You may not know or understand the oppression of the British," he said hoarsely, "but there's a heavy weight already upon our shoulders, and they would only increase the burden if they could to keep us as their inferior subjects."

His breath was hot and his body tense, and she tried not to think about how close he was.

"You can try to justify your crime all you want," she said, "but any knowledgeable statesman knows he cannot pick and choose which laws he'll obey. If every person obeyed the law based upon his whims, we'd give birth to anarchy."

"Sometimes in the course of history, man must look at whose laws he is obeying and determine whether they are just and right and merciful. If the laws are based on tyranny, for the good of only a few instead of for all, then it becomes the duty of man to institute fairer laws."

He was indeed eloquent with his words, just as he'd been that day at the trial of Hermit Crab Joe. But that didn't change the fact that smuggling was wrong. "You can speak all you want, Mr. Ross, yet you won't convince me that breaking the law is justifiable."

"Not under any circumstances?"

"Of course not—"

"Then you'll have to reevaluate whether you really want to help that runaway indentured servant, won't you? After all, aiding her is also an illegal act."

His words stopped her rebuttal and unleashed the inner turmoil that had been growing since the day she'd discovered Dotty. She *did* want to help Dotty. Everything within her told her she needed to comfort and shelter the young woman, that Dotty hadn't deserved her cruel treatment.

On the other hand, the longer she hid Dotty and the more she assisted her, the more she was slipping down the slope of disobedience. And once started, where would it lead?

As if sensing the conflict raging through her, Ben's tight grip on her arm relaxed. "I know everything I'm saying is difficult to digest, but all I ask is that you reflect on the issue before you take any action."

She could only stare at him. She didn't know what was right anymore. If she could find justification for breaking the law to help the poor girl, then why shouldn't Ben do the same for something he felt was important?

He leaned closer. "Think about all the lives and families you'll put at risk if you go to Lieutenant Wolfe and disclose our activities."

Mr. Arnold's voice echoed faintly from the root cellar.

Ben cocked his head. "Do you want to see Mr. Arnold and numerous other men hanging from the end of a noose?"

Of course she didn't. She couldn't imagine losing any more of the men of their community, not after the war, not after they'd already lost so many, not after seeing the way the poor widows had to struggle to clothe and feed their families.

"Very well, Mr. Ross," she said. "I shall think very carefully before I take any action."

Mr. Arnold's voice called louder from the other side of the tunnel.

Ben took a step away from her.

And her heart pinched with an unexpected ache.

He'd been right. All that he was involved in, at this time, in this place—it was all too dangerous for her.

She had to stay away from him.

Chapter
10

"Then it's settled," Ben said. "I'm going to propose to Hannah Quincy tonight."

Parson Wibird squinted. "If you really think this is what the heavenly Father is leading you to do."

Ben sat back in the desk chair of his law office—a small office at the back of his parents' home. His eyes returned to the paper on his desk, to the drying ink of the letter he'd penned earlier to Susanna and the scrawling script at the top: *Dear Diana . . .*

Diana. Yes, she was indeed a dark, spirited goddess of the moon. But why had he written *dear*? She wasn't dear to him.

And yet, even as he tried to deny his right to claim any affection for her, his heart stirred like it did every time he thought about the crushing pressure of their lips together.

She hadn't been afraid to kiss him back. She'd been every bit as ardent as he'd expected.

Ben tore his attention away from the letter he'd written in response to the one she'd given him yesterday at Arnold Tavern, after the storm, after they'd crawled out of the cellar.

She'd given it to him reluctantly, her eyes overflowing with accusation and doubt. All the trust that had glimmered there earlier was gone.

If there had ever been a flicker of hope that Susanna Smith might care for him, the revelation of his clandestine activities had snuffed it out.

"The truth is, Parson," Ben said, "I don't know what God wants." Even after talking with the parson most of the morning, his thoughts were tossing like a vessel upon the waves of a stormy sea.

Parson Wibird scratched the back of his neck and closed the pages of Benjamin Franklin's *Reflections on Courtship and Marriage*. They'd spent the past hour reading through selections together.

"You know I'm striving to improve my situation and my reputation," Ben continued, "and Hannah Quincy is the perfect match for a man like me."

"Sometimes what God wants is clearer than we realize. It's merely obscured by our own selfish desires."

"So you're saying my desire to marry Hannah is selfish?"

Parson Wibird grinned, revealing his crooked and discolored teeth. "Maybe you first need to evaluate why you're chasing so hard after improving your situation and reputation."

"There's nothing wrong with trying to better oneself."

"But at what cost?"

Ben crossed his arms behind his head and watched the raindrops splatter against his office window. The waft of freshly baked bread had crept under the door from the big kitchen where his mother worked hard day after day, a place he could never imagine Hannah Quincy working.

As much as he loved his parents and being with them again, the little saltbox house wasn't the type of dwelling Hannah would ever want to live in. She'd have a large enough dowry to afford something bigger and newer that would suit her tastes.

The steady tap of his father's hammer came from the kitchen, where he'd set up his shoemaker bench, having sacrificed his workspace so that Ben could have an office in which to meet with clients.

Ben sighed. His father was always sacrificing for him.

Surely now it was his turn to do whatever he could to repay his father for his kindness over the years. And if he hoped to do so, he needed to propose to Hannah Quincy—tonight. Her attention was starting to fade, and she'd already begun to show interest in several other admirers. He needed to make the most of her ardor while he had it.

Parson Wibird stood and returned Benjamin Franklin's book to the shelf lining the wall across from Ben's desk. "Is it fair to Miss Quincy that you marry her for what she can do for you with no thought of what you can do for her?"

"You know I'd do my best to give her my utmost devotion." But even as he tried to justify his aspirations, a sliver of guilt pricked him. He hadn't been faithful to Hannah yesterday when he'd pulled Susanna Smith onto his lap and kissed her. Even if the kiss had been for the benefit of Lieutenant Wolfe, Ben couldn't deny how much he'd enjoyed the brief passionate encounter.

But passion wouldn't get him where he needed to go. He couldn't let emotions dictate his decisions. He needed to stay sensible about the best course of action for his future.

"I know you'll make any woman a fine husband," Parson Wibird said with kindness in his squinted eyes. "But if you marry for ambition, will it only be the first of many compromises you make for the sake of improving your reputation?"

Ben couldn't find an answer. He wasn't sure he *wanted* to find the answer.

The parson rocked back and forth on his heels.

For all the parson's quirks and his craggy appearance, the man had more wisdom than all the reverends of Massachusetts Colony put together. He'd seen old Joe Sewall's innocence. He'd never once condemned Joe like everyone else and was offering the man shelter when no one else cared.

Ben knew he couldn't find a better, more honest and wise friend than Parson Wibird.

Yet, today, the parson's words didn't seem quite as wise as they usually did.

Surely God didn't disapprove of his trying to make a better life for himself. Surely He wouldn't find fault in him for marrying a woman of means, not when so much good could come of it, for him and for his family.

And what of Cicero's words? *"The first way for a young man to set himself on the road towards glorious reputation is to win renown."*

Ben knew he was living in a society where one's status and reputation were counted above everything—even intelligence and hard work. Marrying Hannah Quincy would be one more step down the road toward finally gaining the respect of the many men who'd always regarded him as inferior.

Yes, he would propose to her tonight at the party at Mount Wollaston.

He glanced back at the letter he'd written to Susanna.

She'd likely be at the party too. He'd deliver the letter to her, but that was it.

He'd keep his distance. Not that she'd want to be around him anyway, not after discovering the secret tunnel and the smuggling ring.

In fact, after the loathing written all over her face yesterday, he had the feeling she'd make it easy for him to stay away since she wouldn't come anywhere near him now.

Susanna wanted to escape from Elbridge's clammy grip and sneak away to a secluded spot to read. Even though she'd already devoured nearly every volume in Grandmother Eve's house, she still preferred burying herself in a book—here, without the worry of Mother catching her and trying to make her stop.

But she couldn't leave, not yet. Not after Mary and Mr. Cranch had just announced their engagement. He'd discoursed with Father privately earlier in the day. Then he'd proposed to Mary in the parlor shortly after he'd arrived. And they'd decided to get married in November in just a month's time.

Across the dining room, Mary hung onto Mr. Cranch's arm. Her smile rivaled the sun in its brightness. Then again, Mary *was* the sun. Susanna couldn't begrudge her sister the glory she radiated.

"Maybe we'll have another engagement soon." Elbridge patted Susanna's hand and then adjusted it more snugly within the crook of his arm.

"Perhaps we shall," Grandmother Eve said through a bite of one of the tiny cakes the servants had passed among the guests after dinner. Her plump cheeks were rosy and her eyes twinkled.

"All in due time." Elbridge glanced at Susanna in an altogether familiar manner, one that made her want to pull away.

"I have a feeling the engagement will be sooner rather than

later." Grandmother stared openly at Ben Ross as he hovered near Hannah Quincy.

Although Susanna had done her best to avoid him for the past hour, she'd at least expected him to look at her, even sneak a peek in her direction. But he'd been too focused on Hannah to see anyone else.

He'd hung upon her every word, jumped at her every beckon, and practically groveled at her feet.

Irritation wound through Susanna.

Weren't there any men who cared about the beauty of a woman's inward qualities rather than her outward appearance and qualifications?

Elbridge looked around the room and stiffened at the sight of Ben guiding Hannah away from the group. His eyebrows arched high on his forehead near his powdered wig. "You don't think Ross will attempt to propose marriage to my sister, do you?"

Grandmother Eve gave a weak laugh. "I've heard rumors we'll have another engagement tonight."

Against her wishes, Susanna found herself staring at Ben's broad shoulders as he led Hannah out of the room.

Would Ben really marry Hannah?

A momentary twinge of panic urged her to rush after him and stop him. But the panic made no sense. Why should she care whom Ben Ross married? It wasn't any of her concern.

Elbridge's attention was riveted to the retreating couple. "Mrs. Quincy, are you insinuating that Ross is proposing to Hannah this very evening?"

"I'm not insinuating. I'm quite positive he's planning to ask her. He told me so himself when he arrived."

Elbridge frowned and quickly extricated Susanna's hand from his arm. "Excuse me. I shall be back shortly."

He strode across the room toward the door, obviously intending to follow his sister and Ben.

Grandmother Eve's smile widened.

"Do you think Elbridge will disrupt Ben's plans?" Susanna was surprised that she secretly hoped he would.

"Why else do you think I told him?"

"Grandmother Eve!" Susanna feigned indignation. "Why on earth would you do such a thing?"

"Because Benjamin Ross is falling in love with someone else."

"He is?"

"Of course he is. He just doesn't know it yet."

The voices of the guests around her seemed to fade away. What other woman could claim Ben's affection if not Hannah Quincy?

Susanna swallowed a tight lump. "Are you sure? I haven't seen Mr. Ross with anyone else."

Grandmother Eve turned to Susanna, and her eyes twinkled. "I've seen him with *you*, my dear Susanna."

Did Grandmother Eve think Ben was falling in love with her? Susanna shook her head. "You're quite mistaken. Ben doesn't like me any more than I like him."

Grandmother Eve pinched Susanna's cheek. "Come now, darling. I'm not blind. I've seen the way he looks at you. And he's never come close to looking at Hannah that way."

"It doesn't matter if Ben has some fondness for me or not," Susanna said. "He's not the sort of man I can associate with."

"Oh, you silly wild colt. He's exactly the sort of man you need."

"I'm not sure Mother would think so."

Grandmother Eve's smile disappeared. "Ah, Susanna darling. As much as our dear mothers love us, sometimes fear can hold them back from seeing the good in others."

Sadness crept across Grandmother Eve's features, and her eyes took on a distant look as if remembering an occasion with her own mother. It was hard to imagine that her cheerful, easygoing grandmother had ever had any conflicts in her life.

"'Tis exceedingly easy," Grandmother Eve said, "to get caught up in the way things have always been done and never question if that's the way they should continue."

Before she could question her grandmother or find the words to explain why she could never harbor affection for Ben, the shouts from the parlor across the hallway stopped her.

Ben's voice rose in tempo, followed by Elbridge's.

Mr. Cranch broke away from Mary and started toward the commotion as did several other guests. And although Susanna wanted to rush after them, she decided she'd better make use of the distraction to escape the party.

It didn't matter what her grandmother thought about Ben. She doubted the dear woman would be matchmaking if she knew the truth about Ben's illegal involvements. Instead she'd ban Ben from coming to her house ever again.

Susanna made her way down the hallway past the parlor. She slipped into her grandfather's study. And after several moments browsing his shelves, she picked a volume of Shakespeare she'd already read a dozen times.

She wrapped a knit blanket around her shoulders and settled in the hard desk chair. The dustiness of the books and the spiciness of her grandfather's rum were comforting scents. The rhythmic ticking of the mahogany wall clock soothed her as it always had.

Her grandfather didn't complain often, but he'd grumbled about how much the clock had cost. Of course, the polished wood with its scalloped pediment and its front opening door made of real glass was not the kind of item most people owned. Even so, her grandfather had one of his rare moments of consternation at the exorbitant price of the British imported clock.

Susanna perused the small study, suddenly wondering how many other items her grandfather had purchased from the British and at what cost. The shelves of books, the framed map of the world, the painted porcelain vase, even the tasseled carpet covering the wood floor—all of it had been imported and quite expensive.

They were the kinds of items ordinary colonists couldn't afford. But would they be able to buy more if the British didn't have the monopoly and charge higher prices and taxes?

Why were the British charging them so much anyway?

Susanna sat back in her chair, and the fiery passion in Ben's eyes flashed through her mind. He'd seemed so certain of what he was doing and so convinced the British rule was oppressive.

Maybe there was a grain of truth to what he was saying. And maybe she'd rushed to judge him yesterday.

Whatever the case, she could admit that even if she disagreed with what he and the others were doing, he was a kind and helpful man. And whether she liked it or not, she still needed his assistance with Dotty.

She'd only just managed to read through Act 1 of *Romeo and Juliet* when the door of the study squeaked open and Ben poked his head in.

At the sight of her, he slid into the room and closed the door behind him. The quiet click sent her heartbeat scampering.

He leaned back against the door and crossed his arms. "I thought I'd find you reading."

"I'd much rather read than hang on Mr. Quincy's arm all evening." She uncrossed her legs and smoothed her gown.

She'd gotten into the impolite habit of crossing her legs while she read, and everybody knew sitting with legs crossed was a social taboo for ladies like herself.

Through the dim light coming from the candles in the wall sconces, the glimmer in his eyes told her he'd noticed her mishap.

She wanted to ask him the outcome of his proposal to Hannah, whether he'd had time to confirm marriage plans before Elbridge barged in on them. But she was surprised to find herself too afraid to ask.

"I'm taking my leave," he said.

"Oh." The word came out in a breath of disappointment. She was sure she should have been relieved. After all, since yesterday's discovery, she'd told herself she would have to limit her contact with Benjamin Ross most severely.

"I'm riding circuit with the judges starting tomorrow and need to retire early tonight. But I wanted to give you something before I go."

It was only then she noticed he was holding a book.

He turned it over, revealing the title: *The Odyssey* by Homer. Then he held it out to her. "For you."

She pushed out of the chair and stood, letting the blanket fall to the floor. "Alexander Pope's translation from the Greek?"

"It's only volume one, but I thought you might like to borrow it."

"Is it yours?"

"I may not have much, but I do have a plentiful supply of books I've collected over the years."

"What more do you need?"

He grinned. "I agree with Erasmus: 'When I have a little money, I buy books; and if I have any left, I buy food and clothes.'"

She laughed softly. "And I agree with Cicero: 'A room without books is like a body without a soul.'"

He shoved away from the door and started across the study toward her. The light in his eyes flashed with the warmth and merriment she was finding altogether too attractive.

As much as she knew she should resist being in close proximity to this man, she couldn't make herself move, even when he stopped directly before her.

"I see I have finally met someone else who loves books as much as I do."

"Or perhaps more." She caught the scent of him—the unique combination of wet soil and soap—the sign he'd attended his farm duties but had taken the time to attempt to present himself as a gentleman.

"Maybe we have more in common than I realized." His voice was low, and his gaze traveled around her face languidly.

At his boldness, heat flushed her cheeks and she lowered her lashes. Perhaps Grandmother Eve had been right about the way Ben looked at her. His bold stare certainly went beyond ordinary interest, especially for a man who had just proposed marriage to another woman.

She took a step away from him but bumped into the desk chair. "Do tell me. How are you and my dear cousin Hannah faring?"

He stiffened almost as though her words had punched him. "We're faring well enough, thank you."

So, were they betrothed or not? The question hung at the tip of her tongue.

He refused to look her in the eyes and instead peered at the book.

She swallowed her curiosity. She certainly wasn't planning to pester him about his plans and have him think she cared about his relationship with Hannah. What did or didn't happen between them wasn't any of her concern.

He held out the book. "Make sure you read page twenty-five first."

She took it and slid her fingers over the cover reverently. The pages fell open to the place he'd indicated, revealing a folded sheet of paper.

A letter.

She caressed it, relief swelling through her. And gratefulness.

He gently closed the book, forcing her to remove her fingers from the paper. "It would be better—safer—to read it later in private."

She nodded. "I don't know how to thank you. I was worried after our disagreement you might not want to help me."

"I'm not petty, Susanna. If I said I would help you, then you can count on it." The swirling blue in his eyes held traces of both warmth and worry. "Just be careful and don't do anything rash until I have more information and can ride to Boston to investigate the situation more fully."

"It will soon be rather cold for her to live outside—"

Ben lifted his fingers to her lips and cut off her words with his soft touch. He tossed a glance over his shoulder toward the door.

She held her breath and listened, catching a faint creak in the floorboards in the hallway.

Was someone listening to their conversation?

They stood silently for a long moment, Ben's finger against her lips.

The pressure seemed to grow, and finally his gaze dropped to her lips. But instead of pulling away, his eyes darkened and his finger slid to her lower lip. He grazed the rounded curve starting on one end and slowly working toward the other.

The touch left her breathless.

And when his finger moved to her top lip and began tracing the sensitive skin there, her body trembled.

What was it about Ben Ross that made her ignore reason? Why did his merest contact ignite her?

Certainly she'd never met another man who could so easily make her forget about everything but him.

He sucked in his breath, and something about the intensity in his eyes told her he was contemplating kissing her again. And this time he wouldn't be kissing her to put on a show for Lieutenant Wolfe. No. If he kissed her again, it would be because he wanted to.

The door of the study swung open and banged against the wall, making it shudder.

"Ben?" Mr. Cranch barged into the room.

Susanna scrambled to put distance between herself and Ben, but only managed to fall backward into the desk chair Ben turned to face his friend.

"Come quick," Mr. Cranch said. He was out of breath, his face devoid of the usual merriment. "We just got news from one of the neighbors."

"What news?" Ben's voice hardened.

"There's been another murder."

Chapter
11

"It's another young woman," Ben's father called from a patch of salt hay on the wide expanse of beach.

Ben slid off his horse. The half-moon faded in and out behind a gauze of clouds, providing intermittent light. Alas, he wished there was nothing but darkness to obscure what he must look upon.

The wind taunted the lantern Cranch had carried during the ride down from Mount Wollaston, making it throw strange flickers of light over the beach. One of the other farmers standing near his father also held a lantern that cast long eerie shadows over the sand that was covered with tangles of seaweed deposited by the recent storm.

"She's not from our community," his father said. "A stranger, just like the last girl."

Ben started toward his father, but at the movement by his side, he stopped.

Susanna had dismounted.

He spun upon her with all the frustration rampaging through his chest. "You may have convinced me to allow you to come along," he said between clenched teeth, "but you need to stay with Cranch and Elbridge. You're not stepping one foot closer to the body."

"Please. I have to know her identity." Her voice quavered, and she looked at him again with the same beguiling plea that had made him toss reason aside and allow her to accompany him.

"If you come any closer, I'll have Cranch sling you across his saddle and take you right back to your grandmother's house."

She leaned toward his ear and whispered, "I'm afraid it's Dotty." She was obviously thinking the same thing he was, that perhaps the man who had chased Dotty the first time had captured her again, and that instead of taking her back to Mr. Lovelace, he'd killed her instead.

"I'll let you glimpse her face," he said hesitantly, "but only after I have the chance to evaluate the situation first."

Elbridge had joined them, and he slipped his arm around Susanna's waist. "I won't allow it. Susanna will stay right here by my side."

For once, Ben was relieved at Elbridge's possessiveness, and he couldn't muster the frustration from earlier in the evening whenever he'd seen Elbridge hanging on Susanna.

Susanna tried to shrug out of her cousin's embrace, yet he pulled her closer into the crook of his arm.

"Stay with Elbridge." Ben hoped to convey a calmness he didn't have. But her eyes contained turmoil that was crashing and foaming like the nearby waves on the shore. There would be no calming her.

Her insistence upon coming with him certainly wasn't helping to keep their activities regarding Dotty as clandestine as he'd hoped. Surely Elbridge would suspect something now.

Ben tramped toward his father and the other farmers who'd gathered at the shore. The cold, salty sea breeze blew against his face and sent chills down his spine.

His father shook his head, his weathered face wrinkled with sadness. "Looks like she died the same way as the last girl."

"I told you we should have hung Hermit Crab Joe," mumbled one of the farmers.

"Can't blame Joe this time," Ben said, not caring that his tone was sharp. "I swung by the parsonage on the way here, and Joe was with Parson Wibird. He's been there all day and all evening."

Ben had known the men would point the finger at Joe first, and this time he was determined not to let the old fisherman take the blame.

"Maybe he murdered her last night," suggested one of the others.

"This is a recent murder," his father said. "If she'd been here all day, someone would have seen her earlier. And besides, if she'd lain here overnight, her blood would have dried by now."

Ben parted the tall grass, not wanting to look at the carnage, but knowing he had no choice.

A half-clad woman lay in an awkward sprawl. Her wet skirt twisted around her thighs, and her bodice was ripped, revealing too much of her flesh. He had no doubt she'd been violated, just like the last murder victim.

Disgust churned through his stomach.

Rain-drenched hair lay plastered to a bruised neck and a pretty face as fragile and pale as cracked porcelain. The woman's eyes were open and stared unseeingly at the sky overhead.

"Where's the blood?" he asked, trying to make himself remain objective and distant even though everything within him wanted to lash out at whoever was responsible.

"Her feet." His father stepped on the wilted sea grass, pushed it aside, and revealed bloodied, lacerated feet. "She's missing her shoes."

Dotty. So the murderer had taken her shoes again, shoes Susanna had given the young runaway.

Ben gulped a breath of the frigid night air and peered straight ahead to the waves slapping the beach. Dark clouds billowed past the faint moon, shrouding the nightmarish scene. If only he could make it truly disappear.

The inquisitive gazes of his father and the other men smoldered through him to his heart. Ever since he'd returned to Braintree after his time at Harvard and his lawyer training, they'd started looking to him for answers and advice.

"Ben?" His father's voice contained only the utmost respect. "We'll do whatever you think is best."

Ben met his father's blue eyes, so much like his own—only wiser and kinder. He knew his father was proud of him for all he'd already accomplished. To his father and the other farmers of Braintree, Ben was already famous, had already made a name for himself. They certainly didn't expect any more of him.

It was men like Elbridge who considered him ignorant.

He wanted to be angry at Elbridge for barging in on him just when he'd finally mustered the courage to pull Hannah aside and propose to her. And yet he'd been strangely relieved at the interruption and had decided to put off the proposal for another night.

"I concur. She's obviously been murdered the same way as the last girl," Ben finally said. "Chased, violated, and then strangled to death."

"Chased?" Susanna struggled to pull away from Elbridge.

Ben gave a curt nod. He was afraid Susanna's efforts to help Dotty had been for naught.

"If she's been murdered the same way as the last girl," the farmer said, holding his lantern higher, "then we know Hermit Crab Joe did it."

"How many times do I need to tell everyone? Joe didn't kill the last victim." Ben tried to keep from shouting, but he was much louder than he'd anticipated. "And now, fortunately, Joe's got an alibi who will verify he wasn't anywhere near this beach or near this girl."

"If Joe didn't kill the girls"—his father spoke in the same level tone he always used—"then who could it be?"

Whoever it was obviously had some twisted pleasure in taking his victim's shoes and chasing them barefooted.

"I don't yet know who's responsible for both of the murders," Ben said. "But I do have a lead. With a little investigating I'll likely be able to narrow my search."

Surely he could discover the man Mr. Lovelace had hired. And if Mr. Lovelace wouldn't disclose the name, he could check around with other merchants to find the information he needed.

But even as Ben plotted his course of action for his next visit to Boston, nagging doubt plagued him. He couldn't shake the question that if the murderer really was the same man Mr. Lovelace had hired to track Dotty, why kill her and his other victim instead of returning them for the monetary reward?

"May I see the woman?" Susanna pleaded, straining to release herself from Elbridge's hold.

Ben's father glanced at Susanna and then back at Ben, his brow rising with unasked questions.

"Father, this is Susanna Smith," Ben said, fumbling for the

words to explain Susanna's presence without giving away too much information about her part in sheltering Dotty. "She and her mother, Mrs. Smith, help many of the poor widows and young women of their community. And Susanna is worried the victim might be someone she knows."

It wasn't exactly a lie. Even so, Ben couldn't meet his father's gaze.

Somehow Susanna managed to extricate herself from Elbridge's grip. And before Ben could stop her, she darted toward the body.

"Wait!" He lunged for her.

"Susanna," Elbridge called, "I command you to stop this instant."

But she'd already reached the young woman and skidded to an ungracious halt, taking in the ugly scene in one swooping glance. Her eyes widened and she brought trembling fingers to her mouth, stifling a cry.

Ben wanted to grab her and turn her away, but Elbridge quickly put a hand on her shoulder, claiming her.

Instead of finding comfort in Elbridge's open and waiting arms, she pushed away from him, stumbled toward Ben, and fell against his chest. She buried her face into his shoulder, and her body shook violently against his.

He knew he ought to direct her to Elbridge. But he couldn't keep from wrapping his arms around her and drawing her close. He pressed his nose into the hood of her cloak and drew in the scent of roseleaf.

Elbridge's brows arched up into his cocked hat and then came quickly down into a sharp V.

His father glanced between him and Elbridge and then settled upon Susanna.

Ben couldn't bear to imagine what his father was thinking.

Although he hadn't said anything to his father about Hannah Quincy, surely he'd heard the rumors about his courtship of the wealthy young woman. And now here he was holding Susanna Smith.

She clutched the front of his overcoat, her breathing labored.

He brushed aside the wisps of her hair that had blown free. "I'm sorry, Susanna."

He didn't have to look at Elbridge to know he was only making more of an enemy of the man than he already had.

"I'm so sorry for that young woman too," Susanna whispered near his ear. Her warm breath tingled his skin. "But I'm relieved she's not Dotty."

"She's not?" Ben pulled back from her.

Susanna shook her head. "I've never seen that woman before."

"Then who is it?" And more important, who was the monster ravishing these pretty young women?

"I wish I knew. Hence I must return home," she said softly so that no one else could hear their conversation. "I need to make sure Dotty's safe and unharmed."

"I don't think it's wise for you to be involved with her any longer." If the murderer of the two women was indeed the same man who'd been chasing Dotty, then he was a twisted, evil man—and Susanna could be placing her own life in jeopardy by helping the young runaway.

"What would you have me do?" she asked. "I can't allow her to fend for herself, can I? Not when she is clearly in so much danger."

He admired Susanna for her willingness to help those less fortunate than herself. Nevertheless, the situation had become too precarious. A murderer was roaming the countryside, and

Ben had the premonition it wasn't a matter of *if* he would strike again but *when*.

"My dear cousin," Elbridge said, stepping behind Susanna, "I really must insist on taking you back to Grandmother Eve's."

Elbridge glared down his nose at Ben. In the overcast night, the shadows lining Elbridge's face made his disapproval and dislike of Ben more prominent.

"I'm sure your mother wouldn't want you to be here." Elbridge touched Susanna's elbow. "This is no place for a lady."

From beneath the hood of her cape, Susanna's eyes flashed with uncertainty.

For all her spirit, she still accepted the authority and approval of her mother—even when the woman was absent.

"Come," Elbridge said gently. "If we go now, I'll be sure to stay silent about your unseemly display with a man who's practically engaged."

"Practically?" She allowed Elbridge to tug her away.

Ben had to force himself not to pull her back into his arms. The damp ocean breeze moved in to replace her warmth with its biting chill. "I'm not engaged yet. Just ask Elbridge."

Elbridge smirked. "If you're planning to propose to one woman, don't you think it's rather immodest to frolic in public with another? What if word of your display reached my dear sister, Hannah?"

"I'm sure you'll make it your duty to personally deliver the rumor."

Susanna glanced to his father and the others who were watching the exchange like playgoers at the theater. In fact, if the situation hadn't been so serious, Ben might have classified the look on his father's face as humorous.

Elbridge drew her farther away from Ben. "My dear cousin,

I must ask that you refrain from any future embraces with Mr. Ross."

The muscles in Ben's jaw flexed. "She's done nothing for which to be ashamed. You're merely upset that she took comfort with me instead of you."

Elbridge puffed out his chest like a scavenging sea gull. "There can be nothing comforting about you, Ross."

"Oh, stop it, Elbridge." Susanna wrenched out of his grasp. "I may not see eye to eye with Mr. Ross on some issues, but there's nothing wrong with our being friends, is there?"

As she asked the question, her inky eyes held his, and he knew she'd meant the question for him and him alone.

Friends? With Susanna Smith?

She'd asked him that once before, and he hadn't believed it was possible.

Cranch's lantern illuminated her fine complexion, her slender cheeks, and a tantalizing stretch of her neck that dipped down to her triple strand of pearls.

He was surprised to realize the sight of the pearls hadn't bothered him all evening. Even now, the jewels didn't elicit any reaction in him the way they had initially—when they'd seemed pretentious.

Was it possible he could set aside his reservations about her?

Apparently she was willing to offer him the hand of friendship in spite of his political leanings, something he hadn't deemed possible.

Elbridge shook his head at Susanna and his frown deepened.

"Of course we can be friends," Ben said quickly, unwilling to let Elbridge interfere again.

A glimmer sprang into Susanna's eyes, and her mouth curved up just slightly on one side—the start of a smile.

In spite of the grimness of the circumstances, Ben couldn't keep from wishing her smile would blossom all the way so he could see her dimple.

Elbridge tugged Susanna toward their horses.

As he watched her stumble along, his heart drummed with what was becoming an all too familiar longing for her.

Could he really *just* be friends with her and nothing more? When every time he was around her he could hardly keep from wanting to hold her?

A gust of wind slapped his face, reminding him of the gravity of the situation. And the danger . . .

His father and the others remained silent as they watched Elbridge help Susanna mount and lead her away.

Finally his father spoke. "Friendship is a good place to start." He wiped his mouth as if trying to contain a grin.

There was a chorus of ayes from the men.

A cord of embarrassment wrapped around Ben, and he shrugged, hoping he appeared more nonchalant than he felt.

How would he ever stay mere friends with such a beautiful woman? He had a feeling it would be one of the hardest things he'd ever have to do.

They wrapped the body in a sheet and left it with the constable in his shed with guarantees that on the morrow he would search the coast for any further clues that might reveal the murderer.

"I'm confident you'll find the right man to hold accountable for these crimes," his father said as they trudged down the dark Braintree lane toward home.

"Let's hope so." Ben hunched into his cloak, the chill of the night piercing through the homespun wool. He led his horse behind him and slowed his gait to match that of his father.

He wouldn't have the chance to investigate until he returned from riding circuit with the judges. And in the meantime he'd have to pray nothing else happened and that Susanna and Dotty would use extreme caution and stay safe.

The clop of hooves and the distant bark of a hound echoed in the crisp fall air, which was quickly turning into winter. Even the scent of woodsmoke from a nearby farmhouse had taken on a distinct life against the changing of the seasons.

"So, you're in love with the Smith girl?"

Ben stumbled at his father's question that was really more of a statement. "No. Not at all." He forced a short laugh. "Of course I'm not in love with Susanna Smith."

"Well, you certainly fooled me tonight."

"I cannot deny I'm attracted to Susanna," he admitted. "Who wouldn't be? She's intelligent, witty, and interesting."

"She sounds like the perfect match for you."

He wanted to agree. Susanna was everything Hannah was not. He thought about her more than he should. And even in her grandfather's study earlier, he'd felt a pull toward her that was unbearably strong and difficult to resist.

He knew he needed to control himself better around Susanna. Surely he would have less trouble with his attraction once he was finally engaged to Hannah.

"I'm in the process of trying to propose marriage to Hannah Quincy."

His father plodded forward without missing a step. "Then you love Miss Quincy?"

Did he love Hannah? Ben shook his head. "Sometimes there are factors more important than love."

"Then you are in love with her wealth rather than her person?"

Ben wanted to rebut his father's words—similar to those of Parson Wibird from earlier in the day—but something about his father's bluntness kept him from doing so. "Hannah Quincy will give me what I currently lack, namely the status and approval of my peers."

His father was silent for a long moment, the steady scraping of their boots against the dirt road reminding Ben of the steadiness of the man by his side. He was a deacon of the church and had been the selectman of the town for years. There was not a nobler or more respected man among the community.

"There's more than one way to earn the approval of your peers." His father spoke slowly as if weighing his words carefully. "And often the best way is through strength of character."

His father's integrity, honesty, and diligence had gained him his reputation among the Braintree farmers. Maybe he hadn't risen higher in status, but he was held in the highest esteem by his friends.

"Just remember whose approval matters the most, and ask yourself whether you should be seeking man's favor or God's."

As his father's words sank deep inside him, Ben didn't even try to formulate a response.

They rounded the winding road lined with the stone wall that bordered their farm. Ben stared over the dark barren fields resting after the harvest.

It was land. It was better than nothing.

Even so, Ben couldn't keep from longing for more for his future. Surely his father wanted more for him as well. He hadn't sold acreage to pay for his education only to have Ben end up a farmer in Braintree.

"You're a man now, son," his father said at last. "I trust you'll make the right decision."

Ben nodded, hoping he wouldn't let his father down.

Chapter
12

Susanna stood in the enclosed yard and watched the girls hasten down the winding road, the wind teasing the ribbons that dangled from their straw hats. They didn't chatter and play as they usually did. Instead they huddled together and scurried through the last of the fallen leaves, their gazes darting to the scraggly oaks and maples. Without leaves, the bare branches were gnarled and reached twisted fingers toward the girls as if to snag them.

"Keep them safe . . ." Susanna whispered a prayer through the trembling in her heart. Even with her father riding alongside them on his way to the tavern, no one could rest easy after last week's murder.

She'd only had a scant handful of girls arrive that afternoon for dame school, and they hadn't stayed as long as usual. She didn't blame the mothers for not wanting their daughters to traverse the country roads.

Mother had restricted her and Mary from going anywhere. With all the preparations they must make for Mary's wedding, they didn't have time to go visiting anyway.

Susanna shivered and hugged her arms against her caraco jacket. Low, gloomy clouds draped the sky like a sea of murky gray waves. Now that shorter November days were upon them, they wouldn't have long before they'd have snow and ice.

How would Dotty survive then?

Susanna glanced at the barn and then beyond to the barren fruit trees of the orchard.

Dotty couldn't last much longer in the wild. She needed a warm place to stay and steady meals. And safety.

Susanna slipped her hand through the slits in the layers of her petticoats to the embroidered pocket hanging next to her shift. Her fingers caressed the crisp sheet of Ben's letter.

Dear Diana.

Dear.

She warmed once again at the memory of the intimate greeting he'd used.

Although his note had been short, he'd indicated he would be searching through records of previous cases regarding runaway indentured servants, checking for precedents and determining if he could find a judge who might be sympathetic to Dotty's cause.

After last week's murder, Susanna had tried to use even more care. She didn't want to chance drawing any attention to Dotty's whereabouts.

Susanna had only sneaked out of the house one other time to visit Dotty in the barn at night. Most days she passed food to Tom through the milk pail. And Tom in turn hid the food in the loft for Dotty when she slipped into the barn under the cover of darkness.

"Susanna," Mother called from the open door of the kitchen, "you need to finish sewing the lace onto Mary's new apron."

"Yes, Mother," she called back and then sighed, her breath leaving a white cloud in the air.

If only Ben would write her another letter and advise her further . . .

During Mr. Cranch's visits over the past week, she'd learned Ben was still riding the circuit with the judges, that he was traveling as far west as Worcester. According to Mr. Cranch, Ben was handling every kind of case and was as honest a lawyer as ever broke bread.

Of course, Mother didn't think Ben was honest. In Mother's opinion, no lawyer was truthful. They were in the business of defending crooks, debtors, thieves, and smugglers.

No amount of Mr. Cranch's praise on behalf of Ben could sway Mother's disdain of him, not even the knowledge that Ben had been justified regarding Hermit Crab Joe's defense.

There were many who continued to blame the old man for the latest murder, regardless of the evidence that suggested someone else was responsible. But after witnessing the latest victim, Susanna couldn't imagine that anyone but the devil himself was responsible.

She pressed her hand against her chest in an unsuccessful attempt to ward off the anguish that came whenever she thought about Hermit Crab Joe. Hence the poor man would have the M branded on his cheek for being a murderer even though he was innocent. Wherever he went, whatever he did, people would always view him as a killer.

A spot of blue near the barn caught Susanna's attention. The tattered edge of a drab blue skirt flapped in the wind.

Dotty's skirt.

Anxiety spurted through Susanna. She started forward heedless of the cold and the fact that she wasn't wearing her cloak.

Why had Dotty come out of hiding during the middle of the day?

With long strides, Susanna crossed the enclosure, unhooked the gate, and ran the distance to the barn.

As she rounded the corner, she barreled into Dotty.

"Oh, miss, I beg your pardon." Dotty steadied Susanna, giving her a glimpse of chipped and dirt-encrusted nails, and hands that were red and cracked from the cold.

"Why are you here?" Susanna asked. "Are you in trouble?"

Dotty cast a glance over her shoulder toward the apple orchard and the woodland beyond. "I think he's discovered where I'm hiding during the days."

"The man that chased you?"

The young woman nodded. Her lips were dry and cracked like her hands. Her hair was dirty and lifeless beneath her muslin cap. And the hem of her cloak was frayed and caked with mud. "I noticed that someone had been inside my cave—"

"Your cave?"

"Aye, miss. I found a small cave up in the rocks where I can hide during the day. And I have some apples and berries and a few other things."

"Do you know for certain your pursuer was prying?"

"I never saw anyone, miss. Not anyone at all. But who else would be looking for me out there?"

Susanna wanted to believe one of the local farmers and his boy out hunting had come upon Dotty's cave. But she couldn't ignore the buzzing at the back of her mind. If the murderer had found Dotty's cave, then she wasn't safe in the woods any longer.

"You'll have to stay here. In the barn." The words came out before Susanna could stop them. But once spoken, she knew it was the right decision, even if it meant she was slipping further down the slope into disobedience.

"Oh, I couldn't, miss. I just couldn't."

The skin at the back of Susanna's neck prickled. She glanced over the cornfield her father and his hired workers had recently harvested and then to the woodland across the road.

Was someone watching them even at that moment?

A lone doe stood at the edge of the woods, its ears perked in alertness as though it too sensed the presence of danger.

Susanna tugged Dotty toward the side barn door. "Let's get you into the barn before someone sees you."

"But you've already done enough for me, miss," Dotty protested.

Susanna pushed open the door and hustled Dotty inside. The body heat of the animals gave warmth to the barn and took the edge off the coldness of the day. The scent of horse-flesh, damp hay, and manure wouldn't make the barn the homiest of places to live. Still, it would have to do, at least until Susanna could determine what might be the next best option.

A lantern hung above one of the horse stalls, signaling Tom's presence. And as the door creaked closed behind them, Tom rose and peered over the rail. His gentle eyes widened at the sight of her with Dotty.

Even behind the horse stall, Tom's dark shadow leaped out at them. Dotty jerked away from Susanna and scrambled backward.

"Tom knows about you," Susanna rushed to explain. "He's the one bringing you food every day."

Dotty pressed against the pigsty and eyed the door.

"I won't hurt you, child," Tom said in his low, kind voice.

"You'll be safe here with Tom," Susanna promised. "He's like an uncle to me."

Dotty nodded, but her face had turned a sickly pallor. She lifted a hand to her mouth, then doubled over and retched in the hay. The heaves wracked her thin body, draining her until she had nothing left to give.

Susanna rubbed Dotty's back while looking into Tom's worried eyes.

"It's all going to work out just fine," she said, not sure who she was trying to reassure more—herself or Tom.

When Dotty finally straightened, tears streaked her dirty cheeks. "I'm sorry, miss."

"You have no need to apologize." Susanna brushed a tangled lock of Dotty's hair away from her face. "If you're ill, then I must insist you come into the house where I can care for you properly."

She trembled at her own bold words. She knew Phoebe would willingly help her. But what about Mother? Would she turn away a helpless vagrant simply because she'd committed a crime in running away from her cruel master?

Dotty shook her head and her eyes turned frantic. "Oh no, miss. I couldn't. I just couldn't."

"But if you're suffering from distemper—"

"This is no distemper." Dotty hung her head. Then she splayed her hand over her abdomen.

Susanna's heartbeat clattered to a stop. She was innocent in the ways of men and women, yet she wasn't naïve and knew a woman could beget a child outside of the proper bounds of marriage.

"How . . . I mean, when . . . ?" She couldn't get the words past the embarrassment that bridled her tongue.

Dotty continued to hang her head.

The furrows that appeared in Tom's forehead only twisted at Susanna's stomach. She was sure he was remembering just as she was the young woman who had been punished the previous summer for begetting a child without a husband.

The elders had gathered at the meetinghouse and had determined the young woman needed discipline for her sin. The men had declared they wanted to make an example of her in order to deter others from fornication.

So they'd marched the pregnant woman out to Mill Cove, strapped her into the ducking stool, and proceeded to lower her in and out of the water until she'd almost drowned.

Like most of the parishioners, Susanna had gone to watch. Every time the group of strong men had lowered the beam that supported the wooden chair, Susanna had wanted to cry out. She'd wanted to ask why no one would hold the father of the unborn child responsible too. She'd been furious at the thought that perhaps one of the men doing the ducking might even be the father of the unborn babe.

But apparently no one had known or cared.

No one except Susanna.

Susanna slipped her arm around Dotty. "You don't need to say anything more about your condition. We'll make do." At least she hoped they would, though she had no idea how she would keep Dotty's presence in the barn a secret.

"It weren't my choice, miss," Dotty whispered. "I didn't ever want to be with any of the men."

Bile rose in Susanna's throat at the thought of the nightmare this woman had experienced.

No matter how grievously she'd already suffered, Susanna had no doubt the elders would stick Dotty onto the ducking stool if they discovered her pregnancy. They wouldn't care whether the begetting was the result of her being violated numerous times by many different men.

If anyone should suffer for Dotty's predicament, it should be Mr. Lovelace and the other men who had taken advantage of her. But Susanna was quite certain the elders wouldn't make any of the men pay for their sins.

"You're not to blame," Susanna said. "We'll do the best we can to get you settled into the loft. You'll stay there henceforth."

"But, miss, I'd be putting you and your slave into much danger."

"I don't mind." Susanna tried not to breathe in the sourness of Dotty's odor. Maybe Phoebe would help her drag a hot tub of water out to the barn so that Dotty could bathe. "And if anyone should ever question Tom about his involvement, I'll be sure to tell them it was all my idea."

"Now, Miss Susie, you know I ain't gonna turn my back on anyone in need." Tom rested his arms on the top railing of the stall, dangling the hoof-pick and wire brush he used for cleaning the horses' hooves. "But I don't like seeing you sneaking around again."

"I don't have a choice."

"We could tell your mama and papa." His wise eyes urged her to stop now while they could. "They're good people, and they'll get help for Dotty."

"I'm getting assistance. From Mr. Ross." She was glad Tom didn't know about Dotty's stalker and the possibility that he was the same man who had murdered the two women on the beach. If Tom was hesitant about her involvement now, she didn't want to think about the opposition he'd give her if he discovered the truth.

And even though Tom thought her parents would support her efforts, she wasn't so sure Mother would approve of what she was doing. Yes, Mother had compassion for the misfortunate. She'd always taken her duty to aid the poor and the widowed seriously. But she also had given unquestioning obedience to those in authority over her—her husband, the king, and God. And she'd taught her daughters to do the same. In fact, Mother had instructed them that they would learn to obey God by learning first to obey their earthly authorities.

Susanna had always believed Mother, had always wanted to obey, but somehow in Dotty's situation unquestioning obedience didn't seem appropriate.

Ben's words from when they'd been in the secret underground cavern came back to her. *"Sometimes man must look at whose laws he is obeying and determine whether they are just and right and merciful."*

Hadn't he said if the law was tyrannical, then it was their duty to institute fairer laws? Perhaps the system regarding indentured servants was one of those tyrannical practices that needed changing the same as slavery. If a man-made law was in opposition to God's ultimate law of loving Him and loving their neighbors, did He require His children to obey those laws?

Tom pointed heavenward. "What do you think the good Lord wants us to do?"

"I don't know." She wasn't certain about anything anymore—not since meeting Ben.

"Susanna?" Mary called from outside the barn door.

"Quick, hide!" Susanna said to Dotty.

But Dotty was already scrambling up the ladder.

With the side of her boot, Susanna scraped hay over the puddle of Dotty's vomit.

The door opened, and Mary poked her head in. "There you are, Susanna. Mother sent me to fetch you."

"Tell her I'll be along shortly." Susanna straightened. "I was just having a conversation with Tom."

Her words weren't a complete lie. She *had* been talking with Tom—among other things. Even so, guilt whispered in her ear that she was only piling up sin upon sin.

Mary stepped inside. Her features were serious and inquisitive, although as pretty as always, especially framed by the lacy ruffles of her cap.

Susanna wanted to turn around and make certain Dotty had hidden herself, but she forced herself to face her sister and smile.

"I've been worried about you," Mary said.

"Oh?" A scraping noise in the loft made Susanna flinch.

"Yes, with all the planning for my wedding and with all my happiness, I wanted to make sure I wasn't causing you undue turmoil." Mary grasped the knot of the woolen shawl she'd draped around her shoulders.

Something clanged overhead, a hollow ring like a pitchfork hitting a pail.

Mary glanced upward to the dark beams and the shadows beyond.

Susanna held her breath.

"Don't worry about me." Susanna prayed Mary would assume the noises in the loft came from the barn cat. "I'm faring as well as can be."

"Are you happy?" Mary asked as she stepped gingerly across the hay-strewn floor.

Tom hadn't moved, except for the deepening of the creases in his forehead.

Susanna wanted to motion to him to return to his work,

afraid that if Mary looked at him, she would suspect something was wrong.

But Mary passed him without even the slightest acknowledgment, as if he were no more important than one of the barn animals.

"There's nothing wrong with me, Mary." The sour stench of Dotty's vomit rose up around her. She knew she needed to get Mary out of the barn before she suspected anything.

Mary stopped in front of her. "Are you sure, Susanna? You seem rather melancholy this week."

It would be only a matter of seconds before Mary caught a whiff of the vomit and began to question her. How could she answer without having Mary believing *she* was ill and then running back to Mother with the news?

"I'm perfectly happy for you and your Mr. Cranch."

Mary's nose began to wrinkle.

"Come now." Susanna linked arms with Mary and led her toward the barn door. "If I have reason to be melancholy, it's only because I'm pining at the thought that I may never find love quite as ardent as that which you share with your beloved."

"Oh, my dearest," Mary said as she ambled along next to her, "I was afraid you might be feeling that way."

Susanna swallowed her guilt. She wasn't exactly lying again. From time to time she did wonder if she'd ever find a worthy match, a man who would accept her for who she truly was—for her questions and interests, some of which seemed to push the bounds of propriety.

"Be of good cheer." Mary squeezed her arm when they reached the door. "You'll find a good match . . . eventually. I'm sure after my wedding, Mother will begin working in earnest to find you a suitable husband."

"I have no doubt she will." Mother had always insisted that Mary be the first to wed. Susanna had wanted to tell Mother not to fear, that there would never be any chance Susanna the moon would outshine her fair sister.

Now that Mary's future had been secured, Susanna's turn was next. Mother would indeed appoint her attention to finding Susanna's husband. She would make it her full-time occupation as any good mother would.

Susanna opened the barn door and ushered Mary outside. As soon as the barn door clicked shut behind them, Susanna released a breath, grateful her sister was so easily distracted, that Dotty's presence had gone undetected for the time being.

But how long could she hope to hide the girl before someone discovered her?

Mary smiled at her, and in the grayness of the afternoon Mary's joy was like a beam of sunshine.

"Perhaps you'll find contentment with Elbridge?" Mary said hesitantly. "He's been rather kind and attentive to you of late."

"At least he's not mercilessly teasing me anymore." Susanna didn't harbor any affection for her cousin, but she knew she couldn't disregard the possibility of a match with him.

"And what of Mr. Ross?" Mary asked as they strolled arm in arm across the barnyard.

Susanna's heart gave a strange skitter forward at the mention of Mr. Ross's name, but she rapidly brushed aside the thought of a match with him. "Mother would never allow me to consider him. Not in a thousand years."

Mary nodded.

"And besides," Susanna continued, "hasn't he set his sights on Hannah? Who could ever compete with our dear cousin for a man's affection?" Susanna was surprised at the bitter tone that seeped out.

For a reason she couldn't explain, she'd been relieved that Elbridge had foiled Ben's proposal plans. But he was a determined man, and she had the feeling he wouldn't give up his aspirations toward Hannah quite so easily.

Mary plucked a piece of straw from the sleeve of Susanna's jacket. "Don't worry. The right young man will come along soon enough."

"Perhaps." But she wasn't holding out much hope, because she was becoming more convinced with each passing day that she couldn't marry someone unless she counted him as both a friend and admirer.

Chapter
13

Ben shoved against Parson Wibird's door and stopped short when it didn't open. The parson never locked his door. Something was wrong.

"Who's there?" came the parson's voice on the other side of the thick door.

"It is only I, Benjamin Ross."

The lock rattled for an eternity, then finally the door opened, but just a crack. Parson Wibird's face peeked out, his squinty eyes narrowing upon Ben.

"Where's Joe Sewall?" Ben peered past the parson into the hallway cluttered with books, crates, and an assortment of papers. "And why are you locking your door?"

"I've had some threats." Parson Wibird swung open the door and motioned Ben inside with a wave of his hand.

Ben slipped through and was surprised when the parson slammed the door closed behind him and relocked it.

Parson Wibird straightened and then massaged the back of his neck, weariness drawing tight lines across his usually composed face. "Mr. Sewall is safe. But if some of the men had their way, they'd drag him out and hang him."

Ben shook his head at the ongoing ignorance of the men. If only he was at liberty to share his suspicions about who was really behind the murders. Just the thought again of what he'd discovered sent a chill up his spine.

"Mr. Sewall is tucked safely away in my keeping room." The parson cocked his head toward the lean-to along the back of the parsonage, which served as a kitchen and sitting area.

As a bachelor, the parson had hired one of the poor women of Braintree's First Church parish to come several times a week and do his cooking and cleaning. But Ben had the feeling the woman was forever facing an uphill battle in keeping the parson's home clean and organized.

Parson Wibird fidgeted with the lock again. "I told him he had to stay with me—at least until you can find evidence for the real murderer."

"I'm getting closer."

"Then you know who did it?"

Ben swallowed his frustration. It hadn't taken him long to get the information he'd needed. A few well-placed questions with the right people had given him the name of the man some of the merchants hired to track their runaways.

It was the name of the person he most wanted to avoid. . . .

"Lieutenant Wolfe." Ben's muscles tightened just thinking about the lieutenant quartered in Weymouth in such close proximity to Susanna and Dotty. His heart had urged him to ride out to Weymouth and warn Susanna. He'd wanted to do it ever since he'd heard the name. And even tonight, as weary as he was, he wished he had an excuse to ride the four miles to visit her.

Parson Wibird crossed his lanky arms and rocked back and forth on his heels, obviously waiting for further explanation.

"Apparently the lieutenant has gained quite the reputation in Boston for being able to locate runaway slaves and indentured servants. He's had a high success rate in returning the runaways, even if some of his methods are a bit cruel. But no one seems to mind so long as he does the job."

"So you think those murdered girls were runaways?"

"I have no solid proof now that they're dead and buried."

"And even if we knew for certain the girls had been runaways, how can we connect the lieutenant to their murders?" The parson's forehead furrowed.

The impossibility of the situation weighed upon Ben, slumping his shoulders. "I'm afraid we don't have much evidence of anything. At this point I'm merely speculating." The only proof he had that the other two girls were runaways was the similarity of their situation to Dotty's, except that in Dotty's case, so far she'd managed to outrun and outwit the lieutenant in his twisted game of cat and mouse.

Even if Ben could prove Lieutenant Wolfe had been tracking the murdered women, Parson Wibird was right. Ben still wouldn't have evidence that the lieutenant actually killed them. Unless he involved Dotty. She could identify and testify against the lieutenant. The scars on her feet would link her to the murdered women. But would that be enough?

"I trust that you have reasons to suspect the lieutenant that I don't know about," said the parson, studying Ben's face.

Ben nodded. As much as he wanted to disclose the information he had about Dotty, he couldn't. Not yet. Not until he knew Susanna would be safe from any repercussions in helping the runaway.

"Nevertheless," Parson Wibird continued, "it would be

a very serious matter to press charges of murder against an officer of the king, even if we had solid evidence against him. But to level accusations against the lieutenant when we have nothing but speculations? We would only bring trouble upon ourselves and perhaps our community if we were to do so."

"Then I guess I'll need to search for something we can use against the lieutenant, something that would prove he's indeed the murderer."

Parson Wibird widened his permanently squinted eyes, giving Ben a glimpse of the same doubts that had been plaguing him in recent days. "In the meantime, it doesn't appear we're much further along in defending Joe, does it?"

"I'm sorry, Parson." If Ben couldn't prove Lieutenant Wolfe was the murderer, how would he be able to keep the townspeople from acting on their fears and hanging Joe Sewall?

"I guess this means I've got a permanent houseguest and will need to install several more locks."

"I'd be indebted to you if you'd continue to keep Joe safe until I can sort out my next plan of action and talk more with the constable."

Parson Wibird clamped him on the shoulder. "You don't even need to ask. You know I'll do whatever I can to help."

Ben wiped his tired eyes, freeing them from the dust and grit that had built up from his long ride that day. He'd finally left the circuit and stopped in Boston to see Hannah in the Quincy mansion at the top of Beacon Hill.

And now he regretted he'd wasted the time visiting her.

Of course he'd planned to propose again. But she'd had other guests and had been distracted. Besides, he'd been just plain tired and anxious to get home after several weeks away. At least that's what he'd told himself during the ride back to Braintree.

But the truth was, as much as he needed a woman like Hannah, he hadn't thought about her once during the time he was away. He hated to admit it, but he'd thought much more about Susanna. And a part of him rationalized that he couldn't marry one woman when he was clearly enamored with another.

Whatever the case, he hadn't been able to muster the enthusiasm or desire to propose to Hannah. In fact, he was irritated more than anything. If he hadn't made the stop to visit her, he might have had time to ride out to Weymouth and see Susanna to warn her about his suspicions regarding Lieutenant Wolfe. Surely he could have derived some excuse for a visit.

But even as he gripped the door handle, he knew he had to proceed carefully. He'd only jeopardize the secrecy of the Caucus Club and the safety of the underground smuggling operations if he made an appearance in Weymouth without a solid reason. Lieutenant Wolfe already suspected his involvement. He couldn't give the man any more reasons to question him.

No. He'd have to wait for Cranch's wedding on the following Friday, and then he'd have to find a way to talk with Susanna alone.

In the meantime, he'd write her another letter and warn her to stay as far away from Lieutenant Wolfe as possible.

Susanna dipped her rag into the soft soap Phoebe had recently made from the barrel of ashes, along with the grease they'd accumulated during the fall butchering. With the clear jellylike soap, Susanna wiped the marble surrounding the fireplace, rubbing away streaks of soot and bringing the speckled stone to a gleaming shine.

The rancid odor of the lye stung her eyes, and she paused in her work to blink back a watery tickle.

"Keep working, Susanna," Mother said from the side table where she stood polishing several silver candle holders. "There's no time to dawdle."

With only two days until Mary's wedding, Mother was in a frenzy to make the house spotless, in particular the large front parlor where they would hold the matrimonial ceremony.

The wedding wouldn't be a large affair, mostly attended by close friends and family. There were still those Puritans among their community who shunned any ostentatious displays at weddings. They had opposed the changes in the law which had allowed weddings to be performed by ministers at home rather than civil magistrates in a public building as had been the custom.

Nevertheless, Mother expected nothing short of perfection for the day.

Mary was washing the window with such vigor that Susanna wanted to ask her if she expected to transform it into a diamond. But Susanna only smiled and bit back the words.

She couldn't fault Mary's nervous excitement. She was marrying a man she loved. That was indeed cause for rejoicing.

Phoebe's footsteps in the hallway were quick and urgent. When she charged into the room, her thin face was creased with anxiety.

"What is it, Phoebe?" Mother asked. "I thought you were cleaning the guest rooms."

"Yes, Mrs. Smith." Phoebe's gaze darted around the room and landed upon the carpet that graced the center of the room. "But I came to ask Miss Susie to help me shake out the carpet."

Susanna's pulse quickened at the unusual request, which was obviously Phoebe's excuse to speak with her. Was something wrong with Dotty?

They'd been able to keep her presence in the barn a secret so far. But Susanna had the feeling that sooner or later someone would walk into the barn unexpectedly and find Dotty conversing in hushed tones with Tom or helping him with the barn chores as she'd been doing of late.

"The carpet needs a good beating," Phoebe said, pulling herself up to her full height, "but I can't manage it by myself."

Phoebe met Mother's stern glower without blinking. She held her turbaned head tall and her chin almost jutted with defiance. When it came to Dotty, Phoebe had been all too willing to do whatever they needed to in order to help the young woman. Phoebe's enthusiasm had overshadowed Tom's hesitancy and had helped Susanna forget her own uncertainties about sheltering Dotty so freely.

"Yes," Susanna said, not wanting Phoebe to bring trouble upon herself. "Once the carpet is out of the way, Mary can more easily sweep the floor."

Mother pressed her lips together. "Phoebe may find one of Grandmother Eve's servants to help her."

"They're busy upstairs," Phoebe persisted.

Urgency nudged Susanna harder. If Phoebe was refusing the help of the servants Grandmother Eve had sent to assist with the wedding preparations, then the situation was indeed serious. "Please, Mother. After inhaling these cleaning fumes for so long, I have need of a breath of fresh air."

"Very well." Mother gave a dismissive shake of her hand. "You may beat the carpet. But be quick about it."

After donning their cloaks, Susanna and Phoebe rolled the

carpet and half carried, half dragged it out the front door to the patch of lawn.

"What's wrong?" Susanna whispered. "Not something with Dotty, I fear."

Phoebe dropped her end of the heavy mat. Susanna then lowered her end of the carpet onto the yellowing grass that was crusted with a layer of frost. Even though the November morning was filled with sunshine, the bitter edge of a cold breeze sliced through her cloak, making her shiver.

"When I was upstairs making the guest bed, I looked out the window—the one facing the orchard. There are a couple of soldiers in the woods beyond the orchard."

Susanna's heartbeat kicked into a gallop. "Do you think one of them was Lieutenant Wolfe?"

"I wouldn't know. But who else could it be?"

Susanna had no doubt Phoebe was thinking the same thing she was—that Lieutenant Wolfe was closing in on Dotty's whereabouts.

After the letter she'd received from Ben only yesterday, she'd been uneasy. Ben hadn't disclosed much, only that *dear Diana needed to avoid wolves*. He'd told her he would explain more when he came to the wedding on Friday.

She hadn't needed to read between the lines to suspect that Lieutenant Wolfe was somehow involved in tracking Dotty and perhaps connected in some way to the murders of the young women. What would Ben say if he knew Dotty was living in the barn all the time now?

A tap on the front parlor window and Mother's frowning face peering out at them sent Susanna scurrying for the broom on the front porch while Phoebe made quick work of unrolling the carpet.

"Dotty's not safe here." Phoebe hefted up one side of the

heavy mat as Susanna returned. "We need to find a new hiding place."

"Do you think they'd dare snoop around our home or the barn?" Susanna lifted a broom to beat it against the rug. "They wouldn't dare, would they?"

Before Phoebe could answer, two horses with Redcoat riders came trotting around the side of the house.

Susanna sucked in a cold breath.

There, sitting tall and straight upon his gleaming black steed, was Lieutenant Wolfe. Next to him rode his freckle-faced, redheaded assistant. The brilliant sunshine turned the crimson of their coats into the color of freshly spilled blood.

Every nerve in her body screamed at her to get away now. She suspected that Lieutenant Wolfe would devour her if he could.

She took a step back, needing to escape into the safety of the house, but Phoebe stopped her with a jab to her side. The sharpness in the slave's eyes shouted an unspoken warning: What would Lieutenant Wolfe think if they turned and ran?

Surely he would think they were afraid of him and that they had something to hide.

If they stood their ground and faced him with unswerving determination, perhaps they would be able to divert him from Dotty's presence, if indeed that's why he was there.

She steeled herself. "Lieutenant Wolfe, what a surprise."

He reined his horse, but not before he allowed the beast to step upon the carpet and leave muddy hoofprints along its edge.

Phoebe jerked the floor covering away from the horse.

The lieutenant glanced at Phoebe and then dismissed her as though she were nothing more than a discarded thread of yarn. Instead he forced a stiff smile to his lips. "Miss Smith."

"What brings you west this morning, Lieutenant?" She willed her voice to hold steady. "Surely your search for illegal activities hasn't taken you this far from the coast?"

"There's more than one form of illegal activity that I'm investigating."

So, he *was* searching for Dotty.

Her mind urged her to stay calm even though she could hardly breathe with the panic that was beginning to suffocate her. "As you well know, Lieutenant, I am a loyal subject of the king, as is the rest of my family. If we suspected any illegal activities in this part of Weymouth, we would notify you."

The lieutenant narrowed his eyes and peered first at the parsonage and then at the barn.

Would he insist upon searching the premises?

Oh, God, help . . . The desperate plea echoed in the deep chambers of her heart.

She'd begun to believe she was justified in breaking the law to help Dotty, that there were times when one had to choose God's greater edicts of kindness and love over the regulations of sinful men.

But what if she'd been wrong? What if she'd only brought danger to her entire family?

"Today, my assistant and I are hunting for a runaway indentured servant." The lieutenant studied her face as if searching there would lead him to the one he sought.

"And what reason do you have to believe such a runaway would be in this area of Weymouth?"

"It appears you and your mother have gained quite the reputation in this community for your service to poor, helpless women."

"Of course we have always thought it our God-given duty to help those less fortunate than ourselves."

The lieutenant didn't reply, except to smile.

"There's never been anything illegal about our help." She spoke rapidly, realizing how incriminating her words sounded.

But the lieutenant was already dismounting. "Sergeant Frazel, you may search the barn. And I'll search the house."

"Yes, sir." The young assistant nodded and lowered himself to the ground.

Phoebe started toward the barn. This time, Susanna had to do the stopping, snagging Phoebe's cloak and holding her in place.

The lieutenant repositioned his hat and then started toward the front steps of the parsonage.

Susanna couldn't move. She knew she needed to do something—anything to prevent the sergeant from going into the barn. Even if Dotty had the chance to hide herself under the hay in the loft before the soldier stepped inside, anyone with a modicum of investigative skills would have no trouble seeing that the young woman was living there. The sergeant would stumble upon the old chamber pot she was using, locate leftover crumbs or mussed hay.

Susanna stared at the sergeant striding toward the barn. She wanted to race after him and block his way, distract him, at the very least shout out and give Dotty a chance to escape through the side door before he walked in.

She could feel Phoebe's wiry body tense, ready to spring into action. But Susanna kept her grip upon the slave's cloak, rendering her immovable.

Lieutenant Wolfe had already ascended the porch steps and was knocking.

Mother opened the front door, and her surprised greeting carried a hint of worry. Yet Susanna couldn't focus on the exchange between her mother and Lieutenant Wolfe. The only thing she could hear was the thud of her heartbeat as Sergeant Frazel entered the barn.

She cringed and waited for his shouts of discovery.

But the only other sound was the voice of her father at the doorway. "Lieutenant Wolfe, I must respectfully insist on knowing why you intend to search our house."

"Reverend Smith, I have reason to believe you're harboring a runaway."

Mother's gasp was followed by Father's denial.

Susanna couldn't tear her gaze from the half-open barn door.

"Pardon me, Lieutenant, but you must understand how completely shocking such an accusation is to me, considering I'm one of the most law-abiding members of this community. How could I do anything less than set a stellar example for my parishioners?"

Her father's tone was much harder and louder than Susanna had ever heard it.

"Perhaps *you* are law-abiding, Reverend. But I have reason to suspect that other members of your family don't share your principles."

The lieutenant's attention shifted to Susanna.

She lifted her chin. "You're terribly mistaken, Lieutenant Wolfe. I most certainly share the same principles as my dear parents."

"Then if you have nothing to hide, you won't mind if I look through your house."

"I must strenuously protest, Lieutenant," Mother said. "We are in the midst of preparing for my daughter's wedding, and we cannot have you and your soldier tramping through our house—"

Her father put a steadying hand on Mother's arm, silencing

her. He puffed out his chest and straightened the silk cravat at his throat. "Lieutenant, just because we are colonials doesn't mean we have relinquished the rights of English citizens. Since when can an officer search a house without first obtaining a writ of assistance?"

"When someone is obviously involved in criminal activities," the lieutenant said, "then I see no need for a writ."

"I assure you," Mother spoke again, "we are not harboring a runaway in this house."

"Mother's right." Susanna forced more courage to her words than she felt. "But since we have nothing to hide, I suggest we let the lieutenant search the house and see for himself. Perhaps he will take care not to disturb the hard work we've accomplished in preparation for the wedding."

"Absolutely not." Father spread his feet and blocked the doorway. Behind him in the hallway stood William and his tutor, obviously disturbed from their studies, which of course William had the good fortune of continuing in spite of all the work needing to be accomplished before the wedding. "If the lieutenant wants to search our home—or anything on our premises—then he needs to do so after obtaining the proper permission."

The lieutenant gripped the hilt of his saber.

Would he pull his weapon and strike Father?

Susanna started toward the porch. She couldn't let him hurt Father—not when she was the one who'd brought all this trouble upon them.

The barn door squeaked open and Sergeant Frazel stepped out. "No sign of her in the barn, Lieutenant."

Susanna's footsteps faltered. She stared at the young soldier. How could he have missed all the signs of Dotty's presence?

Lieutenant Wolfe frowned at his assistant.

"Am I to understand you've already invaded my property without the writ?" Father asked. "Your behavior is quite out of line, Lieutenant. And I intend to make sure your authorities are aware of your blatant disregard for the rights of a freeholder."

The lieutenant spun away and stomped down the steps. "My authorities won't care in the slightest what you have to say."

"Any luck in the house, sir?" the sergeant asked.

"Not today." Lieutenant Wolfe walked through a patch of mud, and before Phoebe could move the carpet out of the way, he marched directly across it, smearing streaks of mud with each step.

Mother gave a sharp cry of protest.

Lieutenant Wolfe brushed past Susanna, close enough that the staleness of rum on his breath fanned against her cheek. "Just wait, Miss Smith. I know you're guilty. I can see it in your face. I will catch you eventually. And then you'll wish you'd never crossed me."

She tried to keep her expression neutral and was relieved the lieutenant couldn't see just how badly her legs were trembling.

He examined the yard one last time, not seeming to miss a single detail, then mounted his horse and kicked it savagely.

Sergeant Frazel moved at a much slower pace, apparently used to the antics of his commanding officer. As he climbed into the saddle of his horse, he glanced at Susanna.

There was a knowing light in his eyes that made her breath stick in her lungs.

What had he really seen in the barn? Did he suspect Dotty was there after all? And if so, why had he lied to his commander?

Once Sergeant Frazel was astride his horse, he nodded at her. He then turned to her father and mother and gave them an apologetic nod before he kicked his horse into a gallop and raced after the lieutenant.

It wasn't until they were well out of sight that anyone moved or spoke.

Susanna collapsed to her knees—out of relief or fear, she didn't know. All she knew was that Dotty was in terrible, life-threatening danger.

And now so was she.

Chapter
14

The wedding feast was grander than any Susanna had ever seen before. She stood next to Mary, who couldn't stop smiling, even after nearly every gentleman in attendance had come by to kiss the bride in the usual tradition—that is, every gentleman except Benjamin Ross.

Susanna searched the dining room for him again. But amidst the crowd of guests—the men with their powdered wigs and the women in their ribbons and rosettes—she couldn't locate him.

Of course she'd seen him in the parlor earlier when Father had performed the wedding ceremony. Ben had stood in the back of the room, dressed in his finest like everyone else. In dark blue broadcloth and a white satin waistcoat, he'd been striking and difficult to miss.

From time to time during the Psalm reading and her father's short lecture, she'd felt the intensity of his attention upon her, but anytime she'd chanced a glance at him, he'd been otherwise occupied.

She desperately needed to talk to him. After Lieutenant

Wolfe's visit two days ago, she hadn't been able to shake the feeling that something terrible was going to happen to Dotty. Susanna could only pray their charade had thrown him off the girl's trail.

She hadn't admitted the truth to her parents, even though Tom had urged her again to tell them about Dotty, especially since Sergeant Frazel had almost caught sight of the runaway before Tom could finish burying her in the soiled hay behind the mare's feedbox.

Phoebe had insisted the lieutenant wouldn't dare attempt another search—not after both Father and Mother had made a point of speaking out so publicly against the unlawful search. And Susanna had decided she wouldn't take any more action until she'd had the opportunity to confer with Ben.

If she could ever find a way to speak privately with him . . .

She fanned herself, the heat of the room and the tightness of her stays stifling her. The scents of smoked ham and roasted squabs stuffed with dressing and wrapped in bacon wafted across her face and would have tantalized her had not the worry been mounting inside her.

The dining room table had been pushed against one of the walls, allowing room for all the guests—the Quincys, Smiths, Mr. Cranch's family, along with friends from the parish. The table, arranged with the glimmering freshly polished candelabras, was also laden with apple dumplings, plum tarts, and spicy puddings that Phoebe had spent the week baking in the spare moments Mother hadn't demanded her assistance with the cleaning.

Grandmother Eve's servants mingled among the guests with trays of nuts, raisins, cakes, and punch. Even though Phoebe had worked nonstop all week, they had still required the extra help.

Mr. Cranch approached Mary and reached for her hand. "Mrs. Cranch," he said with a dashing smile, "since we've fulfilled our obligation to kiss our guests, I've come now to claim a kiss from the one I most desire."

Mary smiled in return and her eyes lit with an eagerness that made Susanna smile.

When Mr. Cranch bent his head toward Mary's, Susanna found herself looking directly into the intense blue eyes of Ben, who stood behind Mr. Cranch.

He didn't say anything to her. Instead he shifted to look at Mr. Cranch, who'd captured Mary in a shockingly passionate kiss. With his hand upon her neck, he'd tipped her head back, covered her mouth completely with his, and drank of her with a fervor that sent heat into Susanna's middle.

She couldn't keep from thinking about the fact that in a few short hours, Mr. Cranch would carry Mary upstairs to the bed they would share for their first night together as man and wife.

Warmth flooded Susanna's face, and she tore her gaze away only to find it colliding with Ben's. His lips curled up in a slow smile, almost as if he knew what she'd been thinking.

Susanna retrieved a cup of punch from the tray of a passing servant and lifted the cool sweet liquid, hiding behind the drink as best she could.

Ben slapped Mr. Cranch on the back, whispering loudly, "Save it for the bedchamber, my dear fellow. You'll have plenty of time later to enjoy your wife."

At that, Mary broke away, her flushed cheeks growing rosier.

Mr. Cranch gave a shaky laugh. "I don't know if I can wait until later."

Susanna choked on her punch and had to swallow quickly before she sputtered it all over her best azure silk gown.

The flecks in Ben's eyes danced, and he squeezed Mr. Cranch's shoulder. "I'm sorry to say for the time being you'll have to satisfy yourself with a few stolen kisses."

"Ah, Ben, my stuffy friend." Mr. Cranch intertwined his fingers with Mary's. "If you had the right woman, you'd know that a man in love can't be satisfied with a few stolen kisses."

Susanna flipped open her fan again and pumped it to cool her overheated face. The conversation was almost scandalous, even for a wedding.

Ben glanced at her again, and this time his eyes landed straight upon her lips. Something flared there. She had the distinct impression he was remembering the kiss they'd shared at Arnold Tavern. She hadn't been able to forget about the moment of passion that had ignited between them when he'd dragged her down onto his lap and given her a kiss that had left her breathless.

"There's always the closet under the stairway," Ben said softly.

Mr. Cranch grinned.

Mary's blush deepened.

"You weren't supposed to say anything about our hiding spot," Mr. Cranch said with a quick glance around. "But now that you mention it, I may have to sneak my wife away."

Ben hadn't moved his focus from Susanna's lips. "I may have need of the closet this evening too."

Embarrassed, Susanna looked away. Surely he couldn't mean what she thought he did.

Did Ben want to kiss her again?

Mr. Cranch's eyebrows shot up. And when he noticed Ben's

attention directed at Susanna, his grin widened. "You old dog. I guess this means you're conceding Hannah to Bela Lincoln?"

Ben shrugged and glanced across the crowded room. There, next to Grandmother Eve, stood Hannah arm in arm with Bela Lincoln.

Susanna had heard rumors that her cousin was entertaining the interest of the Hingham physician. But she hadn't guessed Ben would give up his aspirations for Hannah—not without a fight. She'd assumed he would work even harder to gain Hannah's affection now that he had competition.

She searched his face. Was he hurt that Hannah had easily discarded him?

"There you are, Susanna." Before she could probe any further, Elbridge sidled next to her and took hold of her arm. "I've been looking for you, my dear cousin."

"She's not hard to miss," Ben said wryly.

Elbridge glared at Ben. "I'm surprised you have the audacity to show your face here, Ross."

"I was just thinking the same thing about you. I mean, after losing the Pepperidge case last week in Boston."

The muscles in Elbridge's face flexed. "At least I'm not locking a murderer away in my minister's house."

"Joe Sewall has committed no crime," Ben growled. "But then again, you wouldn't know how to identify a murderer even if he tossed the evidence straight onto your desk."

Susanna wanted to rise to Hermit Crab Joe's defense, but she didn't know what she could possibly say without divulging too much information about Dotty.

As if sensing her need to speak, Ben shot her a warning glance. Then he stepped back and dipped his head toward Mary. "Excuse me, Mrs. Cranch. I shall leave you to your lovesick husband."

Susanna wanted to tell him not to desert her with Elbridge, that she'd much rather talk with him. She had,
after all, read *The Odyssey*, and she'd been waiting for the
chance to thank him and tell him how much she'd enjoyed
the book.

He started to leave, but then surprised her when he leaned
into her ear. "Meet me in the closet in one hour," he whispered
before turning and slipping through the crowd.

He must be planning to kiss her again. Why else would he
want to meet her in the closet?

Her heart floundered with wild anticipation. If only she
didn't have to wait an entire hour.

Ben crossed his arms.

The slit in the door left enough light for him to see the
tiny closet crammed with an assortment of wooden buckets,
brooms, and crates. The scent of linseed and vinegar permeated the cubicle.

He wasn't sure if Susanna would really meet him there.
But he'd been anxious to talk with her ever since he'd heard
that Lieutenant Wolfe had shown up at the parsonage. In
fact, he'd been nearly sick with worry, and he needed to find
out from her what had really happened.

They didn't have much time left before the men and the
women split into separate rooms so that the men could share
a bottle of wine and tease Cranch endlessly about the coming wedding night.

If he hoped to discuss anything with Susanna without their
absence being detected, it would have to be soon.

He tapped his foot.

Maybe she was too scared to meet him alone in the closet,

especially after the way he'd joked with Cranch about using it as a kissing spot.

At a light rap at the door, Ben straightened only to bump his head on the overhanging step above him.

The door opened a sliver and she peeked inside. "Ben?"

He reached for her arm, tugged her inside, and closed the door swiftly behind her.

Darkness enveloped them.

Her breath came in short spurts in the slight distance between them.

He didn't release her, although he had the feeling he ought to put a good arm's length between them at the outset of their conversation.

But she shifted and somehow in the process bumped against him. Tendrils of her hair tickled his cheek, and her breath hovered near his chin.

Even though he couldn't see her at that moment, he knew she looked stunning. She was more beautiful than the bride. Indeed, she was more beautiful than any other woman there, with her dark enchanting eyes and with stylish curls dangling near her ear . . . tempting him.

Before he could stop himself, he skimmed her arm all the way to her neck, to the spot below her ear.

Her breathing turned ragged.

The warm bursts of air spread over his chin. Her mouth was close enough to claim with his—if he dared.

She shifted, and in the crowded closet her lips accidentally grazed his; at least, he didn't believe her to be so bold as to initiate a kiss.

He hadn't asked her to meet in the closet so that he could kiss her, but suddenly that was all he could think about.

She didn't move away from him but hovered near, as if

giving him permission. For a long agonizing moment he let his lips linger against hers, barely touching. The fullness of her lips taunted him.

Even though every fiber in his body urged him to press closer, he knew he shouldn't. She wasn't his, and he had no right to pretend otherwise.

They were just friends. Wasn't that what they'd agreed upon the last time they'd been together that night of the murder on the beach?

And if he ever wanted more than that, her mother would never allow it.

Mrs. Smith had made a point of ignoring him all evening as though he amounted to nothing more than one of the slaves, unworthy of her acknowledgment or attention.

The truth was, no matter how willing Susanna was to let him steal a kiss from her, he wasn't good enough for Mrs. Smith and never would be.

He stifled a sigh and dropped his hand from her. "Susanna," he whispered, dragging away from her, "as much as I would enjoy sharing a kiss or two with you, I don't think it's a good idea."

"Oh . . ." Her quick intake of breath was followed by a scrambling to put distance between them. "I beg your pardon. It's just that I thought . . . you insinuated earlier—" A bucket toppled with a clatter.

So she'd come to him because she'd wanted to kiss him?

He couldn't contain a grin and was glad for the darkness that hid it from her.

She'd wanted to kiss him.

The thought made his chest swell with the desire to draw her back into his arms and bestow upon her a kiss that would leave her wanting more.

The door rattled. Was she fumbling to find a way out of the closet?

"Don't go." He lunged for her. His fingers made contact with her arm and the fluffy ruffles of her sleeve.

She stopped, yet from the stiffness of her body, he could tell he'd embarrassed her.

"You weren't mistaken," he whispered hoarsely. "Every time I'm around you, I think about what it would be like to pull you into my arms and kiss you again."

She didn't say anything, but at least she didn't move to leave the closet.

"You're a beautiful and irresistible woman," he said, not quite sure why he felt the need to put her at ease, except that suddenly he loathed the thought that he may have hurt her—even if unintentionally.

The rigidness of her stance began to melt.

"And as hard as you are to resist, I must do the best I can." Even as he spoke, though, his fingers slid down to the bare span of her arm toward her wrist before letting go. "You and I both know there can never be anything between us."

She didn't deny him.

And suddenly he wished she would. Why did she have to let her mother dictate her future? And did she really need to put so much weight upon a man's worldly estate?

If only she had the freedom to marry a poor man. Instead she would likely end up with a pork sausage like Elbridge Quincy, who could give her everything she wanted.

But what could a country lawyer offer her, except himself and his high aspirations for the future?

He shook his head.

Aspirations weren't enough for a woman like Susanna Smith.

"There can be *something* between us," Susanna finally said softly. "I thought we'd agreed to be friends."

"Friends. Of course." But the word stuck to the roof of his mouth like day-old hasty pudding.

"You have indeed become a valued friend, and I treasure your honesty and wisdom."

So was that all he was ever to be to Susanna? A treasured friend? He swallowed the protest, reminding himself that she was right. "I wouldn't want to overstep the bounds of our friendship and put it in jeopardy because of a kiss."

"We certainly wouldn't want that," she said.

"Exactly." He had the overwhelming urge to sweep her into his arms and kiss her until they were both swooning.

Instead he took a step back. "How's Dotty?" He needed to steer the conversation to safer ground.

"She's living in the barn loft now. And she's with child." Susanna spoke with a rush as if anticipating his disapproval. "It was too cold. She was ill—"

"I understand." He touched her arm to stop her. "You had no other choice."

She released a breath. "After the lieutenant's appearance this week, she's scared. She's talked about running farther south, perhaps trying to make it to Plymouth."

Although a part of him wanted to tell Susanna to let Dotty go, to send her on her way so that Susanna wouldn't be in any more danger, he knew Dotty would have a hard time surviving the trip and besides, where would she go? She'd likely be captured there and returned to Mr. Lovelace in Boston.

"We need to find another place to hide her," he said. "But where?"

"You don't think Lieutenant Wolfe would come here again, do you?"

"If he's as good at locating runaways as they say he is, then I suspect he'll be back."

She didn't speak, but through the darkness the heaviness of her fear slithered around him.

"Perhaps it's best if she comes to Braintree and hides in my father's barn. I know he won't object."

"But if she's found with you, think of the damage that could do to your reputation."

"And think of the damage to yours." In fact, he hated to think of the harm that could come to Susanna as a result of harboring Dotty. Now, after seeing the two murder victims, Ben shuddered whenever he thought of what Lieutenant Wolfe was capable of doing to Susanna should he ever get her alone.

"I'm more afraid of what could happen to my family than to myself."

Ben feared that his father's farm wouldn't be safe enough—not with all the people that came and went on a daily basis, either meeting with him in his law office or to visit his father.

"What about your grandmother Quincy?" he asked. "She was sympathetic to Joe Sewall, even sheltered him before the trial to prevent a lynch mob."

"I'm not surprised."

"She told me her grandfather built an underground escape route to protect his family back during the days when the Indians were attacking. And that if anyone came looking for Joe, he'd have a way to avoid capture."

"Then you think Grandmother Eve might be willing to hide Dotty?"

"I'll ask her when I return to Braintree on the morrow. If she's agreeable, I'll ride out again to Weymouth tomorrow night and take Dotty under cover of darkness to your grandmother's."

"Then I'll warn her to be ready." Her fingers found his.

"Your grandmother is a kindhearted and brave woman." He relished the softness of her hand upon his. "I can see now that you take after her."

A rap at the closet door made him jump, and he knocked his head against the stair again. He muttered under his breath.

"Shh," she whispered.

They both stood silent and unmoving.

But someone on the other side rapped at the door again.

Susanna made a move as if to open it, but Ben squeezed her hand, hoping she'd heed his caution. If they didn't respond, perhaps the interloper would move away without detecting them.

"Miss Susie" came a muted voice through the wood. "Miss Susie, I know you're in there."

This time, Susanna broke away from him and swung open the door.

There stood one of the Smith slaves, a tall, spry woman who'd been running nonstop all evening from one task to the next. Sweat darkened the band of her turban that crisscrossed her forehead.

"What is it, Phoebe?" Susanna asked.

The woman's eyes darted around the empty hallway before she turned back to Susanna. "There's a soldier at the back door. He's asking for you."

"Soldier?" Ben asked at the same time as Susanna.

"He says he's got a message for you, Miss Susie. And that it's urgent."

Upon hearing the news, Susanna dashed past the slave and down the hallway toward the back of the house.

Ben raced after her. "Let me handle it, Susanna. Please."

But her steps slapped only faster. As she entered the kitchen, she stopped short at the sight of the young attendant that normally rode with Lieutenant Wolfe. He wore a long dark cloak that covered his red uniform, and he'd pulled his cocked hat low, hiding his face.

"Miss Smith," he said to Susanna. But at the sight of Ben behind her, the sergeant pulled back.

"What is it, Sergeant?" She glanced around the large kitchen as if she expected Lieutenant Wolfe to spring out from behind one of the mounds of food left from the wedding feast or the piles of crusty kettles that needed scrubbing.

"I have a private message for you, Miss Smith." The sergeant glanced at Ben and then at the slave woman who'd returned to her worktable and was already scraping one of the kettles.

"They're trustworthy," Susanna said.

His freckled face was pale. And though his eyes flashed with worry, they contained a kindness Ben had not often noticed among the king's soldiers.

The sergeant seemed to be debating whether to stay or leave.

"Benjamin Ross is my friend. You have nothing to fear from him."

Sergeant Frazel finally nodded and then spoke in low tones to Susanna. "Lieutenant Wolfe has obtained a writ of assistance today. He's planning a surprise visit on the morrow with the claim that your father is involved in the illegal smuggling and that therefore he has the right to search the premises."

"Why would you have reason to warn us, Sergeant?" Susanna said with a casualness Ben wanted to applaud. "Surely you know we aren't involved in any smuggling here."

Ben had been afraid she'd give away Dotty's presence all too easily. Even if the young man seemed kind, Ben had never met a British regular who could be trusted.

The soldier glanced at his tall leather boots, red creeping up his cheeks. "I have the feeling you'll want to find a way to hide the young woman in the barn just a little better."

Susanna's face paled and she steadied herself on the edge of the worktable.

Ben moved next to her and resisted the urge to slip his arm around her waist. "We don't know what young woman you're speaking of—"

Sergeant Frazel's clearly anguished expression silenced Ben. "The lieutenant is vicious. I beg you to heed my warning before it's too late." One look into the soldier's eyes told of unspeakable horrors the man had witnessed, of sins committed, of crimes that would happen again if he didn't break his silence. "Please use all caution and make haste."

Ben nodded. "We will."

"I can't stay." The soldier pulled his damp cloak closer. "The lieutenant would whip me if he learned I was here, and then hang me."

"You've been very courageous to come warn us," Susanna replied. "Thank you, Sergeant. I'll pray God rewards you for your sacrifice tonight."

The soldier tipped his hat back down and then spun away. He opened the door soundlessly and disappeared into the dark night. The spattering of sleet that had begun to fall earlier when some of the older guests had made their departure had turned into a steady cold drizzle.

Susanna closed the door behind him, then leaned against it and shuddered. "I'd desperately hoped he hadn't seen her on that day he searched the barn, but he must have noticed more than we realized."

"It's a good thing he did. Otherwise he wouldn't be here tonight with his warning." Phoebe crossed to the hearth to the pot of cider bubbling over the low flames and giving off the spiciness of cloves and nutmeg. "God's watching out for you, Miss Susie. That's for sure."

"I hope you're right."

Ben moved to the window and peered outside. He'd hoped to avoid any further involvement with Lieutenant Wolfe. He hadn't wanted to bring any more attention to himself for fear of causing more danger for the others of the Caucus Club. But with each passing day, his entanglement with the lieutenant seemed to be growing.

"What should we do, Ben?" Susanna asked.

"We're moving Dotty to your grandmother's tonight. And I'm moving you too." Ben's body tightened at the thought of Susanna being anywhere near the lieutenant when he came to the house in the morning and discovered that Dotty was gone. They couldn't wait to go to Mount Wollaston until tomorrow. They'd leave tonight. Now.

Susanna didn't argue. She only hugged her arms, failing to stifle another shudder.

"The rain's coming down hard." Phoebe paused in stirring the cider. "It'll provide good cover for leaving. No one else will be out to see or hear you."

Ben hesitated. He didn't relish the thought of making Susanna or Dotty ride in the icy rain. But what other choice did he have?

Susanna straightened her shoulders. "Phoebe's right. Besides, no one would suspect anything if I left tonight. Everyone's busy. And if anyone asks where I went, you can tell them I went to Grandmother Eve's. In fact, I'll tell Mother I'm going to Mount Wollaston so there will be more room for the other guests."

"Don't you worry," Phoebe said, "I'll cover for you."

If Phoebe's words were meant to reassure Susanna, they did the opposite. Doubt crowded away the confidence that had been on her face.

"Let's go." Ben started toward the door that would lead him back to the hallway and his cloak. "I'll sneak out first and saddle your horse. Meet me in the barn."

She didn't move.

"Remember," he said, "you're standing up for the rights of a person made in the image of God. She shouldn't be denied counsel and a fair trial. No one should be."

"Yes, though I've put so many lives in danger . . ."

"Sometimes doing what's right is dangerous, even life-threatening."

If they didn't stand against injustice and tyranny now, they'd only leave the problems for future generations. He was convinced, like so many others in the Caucus Club, that it was merely a matter of time before they would need to fight against Great Britain for freedom.

Her dark eyes seemed to draw courage from him. He nodded. "I'll do everything in my power to keep you safe."

Although he wouldn't admit it to her, he knew very well he would never let anything happen to her. He'd lay down his life for her.

His gut wrenched with a sudden surge of protectiveness. And he had to spin away from her perceptiveness before she saw the truth in his eyes. The truth he'd been trying to deny these past weeks. A truth he finally had to face . . .

He was falling in love with Susanna Smith.

Susanna's fingers had turned to ice. She wasn't sure if she was holding the reins anymore. She couldn't see anything either, not past the ice on her eyelashes and the ice-crusted hair hanging in her face. She was glad her mare was smart enough to follow Ben's lead.

Through the cloudy night and the steady drizzle of the freezing rain, she fought to stay in her sidesaddle. The only thought that kept her from allowing herself to slide off was that she had to get Dotty away from her home and her family before it was too late.

The young woman sat behind her, clinging to her, pressing her face into Susanna's back. She had to see Dotty safely to Mount Wollaston. Tonight. The girl's life depended upon it.

"We're almost there," Ben called over his shoulder. In the howling wind, his voice was faint.

He'd taken them on an irregular route, off the main roads, with the hope they wouldn't cross paths with any other travelers. They couldn't chance anyone seeing them.

But Susanna also knew Ben was trying to cover their tracks as best he could. If Lieutenant Wolfe suspected she'd left to hide Dotty, they didn't want him attempting to follow them to Mount Wollaston.

Their course had turned rocky and steep during the final climb up the hill to her grandmother's home.

A jolt from the horse's slow trod sent shards of pain up Susanna's frozen arms, and suddenly she found herself slipping. She tried to grip the reins, the saddle, anything, but she couldn't make her fingers work.

With a cry she slipped farther.

Dotty grasped her tighter, but the mare stumbled over another slick rock. And Susanna lost her hold on the beast completely.

She plummeted into the darkness. The icy branches of the brush snagged her full skirt and cloak and slowed her descent. Even so, her body landed against the hard earth with a thud that pounded the breath from her lungs and sent agonizing pain through her back.

She could hear Dotty call out to Ben, but she couldn't get her own voice to work past the tightness in her chest. The leafless canopy of brittle branches overhead provided no shelter from the elements as the freezing rain pelted her face. Yet her lips and cheeks were too numb to feel the sting.

"Susanna!" The wind carried the panic in Ben's tone.

She couldn't muster enough strength to respond.

"Susanna." Ben had dismounted, and he scrambled down

the slope until he reached her. His shaking hands seized her shoulders. "Are you hurt?"

"I don't know," she managed.

His face hovered above hers. Although she couldn't see the features, the short burst of his breath testified to his worry. His trembling fingers moved to her face, sweeping the frozen strands of hair back.

"I pushed you exceedingly hard," he said hoarsely.

"No—"

"I'm sorry, Susanna." He slid his arms underneath her, cradled her, and brought her against his chest.

"It's not your fault." She knew she ought to protest his hold, but the heat of his body and the closeness of his embrace were much too comforting.

He struggled to stand, his muscles hardening and straining as he unbent his body.

"You can't possibly carry me." But even as she spoke, she bit back a cry at the pain shooting through her hip and leg.

"We don't have far to go."

She wound her arms around his neck and clung to him.

"Ride ahead!" He shouted instructions to Dotty, who had managed to stay atop the horse. Then he started up the incline, sliding on the damp leaves and tripping over the rocks.

With each step his breathing grew more ragged.

"I'll try to walk." She squirmed against him.

"I won't let you down," he panted. And even though he slipped and stumbled the rest of the distance up the hill, his hold on her remained constant. When he finally arrived at the top, he stopped for a moment and dragged in a deep breath.

A light glimmered in the distance.

Dizziness washed over Susanna, and she wanted to keel over and release the contents of her stomach.

"We're almost there," he whispered, his lips brushing against her temple.

The gentleness soothed her. She wanted to tell him not to pull away, to go on pressing kisses against her skin forever.

But he started forward again, stumbling toward a flickering light in the distance. In a matter of moments, voices surrounded them. Her grandmother's worried face hovered near. But at Ben's whispered instructions about Dotty she disappeared.

"I'll carry her up," Ben insisted when one of Grandmother Eve's servants attempted to help him. "Tell me where to take her."

He followed the servant inside the house. The warmth enveloped her, along with the familiar scents of her grandfather's pipe tobacco and her grandmother's bayberry candles. Ben's footsteps clattered on the stairway and through the hallway as he tramped behind the servant to the second-floor bedchamber.

When he lowered Susanna to the feather mattress, she cried out at the burning agony in her back. He kneeled beside the large canopied bed, tugged off his gloves, and tossed aside his hat.

In the low lamplight, the crevices in his forehead were deep. He'd long past taken off the queue wig he'd worn at the wedding, and now his sandy-brown hair plastered his damp cheeks.

She wanted to lift her stiff fingers and smooth away the strands and the wrinkles and tell him not to worry. But her fingers shook, and her body trembled from the cold and the pain.

The servant bustled around the bed, laying out towels, a second coverlet, and a night shift. "I must be getting the young miss out of her wet things." Another servant heated a warming pan over the fire in the small hearth.

Ben nodded but didn't make a move to leave. Instead he lifted a hand to Susanna's cheek and gently cupped her face. The work-roughened calluses were warm, and she leaned into his hold.

He bent his head closer as if to place a tender kiss upon her brow.

But the servant stepped next to him. "You must let me attend to Miss Smith. You wouldn't want her to get sick, now, would you?"

Ben let his hand fall away. He stood, clutched his hat, and twisted it in his hands.

"I shall be just fine," Susanna whispered, trying to smile at him with lips stiffened with cold.

His gaze met hers, and amidst the churning of worry the window to his soul was open. She could see inside to something else, something that sent waves of eagerness through her heart.

Was it love?

Did he love her?

For a moment, a well of emotion rose inside her. The words *I love you* pressed for release.

But she swallowed them. In the haze of her pain, she was surely only imagining his ardor. The borders of his affection ended at friendship.

After all, during their tryst in the closet under the stairs, he'd made his position quite clear. He'd said there could never be anything between them. She was not the type of woman he'd seriously pursue.

"Please, Mr. Ross," the servant pleaded. "The most helpful thing you can do for Miss Smith is leave."

Ben jammed his hat on his head, gave Susanna one last intense look, then spun out of the room, taking her heart with him.

Chapter
16

Ben rounded the bend at a gallop. His heart pounded harder than the horse's hooves hitting the ground. The anger inside had been building with each mile he'd traversed since he'd left the Smith household that morning. The decimated Smith household . . .

Ben spotted the Redcoats through the leafless trees on the edge of Cranberry Pond, and he steered his horse in their direction. He didn't care if he disturbed their duck hunting or their leisure. His wrath demanded he confront Lieutenant Wolfe once and for all.

At his approach, a pair of mallards exploded from the marshes along the north end of the pond. The hunters had their fowling guns aimed and ready to shoot, following the trail of the birds as they spread their wings and climbed for the sky.

Lieutenant Wolfe stared down the barrel of a fine walnut flintlock. The crack of his discharge was deafening in the stillness of the secluded pond.

For a moment, the greenhead kept climbing, and Ben hoped

the lieutenant had missed. But then the bird fell away from its companion, diving back into the marsh from which it had arisen. In the grayness of the morning and the barrenness of the land that was now ready for winter, the fallen mallard would be easy to locate.

The lieutenant shared congratulations with his hunting companions, several of the landed gentry from the area that were loyal to the Crown. He then gave his assistant a command to retrieve the fowl before finally turning to Ben.

"My deepest gratitude, Mr. Ross," called the lieutenant. "You helped to flush out my prey."

Somehow the lieutenant's words were not at all reassuring.

Ben reined his horse next to the small hunting party and glared down at the officer. "I've just come from Reverend Smith's home. You've overstepped your bounds this time, Lieutenant."

The lieutenant only lowered his gun and proceeded to rub the engraved serpent side plate. "Perhaps you're the one who's overstepping his bounds, Mr. Ross. What does or does not happen to the Smiths is hardly your concern." The lieutenant paused and then pinned Ben with his sharp eyes. "Is it?"

The young assistant stumbled at the lieutenant's words and cast Ben a shadowed look over his shoulder.

Ben didn't dare to even nod at Sergeant Frazel. "Regardless of my relationship with the Smiths, no one in the colonies deserves the kind of disregard and mistreatment that you meted upon them this morning during your search."

Ben had been shaken to the core when he'd returned to Weymouth early that morning only to find that Wolfe had already visited and ransacked the parsonage and barn in his search for what he claimed was smuggled goods. He'd even beaten one of the slaves.

"Everything I did was completely legal," Lieutenant Wolfe

replied. "I had just cause to believe the Smiths were harboring illegal goods."

"There's nothing legal about what you did." Ben fought to control his rising temper. "You acted on suspicion alone, without evidence, and with brutish force that defies common decency."

"Those who are breaking the law must be prepared to suffer the consequences."

"Every man deserves to be treated as innocent until proven guilty."

The other gentlemen in the group had stopped their bantering. They stood silently watching the exchange, a cold drizzle beginning to fall against the brims of their hats and onto the shoulders of their heavy wool cloaks.

"One must wonder why you'd deserted the wedding party last night, Mr. Ross. Why you weren't with the other guests this morning when I arrived."

"The Smith home was already crowded enough and so I decided to return home to my own bed."

"On such a dismal evening?" The lieutenant cocked a brow. "And during such a merry occasion? You surely had other reasons for departing."

"Yes, like many of the other guests."

"Like Susanna Smith? I suppose she had the same reason for departing that you had?" The lieutenant forced a pinched smile. But the look in his eyes told Ben he knew—not only of his connection with the smuggling but also his involvement with Dotty.

"There were many coming and going all evening. I cannot presume to know when and why Miss Smith left."

"After your ardent portrayal of affection for Miss Smith that day at Arnold Tavern, your declaration rings false."

Ben could feel the inquisitive stares of the other men, and heat crawled up his neck. He'd made Mr. Arnold promise not to breathe a word of his kiss with Susanna to anyone. And so far the kiss had been their secret. "Miss Smith and I share a fond friendship, 'tis nothing more."

A slow smile twitched at the lieutenant's lips. "Very well, Mr. Ross. Friendship it is."

"Stay away from the Smiths and Susanna, Lieutenant Wolfe, or I'll make a point of alerting your commanding officers in Boston about your unlawful conduct here in Weymouth. I'm sure they won't be pleased."

Dark shadows swarmed across the lieutenant's face. For a long moment he fingered the serpent on the stock of his gun, his thumb polishing it into a gleaming silver.

Although Ben didn't know the extent of the lieutenant's situation, he knew the man had failed his commanding officers in Boston once before, and he couldn't afford to disappoint them again.

"Be careful how you tread," Lieutenant Wolfe finally said in a low, tight voice. "I'm sure you wouldn't want to see undue harm befall any of your friends—your *fond* friends."

The threat pierced Ben with the keenest of fears. And as he spurred his horse away from the lieutenant, he knew deep in his heart once again that he'd rather die than let any harm befall Susanna.

⁓

Ben's pulse slammed with each hollow stamp of his boot in the stairwell. He was tempted to take the steps two at a time, but he forced himself to ascend in a manner befitting a gentleman.

After three days, Mrs. Quincy had finally given him permission to visit Susanna. The three days had been the longest he'd lived through.

Every time he'd come calling at Mount Wollaston, Mrs. Quincy had told him Susanna was not well enough to receive visitors but was recovering from bruises to her tailbone and a chill from the wet ride.

From the twinkle in Mrs. Quincy's eyes, he had the suspicion she was purposefully taunting him with the wait. And when she'd patted his hand only moments ago and quoted an old Roman poem, "The absent lover's tide always flows stronger," he'd certainly been able to confirm the truth of the quote.

Of course she'd laughed at him. He didn't doubt she'd discovered the true depths of his feelings for Susanna. After all his pestering over the past several days, he supposed even a dead man could have seen how enamored he was with Susanna.

At the top of the steps, he halted and straightened the lapel of his fashionable new coat.

After the morning chores, his father had quirked a brow at him when he'd changed into one of the suits he'd had tailored in Boston during his last round with the circuit court. And when Ben had explained that he was riding to Mount Wollaston again, he'd pretended not to notice his father's smothered grin or the teasing look that said *I told you so.*

Ben drew in a deep breath to still himself. He hid the book he was carrying behind his back. Then he trod quietly down the hallway toward the open door of the bedchamber where he'd deposited her after their difficult midnight ride.

His excitement over seeing her had pushed the heavy weight of his anger and frustration at Lieutenant Wolfe to the back of his mind. Even so, he paused before the door, tugged at his cravat to loosen it. Mrs. Quincy had warned him she hadn't yet told Susanna of the destruction to her parents' home, that she hadn't wanted to cause her granddaughter undue anxiety when she'd been ill.

Ben wasn't so sure that was the kind of news to keep from Susanna, ill or not.

He brushed a speck from his coat sleeve, then stepped into the room.

She was propped against a cushion of pillows at the headboard, her coverlet smoothed and tucked neatly around her. Her hair, gleaming and brushed into submission, fell in long waves over a lacy night shift.

The contrast of her dark beauty against the mounds of white linen surrounding her stunned him so that he couldn't speak.

As if the intensity of his attraction had announced its presence, she glanced up from the book she was reading.

"Ben," she said softly. First her eyes lit, then her lips formed into one of her slightly cocked smiles that made her dimple bloom.

His breath hitched in his chest. For a moment he could only let himself feast upon her beauty.

She laid her book facedown upon her lap and held out a hand to him. "I've been waiting for you."

She had?

His pulse clattered forward at twice the pace.

"I'd hoped you'd come visit me sooner."

"I tried." He swallowed the lump of nervousness that had been lodged in his throat and forced himself to cross toward her. "But your grandmother was beating me away with an iron skillet."

Susanna's smile widened.

"If she hadn't let me past her today, I was considering climbing the trellis and sneaking in through the window."

When he reached the edge of her bedstead, he was helpless to do anything but put his hand into her outstretched one.

Her fingers intertwined with his, and her eyes sparkled. "Maybe you can still consider sneaking in later."

If not for the teasing half smile, he would have believed she meant the invitation.

"Don't tempt me." He brought her hand to his lips and pressed a kiss there with a gallant flourish, hoping to hide his desire behind his bravado.

When he straightened and let go of her, a pretty flush had stolen over her cheeks.

"You look well, Susanna."

"I'm all but recovered, except for a slight chill and sore back. Nevertheless, Grandmother Eve insists I stay in bed for a few more days."

"I see you're not protesting overly loud." He nodded at the copy of Samuel Richardson's *Clarissa*. "Perhaps there are advantages to lying abed."

Her smile was bright enough to bring in the sunshine that the late November day lacked. "I'm taking full advantage of Grandmother Eve's tendency to indulge me—even if I have already read the book often enough to commit it to memory."

"Then I hope you won't think it presumptuous of me to have brought you this." He took his hand out from behind his back and extended the second volume of Pope's transla-tion of *The Odyssey*.

"Oh, Ben." She breathed his name like a caress, took the book from him, and stroked it.

The tension in his shoulders eased. He'd wanted to give

her something, a small token to show his affection, but he'd had a difficult time deciding what to bring.

Hannah Quincy had been satisfied with baubles and ribbons and flowers. But Susanna wasn't like most girls. In fact, if he were honest with himself, that was exactly why he liked her—because she was different, because she wasn't afraid to think and speak her mind and follow her passions.

Why couldn't he pursue Susanna Smith? What was stopping him?

She certainly hadn't resisted his attention. She'd even sought him out under the stairs because she'd wanted to kiss him. She wouldn't have met him there if she didn't have at least a little interest in him.

Over the past several days of pondering his feelings for her, he'd decided that even if a match with her wouldn't be quite as advantageous as one with Hannah Quincy, he'd still gain much in a union to a woman of Susanna's position.

Besides, his aspirations for Hannah had died. He had no desire for her and had to admit he never really had. He'd willingly conceded her to Bela Lincoln. He was better off putting his attention elsewhere . . .

Upon Susanna.

She hugged the book, then looked up at him, her eyes shining. "You are indeed a true friend. The truest friend anyone could ask for."

He wanted to tell her he'd never be satisfied with *only* being her friend, that he longed to be something infinitely more dear to her.

But at that moment a servant strode into the room carrying a tray with a serving of tea and cakes. The old woman bustled over to the bed, stepping next to Susanna, forcing Ben to move away from the edge of the bed.

"Mrs. Quincy thought you might like tea." The servant placed the tray onto the bedside table and nodded to the chair placed in front of the window, a safe distance from the bed. Her frown scolded Ben for taking the liberty of standing so close to Susanna.

Ben hesitated, but then crossed to the chair. He wanted to drag it across the braided rug and position it next to the bed where he could hold Susanna's hand. But the servant directed another scowl at him, and he forced himself to sit.

The servant was only right in admonishing him. He needed to be careful lest he do anything that might soil Susanna's reputation.

"Grandmother Eve has been unwilling to share any news regarding Lieutenant Wolfe for fear of upsetting me." Susanna took the cup of tea from the servant. "But I know I can count on you to share the truth of what's happened, regardless of my sensibilities."

Ben sat back and eyed the servant now pouring a second cup of tea. Even though she was Mrs. Quincy's most trusted servant and had been taken into their confidence regarding Dotty, who was now tucked into a safe out-of-the-way room, Ben still didn't want to discuss the matter openly.

The servant handed him the tea, letting the hot liquid slosh out of the cup onto his fingers. He tried not to grimace.

Perhaps the old woman was only being protective of the grandchild of her mistress. He couldn't blame her. Nevertheless, he wished she'd finish her business and leave the room.

She went to the high chest with its scroll top and opened one of the drawers. With a sideways glance at him, she began to refold the linens that were already crisply pressed and arranged in immaculate rows.

Alas, they were to have a chaperone.

Ben took a sip of the black tea with its sweet citrus tang and hid his smile. Apparently Mrs. Quincy didn't trust him alone with Susanna. He drank another mouthful to conceal his widening grin. He didn't trust himself alone with her either.

"So, will you tell me what happened with Lieutenant Wolfe's visit?" She fixed expectant eyes upon him. "Was he terribly upset when he couldn't find Dotty?"

His mirth evaporated, and renewed frustration soured his stomach at the remembrance of what he'd seen the morning after Cranch's wedding. After his bitter confrontation with the lieutenant near Cranberry Pond, he'd been all the more relieved he'd pushed Susanna to leave when she did.

"So it was that bad?" she asked.

Ben didn't dare look at her. "I think your grandmother was right. We ought to wait until you're fully recovered—"

"I'm a strong woman." She sat forward, nearly spilling her tea onto the coverlet. "I didn't think you'd treat me like a helpless, witless female. I expected more from you."

"Very well." He did admire her strength and intelligence, and she was bound to hear eventually. She would most certainly learn of it when she returned to Weymouth. "The dressed-up red monkey and several other soldiers ransacked your home."

She blanched. "So that's why Mother hasn't visited me yet."

"Lieutenant Wolfe and several other soldiers pulled the wedding guests out of their beds at the points of their bayonets and marched them out onto the front yard. Then they went through the house room by room, overturning furniture, breaking valuables, and dumping out drawers."

Susanna shrank into her pillows.

Ben stopped. Had he divulged too much for her to handle in her weakened condition?

"Go on," she said. "Please. The guests? Father, Mother, William? They were unharmed, were they not?"

"Yes, they're fine."

"Don't coddle me, Ben. I don't need it. Not from you."

How could he refuse her? "The lieutenant found evidence Dotty had been in the barn."

"But didn't Tom get rid of anything that might have proven she'd been there?"

"Lieutenant Wolfe isn't hired to track runaways without reason. He's good at what he does."

"And?"

"And . . ." Ben pushed aside his hesitation. Susanna deserved to know the truth. "And he beat Tom. Until he collapsed unconscious."

She cried out and then cupped trembling fingers over her mouth.

Ben shot from his chair and went to her. Ignoring the glare the servant aimed at him, he lowered himself to the edge of the bedstead. "He's still alive." He pried the cup of tea from her and set it on the bedside table. Then he folded her fingers into his. "He's battered. But alive."

She nodded and blinked back tears.

Ben wanted to pull her into his arms, but the old servant had turned away from the chest of drawers and was now folding a linen on the end of the bed.

"Apparently Tom wouldn't speak to the lieutenant."

Susanna nodded. "I know he'd never say anything to hurt me or Dotty."

Her inky eyes were wide with the horror of what had happened. He could almost see through the whirling inside her mind, to all her regrets.

"Tom didn't want me to disobey the law." Her lips quivered.

"He didn't want to be involved in the deception. He didn't think it was right."

Ben wanted to remind her that sometimes in the cause of justice against tyranny they would experience danger and perhaps even sacrifice their lives. But at that moment, in the face of her pain, he held back his soliloquy.

"It's my fault he's hurt," she continued. A tear spilled over and rolled down her cheek. "He warned me I would get myself in trouble. But instead I got *him* in trouble. If only I'd obeyed the law . . ."

"And what? If you'd obeyed, you would have sent another young woman to her death at the hands of a crazed murderer. You did the right thing. Don't doubt it for a single moment."

"I do doubt it." Her words rang with passion, and she yanked her hand out of his grasp. "I brought destruction to my family and nearly caused the death of a man who is very dear to me. How can I not doubt it?"

He brought up his thumb to brush the tear from her cheek. But she turned her head, moving out of his reach.

"Susanna," he pleaded, "don't blame yourself—"

"But I do." Her voice was choked. "I can no longer have anything more to do with Dotty or breaking the law."

Ben knew she was reacting out of the fear of the moment and her concern for Tom. It would pass and she would once again see the right course of action.

"The laws are established for a purpose," she continued. "God intended for us to follow them, even if we don't always like them."

"Sometimes those laws need to be changed."

"Then change them."

"That's what I'm trying to do."

"You may continue with your ambitions," she said. "But I beg you not to involve me anymore."

He was tempted to tell her she was the one who'd initially become involved with Dotty—not him—that he was only enmeshed in the situation because she'd asked for his advice. But he swallowed his retort.

"Bernie," she called to the old servant. "I'm ready for a repose."

The servant furrowed her brow at Ben as if to blame him for wearing Susanna out.

Indignation stirred within his chest. Susanna had been the one to ask him to share the truth about Lieutenant Wolfe's tyranny. He hadn't wanted to upset her.

And now he had. . . .

She leaned back and closed her eyes.

He rose and stood by the bed. For a long moment he gazed down at her, at the sweet fullness of her lips, the sleekness of her cheek, the curve of her chin. She was as exquisitely beautiful as always. But suddenly she seemed hundreds of miles away.

As much as he loathed leaving her, he knew it would be for the best. She needed time to reason out the situation and see it with more clarity.

"I shall leave you to your repose, Susanna," he said.

"Good-bye, Mr. Ross."

He walked from the room, head down, his footsteps faltering and a tiny corner of his heart ripping. If only her good-bye hadn't sounded so final.

Chapter
17

Susanna held the cup of cold buttermilk to Tom's lips. "You must drink all of it."

Tom could hardly lift his head, and when he did, he took only the tiniest of sips. One eye was still swollen shut, and bruises surrounded the other. His nose was bent where it had been broken. And several of his teeth had been cracked or knocked out.

And that was just his face.

From what she'd surmised, the rest of his body was worse: a broken arm, cracked ribs, and damage to his internal organs.

Susanna grasped the old slave's hand, the bony fingers stiff and coarse against hers. "I'm so sorry."

"Don't you cry now, child." His breath came in a wheezing gasp. "I'm just glad it was me and not you."

"I only wish it *had* been me." She shivered, set the cup aside, and then went to add more kindling to the bedchamber's hearth fire.

After a week of recovering at Mount Wollaston, she'd finally convinced Grandmother Eve she was well enough to return home. She only experienced pain when she sat, and even that had dimmed compared to what it had been.

The first task she'd accomplished after she arrived home was to find Tom and move him out of the cold, dingy slave quarters to one of the guest rooms.

Mother had been so distraught over the work necessary to repair and bring order back to their home that Susanna had the freedom to care for Tom without her mother's interference.

The horror of what had happened faced Susanna at every turn, and she couldn't bear to see the damage whenever she walked through the house and glimpsed the mattresses that had been split and emptied of their feathers, the linens that had been slashed, the vases that had been smashed, and the portraits that had been ripped from the walls.

It had been wanton destruction. The lieutenant had no excuse for damaging the lovely items in their home. And outside too.

She parted the ripped window covering and peered out to the gray afternoon. The broken fence posts lay scattered near the garden, the hay strewn about the barnyard—now trampled and wet—and the grain sacks dumped and the seeds scattered in the mud.

Fresh guilt stabbed her, and she pressed her hand against her chest to ward off the pain.

The soldiers had slaughtered over half of their chickens, apparently for no reason other than to quench Lieutenant Wolfe's need for violence. Phoebe had already roasted them, and they'd distributed them to the poor.

But Father wouldn't be able to recover the loss of the mare the lieutenant had confiscated.

Ben's impassioned speeches about everyone having an

inherent right to liberty and his insinuations that the king was a tyrant came back to whisper in her ear.

She couldn't argue with Ben. The king's soldiers had been tyrants, and Father had no recourse to take against them. How could he possibly accuse Lieutenant Wolfe of anything, not when there was no one to stop the man from returning and harming them even more?

Maybe she was finally beginning to understand Ben's involvement in the rebellious activities.

If the people of Weymouth—herself included—had been loyal to the Crown before, they weren't anymore, not after all that had happened to their beloved reverend. The incident had only served to unleash more complaints among their parish, not just about the uncensored power the lieutenant wielded, but about the way they'd been forced to quarter the king's soldiers without compensation, about the rumors of new tax laws, and about not having more representation in the making of such laws.

Whatever the case, even if Susanna didn't like the king's methods, she had to stop breaking the law. Surely there were ways to work out the problems without resorting to illegal activities and outright rebellion. She had to find a way to climb out of the murky abyss of disobedience into which she'd slipped over the past months of trying to show compassion to Dotty.

And she had to stay away from Ben. She'd allowed him to influence her too much.

She let the tattered linen slip back over the window, but not before she caught sight of a horse tied under the towering oak at the front of the house.

The horse belonged to Ben.

Warmth seeped into her blood and sent her heart flying.

When had he arrived?

She started across the room toward the door, ready to run down to the parlor where he was surely waiting for her.

But at the sight of Tom's unmoving frame underneath the piles of coverlets, she froze.

"What are you doing, Susanna Smith?" she whispered. What *was* she doing? Hadn't she just told herself she needed to stay away from him?

He was too dangerous for her. He'd once admitted that very fact himself. And here she was at the first opportunity, tripping over herself in her anxiousness to see him.

She forced herself to return to Tom's side and retrieve the cup of buttermilk. But Tom's eyes were closed, and his chest rose and fell with the steady rhythm of slumber.

The fluttering yearning inside beckoned her to retreat downstairs and see Ben. There would be nothing wrong with glancing at him from a distance, would there?

Perhaps he'd come to bring her news of Dotty. Even though she doubted Lieutenant Wolfe would suspect an upstanding citizen like Grandfather Quincy of harboring a runaway, she couldn't ward off a sudden chill. She pulled her shawl closer and rubbed her stiff fingers together.

She'd told Ben she didn't want to have anything more to do with Dotty, yet she still couldn't bear to think of the young girl's suffering. She cared too much already for Dotty.

But how could she help Dotty without endangering her family even more? She gave a soft moan, the confusion reeling through her. "What shall I do?"

Tom had made her promise she'd pray for guidance. And even though she'd assured Tom she would, she hadn't spent much time on her knees lately.

"I need your assistance, God," she whispered. "I'm afraid. And I don't know what to do next."

Her heart demanded she go speak to Ben. But her mind cautioned her, reminded her that since the moment Ben had walked into her life, he'd challenged everything she'd always held secure.

"It certainly won't hurt matters to go downstairs and make a fresh flax poultice," she said. Or maybe she would locate more of the adder's tongue balsam. It had seemed to suppress Tom's swelling—even if just slightly.

And if she happened to get a peek at Ben in passing, she wouldn't be able to fault herself for that.

As she left the room and descended the stairs, her pulse tapped louder than her shoes. At the sound of Ben's voice in the parlor, she couldn't resist the temptation to cross the hallway and draw nearer.

"I realize I don't have much," Ben was saying. "But I'm a hard worker and have high aspirations."

"Aspirations do not put food on the table" came Mother's clipped reply.

Susanna crept closer to the door.

"What my dear wife is trying to say," Father said in his soothing tone, "is that we only want to make sure Susanna will be well situated in the manner to which she's accustomed."

They were talking about her. . . .

"Reverend Smith, I understand your wife perfectly." Ben's voice turned hard. "Mrs. Smith has always made it clear how much she's disliked me."

For a long moment, silence hovered in the air like a heavy storm cloud. Susanna cringed. She knew Mother didn't much like Ben, but she could at least have issued a polite word or two. After all, even if he was involved in the smuggling, Benjamin Ross was still a good man with a kind heart.

She shuffled closer to the door, trying not to bump into the maze of crates and barrels Mother was using to sort the damaged household goods. Susanna could just imagine Father pacing in front of the fireplace, Mother sitting stiff and straight in one of the wing chairs, and Ben standing near the door—poised to escape the room.

"Mr. Ross," Mother finally said, "you must see the barriers are insurmountable and make it difficult for us to consider a man in your position."

"And what *position* is that exactly?" he asked.

Susanna tensed and prayed Mother wouldn't say anything about Ben's lack of worldly estate.

But Mother's reply was as quick as if she'd rehearsed it. "Why, you're nothing but a shoemaker's son, a nobody, with not a possession to your name."

Susanna dropped her forehead against the cold hallway wall and stifled a groan. How could Mother say such things?

Shame crept through Susanna—shame not only for Mother's attitude, but also because she'd said those identical words once upon a time when she'd been young and foolish. Of course, Ben had begrudgingly granted her forgiveness for her girlish immaturity.

Nevertheless, he didn't need any reminders about her past mistake.

"You're likely a very fine lawyer." Father broke the awkward silence. "And we all respect your father, Deacon John. He's a man of great integrity and kindness. But I'm sure you'll find another suitable young woman."

"I'm sorry for your wasted trip today," Mother said, "but we cannot allow you to court our daughter."

Court her? Susanna's head snapped up. Had Ben ridden to Weymouth to ask her parents for permission to come courting?

Even if she'd been telling herself to forget about Ben and to avoid him, she couldn't keep a thrill of excitement from twirling inside.

He wanted to court her.

She leaned forward. Her foot bumped against a wooden bucket and it in turn knocked against a portrait that was missing half of its mahogany frame. The frame began to topple.

Susanna lunged for it. But it slipped away from her and landed against the wood floor with a slap. As she straightened, she found herself within view of the doorway of the parlor.

Ben stood less than a dozen steps away. His shoulders were stiff and the muscles in his jaw tight. His intense eyes landed upon her, startled at first, but then widening with pleasure.

Beyond him, Father had stopped his pacing to stare, and Mother had risen from her chair, her hands fluttering to her chest.

The parlor was strangely bare without all the usual decorations, wall hangings, and linen coverings. Instead the cloudiness of the cold afternoon had seeped through the large window and draped itself about the room.

"Susanna Smith," Mother said. "Surely you haven't been eavesdropping in the hallway."

"Of course she hasn't." Father beckoned Susanna into the room with a wave of his hand. "She's merely coming to join us, aren't you, Susanna dear?"

"Yes, won't you come join us?" Ben took a step toward her and smiled, the warmth of it driving away the chill of the unheated hallway. His clean-shaven face, the crispness of his attire, and his freshly powdered wig—all attested to the care he'd given in presenting himself to her parents. They could find no fault with his appearance. He was indeed a handsome man.

"Perhaps we should ask Susanna her thoughts on the matter at hand," Ben said. "She is after all an intelligent woman and able to make decisions for herself."

She didn't doubt he meant the words. He wasn't saying them to flatter her, and she appreciated that about him. Even as a woman without a formal education, he accepted her opinions and thoughts, almost as if she were equal to a man.

"I've come to discuss the possibility of courtship. What do you think, Susanna?" He held out a hand toward her. His eyes glowed with all the affection and desire she'd witnessed on previous occasions. Everything about him invited her to put aside her reservations, accept his offer, and care for him in return.

She longed to go to him, slip her fingers into his, and be with him. She loved his passion, his intelligence, and his determination. She could speak freely to him of important matters and know he would listen. He happily indulged her love of reading. And he brimmed with compassion to those less fortunate.

She doubted she would ever find a better man than Benjamin Ross.

Phoebe's footsteps echoed in the hallway behind her. "Miss Susie?"

Susanna tore her gaze from Ben to Phoebe, who stood at the bottom of the stairway holding a tray. "I've got that bowl of hot broth for Tom you wanted. Do you want me to take it on up?"

Suddenly all Susanna could picture was Tom lying in bed, battered and broken and possibly dying. The thought made her sick all over again.

She couldn't—wouldn't—consider involving herself with Ben.

He was too dangerous for her.

"Yes, Susanna is an intelligent young woman," Mother spoke again, her tone as brittle as the shattered mirror above the mantel. "And because she's intelligent, she shall realize just how disadvantageous a match to you would be—that is, if she wishes to continue with the kind of life she appreciates."

Ben continued to look at her, his eyes probing deep into her soul to discover the truth of her feelings.

She wanted to deny Mother's advice. She wanted to declare that she didn't care about the disadvantages of marrying Ben. But could she really marry a man who owned nothing? Could she be content to live as the wife to a husband of little means, hardly better than the women she'd always aspired to help?

His expression silently pleaded with her to refute Mother's claims, to take hold of his hand and join her life with his.

She glanced to Phoebe behind her, to the tray and the bowl of steaming broth reminding her of the perils she'd brought into their lives as a result of her interactions with Ben. Then she looked at Mother, at the stiff lines in her genteel face, warning her of all she'd have to give up to be with Ben.

Susanna took a small step back, and her heels bumped into a crate. Even though the step away from Ben's outstretched arm was minuscule, it wrenched her heart, as if she were leaving part of it with him.

The harsh truth was that she couldn't be with him.

"I really must go and attend to Tom."

First his eyes flashed with the realization of her intentions, then hurt. The acuteness of his pain stabbed her, leaving her breathless. She forced herself to turn away from him before she flung herself into his arms.

With trembling fingers she took the tray from Phoebe. The slave's brows lifted with reproof.

But Susanna spun away from her too.

She couldn't encourage Ben any longer. If she'd ever led him to believe there could be something more between them than friendship, she was sorry. Because there couldn't be anything. Perhaps not even friendship.

He'd agreed to her offer of friendship when they'd been together in the closet under the stairs. In fact, he'd been the one to tell her there could never be anything between them.

Why had he changed his position now? He should have left things the way they were.

She took another step away from him but couldn't keep from glancing at him one more time.

He'd dropped his hand and crossed to the hallway. His face was a mask of calmness, but his eyes had turned the shade of a frigid winter storm.

She shuddered as if someone had opened the front door and ushered in the December wind.

"Very well, Miss Smith. I understand your position very clearly." He swiped his cloak from the coat tree. "It would seem I have made a complete fool of myself today."

"You're not a fool. Not in the least."

"Then perhaps I am a very poor judge of character."

His words stung her.

But before she could say anything to defend herself, he moved to the door, flung it open, and retreated into the wintry afternoon, letting the door slam closed after him.

The sound reverberated in the empty chambers of her heart and ricocheted through her limbs.

She had just rejected Benjamin Ross and driven him from her home.

And from her heart.

She'd never felt more like weeping than she did at that moment.

Chapter
18

The laughter and voices around Ben couldn't penetrate the melancholy afflicting him. Not even the meeting with Cranch had lifted his spirits.

"How much longer is Lieutenant Wolfe planning to patrol the Weymouth coast?" Cranch asked, peering at him through the haze of pipe smoke that clouded Boston's Green Dragon.

In their corner spot of the crowded tavern, Ben took a swig of the hard cider, letting it burn the back of his throat, then brought the tankard down to the wooden table with a *thunk*.

"My father's anxious to resume the usual trading," Cranch continued. For once, there was a complete lack of mirth in Cranch's expression. "The barrels of molasses and other supplies are trickling into Boston rather slowly to keep up with the demand. If we can't supply the distilleries with the molasses they need, they may be forced to buy their sugar from the British."

Ben ran his finger around the sticky ridge of his mug. Of course, Cranch was worried about his margin of profit now—now that he had a wife for whom he must provide. He would surely want to keep her happy in the lifestyle to which she was *accustomed*.

"We only want to make sure Susanna will be well situated in the manner to which she's accustomed."

Bitterness pooled at the back of Ben's mouth. Reverend Smith's words played through his mind for at least the thousandth time in the past three days since he'd made his ill-fated visit to the Smith home in Weymouth.

How could he have ever thought they'd accept him as an equal?

Certainly he knew when he'd ridden to Weymouth that afternoon he'd need to use his best oratory skills to convince Mrs. Smith to allow him to court Susanna.

Yes, he'd expected opposition from her. She was a proud, narrow-minded woman.

But he hadn't expected Susanna to agree with Mrs. Smith's declaration that he was a "disadvantageous match."

The sharp tip of pain pricked his already shredded and bleeding heart.

To be fair, Susanna hadn't actually verbalized her acquiescence with Mrs. Smith. But he'd seen it in her eyes. He wasn't good enough.

"So when do you think we can resume our usual transporting?" Cranch persisted. "Will Lieutenant Wolfe want to return to Boston by Christmas?"

"Perhaps."

Even if he and many of his fellow Congregationalists kept to the Puritan tradition of making Christmas a simple affair, the British Anglicans were much more flamboyant in their holiday celebrations. Lieutenant Wolfe would likely return to Boston for the festivities at the month's end, if not permanently, then at least temporarily.

Maybe they could take advantage of the lull.

"Could you ride out to Weymouth and gather a report on the situation?" Cranch asked.

Ben stared inside his mug to the murky contents there. Part of him wanted to shout that he'd never ride to Weymouth again. But he knew that was irrational. He couldn't put his dealings with the Caucus Club in jeopardy because he was angry at Susanna.

"It's overly risky right now," he finally said. During his last visit to Weymouth, the lieutenant had sent an officer to stalk him. At least he'd spotted someone dodging his every move from the minute he'd left the Smith parsonage. He'd planned on meeting with the Caucus Club, but he hadn't wanted to risk drawing any more attention to Arnold Tavern or the other men involved. So he'd gone home to Braintree without even stopping by Mount Wollaston to check on Dotty.

As if anticipating his resistance, Cranch slid a stack of papers across the table. "You can deliver Mary's letters to her family."

Ben didn't touch the bundle. He didn't want to see Susanna again and Cranch knew it. He lifted his tankard to his lips and took another swig of the cider. The spiciness brought a refreshing sting to his chest.

As he slapped his mug back onto the table, he caught sight of Elbridge Quincy weaving through the crowd toward them. He shoved aside the nagging guilt that he'd placed just as much importance on status and wealth when he'd sought Hannah Quincy's affection.

And he refused to acknowledge the niggling reminder that Susanna had much more to lose in partnering with him than he had to lose in marrying her. She wasn't as wealthy as Hannah, but she was still an advantageous match for a man of his status.

Cranch pushed the letters into his hand. "Take them. Please."

Ben nodded and tucked them into his waistcoat before Elbridge could see them. He could at least take the letters as far as Mrs. Quincy at Mount Wollaston.

And why was it wrong for him to consider Susanna's social position and wealth when he truly did care for her more than any other woman he'd ever met?

But even as he tried to justify his aspirations, Parson Wibird's admonition rumbled through his jumble of thoughts. The parson had warned him that marrying for ambition would only be the first of many compromises he'd make for the sake of improving his reputation.

Ben tried to tell himself he would have made the decision to court Susanna even if she'd been the daughter of a poor tenant farmer. But deep inside, he couldn't keep from wondering if he really would have.

"Well, if it isn't the jilted lover himself," Elbridge called as he neared their table, grinning like an overgrown squash.

Ben had no doubt Elbridge was referring to the news that Hannah had accepted the proposal of the Hingham doctor, Bela Lincoln.

"What are you doing here, Elbridge?" Cranch asked.

Ben forced himself to speak. "I'm surprised you made it inside the tavern. I thought you'd turn tail and run at the sight of the dragon hanging over the door."

"Are you saying I'm not welcome in the Green Dragon?" Elbridge asked, lifting his proud nose.

Ben glanced around the dimly lit tavern, over the powdered wigs of patrons like John Warren and James Otis in heated debate regarding the rumors of a new sugar tax that would be imposed to help pay for the recent war against France.

British officials, military officers, and those who were staunchly loyal to the king tended to congregate at the Crown Coffee House.

Elbridge was as out of place at the Green Dragon as a woman would have been.

Ben cocked his head toward the door. "You'll be eaten alive if you stay here overlong."

"For once, you may be right." Elbridge glared at Otis in disdain. "Nothing good can come of this den of rebellious rogues."

"Then exactly what are you doing here?" Ben asked. "Are you spying on the *rogues*?"

Elbridge's eyes flickered.

"Get out, Elbridge." Unease sifted through Ben's gut. Maybe he'd underestimated Elbridge's stupidity. Maybe the man was smarter than he looked.

"You're so charming," Elbridge said. "I'm guessing that winning charm of yours has made you popular with the ladies lately."

"They can't seem to keep their hands off me, can they?" Bitterness crept into Ben's tone.

"Apparently, Susanna isn't in the least interested in dirtying her hands on you."

So the news about his failed attempt to win Susanna was finally beginning to spread. He'd figured it would be only a matter of time.

Of course he'd already told Cranch everything. And Cranch had assured him Susanna adored him and that she'd eventually come to her senses.

Ben doubted she would. Her mother's hold upon her was too strong.

Even if Susanna did come to her senses and declare her love for him, he wasn't sure he could forgive her this time. Although she hadn't been the one to call him a "poor nobody" again, she hadn't denied it or defended him. How could he love a woman who didn't accept him for who he was?

Cranch glared at Elbridge, and his fingers twitched at the handle of his tankard as though contemplating the idea of tossing the contents into Elbridge's face. "Susanna will be grasping after Ben soon enough. It takes some people a little longer to recognize a jewel when they have one within their hold."

Ben gave Cranch a grateful nod.

A slow grin spread over his friend's countenance. "Then again, some jewels need a little polishing to reveal their true worth, even one as crusty as you, my old friend. Maybe if you'd given her a little more time to see past all your stuffiness . . ."

Had he rushed things with Susanna? Maybe she hadn't been ready for him to declare his intentions. Maybe he should have given her a little more time to return his affection before he'd attempted to court her.

Elbridge peered down his nose at Ben. "You might as well look in the gutters, Ross. That's the only place you'll find a woman who would want you."

Ben's muscles tightened. "Yes, I suppose you would know since you frequent the gutters so often."

"As it turns out, I'll be frequenting the Smith home more often in the coming weeks."

"Then that will be quite a change from the filthy dregs to which you're accustomed."

"Mrs. Smith invited me to call upon Susanna at the end of this week."

Elbridge was exactly the type of man Mrs. Smith wanted for Susanna. He should have known Mrs. Smith would encourage the union.

Even so, it didn't seem fair that a man of such poor character as Elbridge could be given free license to court Susanna simply because of the size of his fortune. Weren't there things that mattered more than wealth?

But even as the thought clamored through him, his own guilt shouted at him again.

The beginning of a grin worked at Elbridge's mouth.

Ben shrugged, trying to throw off Elbridge's insinuations. "Mrs. Smith is obviously deluded if she thinks Susanna is going to be interested in you."

"I've a feeling Susanna will welcome me with open arms," Elbridge said. "I mean, after all the trouble you've caused the Smiths."

"Trouble?"

"Don't play innocent, Ross." Elbridge narrowed his eyes. "While I don't agree with what Lieutenant Wolfe did to the Smith parsonage, I'm certain you played a role in provoking him."

"That's a strong accusation."

"It's the truth and you know it."

The truth was, Ben *did* blame himself for the destruction at the parsonage. If only he'd been able to find a way to help Dotty sooner. If only he'd been able to discover a way to make the lieutenant pay for his crimes. Then the Smith family wouldn't have had to be the recipients of the lieutenant's unbridled anger.

But he hadn't had any success even with Dotty, who was

still patiently hiding at Mount Wollaston. He couldn't determine a way to prosecute Wolfe for the murders, not when he didn't have a solid case or any substantive evidence.

His best course of action was to avoid Lieutenant Wolfe and instead pursue prosecution of Dotty's master, Mr. Lovelace. If only he could get several of Mr. Lovelace's servants to testify to the man's abusive nature.

But every time Ben had made one of his covert visits to the Lovelace mansion and attempted to converse with the servants, none of them had been willing to speak out publicly against their master. Ben suspected several other female servants had also suffered abuse, but they were too afraid and ashamed to admit it. They'd apparently decided to suffer silently, at least until the terms of their indenture ended.

Something ignited in Elbridge's eyes. "I know you're hiding something, Ross. And I'll find out what. Eventually."

"I don't think you'd be able to find anything even if it dropped into your lap and did a jig."

Cranch guffawed.

"Now get out of here, Elbridge." Ben didn't trust Elbridge and hoped he hadn't sorely underestimated him.

Ben nodded at the door, but froze at the sight of Parson Wibird ducking into the Green Dragon. The parson squinted through the smoky haze, and there was an urgent, almost frightened wildness to his expression.

"What's Parson Wibird doing in Boston?" Cranch asked. "I didn't think he liked traveling."

"He doesn't." Ben pushed away from the table and stood.

The parson's darting eyes landed upon him, and he started weaving his way through the crowded room toward Ben.

"Something must be wrong for the parson to seek you out in Boston," Cranch said, voicing Ben's deepest fear.

Parson Wibird was breathing heavily when he arrived at the table. He squinted first at Elbridge, then Cranch, and finally Ben.

"What brings you into town?" Ben asked, attempting to stay calm.

The parson's squinty eyes filled with sudden tears.

Ben's muscles tightened. Had there been another murder? Had Parson Wibird come to recall him to Braintree in order to deal with the matter? What of Joe Sewall?

Cranch rose from the table, his chair scraping against the floor. "What is it, Parson?"

Parson Wibird shook his head.

Maybe something had happened to Susanna.

The question stuck in Ben's throat. As hurt as he was over her rejection, he couldn't bear to think of anything happening to her.

Parson Wibird wiped the back of his gloved hand across his face. He looked Ben in the eyes, and the sadness issuing from the parson's expression stopped Ben's heartbeat completely.

"Your father's dead. From influenza."

Chapter
19

Susanna shifted on the wagon seat and pulled her thick wool riding cloak tighter about her body to ward off the damp winter breeze sweeping off the bay. She cupped her fingers to her mouth and blew warmth in them so she could regain her grip on the reins.

She was more than ready to head home and resume her nursing of Tom, who after many days in bed was finally beginning to sit up.

Mother stood in the doorway of the small cottage, counting coins that would reimburse the widow for the finished cloth she'd woven. Mother had also tucked a fresh loaf of bread and a roasted chicken into the basket of fresh weaving material, always generous with the women.

The young widow bobbed her head at Mother.

Mother pressed the woman's hands and replied to her gently.

Susanna might be able to fault her mother for many things, but she could find no criticism with how Mother treated the poor women in their community. She had always modeled compassion for them.

Susanna released a deep breath that contained all the turmoil that had been building over the past months. If Mother could care about poor, helpless women, then surely Susanna had every right to do the same. Who could blame her for following in Mother's footsteps? Even if the woman in question was a pregnant runaway?

The gray clouds hung low and heavy, ready to dump their burden if only someone would but give them permission. The region hadn't had a significant snowfall yet, at least not enough to warrant using a sleigh.

Susanna shivered and blew into her fingers again.

A lone snowflake drifted to the seat next to her. It wouldn't be long before winter would fall upon them.

She supposed that was why Mother had wanted to make the rounds to the widows that morning in spite of her fear of traveling without Tom's presence. Even though there were many who still blamed Hermit Crab Joe for the murders of the two women, others speculated the murderer was at large.

If only she could share the truth—that Lieutenant Wolfe was the murderer they were seeking and that he was more dangerous than they imagined.

If only she could let go of her need to help Dotty further. She certainly had done enough to aid the girl already.

Why then did she continue to fret and think about Dotty? She simply needed to let go of her need to assist the girl as she'd previously resolved. And she needed to let go of her wistful longings for Ben too. If only it were easier to get them both out of her thoughts . . .

At the clop of hooves on the packed dirt road, Susanna

straightened. Through the shrubs and bare brush hedging the front garden of the cottage, she caught a flash of crimson.

Her body tensed, and she shivered again but this time not from the cold. She wanted to shout at Mother to get in the wagon so they could be on their way. But when the Redcoat guided his horse onto the lane leading to the cottage, she realized it was too late to flee.

Her fingers tightened around the stiff leather reins. She'd dreaded the moment she would have to face Lieutenant Wolfe again, for she knew it was only a matter of time before he would confront her and question her involvement in Dotty's disappearance.

The soldier trotted directly toward her, his cloak flapping in the wind behind him. When he lifted the brim of his cocked hat and nodded at her, Susanna's breath swooshed.

"Sergeant Frazel." She greeted the young man with a return nod.

He reined his horse next to the wagon and glanced toward the cottage, where Mother was staring at him, her face pale and her hand fluttering above her chest.

"Your kitchen slave said I might find you visiting among the parish," the sergeant said, giving Mother a friendly nod before leaning toward Susanna. The usual kindness in his eyes was dim, obscured by a cloud of anxiousness.

"I haven't had the chance yet to thank you," she said.

"No thanks needed."

"If not for your warning . . ."

"That's why I've sought you out again." He lowered his voice. "I have reason to believe the lieutenant is getting close to discovering the new hiding place."

Susanna swallowed the sudden fear that clogged her throat.

She should have known the lull of peace was too good to be true. "How did he learn of it?"

Sergeant Frazel looked around before leaning closer. "I overheard a man giving the lieutenant information this morning. The man said he has reason to believe a runaway is being sheltered in Braintree. And he arranged a meeting with the lieutenant for tomorrow to hand the girl over to him."

"Who would divulge such information? And why?"

"I've never seen the man before."

Susanna's mind spun with the implications of the sergeant's news. She'd hoped Dotty would be safe in Grandmother Eve's house until Ben could find a way to bring about justice for her. But obviously they hadn't kept her whereabouts as secret as they'd hoped.

With all the guests coming in and out of Mount Wollaston, someone had apparently discovered she was there.

The sergeant's expression was grave.

"What do you suggest I do?"

"I think you should relocate her somewhere else as soon as possible."

"But where?"

"I wish I knew." Sergeant Frazel glanced at Mother and the widow who were staring at him with narrowed, angry eyes. "In fact, I wish I knew how to help you more."

"You've already done so much—"

"It's not enough to make up for the other girls." His whisper was harsh and his pale face tight. A nightmare of anguish flashed through his eyes, and he shuddered as if haunted by visions he couldn't forget.

"Why?" The question slipped from Susanna's lips before she could stop it. "Why does the lieutenant do it?"

"I've heard rumors thieves broke into his home in London and murdered his young daughter and wife several years ago."

"That's terrible." Susanna couldn't begin to imagine the horror of losing a family to murder. "But why then is he murdering others? Why wouldn't he be eradicating crime instead?"

"I suppose he thinks he is. He claims he's getting rid of the rogues, misfits, criminals, and poor rabble who have nothing better to do than break the law."

"But he's taken his efforts beyond the scope of decency."

"I realize that quite clearly now. In fact, I realize I've been mistaken in my beliefs about many things when it comes to you colonists."

Susanna couldn't find the words to respond to his confession.

"Now that I've been here for these past months," the sergeant continued, "I can't help but envy your freedom here on this side of the ocean."

"Freedom?" Did they really have more freedom? Was that what Ben was so concerned about?

Sergeant Frazel's voice dropped to a whisper again. "I was pressed into the army, and even though I've resigned myself to my fate, there are times when I see the open land and the space here, and I wish I could have a piece of it for myself."

"Susanna Smith," Mother called, starting toward her with choppy steps. "Please cease conversing with that soldier."

"You'd better go," Susanna said.

Sergeant Frazel had already pulled his hat low. He kicked his mount and spurred it forward.

"I don't want you speaking with the king's soldiers," Mother said when she reached the wagon. She stared after Sergeant Frazel's retreating back, bitterness adding wrinkles to her features. After all the destruction to the parsonage, Mother's loyalties to the Crown had been severely tested. And now Susanna wasn't sure the king would ever be able to regain Mother's affection.

"What did he want?" Mother asked as she climbed into the wagon. "Was he leveling more accusations at us?"

Susanna hesitated. Ought she to finally confess to Mother her activities regarding Dotty?

"He's friendly enough," she said, trying to find the words to inform Mother without jeopardizing Sergeant Frazel. She certainly didn't want Lieutenant Wolfe to find out his trusted advisor was giving her information about his plans.

"I don't want you fraternizing with any of the soldiers again." Mother situated her petticoats on the bench. "The best course of action is to refrain from any involvement whatsoever with the soldiers and to keep to ourselves."

"But what if we come across someone who needs our help—someone we wouldn't normally assist?"

"Providence has given us enough people to help right here in our own neighborhood." Mother straightened her shoulders and stared ahead, as though they had nothing more to discuss on the matter.

Several more snowflakes drifted in front of Susanna. They flittered onto the horse's flank, melting at the contact with the beast's warm flesh.

She couldn't disagree with Mother. There were certainly enough poor women in Weymouth who needed their compassion. But how could they turn away from injustice and problems that were happening elsewhere? Surely God didn't want them to stay insulated in their safe little parish and ignore others who might need their help as well.

They could go on doing what they always had, keep to

themselves and attempt to avoid danger. That would indeed be the safest course of action.

But should she refrain from doing the right thing merely because she was afraid of what might happen as a result?

During the short ride home, Susanna scrambled to find an excuse to travel to Mount Wollaston and to Dotty. She prayed if God truly wanted her to continue helping Dotty, that He would show her how and provide a new hiding place.

When they rumbled into the parsonage yard, Susanna's heart did an involuntary flip at the sight of a horse tied to the oak in front of the house.

If only it was Ben's. Maybe he would be able to help her devise a plan for helping Dotty.

A closer examination of the gelding blanketed her with a strange sense of disappointment. The horse was bigger and the saddle much finer than Ben's.

She climbed down from the wagon and handed the reins to the local boy they'd hired to replace Tom until he recuperated.

Why had she believed Ben would come calling again? The truth was, he'd never want to see her again. Not after the reception he'd received during his last visit.

A familiar ache squeezed her heart, the same ache that had radiated within her since the day Ben had walked out the door of the parsonage and out of her life.

Over the past week she'd composed a dozen letters to him in her head. All of them had started with the words *I beg you to forgive me.*

She couldn't deny she'd come to care about Ben, that she didn't want to lose the connection she had with him. But there was also something slightly terrifying about the thought of giving up everything and defying all she knew to be right in order to be with him.

If only she could put him out of her mind altogether . . .

With heavy footsteps, she followed Mother inside.

As she removed her cloak and hat, she could hear Elbridge in the parlor with Father, and a sense of despair pressed down upon her even more.

Susanna tried to slip past Mother to the stairway, but Mother caught her arm and maneuvered her into the parlor at her side.

"Mr. Quincy, what a delightful surprise," Mother said with a smile. "We're so glad to see you. Aren't we, Susanna?"

"Why, of course." Susanna said what was expected of her. But her shoulders slumped at the thought of having to sit in the parlor with Elbridge and make small talk. She had much more important matters needing her attention—life-and-death matters.

Elbridge rose from the chair across from Father's. He gave a slight bow. "Good day, ladies. You both look lovely."

Mother's smile inched higher. "I do hope you can stay for a day or two?"

"Thank you, Mrs. Smith. How can I refuse your kind invitation? While I have business to attend on the morrow, I could be easily persuaded to stay the night and leave early in the morning."

Elbridge's gaze came to rest upon Susanna with a possessiveness that was more intense than in the past. Now that Mary was successfully married, she had no doubt Mother had begun her earnest task of finding Susanna a suitable match.

And it appeared Elbridge was her first choice. She had likely invited Elbridge today for the specific purpose of discussing courtship.

Frustration wound around Susanna, and she had the overwhelming urge to stomp her foot at her mother and tell her no. No, she wasn't ready to court Elbridge—or anyone—not so soon after turning away Ben, not when her heart was still aching.

She wanted to tell Mother to wipe the knowing smile from her face, that she wasn't going to accept the proper way of doing things this time.

All her life she'd allowed Mother to guide and control her, to keep her within the bounds of propriety. Susanna had tried to accept the boundaries and to follow Mother's example of how a lady should live and behave.

But she seemed to forever be swelling against the constraints, pushing the limits of what was acceptable, constantly longing for more. Part of Susanna wanted to swell until she broke free. But the other part clung to the security of the familiar.

Elbridge crossed the room toward her, took her hand, and lifted it to his lips. The warmth from his mouth and the wetness of his kiss against her cold skin elicited none of the anticipation and spark the merest of Ben's touches brought.

She tried to push aside the sudden longing for Ben and focus instead on generating an affectionate reaction to her cousin. Surely she could create attraction if she worked hard enough. Surely someday she could learn to be content with the way of things for women like her.

As if sensing her lack of excitement, Elbridge retrieved a folded sheet of paper from his waistcoat. "I've come from Mount Wollaston and have a letter for you from your grandmother."

"A letter from Grandmother Eve?"

Elbridge held out the letter.

As her fingers closed around it, he didn't let go right away. Instead he forced her to lift her gaze to his. Something sharp in his eyes sent a shiver of unease through her.

She tugged the letter from his grip. "Thank you, Elbridge."

If she didn't know better, she'd almost guess he was silently rebuking her. But rebuking her for what?

She quickly broke the seal and unfolded the letter. The note was short and to the point, and her throat constricted with each word she read.

Ben's father was dead, had passed away earlier in the week. Ben was in a state of grief that worried Grandmother Eve. Grandmother felt certain a visit from Susanna would cheer him and provide the dose of medicine he needed to revive from his state of melancholy. She was hosting a dinner that very evening with the hope of offering condolences, and she wanted Susanna to attend.

When Susanna finished the letter, she refolded it slowly. Apparently Grandmother Eve hadn't yet heard about her rejection of Ben's offer of courtship. If she had, she would know Susanna was the last person Ben desired for comfort.

Nevertheless, Sergeant Frazel's warning clanged in her mind, growing louder with each passing moment. She needed to travel with all haste to Braintree to alert Grandmother Eve and Ben about Lieutenant Wolfe's plans. The dinner would provide the perfect opportunity to discuss what else they might do to locate a new hiding spot for Dotty.

She appealed to her father, who was standing with his palms stretched toward the blazing fire. "Father, Grandmother Eve has invited me to dinner this evening. Perhaps Elbridge would be agreeable to escorting me."

She turned to Elbridge and clasped his hands. "You'll take

me, won't you, cousin?" She peered up at him with what she hoped was her most beguiling look.

"He's only just ridden from Mount Wollaston," Mother said, but her protest lacked conviction. "'Tisn't fair of you to ask him to ride again so soon."

"I don't mind." Elbridge enfolded Susanna's hands within his. "I want to make Susanna happy in whatever way I can."

She smiled up at him. "Thank you, Elbridge."

"Anything for you."

"You're very kind, Elbridge," her father said. "I'm sure it would lift Susanna's spirits to spend time with her cheerful grandmother."

Of course, her father wouldn't mention Susanna's melancholy ever since Ben's disastrous visit, nor the fact that she'd had so little time to focus on reading or eavesdropping on William's lessons. It wasn't within Father's nature to focus on the negative. But the gentleness in his eyes said he had noticed her languishing and wanted to give her a small gift in the visit to Grandmother's.

"If Elbridge is agreeable," Father continued, "then how can we say no?"

Mother gave a brief nod.

"Thank you, Father," Susanna said quickly before Mother could change her mind. "And thank you, Elbridge. I shall go pack." She spun away from him and made her way from the room before anyone could contradict her.

As she strode through the hallway, her pulse began to thump with an urgency that left her breathless.

She stopped at the door that opened to the closet under the stairs. She laid a trembling hand against the plank and shivered at the remembrance of her time alone in the closet with Ben . . . his hand caressing her neck, his breath against her lips, the tightness of his body so near hers.

She couldn't deny how much she'd wanted to be with him then.

And she still did. She would at the very least pen him a letter and finally ask for his forgiveness.

No matter how dangerous he was, she couldn't cut him out of her life. As much as she'd told herself she needed to stay away from him, she didn't want to. Not now.

Perhaps never.

Chapter
20

The wind lashed Ben's cloak, but he didn't care. He kneeled next to the wall bordering the east pasture and restacked the fieldstone where the old ones had crumbled and fallen away.

His fingers had no feeling. Neither did his toes. But he fumbled with the stones and rubble anyway. At least now his limbs resembled his frozen, unfeeling heart.

Flakes of snow drifted around him, forming a layer over everything, but it wasn't enough to brighten the lifeless gray stones or the wilted grass. The snow couldn't bring life to anything—not to the barren field, the leafless trees edging the creek, or the farmhouse in the distance.

Ben couldn't imagine the farm ever being beautiful and alive again. Not without his father.

He brushed a sleeve across his frozen cheek to wipe away a tear. But his face was dry, his tears gone. He'd already shed enough over the past several days since he'd buried his father, and he had nothing left inside of him.

Nothing but a deep, wretched ache.

Nevertheless, farm life had to continue. For now the farm

belonged to him. His father had left him the house as well as forty acres.

Ben sat back on his heels and looked around at the property. He'd received ten acres of adjoining land and then thirty of orchard, pasture, woodland, and swamp.

He was finally a freeholder. He owned land free and clear. Now he could vote or act as a representative in the legislature. And he would begin to earn the respect of many who looked down upon poor, landless men.

Why did it take land and money to earn respect anyway? Why couldn't men respect him for his merits and his accomplishments rather than his status?

His father's words wafted in the wind. *"There is more than one way to earn the approval of your peers. And often the best way is through strength of character."*

Ben bowed his head. The wind whipped at him again, sending scourging lashes down the back of his cloak.

Maybe he needed to earn the respect of his peers the way his father had, by improving his character rather than status. His father had been a good man, the most honest man he'd ever known.

If not for his father's persuasion, he might not have gone on with his schooling, especially when the teacher at the local Braintree school had paid him no attention, but had in fact drained the love of learning out of him with his cruelty.

He'd come home from school one day and declared to his father that he didn't want to go back, that he only wished to be a farmer. But his father had persuaded him to continue with his education and had even enrolled him in a private school where the new schoolmaster treated him kindly and spurred him to study in earnest.

He owed much to his father. . . .

The distant plod of hooves brought Ben's head up, and he exhaled a weary sigh. He peered down the country road to the advancing forms of two people on horseback.

If they were coming to visit him, he knew he ought to shout out a warning for them to steer far clear of his humble Braintree home. The influenza had struck his mother as well. In fact, she'd been too ill to leave her bed when they'd buried his father.

With a grunt, Ben pushed himself to his feet, unbending his frozen limbs.

Fortunately, under the gentle hands of his brother's wife, his mother was recovering. Even so, the illness was spreading. Earlier in the day he'd heard that several other older men of the community had succumbed to death.

This was not the time for anyone to be out visiting.

As the riders drew nearer, and at the sight of a young woman wearing elegant riding apparel, his pulse lurched. The confident set to the woman's shoulders, the proud tilt of her chin, the wisps of raven hair that had escaped from the hood of her cloak—they belonged to only one woman. Susanna.

His first inclination was to drop his chisel, hop over the stone wall, and run to her. Everything within him wanted to hoist her from her mare, drag her into his arms, and bury his face into her neck. He needed to feel her arms about him, her soothing breath on his cheek, and the comforting thump of her heartbeat against his.

But then his attention shifted to the rider next to her and the door of his heart slammed shut. A blast of wind socked him again, and he sucked in bitter air that flowed into his lungs and stung him.

Elbridge lifted his chin, giving Ben a clear view of his countenance and the pride etched there. His smile sent the message *I told you so*, indicated he was indeed the favored one, and that everything he'd said at the Green Dragon in Boston was true. Reverend and Mrs. Smith had placed their favor upon him as Susanna's suitor.

Disappointment bit at Ben.

He'd thought Susanna more intelligent than to settle for someone like Elbridge. She was much too passionate about life. She'd never be content with a man as narrow-minded and ignorant as Elbridge.

Susanna reined her horse on the other side of the wall next to Ben. Her dark eyes radiated such sorrow and compassion, his throat grew tight. Once again he had the urge to sweep her down and into his arms. A deep part of him—a part he couldn't begin to understand—needed her more than anything or anyone.

"Ben," she said softly.

Just the sound of his name on her lips pushed the ache higher into his throat.

The gentle lines of her face were drawn together. "Please accept my heartfelt sympathy on the loss of your father." She held out a gloved hand to him.

He wanted to put his hand into hers and let her console him, but Elbridge nudged his horse between them, giving her mare little choice but to step back.

Her horse nickered in protest, and Susanna rubbed her hand against the beast's mane. "How are you faring?" Her eyes were full of questions and confusion—the same confusion that had swirled in her eyes the last time he'd seen her, when she'd refused his offer of courtship and shut him out of her life.

All the pain, the heartache, and the anger of her rejection came pounding back into his chest.

"Why are you here, Susanna?" he asked.

She drew back as if his words had slapped her. "I came to offer my condolences," she said hesitantly. "And my comfort."

"I don't need your comfort." He was being hard on her, but at that instant, with Elbridge standing between them, Ben couldn't seem to stop his anger from spilling out. "After our last parting, what would make you believe I'd want your comfort?"

"I only wished to express how sorry I am—"

"Obviously. Now that you know I inherited my father's farm and have become a freeholder."

"That's not true. That has nothing to do with my visit whatsoever."

"Admit it. It has everything to do with your visit. You spurned me when I had nothing. But now that I own property, you're no longer ashamed to associate with me."

"The thought hadn't crossed my mind in the least. Surely you can't think me so callous."

He shrugged.

A smile tugged at Elbridge's lips. He was likely getting the kind of show he'd anticipated.

Ben knew he should refrain from any more conversation, but the hurts pushed for release. "You're more like your mother than you want to admit."

Susanna's shoulders slumped and the life that had been in her eyes drained away. "I can see you're still very hurt. And I don't blame you. Even so, I was hoping—"

"Hoping I'd forgotten what happened? Hoping my grief would make me fall into your arms and cry on your shoulder? Go back home, Susanna. And stay there."

"Very well." She lifted her chin.

"Come. Let's go," Elbridge said, urging his horse forward. "I told you Ross wasn't worth the time."

Susanna gathered her reins. But then she hesitated. "I was

planning to extend an invitation for you to join us at Mount Wollaston tonight for dinner."

"Then it's a good thing you didn't invite me," Ben replied. "I wouldn't have come."

The wind whipped at her already rosy cheeks. It wrenched the hood of her cloak and unleashed more of her hair. She shuddered, obviously chilled in spite of her heavy layers.

The day was too cold for her to be riding about the countryside. Why had Elbridge allowed it? If he cared at all about Susanna, he should have insisted she stay home. Especially with the threat of an influenza epidemic.

"This is no time to be having parties." Ben couldn't prevent anxiety from creeping into his tone. "You were a fool to come into Braintree at all, with the influenza striking so many. Three more died today."

She reached into her cloak, glanced at Elbridge's retreating back, then pulled out a letter. She thrust it toward him. "For you."

The wind flapped the folded sheet, attempting to tear it away from him. But he grabbed it before either Elbridge or the wind could sever his last connection with Susanna.

Because the truth was, in spite of all his hurt, he wasn't ready to let go of her.

He tucked the letter into his cloak near his heart.

As he watched her spur her mare after Elbridge, he pressed his hand against the sheet through the scratchy wool. And he couldn't keep the despair from rampaging through him with renewed force.

She'd come to him.

Why in heaven's name had he sent her away?

Susanna stared out the parlor window into the fading light, which was reflected in the snow that was beginning to fall in earnest. She tried to ignore the chatter of the few friends Grandmother Eve had invited for the evening.

Nothing ever stopped her grandmother from socializing, not even illness. Besides, they had need for the commotion of the guests if they hoped to provide a cover for Dotty's escape.

Susanna grazed her fingers along the cold windowpane, unable to shake the gloom that had settled over her since her visit with Ben. Elbridge had protested riding past Ben's farm, but she'd convinced him it wasn't too far off the route to Mount Wollaston.

Perhaps she should have heeded Elbridge. What had she expected? That Ben would throw open his arms and welcome her back into his world?

She certainly hadn't imagined he'd hate her and order her to leave.

The tinkle of laughter behind her mocked her and only made her want to sneak out of the room and secrete herself in her grandfather's study. Instead she gripped the window-sill and held herself back, knowing she had to play the part expected of her, at least through dinner.

Then after everyone had gone, and the hoofprints and sleigh ruts crisscrossed the snowy roads, she would make her escape with Dotty. If Lieutenant Wolfe tried to track them, he'd have a difficult time following them amidst all the other tracks.

When she'd arrived, she pulled Grandmother Eve aside and shared the warning Sergeant Frazel had brought that morning. She'd also had to explain all that had occurred recently with Ben, the alienation between them and his cold dismissal that afternoon.

Grandmother had insisted Ben didn't mean anything he'd said and that he would still be willing to help them. But after a lengthy discussion, and upon Susanna's persistence, they'd finally agreed the best course of action was to move Dotty to Parson Wibird's home. Grandmother was confident the parson would do his best to shelter the young woman, at least until it was safe to bring her back to Mount Wollaston.

"Come, Susanna," Elbridge called from near the fireplace. "You must stop brooding and join us. We were all remarking on the delicious scents coming from the dining room."

The aroma of the dinner the servants were laying out had indeed penetrated the parlor—the tartness of plum pudding, the juiciness of roasted goose, the sweetness of sugar-glazed carrots.

She couldn't fault Elbridge for his attentiveness. He was only playing the role of a suitor. And he had, after all, been willing to accompany her to Braintree, even though it meant another long ride in the wintry weather.

Yet no matter his virtues, she was well past exhausted at being in his presence, at having his undying attention all day long.

As much as she disliked the thought of having to contradict her mother's choice for her, she didn't know how she could possibly endure being courted by Elbridge. He was a decent man, but she couldn't marry someone whose presence wearied her.

Perhaps this was one of those times when she must stay strong and challenge the old way of doing things, shedding the need to acquiesce like a gown she'd long outgrown.

She could begin by convincing Elbridge she wasn't the right woman for him, that with his wealth and status he would surely find someone more suitable.

She had started to turn from the window when a distant glimmer caught her attention. She pressed her face closer to the frosty glass and peered through the blowing snow and growing dusk. At the bottom of the winding road that led up the hill, a light flickered.

Were more guests arriving?

A flare of a second light shone long enough to reveal a spot of red before the darkness and the falling snow swallowed the rider.

Her heartbeat collided with her ribs.

A spot of red? That could only mean one thing. Lieutenant Wolfe was paying Mount Wollaston a visit that very night.

"Grandmother Eve." Her voice wavered. "I do believe we're about to have uninvited guests."

The room grew silent, leaving only the sound of the soft crackling of the hearth fire.

Her grandmother's petticoats swished with each rapid step she took toward the window. "I hope you're not referring to Lieutenant Wolfe."

"I regret to say that I am."

Elbridge's eyebrows shot up. "Lieutenant Wolfe here? Tonight? He can't be."

"I do not believe I'm mistaken." Susanna met her grandmother's anxious eyes.

Without speaking a word, Susanna knew she was thinking the same thing as Grandmother. They had to get Dotty out. Immediately. Even if they were wrong about the identity of the visitor, they were better to use caution.

Elbridge cursed. "Lieutenant Wolfe assured me he would meet with me on the morrow."

"Since when have you been speaking with the lieutenant?" Susanna asked.

For the merest instant Susanna caught a glimpse of guilt upon his face, but then just as quickly he lifted his nose and stared at her with the same look of rebuke he'd leveled at her earlier in the day. "I've had to make it my business in order to protect you from your own foolhardiness."

Something in his eyes said he'd discovered her involvement with Dotty. Had he been the man Sergeant Frazel had seen talking with Lieutenant Wolfe, the one to betray her presence at Mount Wollaston?

Susanna had the sudden urge to scream at him. "Have you no care for what he shall do to Grandmother Eve's home?"

"I arranged to meet the lieutenant on the morrow at Benjamin Ross's farm since he's to blame for the whole affair." Elbridge's voice was clipped. "I'd hoped to prevent any problems for Grandmother Eve."

"You must leave, Susanna." Grandmother Eve steered her toward the door. "What's done is done. There's no time to waste now."

Susanna nodded and scurried toward the parlor door, ignoring the whispers of the other guests.

"Where are you going, Susanna?" Elbridge called after her. "I insist that you remain here."

Susanna didn't stop but instead ran down the hallway toward the kitchen. Behind her she could hear Grandmother Eve tell Elbridge, "If you care at all about your cousin, then you must stay here and detain Lieutenant Wolfe."

Susanna made her way past the kitchen to the small storage closet at the rear of the house. With only the slightest knock she barged into the crowded room lined with shelves and boxes and smelling of honey and apples.

"Why, miss . . ." Dotty glanced up from a corner chair where she'd sat earlier when Susanna had visited her shortly after her arrival. "I didn't expect to see you again tonight. Didn't expect to see you at all."

"We need to go. Now."

Dotty sprang to her feet. The short gown and petticoat Grandmother had given her pulled taut against her gently rounded stomach, which was growing more prominent with each passing week. Dotty's face paled, and her fingers shook so that she lost her grip on the apron she'd been hemming for Grandmother Eve.

There wasn't time to reassure the girl. Susanna shoved aside the round carpet at the center of the room and tugged at the cord that would lift the trapdoor.

"Here." Grandmother Eve charged into the closet-like room, her arms laden with cloaks, muffs, and mitts. "Put these on."

Susanna and Dotty scrambled to don the apparel while Grandmother Eve stowed Dotty's personal items out of sight, scrambling to hide any evidence that Dotty had been there.

"One of the servants has already tied a horse at the bottom of the hill near the road," Grandmother Eve said, pulling up the hood of Dotty's cloak and then helping to tie the ribbon. "Ride the horse as hard as you can and go straight to Benjamin Ross's farm."

"I thought we'd planned to take her to Parson Wibird's?" Susanna wiggled her fingers into the gloves Grandmother had handed her.

"With the fresh snow, the lieutenant will have no trouble tracking you there. You must ride to Ben's."

She couldn't go to Ben, not after her earlier encounter. "Won't the lieutenant follow us to Ben's too?"

"He probably shall. But Benjamin will know what to do.

He'll find a way to keep you safe." Grandmother Eve guided Dotty to the trapdoor that led to the underground tunnel.

"But Grandmother Eve, he didn't want to see me again. His disdain for me was quite evident." Susanna started down the ladder into the dark abyss below.

"Appearances can be deceiving, darling. You've been putting your consideration into his outward qualifications. It's past time for you to look deeper at the things that really matter."

Susanna stopped short at her grandmother's rebuke.

Grandmother Eve steadied Dotty on the ladder as she began the descent. "Please don't make the same mistake I did."

"What mistake?" Susanna's feet touched the hard earth, and the darkness of the cavern threatened to engulf her.

"I once gave up the possibility of love with a wonderful man because I was foolish enough to care about his lack of position in the community more than the goodness in his heart." Grandmother Eve's face was shadowed.

For a moment Susanna could only stare at the merry woman who'd brought joy and hope to her life for so many years. She wouldn't have guessed Grandmother Eve had experienced heartache.

"I've learned to love and respect your grandfather over the years," she said softly. "But I can't ever forget what a foolish young woman I was."

Susanna didn't know how to respond to Grandmother Eve's confession. Her insides twisted with strange confusion as she helped Dotty descend the last rungs.

Grandmother Eve leaned down and handed Susanna an oil lantern, which illuminated Dotty's frightened face and the starkness of the underground tunnel. Susanna took the lantern and paused again.

"For now you must do as I've said. Please promise you'll go to Ben?"

"Only if you think it's for the best."

"Yes. Trust me." Grandmother Eve glanced toward the door and beyond. Her face tightened with urgency. "You must go. We won't be able to stall the lieutenant for long."

Susanna held out the lantern to reveal the short tunnel. The light touched the other end and a wooden door.

"God be with you, Susanna," Grandmother Eve said, pressing a kiss to her hand and then holding it out to Susanna.

Susanna tried to swallow the lump of fear lodged in her throat. "Will God be with me, Grandmother Eve? Even when I'm breaking the law?"

"A kind action is never wrong."

She nodded at Grandmother Eve and pushed aside the doubts. Hadn't she prayed earlier in the day that if God wanted her to continue to help Dotty, that He would provide a way?

He'd given her a reason to ride to Mount Wollaston. And now surely He would have her do nothing less than show compassion to this woman.

But the truth was, she had no idea how she would keep herself and Dotty safe. Once the lieutenant discovered the presence of the secret tunnel, he'd be able to follow their tracks to Ben's farm.

He'd be able to track them anywhere.

Where could they possibly go that would be safe from the lieutenant? The vision of the murdered body of the woman on the beach rose up to haunt Susanna. A pale face frozen with pain, and lifeless eyes wide with fear.

Susanna shuddered to think what Lieutenant Wolfe was capable of doing if he were to catch them.

"Perhaps this is overly dangerous," she started.

"Sometimes doing the right thing is perilous, darling." Grandmother Eve was already lowering the trapdoor. "But you are brave, Susanna. Braver than you know."

The trapdoor closed, giving Susanna little choice but to run.

She crouched and started down the tunnel. The lantern swung erratically. The light cast eerie shadows on the crumbling dirt walls as if demons had come out of the bowels of the earth to gleefully watch their demise.

"Let me go by myself, miss," Dotty said, following behind her. "The lieutenant is after me, not you."

"I'll see you to safety, Dotty," Susanna said. She came to the plank door at the end of the passageway. "I *must* see you to safety."

Whether right or wrong, Susanna couldn't stop now. Not anymore. God had brought Dotty into her life, and she couldn't turn her back on Dotty any more than she'd been able to resist visiting Ben earlier.

With trembling fingers she opened the door a crack. She peered out, but all that met her view was the darkness of the night and the swirling of snow. In the distance, through the whistle of the wind, she could faintly hear the barking of Grandfather Quincy's hunting dogs.

If the dogs were barking, that meant the lieutenant was at the house, likely dismounting his horse. Once he made his way inside, he'd discover their absence and would rapidly be on their trail.

Susanna took stock of their surroundings. The woodland that bordered Mount Wollaston lay directly before them. Behind them, not far up the hill on the plateau, stood the house and barn.

The best course of action was to sprint to the woods and make their way down the hill under the cover of the trees.

Susanna blew at the flame of the lantern, plunging them into utter blackness. As much as she'd like a light to guide their way, they couldn't risk it. Through the darkness, she groped for Dotty's hand. Their shaking fingers connected.

Susanna swung open the door. "We must make haste."

The wind rushed at them and caught at their cloaks, snagging them and holding them back. But Susanna pulled up her hood, ducked her head, and pushed forward.

"Run!" she called over her shoulder to Dotty.

Susanna raced to the edge of the woods, dragging Dotty behind her. Once there, she started down the hill, moving from one tree to the next, slipping and sliding in the snow.

The brittle branches overhead rattled through the howling wind whose bitterness seeped through her cloak and sent shivers over her skin.

With her ragged breath searing her lungs, she cast a furtive glance over her shoulder. The lights in the windows of her grandparents' home shone faintly through the flurry. But so far she couldn't see Lieutenant Wolfe.

When they arrived at the bottom of the incline, Susanna didn't stop even though she was panting. Instead she sprinted toward the road. Dotty struggled to keep up, her days of inactivity and her growing belly slowing her down.

Susanna rushed blindly ahead toward the tree where she knew she'd find the horse.

"We're almost there." Susanna slowed her steps and linked her arm through Dotty's, helping her through the slippery layer of fresh snow. In a few brief moments they located the horse the servant had left for them, and they made quick work of mounting.

Somewhere at the top of the hill near the mansion, another light flickered and was followed by a shout.

The chill on Susanna's skin seeped into her blood. She wrapped the reins around her gloved fingers and dug her heels into the horse's side.

Had the lieutenant discovered their escape?

She urged the horse forward, faster until they were galloping away from Mount Wollaston. She thought she heard more shouts and the pounding of hooves behind them, but the wind rushing in her ears made it difficult to distinguish the different sounds.

Snow pelted her face, and the wind ripped her hood off her head. And yet she spurred the horse to stretch its legs even harder.

Surely they would need the hand of Providence to reach down and intervene if they were to make it through the night without getting caught.

Chapter
21

Ben sat at his desk and unfolded Susanna's letter again.

From Diana, your moon, here to light the way through this dark travail in which you find yourself.

The words poured warmth over the wounds in his heart as they had every time he'd read them over the past several hours since she'd visited. He smoothed the sheet and traced the hastily scrawled words.

The lantern on his desk cast a cozy glow, and the low flames in the fireplace crackled with a comforting heat. For once, since he'd received news of his father's death, a semblance of peace stole over him.

The calmness permeated his office in spite of the wind rattling the windowpane and wailing low in the chimney. The snow was beginning to plaster the window, and frost would soon form a thin layer over the inner glass.

Thankfully he had no need to be out on a night that was ushering in the first major storm of the winter. He was content to closet himself in his office for the evening, to ponder Susanna's plea for forgiveness.

He studied her letter again.

> *I beg you to forgive me for hurting you, again. It would seem I am destined to repeat my past mistakes. Although I thought I had matured, it is now clear to me that I have much room for improvement in my character.*
>
> *Since the day you walked back into my life, you've challenged me to think beyond the limits of my comfort and to seek out God's higher laws of compassion and mercy. You will have to excuse me as I sort through the confusion that has settled over the depths of my mind. Therewith, I know not what to think about anything anymore.*
>
> *I plead for your patience and goodwill. More than anything, I plead for your undying friendship.*

She asked him to forgive her and extend the hand of friendship to her again.

His eyes shifted back to her opening line. *From Diana, your moon . . .*

He brought the paper to his face and breathed in the lingering scent of dried rose petals. He could almost envision the sweet tilt of her lips when she smiled, the sparkle that lit her eyes, and the saucy quirk of her dimple.

A soft groan escaped his lips.

What was he doing?

He tossed the sheet back onto the clutter of documents and empty inkpots littering his desk.

Alas, she'd only shown renewed interest because of his father's death. Now that he was no longer the pauper she'd believed him to be, she was willing to consider his affection.

Although she'd denied his accusation, he couldn't stop himself from questioning her motives. But even as he did, his own guilt rose up to taunt him.

Was this the meaning of Parson Wibird's warning when he'd wanted to propose to Hannah Quincy? That he would only bring hurt to another if he married for wealth and status rather than the qualities that truly mattered.

He most certainly didn't like the idea that Susanna's feelings for him may have changed with his fortunes. How could he have been so callous as to seek after Hannah for her fortune?

Yet he knew he was only deluding himself to think Susanna was newly attracted to him because of his improved status as a landowner. Even with the acreage and house, he was still insignificant compared to Elbridge. She was a beautiful, desirable woman, and she could command the attention of any man she chose.

Why would she want him—even if he had land now?

He expelled a heavy sigh and sat back in his chair. He needed to accept the fact that she wasn't pursuing him as a potential suitor.

She desired friendship. And that was all.

Could he content himself with merely being her friend? And really, what other choice did he have?

A knock on the door of his office startled him and he sat forward, scrabbling to stuff Susanna's letter into his waistcoat before anyone caught him in the act of pining away for her.

The door opened a crack and his sister-in-law peeked through. "I'm sorry to disturb you, brother, but Mrs. Quincy's granddaughter is here."

"Susanna?" Ben jumped to his feet. Against his will, his pulse sputtered at the thought of seeing her again.

"Yes, it's Miss Smith. And she insists her business is of the utmost urgency."

Trepidation slammed into him like an unexpected fist punch, leaving him suddenly breathless. If she had the need to seek him out on a night such as this, something was terribly wrong.

He wasted no time in grabbing his great coat and outer garb. He raced through the house to the front hallway. And he wasn't in the least surprised to find her with Dotty. Both of their cloaks were covered with a thin layer of snow, their faces red, and their expressions wild with fright.

"Ben." Susanna started toward him but then hesitated. "Lieutenant Wolfe is chasing us."

"How close is he?"

"Grandmother Eve hoped to detain him at Mount Wollaston to give us a lead. But I don't know how long she'll be able to keep him at bay."

"Then we have no time to lose."

At his words, relief flooded her eyes.

Had she been worried he'd refuse to help her? He supposed after his reception of her earlier in the day, he had indeed given her reason to doubt his affection.

He wanted to pull her into his arms and reassure her that he was helpless to do anything but her bidding. But now was neither the time nor the place.

Instead he made haste at donning his winter garments, gathering his musket, and saddling his horse. Susanna and Dotty were waiting when he charged around the house. They cast glances over their shoulders in the direction they'd already come as if they expected Lieutenant Wolfe to ride out of the flurry of blowing snow and descend upon them at any second.

For an instant he thought he saw a flicker of light in the distance. Was Lieutenant Wolfe already catching up to them?

"Let's go," he called, starting forward, digging his heels into his horse. They didn't have a moment more to spare.

Without a word, the women followed.

He didn't need to tell them to hurry. They understood the gravity of their situation. If the lieutenant intercepted them, he'd not only punish Dotty, but he'd also bring charges against Susanna and him for aiding the runaway. And after all the trouble they'd already caused the lieutenant, Ben had the feeling the man wouldn't hesitate to request the fullest measure of prosecution.

In fact, Ben had begun to wonder if the lieutenant had ulterior motivations for pursuing Dotty so relentlessly. Surely one helpless runaway wasn't worth his effort. Surely he would have given up the chase by now, unless he had other, more sinister reasons for capturing her.

Ben forced his horse to plunge into the wind and snow. The pounding hooves urged him to ride faster and harder.

He had to protect Susanna and Dotty from Lieutenant Wolfe, and he knew of only one place where he could take them that would be safe, at least for a few hours until he had the time to formulate a better plan.

They had only gone about a mile at top speed before the women began to lag behind. He finally slowed his horse and rode alongside them.

"With the burden of two people, your horse is wearying under the strain," he yelled through the wind. "One of you will need to ride with me."

He hated to stop their progress, even for the brief instant it would take them to make the switch.

Susanna hesitated and called something to Dotty.

"Make haste." He stretched out his arms to assist her onto his horse.

"Dotty will ride with you," Susanna replied.

"No, miss. You'll be warmer. You go."

Susanna protested. "I insist—"

"Susanna, come to me." He grabbed her arm and dragged her off the horse and onto his.

. She didn't resist. Instead she hoisted herself in front of him, wrapped her arms around his waist, and settled upon his lap almost as if she were relieved to be in his embrace.

A glance over his shoulder revealed a tiny light bobbing on the road behind them. He didn't wait to discover whether it was Lieutenant Wolfe or a figment of his petrified imagination. He spurred his horse onward and yelled to Dotty, "We need to go faster."

Susanna clung to him and buried her face into his cloak. Her body shook like the branches on the trees overhead. If he was frozen down to the bones, he had no doubt she was too.

He needed to get her and Dotty out of the winter storm and somewhere dry before they became ill.

They rode without conversing, the wind making it impossible to breathe much less speak. His only hope was that the increasing winds would blow snow across their tracks, making the chase more difficult for Lieutenant Wolfe.

As they finally neared the bay, Ben galloped down the coastal road until the light from the front windows of Arnold Tavern greeted him.

He knew he was putting the smuggling operation in jeopardy by leading Lieutenant Wolfe directly to the tavern. But at the moment, Susanna's safety was more important than the causes of liberty.

He lowered her to the ground and jumped off behind her.

He helped Dotty from her horse. Then he slashed at the hindquarters of the horses with his riding whip.

"Ride on!" he called to them as he propelled Susanna and Dotty up the front steps.

Spooked, the horses hurtled down the road away from Arnold Tavern. Ben prayed Lieutenant Wolfe would pursue the beasts for a while longer. But the lieutenant was too smart to be fooled for long. He'd come back to the tavern. And when he did, he'd tear it apart in his search for them.

Ben hoped by then he'd have Dotty and Susanna tucked safely into the smugglers' hold.

The women stumbled through the door, and the warmth of the tavern welcomed them with outstretched arms.

At the sight of them, Mr. Arnold shoved away from the table where he sat with several patrons who had been brave enough to venture out on the stormy night.

"Benjamin Ross." He wiped his hands on his apron. "Ye look like ye've seen a ghost."

"I wish." Ben heaved the door closed against the pressure of the wind and then steered the women forward. Seeing a ghost would have been preferable to being hunted by the lieutenant.

Susanna turned her dark eyes upon him, seeking his direction.

"Go to the kitchen." He spun their cloaked faces away from the men and hastened them across the room. The less the patrons knew about the identity of the two women, the safer they'd be.

Mr. Arnold rounded the table, and his thick brows furrowed. "So ye are in trouble, then?"

"When am I *not* in trouble, Mr. Arnold?"

The man followed him. "'Tis true. Ye are a glutton for it, aren't ye?"

Once they were out of the dining room and away from the inspection of the other men, Ben stopped and lowered his voice. "The red monkey will come searching for me here shortly. You'll have to convince your patrons to have a case of blindness in regards to seeing us. Perhaps a few extra drinks are in order?"

Mr. Arnold nodded and was already at work lifting the hatch that led to the root cellar.

Susanna started down the ladder. At least the smugglers' cavern would come as no surprise to her this time.

Within minutes they'd crawled into the hidden underground cave. On the other side of the tunnel, he heard the scrapes and squeaks as Mr. Arnold moved the shelf back into place to camouflage the opening. There were several other bangs and bumps, the sign that Mr. Arnold was shoving barrels around to make the lieutenant's discovery of the door nearly impossible. Nearly.

When all was quiet in the cellar, Ben finally turned. The dim light of the candle he held illuminated the frightened faces of Susanna and Dotty.

They didn't move, and the heaviness of their breathing echoed against the walls and low ceiling of the cavern.

Susanna's cheeks were flushed from the wind, her hair a tangle about her face. "Do you think we've fooled him?"

"He won't find us here." At least Ben hoped not. With as many times as the lieutenant had already snooped around Arnold Tavern, if he'd suspected the room, he would have located it by now.

And since they'd had to cease smuggling molasses into Weymouth, the cavern was nearly empty. Even so, the sweet sugary scent saturated the air, along with the dampness of the earth. The dark coldness of the room circled around them, leaving them without a means to thaw their frozen bodies.

Susanna shuddered. Ben positioned the candle holder atop one of the barrels that remained, and he reached for her. He brushed the snow from her shoulders. Then he gently lifted her hood off her head and combed the loose wisps of her hair away from her face.

She didn't protest. Instead her eyes lifted to his with admiration shining in their depths. "Thank you," she whispered. "Thank you for helping us—even though you had every reason not to."

For all the bravado and false confidence he'd acquired over the years, he was unprepared for the surge of real assurance that came with her admiration. The spark in her eyes said she believed in him enough that she'd entrusted her life into his care. That knowledge was exhilarating and frightening at the same time.

He couldn't find the appropriate words to answer her. For once, he didn't feel the need to hide behind his witty and sarcastic comments. In fact, words didn't seem quite appropriate.

Instead he tugged her closer.

She stumbled against him.

He wrapped his arms around her and drew her into a hug, and was surprised when she slipped her arms around his waist and laid her cheek against his chest.

He let his lips brush against the silkiness of her loose hair. For a long moment, he just held her. They'd outrun the lieutenant. They were safe together. And they were still friends.

Finally she pulled back and looked up at him. "What will we do next?"

"I haven't figured out the next step. But I will."

She shivered again. He grabbed one of the heavy wool blankets Mr. Arnold had given them. He handed one to Dotty, then draped the other around Susanna's shoulders.

"For now we'll wait," he said, lowering himself to the earthen floor and drawing her down next to him.

She snuggled against him. For the first time since they'd shown up at his home, he allowed himself a deep breath.

Dotty melted to the ground too, her face mirroring the exhaustion on Susanna's. She rubbed a hand across the bulge in her abdomen as if attempting to comfort and reassure her unborn baby that they were safe and secure now.

Ben took off his hat and leaned his head against the damp wall, the chill of it seeping into his blood. He held back a shudder.

If only he could reassure the women of their safety. If only he could promise Dotty that she and her baby would survive and have a happy life.

But regrettably, even if Dotty made it through the night without being captured, she was bound to face incredible difficulties in the days to come, as did most unwed mothers. Even if she wasn't at fault for the pregnancy, no one would care. People would still blame her, as if somehow she'd had a choice in the matter.

And Susanna?

Her breathing had turned steady, and she'd stopped trembling.

If she made it safely through the night—and he would do his best to make sure she did—she would still have to face the wrath of Lieutenant Wolfe at some point. For surely the man would now know the extent of Susanna's involvement and wouldn't rest until he'd made her pay for the trouble she'd caused him.

Ben closed his eyes and tilted his head heavenward. God help him. Help him find a way to keep the women safe.

Chapter
22

A distant shout startled Susanna out of a doze. She blinked her eyes open, only to find herself still in the shadowy cavern under Arnold Tavern. She'd desperately hoped to awaken to the heavy quilts and canopied bed in her chamber at Grandmother Eve's house.

Instead she was still in the center of a nightmare—a freezing, dangerous, unending nightmare.

She trembled.

A strong arm tightened around her.

Only then did she realize that during her exhaustion, she'd leaned against Ben and laid her head upon his shoulder. He'd not only permitted it, but he'd slipped his arm around her, allowing her to rest more comfortably in the crook of his body.

She lifted her head and found his face only inches away. The flickering candle illuminated the anxiety there.

"Thank you for lending me your shoulder," she whispered.

He quickly touched his finger to her lips and nodded toward the tunnel and the root cellar.

Another shout was followed by the crashing of glass, possibly the old jars Mr. Arnold had sitting on the shelves.

Even as the warmth of Ben's finger caressed her lips, the warning in his eyes caused her to stiffen with renewed fear.

Was Lieutenant Wolfe rampaging Arnold Tavern in his search for them?

Across from her, Dotty quaked under her blanket, her wide eyes upon the tunnel, waiting for Lieutenant Wolfe to barge in.

Ben let his hand at Susanna's lips fall away and grasped her fingers into a tight hold. With his other hand he gripped his musket.

Was that why her fingers weren't so cold anymore? Had he been holding her hands while she'd slept?

At an angry roar in the root cellar, she flinched.

Ben's muscles flexed in readiness to spring up and fight.

She closed her eyes and fought against the apprehension that had been her constant companion since the moment she'd run away from Mount Wollaston. All of the previous doubts came crawling back to torment her, making her question her involvement in everything.

As if sensing her inner turmoil, Ben's fingers pressed into hers. She lifted her eyes to his again. And they seemed to reassure her that she was doing the right thing, that she couldn't let her fears hold her back.

Somewhere deep inside she knew he was right, that throughout the course of history many people had suffered harm and even death in order to bring about changes that were for the common good of man.

But even with that knowledge, fear was a powerful force to overcome.

There were several more muffled shouts. Then all fell quiet.

Susanna started to breathe again.

But Ben shook his head, cautioning them to stay silent and unmoving.

She nodded and allowed herself to sink back against him, reveling too much in the nearness to him that she'd never expected to experience again after their bitter parting earlier in the day at his farm.

The steady pounding of his heart echoed near her ear, and she couldn't bring herself to remind him of his order to leave him and not to visit him again. She wanted to cling to the peace between them, even if it wasn't real, even if she would wake up tomorrow and find it had evaporated.

At least for this night, at this moment, she could be his friend again.

They seemed to wait for hours, and Susanna felt herself beginning to get drowsy again, when a scraping at the tunnel jolted her upright.

Ben released her and jumped to his feet.

Without the solidness of his presence next to her, the chill in the air crept under the blanket.

Cautiously Ben neared the tunnel, his musket loaded and ready to fire. The taut determination on his face said he was prepared to defend them to the death.

Susanna shrank against the wall. Could Ben really kill another person or would he only make threats? She prayed they wouldn't have to find out.

"Ben?" A soft call with an Irish brogue reached them.

The lines in Ben's forehead smoothed. He lowered his gun and leaned down to squint into the tunnel. "Is the red monkey finally gone?"

"Aye, that he is" came Mr. Arnold's shaking voice. "But not without tearing apart me tavern from top to bottom."

"I promise I'll come back and help you clean it up once I get the women to safety."

"No matter," Mr. Arnold said with a hoarse whisper that echoed through the tunnel. "The important thing is that ye are all right."

"Do you think we're clear to go?" Ben started back through the tunnel, leaving them in the sputtering light of the stub of the candle.

For several long minutes she and Dotty waited. She strained, trying to decipher the murmured whisperings of Ben and Mr. Arnold.

When Ben returned to the cavern, he had several wrapped bundles and extra blankets.

"We'll wait here until just before dawn." He handed Dotty another blanket. "Then we'll leave. Susanna and I will ride toward Boston and act as a decoy. And Mr. Arnold will row Dotty in one of the small fishing vessels around Crow Point."

Susanna nodded. "So if the lieutenant is still looking, he'll see our tracks and follow us north, allowing Dotty time to escape to the south?"

"That's what I'm hoping." He kneeled before Dotty. "I wish I could find a way to send you all the way to Plymouth. But Crow Point is as far as you'll be able to go by sea. After that, you'll have to find your way to Hingham to the home of Mr. Tipton. He's a friend of liberty and justice. Tell him I sent you, and he'll shelter you."

"Thank you, Mr. Ross," Dotty whispered. "You and Miss Smith have been kind to me. Very kind. I can't ever thank you for all your help."

"I only regret I couldn't find a way to prosecute your master, Mr. Lovelace, for all the distress he's caused you. Although

I tried to find other servants who would be willing to testify against him, they were all frightened to speak."

"They're afraid of what he would do to them for crossing him. And rightly so. He's a cruel man. Very cruel."

Ben released a long sigh. "I should have done more for you, Dotty."

"Nay. You've done more than enough." Shadows flickered across Dotty's pretty features, and Susanna couldn't keep from wondering if the young woman regretted running away. Her life had been nothing but hardship since she'd run. And Susanna doubted it would get any easier in the days to come.

"I'll still be working to find a case for you, Dotty," Ben reassured her. "But I must warn you that you won't have an easy path ahead." He glanced at her protruding belly.

"I don't want to go back," Dotty said, splaying her hand over her stomach. "I'd rather die first."

Ben nodded.

Susanna suspected she would have given up long ago. But she supposed she couldn't empathize with the horrors of living under the tyranny of someone who could perpetuate abuse day after day with no recourse.

Perhaps this very situation was beginning to happen between the colonies and Great Britain. They were indeed living under the authority of someone who could perpetuate abuse without recourse.

Would the situation only worsen until they were forced into rebellion—perhaps even war? Would one dangerous situation only lead to another, similar to Dotty's predicament?

"Try to get some rest," Ben said gently to Dotty. "Mr. Arnold will alert us when we need to leave."

Then he straightened, turned toward Susanna, and began to drape the extra blanket across her legs.

She pushed it back at him. "You need it. Please warm yourself."

He shook his head. "I insist."

"Then I must insist that you sit next to me and share it."

In spite of the seriousness of their predicament, a grin tugged his lips. "You need not command me to sit next to you, Susanna. I need no persuasion to have you in my arms."

When his grin inched higher, she had to admit how much she wanted his body against hers, to sit in the shelter of his hold, to hear the steady thump of his heartbeat and feel the heat of his breath against her cheek.

A moment later, after he'd lit another candle and checked to make sure they were secure, he returned to her.

She smiled up at him and lifted the blanket, indicating he should join her.

But this time, he didn't smile. Instead he regarded her with a mixture of desire and caution.

He hesitated, and for a moment she almost believed he would walk away from her, that he was remembering all that had transpired between them, and how he'd wanted her out of his life.

Had he not read her letter? If he had, he would have known how sorry she was for hurting him. But perhaps he'd decided not to forgive her again. Perhaps her pride would at last be her downfall and cast him away forever.

She let the blanket fall, and her smile melted away, replaced by emptiness and utter melancholy.

He sighed and lowered himself next to her, being careful not to touch her this time. When he was seated, he leaned his head back against the earthen wall and stared at the dancing flame of the candle across from them.

She knew she had to say something. No matter his

resolutions, she had to prove to him she'd meant every word of her letter.

With a brazenness that would have shocked Mother, she clutched Ben's hand. She wound her smooth fingers through his thick callused ones and took hope when he didn't pull away.

"I know I don't deserve your forgiveness for the same mistake a second time in my life," she said softly, "but I pray you will grant it."

He placed his other hand over hers, sending more hope skittering through her heart. "I forgive you, Susanna. But if I'm to be completely honest with myself, I cannot lay the blame for what happened entirely at your feet. Since I had considered your wealth and status and the benefits that would come from a union with you, how could I expect *you* not to consider such things?"

"Even so, I was prideful, and I regret the hurt I caused you."

"And I regret asking you for something you weren't ready to give." He finally turned to look at her, and the intensity of his eyes drew her into him like the tide to the shore. "You asked for nothing more than my friendship. But of course, in my own self-seeking, I thought to have more."

"I cannot deny that I have thought of more," she said, glad Mother wasn't there to be scandalized by her boldness.

"But we're both invested in the need to improve ourselves with our matches," he continued as if he hadn't heard her admission. "We have fallen prey to the selfishness of marrying for what our partner can do for us rather than what we can give."

"I'm guilty, although I wish not to be. 'Twould seem that once again I have let my fears dictate my course of action." Her thoughts returned to Grandmother Eve's rushed confession in the tunnel and the admonition that Susanna look past outward qualifications and see into the man's heart to his character.

"Then perhaps it's time for both of us to set aside our selfish aspirations and seek to live sacrificially." He patted her hand. "And because I wish to start, I free you of any obligation to assent to the offer of courtship I placed before your parents."

For a reason she couldn't understand, his declaration left a hollow spot in her chest.

"I'd like to accept your request for friendship," he said. "You've offered it to me all along and I haven't taken it seriously."

She nodded, unable to formulate a response. Confusion wound through her, the same confusion that had been simmering inside her over the past several weeks. The more she was with Ben and the more she came to know him, the more she wanted from him.

"I shall do my best to honor your request of friendship." The warmth in Ben's eyes reached out to caress her. "You're intelligent, easy to converse with, and compassionate—all traits I highly value in a friend. In fact, I have found very few men equal to you, Susanna."

His praise stirred the ache inside her, filling the hollowness with a mixture of sweetness and sorrow.

"I guess what I'm trying to say," he continued at a whisper, "is that I'd be a fool to do anything to jeopardize our friendship."

And she'd be a fool to do likewise. For now, she would need to put aside her confusing thoughts about Ben and find gratefulness in his willingness to renew their friendship.

"You're a good man, Benjamin Ross," she said softly. "In fact, you're a better man than most."

"Better than Elbridge?" Even though his voice was light, there was something in his gaze that demanded to know where her relationship with him stood.

"I have nothing in my heart for him but the utmost scorn. He's the one who betrayed Dotty's whereabouts to the lieutenant."

"I should have deduced he was sneaking around and putting the clues together."

"He met with the lieutenant privately and arranged to bring Dotty to your home so they could implicate you in sheltering her."

"I'm not surprised. I've made enemies of them both."

She hated to think what could have happened if Elbridge had succeeded in implicating Ben for harboring Dotty. Since Lieutenant Wolfe already suspected Ben's involvement in the smuggling activities, he'd likely take any opportunity he could to arrest and prosecute Ben.

"I believe Elbridge also thought he'd protect me," she said, "if he could shift the blame to you."

"Get rid of me and save you at the same time. I guess he's smarter than I realized."

"Regardless of how smart he's proven himself to be"—she tried to infuse her tone with a lightness she didn't feel—"I've realized today he's clearly not the man for me."

"Then perhaps something good has come out of all this after all," Ben responded with the wry humor she was growing to love.

She tried to smile. But she knew if she lived through the night, she would have to explain everything to Mother. And that thought was enough to squelch any mirth.

Susanna believed Mother and Father were wise and only wanted what was best for her. They truly did want her to have a prosperous and happy future. But their idea of what constituted happiness was growing further at odds with hers.

Even if she could use all her wiles of persuasion and logic to gain Mother's agreement to stop pursuing Elbridge, what would she gain from it?

Mother would only seek after some other gentleman of means. And Susanna would be stuck again . . .

Unless she broke free.

If she could be brave enough to free Dotty, surely she could be brave enough to free herself.

Chapter
23

They left through the smugglers' tunnel at the first hint of dawn. Faint sunlight streaked the sky and the calm waters of the bay. The winter storm had finally blown itself out to sea and had left a crisp, bright day in its wake.

Ben rode next to Susanna on horses they borrowed from Mr. Arnold. After the sleepless night, she'd proven herself much stronger than Ben expected.

But finally after riding the fourteen miles north to Boston, she'd sagged in her saddle like a soggy gown out of the washing tub. When they rode into the city, she could hardly hold her head up or cling to the sidesaddle.

"Hang on, Susanna," he said, leading her horse by the reins.

If *he* was exhausted, he could only imagine how bone weary she was.

They hadn't seen any trace of Lieutenant Wolfe, even after stopping several times to warm their frozen limbs at wayside taverns. Their tracks in the freshly fallen snow—at least three inches of powder—would surely make it easy for the lieutenant to follow them if he'd wanted to.

But over the course of the day, the glances over their shoulders had only shown an empty road. Ben hoped the lieutenant had finally given up his need to find Dotty, that he'd just let her go. And he prayed Mr. Arnold had safely stowed the young woman in the bottom of the fishing vessel after they'd left, that nothing had gone wrong in rowing her to Crow Point.

Ben's frozen feet slipped in the dirty gray slush that formed puddles on the cobbled street. He caught himself and filled his lungs with the crisp air that hinted of the sea. Now that they were away from the market and the wharves, blessed silence had replaced the calls of peddlers, the clatter of carriages, and the clamor of the farmers come to sell plucked turkeys, pumpkins, and cheese.

Ahead the looming mansions of Boston's richest merchants rose up to tower over the waterfront city.

They were almost there.

The Cranch home, while not as imposing as some of the mansions of the Boston elite, was still an enormous brick structure that rivaled the Quincy mansion on Mount Wollaston.

Even if the day had been long and the travel wearisome, his heart was content for having conversed for hours with Susanna about *The Odyssey* and other books they'd both read. With each passing mile, his admiration for her brilliance had grown. When she'd shared her frustration once again at having been denied the same quality of education as her younger brother, he could finally begin to understand why. Her mind was no less capable than that of a man. Why should she be forbidden an education simply because of her gender?

He'd been able to understand why her dame school meant so much to her, that she was wanting to do her part in giving women a chance at bettering their minds and lives.

"Ben?" Susanna's voice was groggy, and she began to slip from the saddle.

He lurched toward her, lifted her from the horse, and cradled her in his arms.

"I'm so tired." She laid her head against his shoulder.

He'd been foolish to bring her along to Boston on a wintry December day. He should have made the trip by himself, given the last time he'd fled with her and the chill she'd developed as a result.

With a rush of worry propelling his steps, he strode the rest of the distance to the Cranch home, bounded up the steps, and banged the gleaming brass knocker on the paneled front door.

In a matter of moments, Cranch greeted them. His surprise at seeing them vanished in the shadow of Ben's concern over Susanna. Cranch ushered them in and led the way to an upstairs bedchamber. Ben deposited Susanna onto the bed and was determined to stay with her this time. But Mary insisted that Susanna needed privacy, and Cranch guided him back downstairs to his father's study.

Ben tried to explain their predicament to Cranch, who grinned. "Oh, sure. You can speak of being a decoy and trying to outwit Lieutenant Wolfe, but you can't fool me, you old dog."

A servant handed Ben a tankard of flip. Steam spiraled from it and brought the waft of nutmeg. He nodded his thanks and took a swig. The creamy liquid made a path down Ben's throat.

Cranch leaned back in the desk chair, letting the front two legs rise from the floor. He crossed his arms behind his head and then propped his boots onto the large mahogany desk in front of him. "I know exactly why you came."

The hollow slap of footsteps overhead drew Ben's attention to the high ceiling, to the room where Mary was tending Susanna. "If I'd had my way, I wouldn't have involved Susanna in this whole escapade."

"Just admit it. You wanted the chance to sneak her out of her home and spend time with her away from Mrs. Smith monitoring your every move."

Ben lowered his gaze to the window next to the desk. The glass pane overlooked the spacious snow-covered gardens at the rear of the house, and in the appearance of the late afternoon sunshine, the crystals of fresh snow glinted like a sea of brilliant gems.

The time with Susanna had been equally beautiful in spite of the hard travel. She was like a sparkling gem. And after spending the day with her, he couldn't imagine ever meeting another woman whom he could converse with as readily or speak with as openly about subjects that were both interesting and important.

But if he'd ever thought to win Mrs. Smith's favor and fall into her good graces, the day with Susanna had most certainly destroyed any sliver of hope.

"Mrs. Smith will murder me when she learns Susanna isn't at Mount Wollaston, and that I've brought her to Boston instead. And if she doesn't kill me, then she'll surely ban me from ever seeing Susanna again." At least when he returned Susanna to her home, he would be able to lay claim to the desire to see Mary and Cranch, even if that wasn't the real reason for their foray.

"Yes, I can think of better ways to endear yourself to Mrs. Smith's good favor besides abducting her daughter and then marching the girl through the snow and cold all day."

Ben sat back in the chair he'd taken near the fireplace. His shoulders sagged with fresh discouragement. "Don't worry. I didn't have Mrs. Smith's favor to begin with. If she had her way, she'd toss me on the ground like carpet and wipe her feet on me."

"I don't think it really matters terribly much what Mrs. Smith thinks. Do you?"

"Of course it matters." Ben took another gulp of the hot flip. "She wields a great deal of influence over Susanna."

"Perhaps not as much as you believe. Susanna's here, isn't she? She obviously has a mind of her own and doesn't want her mother telling her everything she should do and believe." Cranch sat forward, letting the legs of his chair hit the floor with a thump. His eyes flashed with mischief. "Or perhaps she likes you enough to defy the wishes of her parents."

"She might be saucy, but she won't defy them when it comes to me." She'd already proven she wasn't willing to court him without their consent. "And I'm resigning myself to the fact that no matter how attractive I find Susanna, I'll have to satisfy myself with friendship."

"Friendship?" Cranch snorted a half laugh. "I'd like to see that."

Ben started to shake his head.

But Cranch cut him off with another snort. "You won't be able to maintain a platonic relationship with a woman you want to pull in your arms and kiss every time she steps near you."

"I don't want to kiss her every time."

Cranch's brow quirked. He dragged his feet from the desk and plopped them back to the floor. Then he reached for his tankard. He took a long drink, unable to hide his humor behind the tall mug.

They both knew how attracted Ben was to Susanna. There was no sense pretending otherwise, especially with Cranch.

"Perhaps I don't want to kiss her *every* time I see her, but very close to that."

Cranch swallowed his flip and then his grin spilled over again. "You mark my words, you'll be married to her within six months."

Ben shook his head. "I won't pursue it. Not after I pledged to her that I would do my best to honor her request of friendship."

Besides, didn't he need to prove to himself that he was giving up his self-seeking ways when it came to a marriage partner?

For too long he'd believed he needed a suitable match in order to gain a reputation. He'd placed his hope in earning fame and prominence in the eyes of man. But he was finally beginning to understand his father's admonition—the need to live with integrity, loving justice and mercy, and walking humbly with God.

With the dangerous course he'd embarked upon—defending the colonists against British oppression—he would likely face many difficult days ahead. If he chose to continue doing the right thing, he would have to sacrifice a great deal, including his reputation, fame, and fortune. He could very well become a wanted man, a criminal, a man condemned.

In fact, he had the feeling after yesterday's chase he'd only made an enemy of Lieutenant Wolfe. And if the man had been dangerous before, he'd be even more so now. Nevertheless, Ben would take hope in the fact that the lieutenant's days in Weymouth were numbered. He'd soon need to report back to his superiors in Boston his findings on the smuggling operations, which would amount to nothing if they were lucky.

And if they got even luckier, the general would send Lt. Wolfe back to England for his failure.

Even so, the days of easy smuggling were over. They would have to continually be alert for searchers like Lieutenant Wolfe and for collectors and comptrollers who would squelch their freedoms.

During the past several weeks the colonists had started carting some of the molasses from Plymouth to Boston over-land and storing it in barns and warehouses, smuggling it into Boston however they could—in farm carts, in fishing dinghies, and even in the back of chaises. Ben suspected they would have to continue with such underhanded methods in the days to come.

As if sensing the turn of his thoughts, Cranch's smile faded, and he sat forward. "Susanna Smith is the right woman for you, Ben. Together the two of you will set out to conquer all the injustices in the world."

Ben met his friend's serious gaze. They both knew involv-ing any woman into their lives was risky, that should either of them be captured for their rebellious leanings, their families would surely suffer.

But Susanna had proven she was willing to face adversity. She wasn't afraid of doing what was right in the face of in-justice. Maybe she wasn't completely won over to the cause of liberty for the colonies, but she was moving in that direction. He'd seen the shifting tides within her.

Ben expelled a sigh. "I've already pushed Susanna away once in my eagerness for her. And I cannot risk it again. As much as my entire being longs for more, I must resist. I shall endeavor to remain friends, and friends only."

Susanna's body sagged with exhaustion. During the short time they visited with Mary and Mr. Cranch in Boston, Susanna slept overlong—to the point of embarrassment. The harrowing escapade outrunning Lieutenant Wolfe had surely taxed her beyond her capacities.

Ben insisted on leaving the following morning, and Mr. Cranch provided them the use of his sleigh. On one of his errands about town, Ben had heard rumors of a smallpox outbreak in Boston. And although he didn't know if the news was true, Ben was anxious to see Susanna safely home, declaring that after the influenza epidemic, he didn't want to chance any further exposure to illness.

As delighted as Susanna had been to see Mary again, she was anxious to travel home and ensure Dotty was safely in Hingham and that no harm had befallen any of her family on account of her actions.

The return trip to Weymouth with Ben was a quiet one, and she slept most of the ride there. As the sleigh crunched to a stop in front of the parsonage, Susanna tried to blink away the drowsiness that wouldn't let go of her, along with the headache that had plagued her for the last half of the trip.

She lifted her head from Ben's shoulder and stifled a shiver, even though her body wasn't cold. Ben had stopped several times to refill the warming box under her feet, and the pile of robes Mr. Cranch had sent along had more than adequately kept her comfortable.

In fact, she was overheated.

Ben jumped from the sleigh and lifted a hand to assist her down. She pushed the blankets aside and let the coolness of the air bathe her hot skin.

"Are you ready to face the firing squad?" He glanced at the

front window of the parsonage as if expecting her parents to storm outside with guns and swords.

Susanna's gaze swept over the house, yard, and barn. From all appearances the home hadn't suffered any more damage. Lieutenant Wolfe hadn't come to seek revenge. She could only pray he hadn't wrecked Mount Wollaston or hurt Grandmother Eve.

"Mother won't be pleased with me." If only she could take all the blame and save Ben from Mother's wrath.

"Remember, you've done nothing for which you should be ashamed." Ben's outstretched hand waited for hers. "You've protected an innocent life from the hands of a brutal murderer."

She placed her fingers into his, letting his strength soak through her skin. She looked into his eyes and allowed his clear honesty to infuse her with courage. No matter the consequences, no matter what happened, she'd done what was right. She couldn't let fear slip back in and make her second-guess herself this time.

"Thank you," she whispered. "I wouldn't have been able to save Dotty without your help."

He smiled. "That's what friends are for."

She tried to smile back, but her lips couldn't quite bend. Ben had certainly taken her request of friendship to heart over the past two days. In fact, she was almost disappointed with his ardency toward their friendship. He seemed determined to erect proper boundaries between them and not allow himself to cross them—not in the least.

And as confused as she'd been about their relationship, and as much as she'd wanted friendship with him, she had to admit, she longed for him to resume the affection he'd shown her previously.

"There you are, Miss Susie," Tom called to her from the direction of the barn. He hobbled out of the open door, limping slowly, dragging one leg and using a cane. His back was stooped and his shoulders bent, and he still wore a bandage around his head to cover the gash in his scalp.

"You're out of bed?" Susanna asked. "And you're getting around well?"

Tom's craggy face lit and he gave her a half smile, the muscles in one side of his face not working anymore. The lieutenant's beating may have killed half of Tom's body, but it couldn't quench his life. "Don't know if I'm getting around *well*, Miss Susie, but I'm managing."

Susanna stood, but a wave of dizziness nearly sent her back to the sleigh's curved bench. Only Ben's grip on her hand kept her from tumbling.

He helped her down from the sleigh. When her feet touched the ground, she swayed with another wave of dizziness.

A crease formed between Ben's brows. "You're not well."

She swallowed past the twinge of pain in her throat and shook her head. She wouldn't—couldn't—get sick now. "I'll manage better. Once I get inside."

Ben's eyes flickered with concern.

But she glanced away before he could suspect just how much the trip had taxed her. Instead she focused on Tom, shuffling across the soggy farmyard. A hazy sunshine tried to break through a scattering of gray clouds and had already begun to melt the snow, leaving muddy puddles. The light illuminated Tom, revealing all the abrasions and bruises that his hat couldn't hide.

Guilt wrenched her so painfully her knees wobbled. She'd done this to Tom. Her actions had surely battered him as much as the lieutenant's hard boots.

"I think you should still be abed," she said as he neared the horses.

"I couldn't sleep. Not when I've been worried about you, Miss Susie."

"No need to worry," she said. "I've only been visiting Mary in Boston."

Tom reached for the muzzle of one of the horses and stroked it with a soft murmur. But he looked at her with a raised brow, a look that told her he knew what she'd been doing and why, that she wouldn't be able to fool him.

Susanna swallowed past the growing ache in her throat. She wanted to ask him if he'd heard any news about Dotty or about Lieutenant Wolfe. She wanted to discover what her parents knew before she had to face them.

But the front door opened then. "Susanna, my dear, there you are." Her father stepped onto the porch.

Ben's hand against hers flexed, and he set his mouth into a grim line.

She pressed his hand, hoping she could reassure him that she was stronger this time, that she would stand by his side and face her parents together.

"We've been so worried about you, my dear." Wrinkles lined her father's forehead.

Susanna forced what she hoped was a cheerful smile. "Please don't worry, Father. We've only been to Boston to visit Mary and Mr. Cranch." She pushed aside the whisper of her conscience that accused her of telling a half-truth.

"And how are my dear daughter and her new husband faring? Well, I hope?"

"They are perfectly fine." She only wished she could say the same about herself.

She allowed Ben to lead her toward the house and prayed

her parents wouldn't ask too many questions. But her hopes were dashed the moment she stepped inside the house and Mother descended upon her.

"My gracious. Susanna Smith, you are a disgrace to this family," Mother said as she glided down the hallway, her face a mask of calm fury.

Susanna's legs trembled beneath the layers of her petticoats, and she slipped her hand into the crook of Ben's arm, trying to keep herself from sinking to the hallway floor.

Did Mother finally know the truth about Dotty?

Father held out his arm toward Mother. "Now, dear, let's not be hasty. Let's allow Susanna time to explain. I'm sure she has a good explanation."

"There's absolutely no acceptable explanation for running off to Boston with Benjamin Ross." In the dark shadows of the hallway, Mother's face was pale. "No explanation whatsoever."

"I take the blame," Ben started. "I had business in Boston—"

"It was my fault," Susanna cut in, her legs wobbling and beads of sweat forming on her forehead. "I take full responsibility. Ben wouldn't have gone if not for me."

But Mother had already spun to face Ben. "We told you to stay away from Susanna."

The muscles in Ben's jaw flexed.

"It's not his fault, Mother," Susanna said, desperation starting to rise in her. "I went to him."

Mother only took another step toward Ben as if she would slap his face. "And now you've tainted Susanna's reputation."

Susanna waited for her parents to say something about Lieutenant Wolfe and Dotty. But apparently Grandmother Eve had managed to find a way to cover up his visit to Mount Wollaston without revealing his true motivation.

"I'm sorry for putting Susanna in a compromising situation," Ben said.

The kitchen door opened and Phoebe slipped into the hallway, bringing the waft of broiled sturgeon and the sourness of fried cabbage and onions. The dark eyes searched Susanna before settling on her face.

"You ought to be ashamed of yourself." Mother spat the words at Ben.

His shoulders stiffened.

"We've done nothing wrong." Susanna fought back the pounding in her head, which seemed to grow louder with each passing minute.

"You were wrong to leave with this man." Mother turned upon her. "You disobeyed us. We trusted you into Elbridge's hands and expected you to stay with him at Grandmother's home. You shouldn't have gone to Boston with Mr. Ross, not without a chaperone."

Susanna could feel herself slipping under the censure. She didn't want to disappoint them.

"Mr. Ross," Mother continued, "ever since Susanna has met your acquaintance, you've been an extremely poor influence upon her."

Susanna wanted to shout that she'd once believed the same thing, and that of late she was learning much from him about courage and taking a stand for what was right, even when everyone else said it was wrong. But she couldn't muster the energy to voice her thoughts.

Ben held himself erect like an unbending nail, letting Mother hammer him, taking blow after blow. Even though he didn't say anything, Susanna could see his chest expanding, as if he were holding in the angry words he wanted to express.

"I demand you leave our house this instant." Mother

pointed at the door behind them. "And I must request that you refrain from coming again."

Ben didn't move.

From the shadows of the hallway, Phoebe's expression urged her to stay strong, that this was one of those times when Susanna could make a change, that it was within her grasp to bring about a better way of doing things.

Susanna's cloak suffocated her, hot and oppressive. She tossed back the hood and tugged at the strings to loosen it, her fingers trembling as much as her legs.

"I apologize, Mr. Ross," her father offered. "I'm sure you had no intention of tainting Susanna's reputation. But whatever the case, now the neighbors are gossiping about this untimely trip the two of you have taken alone. So I must agree with my dear wife that you abstain from seeing Susanna again."

"I understand, Reverend Smith," Ben said. "If there had been any way to avoid placing Susanna into such a compromising circumstance, I assure you I would have done my best to prevent it."

"We made our parameters quite clear during your last visit," Mother cut in.

Behind her parents' backs, Phoebe nodded at Susanna, her level gaze admonishing her to speak up. But Susanna's lips felt dry and hot, and her tongue seemed to stick to the roof of her mouth.

"You did indeed make your wishes clear," Ben said dryly. "But before I leave, I would like to hear what Susanna wants."

"She'll do as we say," Mother insisted.

Ben shifted so that Susanna had no choice but to meet his gaze. The blue of his eyes was as clear and guileless as Mill Cove on a summer day. "If after all that has happened, you want me to walk out of your house and never come back, I'll respect your wishes."

"Of course she does," Mother insisted.

Susanna refused to look at her mother and instead focused on Ben. His voice was soft and eased the thudding in her temples.

"But if you desire to continue with our understanding, then I will pledge you my undying friendship."

The sweetness of his words filled her. And suddenly she knew she couldn't deny him again. Never again.

He was right. She was a grown woman. And surely there was nothing wrong with being friends with him. If her parents really knew him, they would understand what a good man he was.

God's laws of love and mercy and kindness had to take precedence over the prejudicial and flawed laws of man—including her parents, who were well-meaning yet clearly in the wrong about Ben.

She took hold of Ben's hand and entwined her fingers with his. "I do desire," she whispered.

A gentle smile hovered over his lips, and sunshine flitted into his eyes.

The warm rays went straight to her heart, and she couldn't keep from smiling in return.

"Susanna Smith." Mother took a step back and her hand fluttered over her chest. "I'm utterly speechless."

"Ben is my friend." Susanna gripped Ben's hand tighter. "He's a God-fearing, compassionate, and considerate man."

Ben's smile rose, smoothing the lines in his face.

She had the sudden urge to graze the dark stubble that had formed along his jaw over his normally clean-shaven skin.

"Benjamin Ross is a troublemaker," Mother insisted.

"Ben's courageous, and he's destined for great things because of it," Susanna replied. If only she had half of Ben's courage. "I'm honored that he's willing to consider me his friend."

Mother opened her mouth to speak but then closed it, clearly unable to find a suitable response.

Down the hall, Phoebe nodded, pursed her lips together into the start of a smile, and gave Susanna the kind of look that told her this time she'd done the right thing.

Father cleared his throat. "I don't suppose there's any harm in allowing Susanna to maintain a friendship with Mr. Ross."

A flash of heat hit Susanna, sending a shimmer of pain through her head. It was followed by a tremor of chills that made her dizzy. She swayed and grabbed Ben to keep from falling.

"Alas, I think you *are* ill." Ben slipped his arm around her waist.

"I'm merely tired," Susanna said, but her knees gave way.

As if from a distance, Susanna could feel Ben scoop her up. Her head lolled back, and she couldn't keep her eyes open.

Ben's soothing murmurs blocked out the accusations her mother was leveling at Ben, blaming him again for Susanna's condition.

The odor of onions and the feel of Phoebe's wiry, capable body pushing against hers permeated Susanna's daze. Phoebe's chafed hands pressed against her cheeks and then her forehead.

"What's wrong with her, Phoebe?" Worry echoed in every fiber of Ben's tone and body.

"Influenza," Phoebe said gravely. "She's got the influenza."

Chapter
24

Susanna thrashed in her bed, the fever raging hot then cold. Her lungs constricted, making each breath a struggle. Once when Phoebe and Mother didn't realize she was awake, she overheard their frightened whispers, that the number of people who'd died of the influenza in Braintree had risen to seventeen.

"I'll set with Miss Susie awhile," she heard Tom say to Phoebe at one point. "You go on now and get some sleep before you get sick."

Susanna pried her eyes open to find Phoebe hovering above her, wringing a cloth out in a basin on the bedside table.

"There's a good girl." Phoebe laid the cool rag across her forehead. "Let's get you some more of my boneset tonic."

The mist from a steaming pot next to the bed wafted near Susanna's face, bringing with it the odor of camphor oil in hot water. Susanna dragged in a wheezing breath, along with the sting of onions that came from the warm poultice Phoebe had pressed against her chest.

Susanna shifted her head to find Tom seated in a chair on

one side of the four-poster bed, where the thick bed curtains had been pulled back. His eyes filled with compassion. And tears. "You stay with us now, Miss Susie."

She nodded and shifted her hand, stretching her fingers to him. He laid his gnarled fingers against hers. "I'm rather stubborn to die," she whispered and tried to smile. But her lips were dry and cracked.

Phoebe lifted a spoon to Susanna's lips and forced a bitter liquid into her mouth. "There you go."

"Where's Ben?" she asked after another painful swallow. The angle of the light in the room signaled morning.

She'd survived the first horrible night of the illness. That was something for which to be grateful.

"He didn't want to go. But your mama kicked him out yesterday." Phoebe bounded to the hearth fire and removed another pot of steaming water she had dangling from a grid-iron that belonged to the kitchen.

Susanna fought a wave of dizziness and frustration.

"But don't you worry none." Phoebe returned to the bedside with the steaming pot, the scent of sassafras and rum drifting under the canopy of her bed. "It's gonna take a pack of wolves to keep that man from coming back to see you."

Susanna could only pray Phoebe was right, that Mother's disdain hadn't driven him away.

Phoebe draped a sheet over the steaming pot and formed a tent with it above Susanna's face. "Breathe in the hot air. It's gonna help you get better."

She tried to inhale, but each lungful was tight. The steam bathed her already hot face, plastering her loose hair to her cheeks and forehead. Underneath the coverlets, her nightdress stuck to her skin and tangled in her legs.

"You did the right thing standing up for Mr. Ross." Phoebe hovered above her, holding the sheet. "You made me proud."

Susanna couldn't imagine any other man who would have done what Ben had—for Dotty and for her.

"I know your mama's a godly lady," Phoebe continued, lowering her voice. "And she's been a good missus—taken care of me and Tom better than a lot of owners."

Susanna wanted to say there was so much more Mother could be doing for them, that they deserved to be free of bondage and treated with dignity. But she knew neither Tom nor Phoebe were ready to make that fight yet. Maybe Phoebe would be someday. But Susanna couldn't foresee a day when Tom would ever be interested in freedom.

She supposed not everyone would be ready to take a stand against oppression, that perhaps there were those who were content to live in safety rather than liberty. But could she sit back and do nothing, as she'd done for so long, or was she waking up to the need to fight for justice and freedom the way Ben had talked about?

"Even if your mama is a godly woman"—Phoebe fanned the steam toward Susanna's face—"she was wrong to stick her nose up at Mr. Ross."

Susanna nodded but then coughed. The spasm wracked her body and left her listless.

Tom held her hand tightly. "If my old body can make it, then you ain't gonna have any trouble getting better."

She gave him a weak smile.

"I been praying about what you been up to," he said, gazing tenderly upon her face. "And ever since that lieutenant came—"

"I'm sorry," she croaked, wanting to let him know again how much she regretted his being hurt on account of her.

He shook his head. "Now, hear me out, Miss Susie. I still don't know what to think about all you been doing. But I do know the good Lord's been trying to get through my thick skull that I been letting fear take hold of me more than I should."

"Amen," Phoebe said.

"The Word says, 'For God hath not given us the spirit of fear; but of power, and of love, and of a sound mind.'" Tom's bent fingers gripped Susanna's with the urgency of his words. "The good Lord don't want us to be walking around in fear. He wants us to have courage, love our enemies, and use our minds."

Susanna squeezed his hand as best she could. "It's hard not to be afraid."

"No matter what happens in the days to come," he said with uncharacteristic intensity, "you can't let fear take hold and stop you from doing the right thing."

His eyes held hers as if he could see into her future and the many hardships she was yet to face.

She'd hoped the worst was over. But did God have more in store for her than she'd imagined possible?

"I believe you got what it takes, Miss Susie. The good Lord gave you plenty of love, courage, and a bright mind. And if He gave it to you, He's gonna expect you to use it."

At a shout from somewhere in the house, Phoebe straightened and frowned.

The front door banged, reverberating against the walls of the house. Heavy stomping and more shouts followed.

"Now, why they making such a racket?" Phoebe pursed her lips and started toward the door. "They know Miss Susie has got the influenza and needs quiet."

Before Phoebe could reach the door, it slammed open, revealing the bright red of a king's soldier.

Susanna gave a hoarse gasp.

Lieutenant Wolfe barged into the room. His shiny black boots slapped against the hardwood floor. His saber swung at his side. And his black hat with its silver cockade glinted in the sunlight.

"I demand that you leave this instant." Mother bustled into the room after the lieutenant, breathless, likely having chased him through the house. "My daughter is ill and cannot receive visitors."

The lieutenant stopped abruptly at the foot of the bed. His eyes contained a triumphant glimmer that only served to unleash fear in Susanna's veins.

"You must go," Mother said, following the lieutenant. "And if you wish to return, then you must do so when my husband is home later."

Lieutenant Wolfe didn't smile. Susanna didn't think him capable of a real smile. But his mouth had twisted into a semblance of a grin.

Susanna's throat pinched, making her wheeze. Something had gone wrong. Terribly wrong.

"Lieutenant." Mother grew more insistent. "You are not welcome here. I must demand that you leave our house at once."

Irritation flashed through the lieutenant's eyes. His gloved hand touched the hilt of his saber.

Susanna wanted to call out to Mother to be still, to remind her of all the lieutenant had done to their home the last time he'd visited. But before she could get her voice to work, the lieutenant raised his hand as though he would strike Mother.

"No," Susanna croaked, trying to sit up, horror pressing into her heart and giving her a surge of energy. "Please don't hurt anyone! I'll do whatever you want. Just don't harm them."

The lieutenant paused as though considering her declaration. And then with a slight smile he lowered his hand.

Phoebe bolted to Mother and ushered her a safe distance from the lieutenant.

"Mrs. Smith, I will not be leaving," the lieutenant said, fixing his eyes upon Susanna again. "At least not without your daughter."

Tom's chair scraped against the floor, and he fumbled to push himself upright. He positioned himself next to Susanna like a bent sentinel, ready to do battle for her.

But the lieutenant didn't give Tom even the barest of glances. If he recognized the man he'd nearly battered to death during his last visit, he gave no indication.

"I'm arresting you, Miss Smith," said Lieutenant Wolfe in his clipped tone, "for unlawfully harboring a runaway indentured servant belonging to Merchant Lovelace of Boston."

Mother gasped. "That's impossible." But even as the words left Mother's lips, Susanna could see understanding dawning in her eyes. She was putting together all the events and clues of the past several months.

Finally, Mother knew the truth. She wouldn't be able to hide her involvement with Dotty any longer.

What must Mother think of her now? Now that she'd defied her wishes regarding Ben *and* hidden her involvement with Dotty?

She didn't dare look at Mother and observe her censure.

And now what could she do? How would she resist the lieutenant? Everything in his cocky stance said he wouldn't hesitate to drag her from bed, haul her to Boston, and throw her in jail. And if he did, she'd surely die, given her state of illness.

She had to do something to defend herself. "You cannot arrest me," she said, her voice raspy. "You have no proof—"

"I have every piece of evidence I need." The lieutenant nodded at the window.

The humidity and steam in the room had frozen against the cold glass, forming a layer of frost. Even so, the sunshine streamed into the room, lighting it and bringing a warmth that now felt stifling.

"My assistant is outside guarding our prisoner."

Susanna's heart stopped beating.

"Early this morning we found the young woman hiding in the woods down by Hingham," the lieutenant said triumphantly. "We've captured her, and now we've come to arrest you for aiding her these past weeks."

Mother's face paled, and she had to grasp Phoebe to keep from crumpling to the floor.

Susanna wished she could get out of bed and peer out the window to discover for herself if the lieutenant's words were truthful. Had he captured Dotty? Surely not. Surely Dotty had found refuge in the hands of Ben's friend in Hingham.

Tom hobbled to the window. He scratched at the frost, clearing a circle that allowed him to see outside. He squinted down at the front yard for a long moment. Then he turned away from the window, his shoulders drooping.

His slight nod confirmed that the lieutenant did indeed have Dotty.

Susanna's mind scrambled to find some way of escape.

Lieutenant Wolfe took a step around the bed. He stared altogether too boldly upon the lace of her night shift showing above her coverlet.

"You won't be able to prove anything," she said. "And once Mr. Ross learns you've come into our house again, he'll file charges."

The lieutenant's lips only rose higher. He didn't say anything. Instead he brought his hand from behind his back and dangled something in front of her.

Her boots. The pair she'd given to Dotty that day in the fall when she'd first met her.

"I see you recognize these, Miss Smith." The lieutenant's eyes gleamed. "The Weymouth cordwainer confirmed that he had indeed fashioned these buskins for you."

Susanna wanted to deny the boots were hers, but her mother spoke too quickly. "Yes, those are indeed Susanna's. Where, may I ask, did you locate them?"

"Why don't you ask your daughter?"

Mother frowned. "I thought you gave them to a poor beggar woman. . . ." Mother paused and her eyes widened.

The lieutenant nodded. "Of course Dotty wouldn't admit to your involvement, Miss Smith. But don't worry. By the time I'm finished with her, she'll confess everything."

"No!" Susanna cried, haunted by the memory of the young woman murdered on the beach, the bruises, the agony etched on her face, the shredded skin on her feet. "Please spare her your cruelty. I beg you."

Wolfe drew nearer, his boots scuffing against the floor. "You may as well come with me willingly, Miss Smith. It will be more pleasant that way. And perhaps you'll save Dotty undue punishment."

Helplessness washed over Susanna. What choice did she have? When she'd first gotten involved with Dotty, she'd known the risks and the danger. And while she'd hoped for a happy ending to Dotty's predicament, she'd been well aware that her efforts could end in disaster.

If she didn't go with the lieutenant, she'd only cause more problems for Dotty and possibly her family.

The lieutenant held out a gloved hand. "Come, Miss Smith.

I'm sure you don't want to keep Dotty waiting—now that she has no shoes."

The clamor raging in her body smoothed into an eerie calm. Her fate was sealed. Why fight it?

"Very well, Lieutenant." She tried to push herself up but only got as far as her elbows before collapsing against the feather mattress.

"You can't take Miss Susie!" Phoebe darted away from Mother and flung herself across the room toward Susanna. "She ain't done nothing wrong."

The lieutenant grabbed his saber. It rasped against the scabbard as he unsheathed it.

"Stop!" Susanna croaked.

After what the lieutenant had done to Tom, Susanna knew he would have no qualms about plunging his saber into Phoebe's heart.

Yet from the firm set of Phoebe's lips, Susanna knew the dear woman didn't care what the lieutenant would do to her, that she was determined to keep Susanna in bed.

The lieutenant raised his saber and pointed it in readiness.

With a cry Tom moved away from the window and knocked into Phoebe, pushing her out of the lieutenant's reach.

Phoebe fell against the edge of the bed near Susanna.

Tom stumbled to his knees in front of Lieutenant Wolfe, his cane clattering to the floor. But he made no effort to retrieve it or move out of harm's way. Instead he bent his head in submission. "If you're gonna blame anybody for sheltering that runaway, then you'd best blame me."

The lieutenant's fingers tightened around his saber, and his mouth pinched into a scowl.

"Tom, no!" Susanna called hoarsely.

The slave didn't lift his head.

Mother stepped forward, her face hard. "You know if you lay one hand on my daughter, you'll have every colonist from here to Boston up and to arms."

Lieutenant Wolfe froze. His saber hung in midair.

"I am of Quincy blood, and my relatives are important and powerful members of this community. You have abused us once. We won't tolerate it again."

"Your daughter has broken the law, Mrs. Smith. Surely your family's reputation does not put you above judgment for unlawful deeds."

Mother lifted her chin. "If you must make someone pay for the crime of sheltering the runaway, then you may take the slave. By his own admission, he is to blame."

"No, Mother." Susanna struggled to sit up. She couldn't let Tom take her place.

But Phoebe pushed her back down and shook her head in warning.

A frown creased the lieutenant's forehead, and he glared in disdain at Tom's bent head.

"I won't let you do this." Susanna pushed against Phoebe's hold, knowing she had to get up and go now. She was completely to blame for helping Dotty, and she wouldn't let Tom suffer again—not on her behalf.

But Phoebe's well-muscled arms held her down with little effort.

The lieutenant pointed the tip of the saber against Tom's shoulder.

Tom winced but didn't back away.

Susanna cried out, "Don't hurt him! Please take me instead. Please." She strained against Phoebe.

"Silence, Susanna," Mother said.

The lieutenant stared at Susanna for a long intense moment.

And Susanna could only pray he wouldn't consider Mother's plea. Finally with a muttered curse he sheathed his saber. "Very well, Mrs. Smith. I will take the slave for now. But once I have gained the runaway's confession, I shall indeed arrest whomever is truly responsible. And no one in this community will be able to stand in the way of justice."

With a final glare he grabbed Tom's coat and hauled him to his feet with cruel fierceness.

"No-o-o!" Susanna screamed as she tried to claw her way free of Phoebe.

But in the confusion of the moment, somehow her mother had appeared at her side and joined Phoebe in holding her back. Susanna lashed against the hands pinning her down, knowing she was helpless to do anything but watch as Lieutenant Wolfe dragged Tom away. She couldn't stop struggling regardless.

Tom stumbled after the lieutenant but glanced at her over his shoulder. "No fear, Miss Susie. No fear."

Tears wet her cheeks, and sobs burned in her chest.

The lieutenant yanked Tom through the door, but without his cane, the old slave fell to his knees. With another curse, Lieutenant Wolfe kicked Tom in his ribs with a crack that vibrated through Susanna and sent bile to her throat.

Tom groaned.

A sob burst from her lips. "Please . . . take me . . ." She lurched against the hands holding her down.

"No, child." Phoebe's cool fingers brushed against Susanna's tangled hair and the tears streaking her cheeks.

"Please . . ." Susanna cried. A wave of blackness enveloped her.

"I shall not let you go, Susanna," Mother said.

Susanna wanted to be angry at her mother for sacrificing Tom, wanted to lash out at her and call her a coward.

But in the struggle to restrain Susanna, pieces of Mother's hair had come loose from the tidy knot she normally wore. Through the dangling hair, Mother's eyes swam with confusion, and something Susanna hadn't seen often. Pride.

They were in the midst of the direst of circumstances, and Mother was proud of her?

Another wave of dizziness attacked Susanna, forcing her to close her eyes even though she wanted to search Mother's face again to see if the pride was real or if she'd only imagined it.

Susanna had expected condemnation, anger, and censure now that Mother knew about Dotty. Never in her wildest imaginings had she believed Mother would be proud of her.

"Please . . ." Susanna gasped, fighting the blackness of oblivion. "Please find Ben. He'll know what to do."

Mother squeezed her hands.

And then Susanna let go. She fell into the hole of darkness, letting it swallow her and take her away from all the horror that had swept down upon her.

Chapter
25

Bitter pain gripped Susanna's heart and tore it relentlessly. Not even the world of sleep could shelter her from the heartache. She wasn't sure how long she hovered in and out of consciousness. When she finally started to awaken, she wanted to cry out at the intensity of the injustice that had befallen them.

But she couldn't move. The stiffness in every muscle weighted her down as though someone had tied her to the bedstead. Her eyelids felt heavy and her tongue parched. And even though the fever that had ravaged her body was finally gone, she was still overly warm and sticky with sweat.

She tried to shift her exhausted body and realized someone was holding her hand. Strong fingers intertwined with hers. The rough calluses that brushed against her skin were familiar and welcoming.

She pried open her eyes. There, sitting in a chair next to her bed, was Ben. His head was bent, his hat and wig had been discarded, and the strands of his hair were sticking up in places, the sign he'd rammed his fingers through his hair one too many times.

Relief mingled with the battle raging in her heart. He was there. Finally.

Even if he couldn't make everything better for Tom and Dotty, even if the world collapsed around her, at least he would be by her side. They would be together. And that's what she needed more than anything.

If only she could bury her face against his chest, breathe deeply of him, and block out the nightmare of all that had happened.

With a sigh, he lifted her hand and pressed his lips to the sensitive skin of her wrist. His warm breath bathed her pulse.

He'd obviously not realized she'd awoken. And she held herself absolutely still, relishing his touch and not wanting it to end.

The unshaven stubble on his chin brushed against her inner arm. What would it be like to have him make a trail of kisses all the way from her wrist to her lips?

A flush stole over her at her brazen thoughts. He'd only kissed her once, in Arnold Tavern when they'd tried to fool Lieutenant Wolfe into thinking they were lovers.

Surely another kiss wouldn't harm their friendship.

As if sensing a change in her restfulness, he glanced up. In the dim light of the candle upon the bedside table, his gaze met hers and widened with surprise—nay, embarrassment.

"Susanna." He sat back and put a proper distance between them. He started to pull his fingers from hers, but she grasped him.

"You came back."

"Nothing could keep me away." Something sparked in his eyes—an intensity that stirred her insides.

A quick sweep of the shadowed room revealed they were

alone. She didn't stop to analyze who had let Ben in the house and why he was in her bedchamber without a chaperone.

She didn't pull her hand away from him as she knew she ought. Instead she met his gaze again boldly and couldn't keep herself from thinking about the kiss he'd laid on her wrist and how she wanted more.

As if she'd spoken the words aloud, he studied her lips. He wanted to kiss her too. She could see it in the hot blue flames that flickered to life in his eyes.

With one hand still holding hers, he touched the strands of hair on her cheek, brushing them back.

The gentleness of the stroke sent a sweet ache through her. She wanted to raise herself up and offer him her lips. But he hesitated. His jaw flexed and he closed his eyes. For a moment a battle waged across his features.

She started to reach for him, but a cough scratched her throat and then a spasm of coughing shook her body. When she finished, she was breathless and her lungs were tight.

He sat back and peered down at her, his brow wrinkled. "You're still ill. Just close your eyes and rest."

She couldn't rest now. Not now that he was here. "I'm glad you came." She wasn't ready to end this moment of intimacy.

But he'd wiped his face clear of his desire and had donned a brotherly concern. He was only being chivalrous and trying to preserve her reputation. And he was attempting to remain a friend—just as she'd asked.

Therefore she should be grateful to him. Why then was she frustrated?

"Your mother sent the hired stableboy to retrieve me."

"She did?"

"I was on my way here anyway."

Susanna glanced to the open doorway. From the hallway

and stairwell, the rich aroma of rabbit stew had wafted into the room. The faint echo of clinking plates and tableware signaled the evening repast was under way.

"I'm bewildered that Mother's allowing you to sit with me."

"She invited me in and didn't resist when I told her I wanted to stay by your side."

Why had her mother sent for Ben now after the many weeks of spurning him?

Of course Susanna had told Mother that Ben could help them, but she'd expected Mother to send for Elbridge instead. Her mind flashed to the picture of Mother's face hovering over hers before she'd lost consciousness. Had she really seen pride in Mother's eyes or had it merely been the imaginings of her feverish mind?

"I didn't tell your mother I would have barged in anyway, whether she liked it or not." Ben's fingers caressed hers. "I don't care what she thinks about me. I'm determined to keep you safe."

A blade twisted in her heart at the thought that Tom was somewhere suffering under the hands of Lieutenant Wolfe, that he was imprisoned and awaiting a horrifying fate . . . all because of her. What if the lieutenant decided to hang Tom? Or brand him?

She shuddered at the remembrance of Hermit Crab Joe's screams when the blacksmith had hammered off part of his ear. She could smell the stench again of Joe's flesh when the smithy had pressed the red-hot iron against his cheek and hand.

"Can you help free Tom?" She grasped Ben's hand and tried to sit up. "Please. We've got to do something." The same desperation she'd felt earlier in the day began to seep into her body.

Ben's expression turned grave. "I'm not sure there's much we can do. He's already confessed to the crime."

"But it's not his fault. Sheltering Dotty was my idea. I most certainly won't let him suffer the consequences of my choices."

"I understand," Ben said softly. "I don't want Tom to suffer either. But I'm grateful to him for sacrificing himself for you."

"I can't let him do this."

"I would have done the same thing."

She shook her head. "I'm handing myself over to Lieutenant Wolfe as soon as I can climb out of this bed."

"I won't let you."

"You can't stop me." Frustration pushed up her throat and brought tears to her eyes. She'd let fear hold her back often enough. She wouldn't let it this time. "I need to do the right thing, Ben. I cannot let Tom take the blame for me. Please understand."

"I don't know Tom well, but I know that if he cares about you half as much as I do, he won't allow you to go anywhere with the lieutenant. I know I'd rather die for you than give you over to that man."

She captured his words and tucked them away into a safe place in her heart so she could pull them out and mull them over later. For now, she needed to find a way to save Tom—and Dotty.

"Then what can we do?" she asked.

"Wolfe has arranged for a trial in two days at the meeting-house in Weymouth. I'll have Dotty share her story about the lieutenant capturing her, taking her shoes, and then chasing her. Even though we may not have much with which to accuse the lieutenant, at least we can expose his connection with the other murders and attempt to show why it was necessary to shelter Dotty."

"But that won't save Tom, will it?"

Ben didn't answer.

She knew people wouldn't care what happened to Tom. He was only a slave. And if they needed to blame someone, he'd prove a suitable candidate for their needs. And as for Dotty, would they take her seriously once they discovered she was pregnant? She shuddered at the possibility that if poor Dotty testified, they might only strap her to the ducking stool and drown her in the nearly frozen waters of Mill Cove.

A loud rapping on the front door of the house rattled the walls.

Ben sat up straight.

No one would be out visiting after eventide unless it was urgent.

The murmuring in the downstairs was followed by the sharp tapping of footsteps on the stairway. Was the lieutenant coming to get her after all?

Ben's grip on her hand tightened.

When a Redcoat halted in the doorway of the bedroom, Ben shoved his chair aside and stood.

Susanna tried to sit up, but her body was still too weak, and she could only fall back against the sagging mattress. Even if she wanted to go in Tom's stead, how would she make it out of the house?

The soldier ducked into the room and swept off his cocked hat, revealing a pale, freckled face.

"Sergeant Frazel!" Susanna croaked. "What tidings do you bear? Hopefully good . . ."

The young redheaded soldier shook his head, and his face creased with apology. "I have a message for Mr. Ross from Lieutenant Wolfe."

Her father and mother stood behind Sergeant Frazel, their

faces drawn. Her brother, William, hovered nearby. After all that had happened, Susanna didn't blame them for being afraid.

Sergeant Frazel took a step into the room, glanced at her in the bed, and then stopped. His face flamed a red almost as bright as his hair. "Miss Smith. Mr. Ross. I beg your pardon for intruding. You must know it was not my intention to recapture the young woman."

Ben let go of Susanna's hand and approached the sergeant. "And yet you helped track her down anyway?"

The sergeant hung his head. "I did my best to divert the lieutenant, but he has become a desperate man these past weeks. The general has given Lieutenant Wolfe until Christmas Day to find solid evidence of the smuggling operations. And if he doesn't return with some proof of the smuggling, then the general is planning to send the lieutenant back to England in disgrace."

Ben nodded, his expression suddenly wary. "And what does that have to do with recapturing a poor, helpless runaway?"

"She's the bait." Sergeant Frazel handed Ben a folded sheet and took a step back. "The lieutenant intends to use her to lure in a culprit."

Ben unfolded the letter and read it silently.

Her father stepped into the room and watched Ben. Mother slid around Father and Sergeant Frazel and made her way soundlessly across the room to stand by the bedstead. Susanna was afraid to meet Mother's gaze, afraid of what she might see there this time.

Ben refolded the letter and let out a sigh.

"They cannot take Susanna," Mother said, her voice ringing with her usual determination.

Ben hung his head, and his shoulders slumped.

Susanna's heartbeat slowed. "Ben?"

"I won't let them take Susanna," Mother said again, this time straightening her back with a haughtiness that Susanna realized was intended to frighten Sergeant Frazel.

"Don't worry, Mrs. Smith." Ben finally glanced up, revealing the agony catapulting through him. "I won't let Susanna come to any harm. I promise it upon my life."

"Thank you, Mr. Ross." Mother's fingers trembled, belying her outward calm.

Ben nodded. "If you would all excuse us for a moment, I think I should speak with Susanna. Alone."

Mother shook her head. "While I can admire Susanna's efforts to help an abused young woman, I cannot abide any further deception."

"I'm sorry, Mother," Susanna whispered. "I should have told you about Dotty—"

"Yes, you should have," Mother said with a gentler tone. "But that's in the past. Now we must move forward together."

Once again, the condemnation she'd expected in her mother's eyes was absent. In its place was a compassionate understanding that filled Susanna with a sense of wonder.

"Come, my dear." Father held a hand toward Mother. "Let's allow Mr. Ross a moment of privacy to discuss matters with Susanna."

Susanna was sure Mother would protest, but she hesitated for only an instant before following Father and Sergeant Frazel from the room.

"What is it?" Susanna asked once she was alone with Ben.

He lowered himself into the chair next to the bed. Then he rested his elbows on his knees and dropped his face into his hands with a groan.

Susanna lifted her hand to his bent head. She hesitated, her fingers grazing his hair.

Her heart yearned for him. Why deny what she was feeling any longer? She loved him. Deeply . . .

The truth brought a rush of thick emotion into her throat. God help her. She couldn't love him now. Not when her entire world was tumbling upside down.

She let her fingers slide down into the thick waves of his hair and sucked in a breath at the silkiness against her fingers.

But how could she stop loving him? Not when everything within her was alive with the knowledge that he meant more to her than anyone or anything else. She plunged her fingers deeper.

He gave a sudden pained groan, then gripped her hand and dragged it away from his hair. To her surprise, he brought her hand to his mouth. With his head still bent, he pressed his lips against her palm. His breath was hot and his kiss urgent.

She wanted to drag him forward and move his kiss to her lips. But with another tortured groan he sat up and pushed away from the bed, letting her hand fall to her side.

"He wants me to take the blame for Dotty and admit to my involvement in the smuggling."

"No."

His expression was wild and tortured. "I have to do it, Susanna."

She was panic-stricken. "Ben, I won't let you make that kind of sacrifice."

"I have to."

"No!" she cried. "We can't give in to the lieutenant's demands. If we do, then we've let him win." She forced herself upward, desperation giving her new energy. The coverlets fell away, and she struggled to untangle her feet from her nightdress. "I'll go. This is all my doing and I'll take the responsibility."

"I won't let you go," Ben said with a fierceness that would have scared her had she not been so distraught.

"And I won't let you go either." Beads of sweat formed on her forehead, and she could feel a wave of dizziness crashing over her the more she moved. But she didn't care.

If he thought just because she was a woman that he could coerce her into something, then he hadn't learned yet how strong she could be.

"Think about all the people who are involved in the smuggling," she said. "Think about all the lives you'll put in jeopardy if you turn yourself in. Lieutenant Wolfe won't stop with you. He'll find a way to make you reveal all the names of everyone else involved in the treasonous activities. And when he's done torturing you and sends you to England for trial, what will stop him from going after Dotty anyway? Or me?"

Ben didn't say anything.

A cough rose in her chest and for a long moment it wracked her body, leaving her unable to breathe except in wheezing bursts.

Phoebe came into the room. She'd likely been hovering in the hallway all along. "Time for you to go, Mr. Ross. Your visit is wearing out Miss Susie."

"You can find a different way to help save Dotty and Tom," Susanna said. "You can still put Dotty on the stand and have her testify like you planned. We can try to prove the lieutenant is guilty of the murders."

"I can't prove anything. I'll only be able to arouse suspicion, and that's not going to be enough." His face lacked as much conviction as his voice. "Besides, it's always risky accusing an officer."

Phoebe pushed Susanna back down on the bed and tugged her covers back up. "Go on, Mr. Ross. We can't be making Miss Susie any sicker now, can we?"

At that, Ben jumped to his feet.

Before he could move away, Susanna grabbed his hand. "Please. Promise me you won't give in to Lieutenant Wolfe's demands."

Ben tried to back up, but she clung to him.

"Please."

He hesitated, and she had the feeling there was something in the letter he wasn't revealing to her.

Phoebe poured a spoonful of boneset tonic and shoved the bitter medicine at Susanna's lips. "Be a good girl and swallow this."

Susanna turned her head away from Phoebe. "I won't do anything until Ben promises he won't turn himself in to Lieutenant Wolfe."

Ben's jaw flexed. He stood there motionless in silent contemplation. Then he finally nodded. "I promise I won't do anything until the trial. As long as you promise to stay in bed and let Phoebe take good care of you."

"Very well," she whispered. "I promise to stay in bed." *At least until the trial.* But she wasn't planning on telling him that.

He nodded at their truce.

Even so, there was something about his expression that warned her he hadn't given in, that he was just as determined to do the right thing as she was—no matter the personal cost.

Somehow she had to find a way to turn herself in to the lieutenant before he did.

Ben followed Sergeant Frazel up the plank steps of Wayside Tavern, the inn where the lieutenant had demanded quartering during his stay in Weymouth. After the ride from the parsonage, Ben's fingers and limbs were as numb as his heart.

He had promised Susanna that he wouldn't do anything until the trial. But that didn't mean he couldn't talk with the lieutenant.

Sergeant Frazel put a hand to the door, then turned to Ben, his kind eyes clouded. "I'm sorry, Mr. Ross."

"It's not your fault." He'd already assured the young man a dozen times. "You did the best you could."

"Maybe there was more I could have done."

The laughter from within the tavern sifted out in the cold December night. Overhead, the sky was clear and every star shone with perfect brilliance in stark contrast to the tempest brewing within him.

"I'm going to give the lieutenant exactly what he wants," Ben said. "But first I need the guarantee he won't hurt Dotty or Susanna anymore."

"I'll make sure he leaves Dotty alone," the sergeant reassured him. "I've been guarding her myself."

Ben nodded his gratitude before the soldier pushed open the door of the tavern, letting the boisterous voices and the heavy scent of tobacco fall over them. Sergeant Frazel wound through the crowded room, with Ben lagging behind.

The tavern was frequented mostly by miscreants who preferred to stir up trouble rather than work hard. Immersed in their cards and rum, they hardly gave Ben a second glance.

"This den of thieves is a fitting place for you to stay, Lieutenant," Ben said as he stopped beside the corner table where Lieutenant Wolfe sat alone smoking his pipe.

The lieutenant dismissed Sergeant Frazel with a wave of

his hand before glancing up at Ben. "I thought I might see you here tonight, Mr. Ross."

"Indeed, Lieutenant." He could feel the noose around his neck growing ever tighter. "It would appear that you have gambled and won."

"I'm very glad to hear of your willingness to cooperate finally. I was hoping once you read my letter you'd be more agreeable to assisting me in my investigation."

The letter burned against Ben's waistcoat into his chest. Of course he hadn't allowed any of the Smiths to read the message. He didn't want them to see the true nature of Lieutenant Wolfe's demand—that he hand himself over in place of arresting and hanging Susanna.

He hadn't wanted to scare the Smiths any further. Mrs. Smith had explained how her threats to the lieutenant earlier in the day had deterred him from arresting Susanna and that he'd taken Tom instead. Ben didn't have the heart to tell her that none of her pompous threats would keep the lieutenant from getting what he wanted.

If the officer decided to arrest Susanna, there would be nothing he or any other man could do to prevent it. The lieutenant was within his legal bounds to implicate Susanna after her involvement in breaking the law to help a runaway indentured servant.

And the lieutenant wasn't about to be satisfied with letting a mere slave take the blame in Susanna's stead. No, the lieutenant had laid out in the letter the only possible terms he would accept in place of arresting Susanna. He wanted Ben and Ben alone.

"I will stand up at the trial and take the entire burden of blame upon my shoulders for the indentured servant."

The lieutenant narrowed his eyes. "And . . ."

"And I'll become your scapegoat for the smuggling operations."

"Excellent—"

"Under two conditions."

The lieutenant took a puff of his pipe and spoke with it clenched in his teeth. "You have no leverage for bargaining, Mr. Ross."

"I know you murdered at least two young women found along the Braintree coast, Lieutenant. And although I may not have the means to prove it, I can certainly cast suspicion upon you that will reach the ears of your superiors."

The dim lighting of the tavern shadowed the lieutenant's face, hiding his reaction to Ben's words. He was silent, taking several more puffs on his pipe before extracting it from his mouth. "What are your conditions, Mr. Ross?"

"Leave Susanna Smith alone. Drop all charges. And never come near her again."

"As long as you carry forth your end of the bargain, I'll have no need for Miss Smith, shall I?"

Ben didn't trust the lieutenant. As Susanna had said earlier, what was to stop him from turning upon Susanna again once he had Ben in his custody?

"You must give me your word as a gentleman and an officer," Ben demanded. "And you must also release Dotty and the Smith slave. Absolve them of their guilt and let them both go free."

"You can't possibly expect me to let Dotty go free. She has a contract to fulfill."

"Convince the judge to release her into the care of the Smiths with the option that they may buy the rest of her indenture from Merchant Lovelace."

The lieutenant was silent. The raucous laughter behind

them pounded against Ben. How dare anyone laugh when lives were at stake.

"Bring Dotty to the trial," Ben persisted. "Hand her over to the Smiths along with the slave. Then you may take me in chains to Boston."

The lieutenant sat forward, his expression deadly. "I agree to your stipulations, Mr. Ross. But if you fail me in any way— any way at all—I won't hesitate to go after Susanna Smith. And if I go after her, you won't like what I'll do to her."

Ben swallowed the revulsion that threatened to rise in his throat. "Rest assured, Lieutenant. I won't fail you."

Chapter
26

Ben perched on the edge of the front box pew of Weymouth's North Parish Church. The building was unheated except for the warming boxes that members of the community brought with them. Everyone who'd assembled for the trial wore layers of clothing for extra warmth just as they did for worship services.

With less than a week until Christmas, a winter chill permeated the plain boxlike meetinghouse.

Nevertheless, Ben loosened his cravat, his body already overheated. It wouldn't be long now until he lost all sense of comfort. Once he was dragged off in chains to Boston, the lieutenant would dump him in a frigid, dank prison. He'd likely never feel warmth again.

But he wouldn't hand himself over yet, not until Tom and Dotty were brought to the trial. He wouldn't do anything until he made sure Lieutenant Wolfe kept his word.

From what Ben had heard, the lieutenant had locked the prisoners into a makeshift jail in two rooms at the Wayside Tavern. Over the past two days, Ben had made himself nearly sick with worry as he'd plotted the various options available to them. He'd even considered how he might break Dotty and Tom free of their prisons.

After all the deliberating, Ben had come to the conclusion that the best plan for everyone was that he do what the lieutenant had requested and take the blame for both Dotty and the smuggling. In fact, as far as he could tell, there was no other way to keep Susanna safe.

Ben glanced sideways to the opposite front pew where Lieutenant Wolfe made a dashing figure in his military uniform, complete with sashes and ribbons and silver buttons. The lieutenant's lips curled into a satisfied smile. Somehow he'd guessed the intensity of Ben's ardor for Susanna and realized he'd do absolutely anything for her.

If the lieutenant needed to return to Boston with a criminal, it might as well be him. Ben was strong enough to resist betraying the others. He didn't have a wife and children that he'd leave behind. He was the perfect candidate to take the blame for the smuggling.

He would give up all hope of improving his reputation. He would become reviled, detested, and possibly condemned to die. But at least he would end his days with integrity and honor before God.

A gust of wind rattled the large windowpanes as if it protested the gathering. From the heavy snowflakes beginning to fall, he had the feeling a winter squall was blowing in from the bay.

He looked out over the crowded meetinghouse, to the gallery where the women waited. Mrs. Smith sat stiff and unmoving on the bench next to her mother, Mrs. Quincy, who'd come from Mount Wollaston that morning.

Susanna was nowhere in sight, and for that he was grateful.

He'd been afraid that in spite of Susanna's promise to stay in bed, she would come and offer herself to the lieutenant in place of Tom.

And if she publicly confessed her role in aiding the runaway, the lieutenant would have little choice but to press charges against her, even though he really wanted Ben.

Judge Niles, with his elaborate robe and long white periwig, stood near the elevated pulpit conversing with Reverend Smith. The half-circle window that graced the wall behind the pulpit provided little light in contrast to the large rectangular windows that served the rest of the meetinghouse. Thus, even at midday, the oil lamps near the pulpit had been lit, and they cast flickering shadows across the pew where Ben sat. The murky flutters taunted him, reminding him just how dark his life was about to become.

He tugged at his cravat again, and agony clenched his gut. Could he really willingly place himself into the custody of the lieutenant? He'd be signing his death warrant if he did.

Had he given up too readily on the possibility of trying to prosecute Lieutenant Wolfe? Could he at least try to make the man take responsibility for the murders? Maybe he still should have Dotty testify about the cruelty she'd suffered. But would anyone care, once they saw her swelling abdomen and branded her a harlot?

Ben shook his pounding head. No. He needed to go through with the plan and give Lieutenant Wolfe what he wanted—a criminal to blame for the smuggling.

They needed to start the trial. Now, before he changed his mind.

Ben glanced over his shoulder toward the entrance of the meetinghouse. What was taking the beadle so long to collect the prisoners?

The box pews behind him were crowded with the men of Weymouth, some from Braintree, and others from the Caucus Club. Most of them disliked Lieutenant Wolfe. Their glares, wrinkled brows, and somber expressions all testified to the toll the lieutenant's presence in their community had taken.

They would be grateful to Ben if he could find a way to get rid of the red monkey. And he'd do it, just not in the way they expected.

The meetinghouse door rattled, and suddenly it swung open. The wind caught hold of the door and slammed it against the wall with a bang that brought everyone to silence.

Ben jumped, but relief swelled through him. Finally the beadle was back with the prisoners. Now he could get the dirty deed done. He could hand himself over to Lieutenant Wolfe.

Several loud gasps from the balcony drew Ben's attention upward. Mrs. Smith had risen to her feet. Her eyes widened and dismay carved lines into her face.

Even before a word slipped from Mrs. Smith's lips, Ben knew the prisoners hadn't just walked into the meetinghouse. He twisted in his pew.

There, framed in the open doorway and the swirling snow, stood Susanna. The wind had captured her cloak and swept the hood from her head, revealing her loose hair. It blew in dark tangles about her pale face. Her apparel was askew. She'd likely come straight from bed and only stopped to throw on a gown as an afterthought.

Still, her beauty was utterly breathtaking, with the contrast of her ebony hair against the whiteness of the blowing snow.

The wind whipped at her, and she swayed against the pressure.

In an instant, Ben was on his feet and fumbling at the latch of his pew.

He only had to peer at the determination flashing from her eyes to know why she was there. She caught her balance and started down the center aisle. Each step was halting, but her eyes found the lieutenant and didn't budge from him.

His heart racing, Ben scrambled to exit the pew. He couldn't let her hand herself over to Lieutenant Wolfe. He had to stop her before she confessed everything.

He flung open the pew door and started down the aisle.

She swayed again and then stumbled, obviously still too weak to be out of bed. She grasped the nearest pew to keep from falling.

Ben sprinted the last several steps and caught her by the arm. "Susanna," he whispered, "you're ill, and you should *not* be here."

"Let me go," she whispered back.

"You need to be home in bed."

"I'm not leaving here unless it's with Lieutenant Wolfe."

Her whisper echoed in the silent meetinghouse, and he was sure everyone had heard her announcement, even the women in the galleries.

With a groan he dragged her into his arms.

Her body wilted and she collapsed against him.

How had she managed to leave the house without Phoebe noticing her? And how had she been able to drag herself to the meetinghouse alone?

Frustration pummeled him. He didn't have time to sweep her up into his arms and carry her down the street to the parsonage as he wanted to. He had to stay at the meeting-house and turn himself in to the lieutenant as soon as Dotty and Tom arrived.

"Susanna . . ." He glanced around the building and, seeing that everyone was staring at them, bent lower so that his mouth brushed her ear. "I won't let you say anything to the lieutenant."

"You can't prevent me, Ben," she said.

"I'll tie you up, gag you, and find a place to lock you up."

She tilted her head back, and anger blazed in her eyes, bringing them to life, making her more beautiful than ever. There was so much passion inside her, so much depth. That's why he loved her.

And his love for her could never allow him to let her discard her reputation, her future, and her chances at happiness.

But before he could decide what must be done with her, she wrenched away from him and lurched backward. "Brothers and sisters," she called out.

He stepped toward her. "Susanna, please!"

She held out a hand to halt him. "My brothers and sisters," she repeated, louder this time. "I must make a confession."

He knew he ought to snatch her, cover her mouth, and drag her from the meetinghouse—even if she kicked and screamed. But she looked him square in the eyes, and something new flamed in the dark recesses that took his breath away.

Was it love? Was it possible Susanna Smith loved him?

Or was her love similar to what she had for Tom? After all, she loved Tom and was willing to sacrifice herself for the slave, just as she was willing to do for him.

He reached for her, needing to pull her into his arms, to hear the declaration of love from her lips. But she took another quick step away, her body trembling with her effort to stand. She lifted her chin and pressed her lips together. Determination hardened the usual softness of her face.

"I have to do this, Ben," she said. "I won't be able to live with myself if I allow anyone else to take responsibility for what I've done."

He knew the desperation she was feeling. It mirrored his own. Even so, he couldn't let her hand herself over.

Out of the corner of his eye, he caught the movement of Reverend Smith coming down the aisle toward them, as well as Mrs. Smith descending the stairway from the gallery.

If he could capture Susanna before she blurted out her confession, then he could enlist their help in locking Susanna away until after the trial. They were as determined as he was to keep Susanna free from suffering at the hands of the lieutenant.

But Susanna shook her head—almost sadly. Then she glanced away from him to the front of the building, to the judge.

Even before she opened her mouth to speak again, Ben knew what she would say.

He lunged for her.

"Honorable Judge Niles," she started loudly.

But that's as far as she got. He captured her before she could escape, jerked her against him, and cut off her next words by covering her mouth with his.

She held herself stiff for only a moment before softening and sagging against him, giving in to his tender kiss.

It didn't matter that the whole parish of Weymouth was witnessing his affection for her. He blocked out the eruption of their gasps and murmurings.

He needed to stop her from her foolishness. It didn't matter that she might not be ready for his declaration of love. It didn't matter anymore if he gave away how much he loved her.

As if from a distance, Mrs. Smith's tense whispers urged him to stop, and Reverend Smith stood next to them clearing his throat.

He didn't care what they thought anymore. In fact, he didn't care what anyone thought. He was done living his life at the mercy of status and prestige.

Besides, it was his good-bye kiss to her. For after today, he doubted he would ever see her again.

With one last consuming press of his mouth to hers, he dragged his lips from hers and pushed them against her ear. "I love you, Susanna," he whispered. "I love you with every fiber of my being. And I always will, until the day I die."

She sucked in a sharp breath. Her body trembled against his. And when she leaned her head back so that she could look into his eyes, wonder spread over her face.

Could she return his love?

Mrs. Smith gripped Susanna's arm and tugged at her. The woman's eyes were hard and attempted to shame him with her haughtiness.

He pretended not to notice. He no longer cared if Mrs. Smith liked him. He didn't need her approval or anyone else's.

She wrenched Susanna away and slipped her arm around her daughter to keep her from falling. "I'm taking you home this instant." She propelled Susanna toward the door. "You shouldn't be here."

Susanna allowed her mother to push her along.

With each step she took, agony tore at his heart. This was it. This was good-bye. Only when they neared the door did Susanna struggle against her mother. She glanced over her shoulder.

Something in her eyes spanned the distance and caressed him. It soothed the radiating pain into a dull ache. Her eyes spoke what her lips couldn't. She cared about him. Truly and deeply. Perhaps not with the love he desired, but surely with the affection of the truest friend.

What more could he ask for in life than to have had a friend like her?

Lieutenant Wolfe had risen in his pew box. A smirk curled his lips. He'd obviously watched their display, knowing exactly what Ben would do and why.

Ben's fists clenched at the need to swing them at the lieutenant and knock the grin from his face.

The lieutenant had won. And there was nothing Ben could do about it, except to feast his eyes upon Susanna one last time. He drank in her features, her eyes and slender cheeks, the curve of her lips, the raven waves of her hair.

"Come, Susanna." Mrs. Smith began towing her.

But Susanna resisted and craned her head, as though unwilling to break the connection with him. She seemed to read the truth inside him and realize he was saying good-bye for the last time.

Panic darted across her face. "No!" she cried, trying to twist free from her mother's grip.

"Reverend Smith," Ben said to her father standing next to him, "I believe your wife is in need of your help in escorting Susanna home."

The reverend nodded. His usual benevolent expression had turned grave.

"No!" Susanna cried again.

Ben spun away, her anguished call ripping his heart again. His shoulders slumped, and he shuffled away from her toward the lieutenant.

Her cries mingled with her father's low murmurs of comfort interspersed with Mrs. Smith's rebukes. Every muscle in his body demanded that he turn around, run to her, and crush her in his arms once more.

Before Ben could return to his pew, the door of the

meetinghouse swung open, and the bitter winter air rushed down the aisle to nip him.

"The beadle is back," a voice called.

Ben straightened his shoulders. It was time to give himself over to the lieutenant.

"Where are the prisoners?" Lieutenant Wolfe scowled.

The beadle pushed past the Smiths. His hat was askew, his face flushed, and his chest heaved, as if he'd run the distance from the tavern to the meetinghouse.

"The girl's gone," the beadle finally managed to choke out between breaths.

"You're mistaken." Lieutenant Wolfe exited his box pew. His eyes narrowed to slits. "She's been under constant guard since she was apprehended."

"She's long gone," the beadle insisted, taking a handkerchief out of his pocket and wiping at the perspiration on his forehead.

"You must go back and check again," the lieutenant barked.

"I searched the entire building, the entire premises," the beadle rushed to explain. "There is no sign of her anywhere. Not one."

"You idiot." Lieutenant Wolfe spat the words. "Where is my assistant? He will surely know where the prisoner is."

"I didn't see Sergeant Frazel anywhere either."

"And what of the slave?"

"He's still locked in his room."

The lieutenant turned his glare from the beadle to Ben. The accusation in his eyes sent a ray of hope through Ben.

Had Dotty escaped?

"If the indentured servant has escaped, then apparently someone else is involved in helping her," Ben called out above the murmurs. "It would appear you've accused the wrong people, Lieutenant."

He strode to the pulpit and stood before the judge. "Honorable Justice, I ask for a dismissal of this case. The lieutenant has obviously brought charges against the wrong suspects."

"You know I'm not wrong, Mr. Ross." The lieutenant's boots tapped the floor until he stood next to Ben. His eyes warned Ben to cooperate and follow their agreed-on plan.

But Ben focused his attention on the judge, knowing he had to act quickly and decisively or he'd lose his chance at making his case. "Honorable Justice, how could the slave be involved in helping the prisoner if he's still locked in his room? The lieutenant has been mistaken about who's responsible for the crime."

"You're right," the lieutenant said, his voice hard. "I should have arrested Miss Smith. She's the one who's been sheltering the runaway."

"I think you're confused, Lieutenant," Ben countered. "Miss Smith has been gravely ill with the influenza. There is no way she could have ridden out to the Wayside Tavern and released the prisoner. She could hardly make it here to the meetinghouse from the parsonage without collapsing."

He paused and turned to face Susanna, who had fallen to her knees at the back of the meetinghouse. Her pale face was streaked with tears.

His pointed stare at Susanna drew the attention of everyone else, the way he'd intended. "Honorable Justice, as you can see, it's impossible that Miss Smith, in her condition, could have been involved with the escape of the prisoner. There is absolutely no way she could have overpowered a full-grown man on guard duty to free the runaway. And if she'd freed the runaway, why not free her innocent slave also?"

He didn't know if Susanna had somehow managed to free Dotty. In fact, he didn't really care how Dotty had escaped.

All that mattered was casting enough doubt upon Tom's and Susanna's involvement.

From the increased murmurings of the crowd, Ben could sense he was winning their support. Most of them distrusted Lieutenant Wolfe anyway.

"I don't know how the prisoner could have gotten out of her room," the lieutenant said. "She was under guard at all times."

"Exactly," Ben said. "Since she was under your protection, then we must assume you decided to dispose of her in your own way, perhaps the same way you disposed of other pretty runaways?"

The lieutenant sent him a warning glare.

Ben pushed himself taller, letting the passion that burned inside him swell and find voice. "Lieutenant Wolfe, perhaps you decided you didn't want Dotty to testify in court today because you were afraid she would incriminate you and link you with the two Braintree murders."

"That's *not* true."

"Perhaps you had your assistant remove her so that she wouldn't be able to divulge to this room of people the fact that you'd taken her shoes from her and then cruelly chased her until her feet were mangled and bleeding, which was what happened to the two murder victims found on the beach."

"How dare you!" The lieutenant's face had flushed. His hand went to the hilt of his saber.

But Ben didn't care what the lieutenant decided to do to him. The words wouldn't stop now that he'd started. "You obviously didn't want her to show the scars on her feet because doing so would link you to the two murdered women."

"I am no murderer!" the lieutenant shouted.

The low rumbling and gasps coming from the room only loosened Ben's tongue further. "And I suppose you'd have us believe it coincidental that the murders happened after you were quartered in Braintree?"

The lieutenant glared at him. "You have no proof of anything, and I'm offended by your accusations. I shall see that you are punished for this defamation of my good name."

Ben returned the stare, unwilling to back down. He'd cornered the lieutenant and he knew it. Ben could see it in his eyes.

The beadle stepped forward. "Mr. Ross, I don't know if this will help, but it was sitting in front of the prisoner's room." The beadle held out a bulging haversack.

The lieutenant's face paled at the sight of the bag.

The judge motioned the beadle forward, but Lieutenant Wolfe gave a growl of protest. "I object. The bag is from among my personal possessions. How dare this man presume to meddle in my belongings."

"I didn't know it was yours," the beadle said quickly. "Honest. It was just sitting in the hallway outside the prisoner's door. I figured it might be helpful in determining what happened to her."

"Return it to my room in the tavern at once."

"I agree with the beadle," Ben said. "It may have valuable information that could help us solve the mystery behind Dotty's disappearance. I suggest we investigate what's inside. And if Lieutenant Wolfe has nothing to hide, then surely he won't mind our checking."

"I do mind," the lieutenant said sharply.

But Ben ignored the man and instead nodded at the beadle, indicating that he should open the haversack.

"If you do not obey me," the lieutenant called, "I shall report you for insubordination—"

But the lieutenant's declaration was cut off by the alarmed cries of those gathered, as the beadle had already turned the haversack upside down and spilled its contents onto the floor.

For a moment, Ben could only stare in disgust. How many women had the man murdered? Obviously more than two.

The lieutenant pinched his lips together, his nostrils flaring with barely contained rage.

The judge was the first to speak. "Lieutenant Wolfe, would you care to explain why a bag you admitted was rightfully your own came to be full of women's shoes?"

"I cannot explain it," the lieutenant said. "Someone has obviously planted the shoes in my bag without my knowledge."

The look he leveled at Ben, however, said that he knew how the shoes had ended up in his bag, but that Ben would never be able to prove it. Nevertheless, the shoes provided Ben with enough solid evidence to file a case of murder against the lieutenant.

"Honorable Justice," Ben said, turning to speak to Judge Niles. "I request the case against the Smith slave be dropped and that Tom be set free. We have no reason to hold him any longer. "

"You're absolutely right, Mr. Ross," Judge Niles said, his voice booming through the building. "I hereby dismiss the case against the Smith family and their slave."

Ben's shoulders sagged with relief. The nods and choruses of approval echoed around him. He peered to the back of the meetinghouse in time to see Mrs. Smith assisting Susanna to her feet. He wanted to catch Susanna's gaze and share the moment of victory. But Reverend Smith flanked one side and Mrs. Smith the other, giving Susanna little choice but to accompany them from the building.

Even though he longed to chase after her, he forced himself to stay. He had unfinished business with the lieutenant. And besides, Susanna needed to be back home in her bed as soon as possible.

"Judge Niles," Ben said loudly and decisively, "I propose that if we do locate the runaway indentured servant, we bring her to the meetinghouse for questioning. I'm sure everyone here is curious to hear what she has to say about Lieutenant Wolfe."

Again the crowd mumbled their assent.

The lieutenant squirmed.

"I'm quite certain she would be able to identify her shoes from among those found in the lieutenant's satchel." Ben could only hope that the lieutenant caught the threat behind his words. He wanted the man to stop chasing Dotty. If he knew that capturing the girl would only bring about further connection to the Braintree murders, then perhaps he'd leave her alone, wherever she was.

"I concur, Mr. Ross." The judge folded his arms and gave Lieutenant Wolfe his most sober stare. "If she is able to help us solve the murder mysteries of Braintree, then I daresay we must thoroughly question her."

A silent prayer of gratefulness whispered through Ben. He would file charges against Lieutenant Wolfe in Boston the first chance he had to ride there. And even though he wasn't sure that he could actually win against one of the king's officers, at the very least he prayed that Susanna would finally be out of danger.

His heart thudded with the need to go after her and wrap her in his arms again.

But as much as he wanted to be with her, he needed only to glance at Lieutenant Wolfe's red coat to remind himself of the life of danger he'd charted for himself. If he continued to resist the British oppression, the coming years would be fraught with turmoil.

Now that he'd saved Susanna from one disaster, could he really drag her into more?

He let out a long tense breath. Deep inside he knew she would be much better off without him. But could he live without her?

Chapter
27

Susanna stared at the pages of *The Odyssey*. The book lay on her lap, opened to the same spot she'd turned to when Phoebe had helped her into the chair before the fireplace earlier that morning.

It had been two days since the trial, but Ben hadn't visited her.

She grazed her fingers along the edge of the book, trying to ignore the ache in her heart. But with each passing hour she was having a difficult time overlooking the pain she felt inside.

Why hadn't he come to see her yet?

The knit blanket slipped from her shoulders, and the chill of her bedchamber drifted around her.

He'd told her he loved her.

She'd mulled over his words a hundred times since the trial. The delight she had experienced the first day of his confession had slowly evaporated as she'd waited in vain for him to run to her and confirm his declaration.

Now confusion pulsed through her, leaving her restless and unable to focus on anything except the emptiness inside.

Why had he admitted his love if he hadn't planned to come for her?

She'd asked herself that question over and over. And she didn't want to face the obvious answer—that he'd kissed her and given her his love only because he'd been saying good-bye and going off to face imprisonment and death. He'd had nothing to lose by making his bold declaration.

But now . . . He was putting the distance back between them.

Perhaps he was honoring their friendship and erecting the boundaries of a platonic relationship.

She gave a woeful sigh and smoothed her hand over the page of his book, wishing she were running her fingers over the solidness of his face instead.

He likely had no excuse for visiting her. Why would he create one after she'd rejected him in the past? Why would he risk giving her his devotion now?

At the thump of Phoebe's shoes on the floor in the next room and the murmur of voices, Susanna bowed her head and chided herself. She ought to be grateful. Tom was safely tucked into the guest-room bed, and Phoebe was seeing to his needs. Some of the men of the parish had delivered the old slave home, hungry but alive.

And while she didn't know what had happened to Dotty or where she was, she knew she ought to be thankful the young woman had somehow managed to escape the clutches of Lieutenant Wolfe.

She indeed had much for which to be grateful, especially because Lieutenant Wolfe had returned to Boston in shame. He would likely be prosecuted for murder and then sent back to England and imprisoned.

Why then was her heart so full of melancholy?

The experience with Dotty had shown her the need to stand up for the poor and disadvantaged, to show love and mercy to them, even if she had to disobey her earthly authorities to do so. She couldn't hide behind fear and make excuses for doing what was right.

Surely after such a lesson she could proceed forth with renewed vigor, continue with her dame school, and find additional ways to help women who were disadvantaged.

A soft rap on the door sent a shiver of anticipation through her. Had he finally come? She sat up and smoothed her hair back.

The door opened a crack, and Mother peeked in.

Susanna's heart dipped with disappointment. But she forced herself to offer her mother a welcoming smile. At the very least, she had to acknowledge Mother's support during the past awful days. Never once had her mother reprimanded her for her involvement with Dotty.

Mother stepped into the room, the layers of her gown rustling and bringing the faint scent of her lavender perfume. "I have a letter for you."

Mother crossed to her, and Susanna held her breath, praying she finally had news from Ben.

With trembling fingers Susanna took the crisply folded sheet. At the sight of the scrawled handwriting on the front, she sagged. It wasn't Ben's strong print.

"It's from Elbridge." Mother bustled to the window and threw back the thick curtains. "He called earlier this morning and delivered it."

"I don't want to read it. You can burn it."

"He's only wanting to apologize for his involvement with the young runaway," Mother said as she tied the curtains, allowing the daylight to chase the shadows from the room.

"Perhaps he was misguided in his interfering, but he only wanted to ensure your well-being."

"I won't be courted by him, Mother." Susanna trembled at the defiance in her words.

Mother strode to the fireplace and added another log from the woodbox.

Susanna sat up straighter and prayed for courage. Tom had admonished her not to let fear take hold of her and stop her from doing the right thing. She'd done that with the trial. She'd fooled Phoebe into thinking she was sleeping, but had instead sneaked out of the parsonage and ridden to the meetinghouse. She'd had enough courage to drag her weak and sick body there so that she could turn herself in to the lieutenant rather than let Tom or Ben take the blame for her crimes.

Couldn't she summon the courage to face Mother now?

"I won't marry Elbridge," she said louder.

Still Mother didn't say anything. Instead she poked at the embers, fanning the flames higher.

Susanna clutched the knit blanket. "I know you only want what's best for me, but I can't marry someone I don't love. I don't love Elbridge, and I never will."

Mother returned the poker to its hook and then turned to face Susanna. Disappointment creased her regal features.

Susanna hesitated, fighting the ghosts of doubt that rose up suddenly to haunt her with all the fears she'd once had, reminding her that she needed to marry well. That if she didn't, she'd give up the comforts and status she'd always had.

But what did all the status and wealth in the world mean if her life was devoid of love? Surely she would find greater happiness and contentment if she could spend her life with a man who not only respected and cherished her for who she was, but whom she adored, trusted, and respected as the truest and best of friends. How could she ever ask for anything more?

"I love Ben."

"I know," Mother said softly.

"You do?"

"I've noticed it for some time. I'd hoped to divert you. But I can see now my efforts have been futile."

"I realize all I'd have to give up to be with him," Susanna said quickly, "but I'd gain so much more of what really matters."

Mother smoothed her hand over the silky layers of her skirt. "I have always said you are rather wild, Susanna."

Susanna nodded. Indeed she'd always wanted more of her life than Mother believed appropriate for a woman. Perhaps she would be ever straining against the rules and expectations that restricted her. Perhaps she wouldn't break free, but could she not at least help loosen the constraints for her daughters and the women who would come after her?

"Grandmother Eve once bade me to look beyond the outward qualifications of a man and to consider his heart. She entreated me not to make the same mistake she did by rejecting love for earthly gains." And although Grandmother Eve hadn't divulged the name of the long-ago suitor she'd rejected, Susanna couldn't help but wonder if the dear woman's concern and defense of Hermit Crab Joe had anything to do with the past.

She supposed it would forever remain a mystery.

"I shall endeavor to mark a new course for myself—to marry for love rather than personal gain."

"I think you resemble your Grandmother Quincy much more than you have ever resembled me."

"No, Mother." Susanna gazed into the strong, determined eyes of the woman standing before her. "You have given me much strength in character for which I'm grateful. And you have modeled to me a love for other women—for those less fortunate than myself. I'm indebted to you for much."

"But you will never be content living an ordinary life." Mother's lips curved into a gentle smile. "I believe you were born to do greater things."

The words of confidence spread over Susanna and warmed her.

Mother bent and placed a kiss upon her head.

A joyful swell pressed against Susanna's chest.

Mother took Elbridge's unopened letter, strode to the fire, and tossed it in. Then she stood back and watched the flames turn it into curling black wisps that disintegrated into ash.

"You will do those great things beside a great man." Mother lifted her chin and started toward the door. "And that man is waiting for you downstairs. I shall send him up to see you now."

Susanna's pulse quickened. Ben was there?

Her mother slipped through the door.

Susanna wished she could rush after Mother and wrap her arms around her in a hug. But she knew, even if she had the strength for such a display, Mother wouldn't have approved. A kiss on the brow would have to suffice.

With her heart pounding, Susanna straightened her night-dress and smoothed at the loose strands of her hair again. She closed his book, then opened it again. She crossed her feet, then uncrossed them.

If only she'd had time to change into her new pink polonaise and to dab a drop of rose water to her neck.

But the clomping of heavy boots on the stairs was followed

by rapid footfalls in the hallway. In an instant her door swung open and Ben filled the doorway.

He stopped short as if he'd wanted to charge into the room but had decided at the last second to show restraint. He swiped his hat from his head.

Nervous happiness sifted through Susanna. She wasn't sure why he'd waited so long to see her, but it didn't matter anymore. He was there.

He crumpled the brim of his hat in his fingers and glanced down to his old hunting shirt, stained breeches, scuffed work boots, and spatterdashes. "I apologize for visiting you this way, Susanna."

"Don't apologize." She wanted to say she was glad to see him, but there was something reserved in his eyes that dampened her joy.

"I didn't stop to think. I should have changed." He stepped into the room. "It's just that when I got the letter, I was excited and wanted to share it with you."

"Letter?" So he hadn't come to declare his love for her again?

He glanced over his shoulder into the hallway as if making sure they were alone, then pulled a soggy sheet out of his coat pocket.

"It's from Red," he said in a hushed voice as he moved closer to her.

"Who's Red?"

Ben kneeled in front of her and placed the note in her lap. "Sergeant Frazel."

Since the trial, no one had been able to locate Lieutenant Wolfe's assistant. And the lieutenant had been in too much of a hurry to return to Boston to worry about his assistant's whereabouts.

"He has news of Dotty."

"Oh." The one word contained all the anxiety she'd held in her heart the past days.

"Don't worry. It's good news."

"Then don't delay. Do tell."

He unfolded the letter and spread it out. "They're heading west to the frontier. He wants to find land to farm. He said he plans to marry Dotty the first chance they have."

Susanna could only stare at Ben, trying to make sense of the news.

"He'll take good care of her, and together they can begin a new life where no one will know or care about their past."

"He deserted the army?" She knew she shouldn't be surprised. The young officer hadn't seemed quite suited to his work.

"It happens all the time."

Susanna released the tension in her shoulders, letting the good news sink in.

"He said he was the one who left the bag of shoes for us."

"And the shoes will be enough evidence to convict the lieutenant for the murders?"

"I'll do my best." Ben's smile of excitement wrapped around her heart, and she couldn't keep a smile of her own from forming. "So, what do you think?"

"I think you're an amazing man, Benjamin Ross."

His gaze alighted on her dimple and then dropped to her mouth. Was he remembering the kiss he'd given her at the meetinghouse in full view of the entire parish?

Of course, Mother had been aghast at Ben's brazenness. But Susanna felt fresh longing every time she thought about how his lips had moved against hers and demanded a response from her.

Would he kiss her again?

"Ben . . ." she breathed softly, hoping he'd claim her. Surely he could see her desire and her love for him.

His smile faded and he turned to leave.

"Wait." She captured his hand. For a reason she couldn't understand, she was losing him. He was putting a wall between them just when she'd believed all the barriers were finally gone. "Don't go yet."

"I came to give you the news, Susanna." Gently he slipped his hand out of hers. "But I can't stay. I need to return to the farm to my work."

"You came all this way. Can you not stay for a little while longer?"

He shook his head. "I don't think that's a good idea."

"I thought we were friends." She hated the whine in her voice, but she couldn't prevent it.

The muscles in his face tightened. "I'm sorry, Susanna. I know you'd like to remain friends," he whispered. "But I cannot. Not anymore."

"Whatever for?" The despair churned faster. "After what you said at the meetinghouse, I thought you cared about me."

Pain flashed across his face. "Of course I care about you."

"But . . ."

"But I could never be satisfied with a simple friendship when everything within me demands so much more."

She pushed herself out of her chair and stood, letting the book that had been in her lap clatter to the floor. "I love you, Benjamin Ross. And everything within me demands more as well."

At her declaration, his eyes widened.

"I should have told you much sooner," she said, "but I

didn't realize it until just recently. I was confused . . . and I was a coward."

He studied her. "What will your parents say about your love for me?" He glanced again at his worn, homespun garments.

"It doesn't matter what they think. Besides, my mother allowed you to visit, did she not?" She attempted to give him a smile, but he didn't smile back.

Before he could move away and distance himself from her further, she closed the gap between them. She knew she was being much too forward. But as her mother had said, she was too wild. She wound her arms around his neck. "What matters is us. Our future together. Our love. Our happiness."

For a moment, he held himself rigid.

She was afraid maybe he'd push her away, that she'd hurt him too many times and now he didn't want her anymore.

Finally, he groaned and slid his hands around her waist. "Susanna," he murmured, drawing her closer, "I can't resist you, no matter how hard I try."

She pressed her face into his shirt and breathed the earthy scent that permeated the fabric. Then, closing her eyes, she relished the soft warmth of his lips.

"After all the recent danger, I know I should put you far away from me to keep you safe." His lips grazed her temple. "I have the premonition Lieutenant Wolfe will only be the first of many enemies I'll make in my life. And I don't want to subject you to that kind of life—"

Again she lifted her lips to his, cutting off his words and silencing him the same way he'd silenced her at the trial. She leaned into him with a boldness that contained all the love she had for him. She let her mouth possess his, and he met her with all the heat and force of his passion—his passion for life, for those he chose to defend, for the causes he believed in.

He was a passionate man, just the kind of man she needed. If only she could convince him of the same . . .

"I see what you're attempting to do," he said in a ragged voice, dragging his lips away from hers and making a warm trail across her jaw to the tender spot below her ear.

She gasped and arched to give him admission to more of her.

His hand splayed across the small of her back, urging her closer. "You're trying to make me forget all the reasons why we shouldn't be together," he murmured against her skin.

"Is it working?" she whispered.

He stopped then and pulled back. A gentle smile played at his lips, and his eyes shone with the clarity of his love. "Yes. It's working very well."

She smiled.

His eyes softened even more. "And every time you give me one of your smiles, I'm helpless to do anything but what you wish."

"Then I shall have to smile often."

"But will I be able to give you enough to smile about?" He caressed the line of her cheekbone. "I don't want you to come to regret all that you gave up to be with me."

"I can only think of all I will sacrifice if I do not have you by my side the rest of my life."

"But what about the danger I could possibly bring to you? You know I've not exactly chosen the safest course of life."

"Old Tom once told me that God hasn't given us a spirit of fear, but of power, and love, and a sound mind." She grazed the scratchy stubble on his cheeks that he'd neglected to shave. "I think with the two of us together we'll be unstoppable, don't you think?"

"Is that a proposal, Miss Smith?"

"Why, Mr. Ross." She tilted her head coyly. "I'd like to think of it as an extension of our friendship."

He bent and placed a kiss in the crook of her neck.

Warmth spread through her belly, tightening it with anticipation.

As if sensing his effect on her, he lifted his head and grinned again. "I'll only agree to a friendship if it involves a great deal of kissing."

"Very well." She brushed her lips against his cheek. "Only the utmost of kissing."

His eyes brimmed with adoration. "Then you shall be my dearest of friends."

"And you shall also be my dearest of friends."

"Forever. Until I draw my dying breath."

She nodded, her heart swelling with joy. "Shall we seal our agreement with a kiss, then?"

"Most certainly."

She leaned in and let her mouth linger against the lips of the man she loved.

Author's Note

Rebellious Heart is inspired by one of history's most famous couples, John and Abigail Adams, the second President of the United States and his First Lady. They are often admired for their loving marriage, which spanned a length of over fifty years, the travails of at least two wars, including the Revolutionary War, as well as thousands of miles and long years of separation.

This book is my attempt to loosely recreate the early years of their courtship. While there are countless biographies that bring to life their marriage and all the great things they accomplished during their years of service to the young American nation, there is very little recorded about their early love affair. Only eight of their letters before April of 1764 survived among the hundreds they wrote to each other.

As I studied the information available in biographies and original letters, I tried to piece together John and Abigail's personalities, beliefs, interests, homes, and family backgrounds, along with the assortment of incidents and facts that we know about their early years together. Then as with any work of fiction, I allowed my imagination to invent and weave together the rest of their courtship the way it *could* have happened.

Thus *Rebellious Heart* is truly a work of fiction. I make no claims at being an expert on the lives of John and Abigail Adams. There are those who have devoted their life's work to studying these famous Americans and know far more than I ever could.

While my book is not a perfect or complete representation of the Adamses, I do hope this story will give you a glimpse into their lives and their love, and perhaps a new appreciation for this famous couple. Perhaps you may even go on to do more reading and research about them on your own. If so, I highly recommend three biographies: *Abigail Adams* by Woody Holton; *Dearest Friend: A Life of Abigail Adams* by Lynne Withey; and *John Adams* by David McCullough.

As with my other books that are inspired by real couples from history, you might be wondering what events within the story really happened and what I invented for the sake of telling a riveting story.

Abigail Adams really did have a passion for helping women. She assisted her mother in delivering food and supplies to the poor widows in their parish. Abigail had a charitable instinct and began to argue for the improved legal rights and education of women during a time when women were denied equality.

She was largely self-taught, loved to read, and became known for her brilliant mind. One of her deepest regrets was that as a woman she'd been denied a formal education equal to that of her brother. Later, in a letter she wrote to John during the First Congress, when the founding fathers were developing the Constitution, she said: "I desire you would remember the ladies and be more favorable to them than your ancestors. Do not put such unlimited power into the hands of husbands."

While I found no record of Abigail helping indentured servants (like Dotty), she felt passionate about liberty for those in bondage and had a heart for the unfortunate. In another letter she wrote to John, she said, "I wish most sincerely there was not a slave in the province. . . . We are daily robbing and plundering from those who have as good a right to freedom as we have."

As portrayed in *Rebellious Heart*, Abigail did have a somewhat tense relationship with her mother, who is said to have initially objected to her affection toward John due to his social standing and being a lawyer. Abigail was disappointed in the dearth of suitors who sought after something other than wealth. She's quoted as saying, "Wealth, wealth is the only thing that is looked after now." Even so, she herself knew she must make an advantageous match by marrying up.

When John walked into her life, at first he wasn't impressed by the Smith girls. Essentially he thought they were too proud. Since one of his best friends, Richard Cranch, spent time courting Mary, John was thrust more and more into the company of Abigail. And eventually he grew to admire her qualities, in particular what he called her "sauciness."

It was during this time that they began their lifelong pattern of penning letters to each other. At that time, it was customary for letter writers to adopt classical pen names. And one of the names among many they took were Diana (the goddess of the moon) and Lysander (the Spartan statesman). And while I made up the circumstances of Dotty's plight to initiate their letter writing, they eventually became good friends, prompting Abigail at one point to address him as "My Dearest Friend."

John and Abigail's courtship lasted over the span of approximately four years. Thus I had to condense some of the real events into a shorter time frame for the sake of the story flow, including: the foiled plans to propose to Hannah Quincy; the influence of his friend Parson Wibird; the influenza epidemic; his father's resulting death; his inheriting of the farm; and the wedding of Mary and Cranch. All of these events really happened, but over the span of several years versus the several months in the story.

History also mentions a trip John and Abigail took together in the fall of 1763, apparently alone. No one is certain where they went or why. So I used this fact, along with the disappearance of so many of their early letters, to signify that perhaps they were involved in something secretive—such as I portrayed with harboring Dotty. Whatever the case, the times were not favorable to indentured servants. Many ran away, seeking a better life. Most were recaptured and punished, some severely.

The 1760s and the years leading up to the Revolutionary War were indeed setting the stage for the conflict that was yet to come. The years of 1763–1764 saw the beginning grumblings about new taxes as well as the crackdown by the British on the illegal smuggling that was widespread among the colonies. While I invented Lieutenant Wolfe, the British parliament did attempt to suppress the smuggling by sending out officers to enforce the Acts of Trade.

It was during these prewar years that many like John and Abigail began to resent the control of the British. Although I found no indication that John was involved in one of the Caucus Clubs during this time period, we know that later he supported the Sons of Liberty, a group pivotal in the rebellion.

During the course of their courtship, John and Abigail formed a beautiful friendship, overcame the barriers standing between them, and agreed to get married. They planned a wedding for the spring of 1764. But due to a smallpox outbreak in Boston, they postponed their wedding plans until the fall of 1764. They were married on October 25, 1764. Afterward they moved to John's cottage in Braintree, where they would live the rest of their lives together as the dearest of friends. John said, "Friendship is one of the distinguishing glories of man. . . . From this I expect to receive the chief happiness of my future."

And in her last letter to John before the wedding, Abigail asked him to take all her belongings in a cart to her new home in Braintree: "And then, Sir, if you please, you may take me."

It's my hope, dear reader, that as you close the pages of this book, you will walk away encouraged by the sweet relationship of this famous couple. Even more than that, I hope you will take courage from their compassion, bravery, and willingness to stand against tyranny for God's higher laws of justice and mercy.

Acknowledgments

First, I need to thank my dear husband for *his* friendship. Without his ongoing support, unswerving help with our large family, and constant belief in me, I would be lost. I could not accomplish all that I do without his ever-willing, never-complaining spirit.

I want to thank my wonderful mother for pitching in and helping whenever and wherever possible—including cooking a couple of big meals for my family each week. In addition to her help, I'm grateful for her willingness to listen to me ramble on about my stories and characters as if they were real people.

I can't neglect to thank my Bethany House editors, Dave Long and Luke Hinrichs, for their incredible wisdom, insights, and abilities. I'm also appreciative of the many other people at Bethany House who work so diligently and strive so hard to make each book a success.

I also would like to express my deepest gratitude to my agent, Rachelle Gardner, for her helpful critique on this novel and for brainstorming with me. The additional feedback was invaluable.

As with any historical novel, I also had to consult many resources. Since I'm not an expert on the Colonial or Revolutionary War eras, I'm grateful for the original documents, diaries, and biographies that are so readily available.

I especially appreciate Colonial novelist Carla Olson Gade's generosity in beta-reading for me and providing additional ideas and details to strengthen the Colonial aura of this story. Any historical inaccuracies are completely my own fault.

Finally, I must thank the Lord for giving me the gift of writing, which I enjoy so immensely. I'm deeply grateful I'm able to do something every day that I love so much!

Jody Hedlund is an award-winning historical romance novelist and author of the bestselling *A Noble Groom*, *Unending Devotion*, and *The Preacher's Bride*. She holds a bachelor's degree from Taylor University and a master's degree from the University of Wisconsin, both in social work. Jody lives in Michigan with her husband and five busy children. Learn more at JodyHedlund.com.

More From Bestselling Author Jody Hedlund

For more on Jody and her books, visit jodyhedlund.com.

Annalisa Werner has given up on love, but she needs a husband to save her farm. Desperate, she accepts her father's offer to write to Germany and find her a groom. Then friendship—and something more—begins to grow between Annalisa and her new farmhand. The trouble is, her mail-order groom could arrive any day....

A Noble Groom

Lily Young is determined to find her lost sister or die trying. When her search leads her into the dangerous lumber camps of Harrison, Michigan, this devoted young woman will challenge everything boss-man Connell McCormick thought he knew about life—and love.

Unending Devotion

More Faith-Filled Romance From Jody Hedlund